Praise for Lois Richer
and her novels

"This delicious romance mixes a fun subplot and
a hint of mystery to enhance strong characters
and the enjoyable main story line."
—*RT Book Reviews* on *A Hopeful Heart*

"Once again, Lois Richer delights readers with
an enjoyable romance."
—*RT Book Reviews* on
A Home, A Heart, A Husband

"The perfect book for a cozy evening."
—*RT Book Reviews* on *Heaven's Kiss*

"Lois Richer pens an excellent story in
Spring Flowers, Summer Love."
—*RT Book Reviews*

LOIS RICHER
A Hopeful Heart

❧

A Home, A Heart, A Husband

Love Inspired

Recycling programs
for this product may
not exist in your area.

 ™ LOVE INSPIRED BOOKS

ISBN-13: 978-0-373-68889-0

A HOPEFUL HEART AND A HOME, A HEART, A HUSBAND

A HOPEFUL HEART
Copyright © 1998 by Lois Richer

A HOME, A HEART, A HUSBAND
Copyright © 1998 by Lois Richer

CONTENTS

Books by Lois Richer

LOIS RICHER

likes variety. From human resources manager to entrepreneurship, life has held plenty of surprises.

"Having given up on fairy tales, I was happily involved in building a restaurant when a handsome prince walked into my life and upset all my career plans with a wedding ring. Motherhood quickly followed. I guess the seeds of my storytelling took root because of two small boys who kept demanding 'Then what, Mom?'"

The miracle of God's love for His children, the blessing of true love, the joy of sharing Him with others—that is a story that can be told a thousand ways and yet still be brand-new. Lois Richer intends to go right on telling it.

A HOPEFUL HEART

Therefore I say unto you, Take no thought for your life, what ye shall eat, or what ye shall drink; nor yet for your body, what ye shall put on.... Consider the lilies of the field, how they grow; they toil not, neither do they spin: And yet I say unto you, That even Solomon in all his glory was not arrayed like one of these. Wherefore, if God so clothe the grass of the field, which today is, and tomorrow is cast into the oven, *shall He* not much more *clothe* you, O ye of little faith?

—*Matthew* 6:25-30

This book is dedicated to my grandpa John, and to Papa Richer. Both of them would have loved Melanie's refreshing attitude toward seniors and her efforts to improve the lives of those spending their last years in a nursing home. To you who devote your days and nights to caring for someone's spouse, mother, grandparent or friend, may I say "Thank you." Your labors do not go unappreciated.

Chapter One

Melanie Stewart slipped out of her battered tan car and slammed the door shut, hoping it would catch.

"You're doing fine, Bessie, old girl," she murmured, patting the ancient car's rusty fender. "I know. You need a paint job and new tires, but that will wait. It has to."

She grimaced at the thought of the number of high-priority items on her to-do list that seemed to multiply daily. Oh, for a little spare cash!

"The love of money is the root of all evil," she repeated to herself. "Remember that, and be glad for what you have."

With a sigh, Melanie blew her auburn bangs from her forehead, resigned to both her penurious state and the blistering July heat.

"Just a few dollars would sure be nice, though." She sighed, glancing heavenward. "Just a little spare cash could make a big difference to so many." Unbidden, images of the residents at the Sunset Retirement Home—*her* residents—rolled through her mind. "Give me a sign, Lord, please," she pleaded in a heartfelt prayer. "Just a little hint that better things are on the way."

"Oh, Melanie!" Mr. Jones strode jauntily down the street

toward her, whistling his usual happy tune as he pushed his delivery cart in front of Melanie's redbrick apartment building. "Afternoon, Melanie, my girl."

Fred Jones was a genial man who had been Mossbank's special-delivery officer for twenty years. He knew everyone in town and most of what went on. Melanie had long ceased to wonder how he kept the residents and their stories straight.

"Hi, Mr. Jones. How's your wife doing?" They exchanged the usual banter about the romance Melanie had helped along three years earlier. Then the older man thrust an ordinary white envelope with Official Notice stamped on the front of it into her hand.

"This looks pretty important, Melanie. Thought I'd better bring it over soon as you got off work. It was addressed to the nursing home, but I knew you'd be coming home about now. Sure hope it's good news." He grinned. "You've got a couple more wedding invitations, too. Reckon Cupid and you were real busy last winter," he said teasingly, watching her face flush.

His wiry tanned hand offered the shabby clipboard for her signature.

Melanie shook her head at the suggestion that she was the local matchmaker. In Fred's mind, the two latest invitations confirmed it, even if she hadn't meant to get involved.

"All I did was lend a little advice," she told him. When there was no response, she turned the plain white envelope over. There was nothing to identify it on the back. She peered at the strange letters on the front upper left corner—PJPB.

"Why do those initials seem so familiar?" she wondered. After a few moments of deep thought, Fred Jones answered her.

"It's probably just another of those form letters announcing you have won an unbelievable amount of money." He frowned. "Then, when you read the fine print, there is always a conditional *if* or *possibly* to free the sender of any misrepresentation." He shook his head gloomily and watched while Melanie stuffed the envelope into the outside pocket of her tan leather bag. "Then again, maybe it's a letter from an admirer," he suggested slyly.

"Well, whatever it is, it will have to wait," she told him tiredly. "I need a shower and some supper. Thanks anyway, Mr. Jones."

Fred Jones grinned, waved his hand and strode off down the street to his next destination, still whistling, but this time it was "Here Comes the Bride."

Lethargically, Melanie forced her tired feet up the three stairs and into the blessed coolness of the air-conditioned foyer. The elevator took forever, so she slowly climbed the stairs.

As usual, the events of her day threatened to overwhelm her and she forcibly thrust them to the back of her mind, refusing to allow herself to dwell on the sad situations she often handled as director of Sunset Retirement Home.

At twenty-eight, she had never become resigned to the plight of seniors forced to enter a nursing home when they could no longer care for themselves. Empathy of a world-weary foster child, no doubt, she derided herself.

Melanie spent every minute of her workday trying to make their lives interesting and enjoyable. In short, she hoped to allow the residents the freedom to live as they wished with help nearby when necessary. Since her childish dreams of husband and children had never been fulfilled, the small community of Mossbank, North Dakota, but especially the residents at Sunset, had become her special family.

Melanie placed the letter on the hall table just as the phone rang.

"Oh, hi, Mom." She smiled at Charity Flowerday's excited rush of words. "Yes, Mother. I'm perfectly fine." She grinned at the familiar question. "I will eat supper, Mom. A lovely Chinese dinner that Shawna left for me. She's gone out on another date, I think."

"Aren't you going out, dear?"

Melanie burst out laughing.

"Me? No way. I'm dead tired and I just want to relax." She groaned inwardly. "No, Mother, I don't know Judge Conroy's grandson. You said he's moved here?"

Melanie eyed her letter longingly, knowing that her adoptive mother took a special interest in each and every newcomer to their small, closely knit town and would relay every morsel of information she'd found out about this most recent arrival. It seemed Charity had found yet another homeless chick to spread her wings over. For her own sake, Melanie just hoped this grandson was happily married.

"No, I hadn't heard anything, but then I don't know Judge Conroy all that well. If his grandson's been here for two weeks, I'll probably meet him at church soon. If I ever get another Sunday off!" Melanie smiled at the abrupt change of topic.

"Yes, Mother, I know there are some good men in the world. I just haven't met many of them, and those I think I might be interested in usually want my help to attract someone else." She smiled at the volume of reassurances that issued over the phone.

"Listen, Mother, I was just going to start dinner when you called. I have to go now. I'm starved. Have a good time with Faith and Hope. Bye, Mother."

The letter on the hall table stared at her all the while she ate her dinner. Knowing she could procrastinate no longer, Melanie finally carried her tea to the living room and sank into the depths of her overstuffed sofa. Yawning widely, she slit the slim envelope and drew out a single sheet of heavy white paper.

We are pleased to announce that M. Stewart of Mossbank, North Dakota, has been randomly selected by our computer as the grand prize winner of 50,000 in our recent Papa John's Peanut Butter contest.

This will advise you that prizes will be awarded Thursday, July 15, during a televised announcement at WMIX-TV13. Please be at the station no later than 1:00 p.m. of that day. A company representative will contact you within the next few days to confirm your win and to give you additional information.

There was another paragraph offering congratulations and asking her not to talk to the press, but Melanie absorbed none of it. Her eyes read the words, but her mind couldn't comprehend their significance.

She turned it over to check for the usual qualifying sentences and found nothing. There was only a scrawled signature at the end of the letter which was identified as the CEO of Papa John's Peanut Butter. Stupidly, she stared at the embossed golden logo, afraid to believe it.

"He answered," she muttered to herself, dazed. "I've actually won some money!"

Melanie read the wonderful letter three times before her mind acknowledged and processed the information, and then she let out an unbridled squeal of joy.

"A grand prize winner," she mused, twisting one curling lock of her shoulder-length hair. "Thank you, Lord. As usual, Your timing is perfect. Maybe Mr. Henessey will get his wish after all. And of course, Mrs. Blair."

One by one, the residents of the special-care home flew through her thoughts. Many of the seniors had little or no family nearby. Some, like Mr. Henessey, had very little money for things that would make his last few years so enjoyable. A windfall of cash would be just the thing.

When Shawna sauntered through the door three hours later, Melanie had finished drawing up her list of future expenses. She pounced on her friend eagerly.

"I won, I won," she squeaked, thrusting the letter in front of Shawna's sunburned nose.

Her roommate was cool and efficient, well used to Melanie's bursts of excitement. Calmly she laid her jacket and purse on a nearby chair, wished her gaping date a good evening and closed the door on him firmly, then reached for the letter. After a careful scrutiny, she grabbed Melanie and they danced giddily around, laughing hilariously.

A week later, the thrill of excitement had not diminished as Melanie found herself ushered into the makeup room of WMIX, a Bismarck television station that specialized in North Dakota's news events. Melanie sat nervously while a teenage girl applied a thick layer of shadow and mascara. She felt butterflies dance an entire ballet through her midsection. Finally, eons later, a short, frumpy woman bustled into the room.

"M. Stewart?" Accepting the nod, the older woman wrapped her vivid purple nails around Melanie's arm and led her through a maze of corridors to a busy sound stage.

"Now, dear," she said over her shoulder, "we'll be broadcasting shortly. Don't move from this spot. When it's your turn, I'll be here to guide you on."

Like a plump, busy robin, the woman in the bright red shirt whisked through the menagerie of sound men, cameras and directors to the booth across the room.

From behind the curtain, Melanie saw part of the stage setting. A huge structure meant to represent a peanut butter jar full of gold coins sat front and center with the famous glittering golden letters PJPB on its side. Standing beside it was a man Melanie identified as Papa John, clad in his white shirt, bow tie, blue jeans and red suspenders. Snowy white hair looked exactly as it did on the commercials that flashed across the television screen every night.

In the last forty-eight hours, Melanie had spent valuable hours at work wracking her brain, trying to remember entering any contest to do with Papa John's Peanut Butter. Nothing specific came to mind, but then she had been in such a fog during a particularly low period in her life a few months ago. Right after poor old Mrs. Peters had passed away.

Suddenly the announcer's voice penetrated her thoughts.

"The winner is M. Stewart!"

Melanie felt a hand on her back propelling her forward. As she moved toward the grinning announcer, she noticed a tall, dark-haired man moving from the wings on the far side of the stage. Slim and muscular, he exuded the very essence of a man-about-town. He had rugged, chiseled features and the bluest eyes she had ever seen.

And those eyes were fixed firmly on her!

Melanie gave herself a mental shake and focused on the task ahead. Nervously, she wiped her sweaty palms on her skirt before moving to stand beside the announcer.

"M. Stewart," he boomed in his loud, TV personality voice.

"Yes," Melanie answered, and then heard a yes from directly behind her. Turning her head, she found those deep blue eyes glaring at her.

"I'm sorry, miss, but I think he asked for me." Low and rumbling, his voice rolled past her left ear as the man carefully but still rudely elbowed his way past.

"But my name is M. Stewart," Melanie insisted, wondering if the whole thing was a hoax. The announcer was obviously at a loss as he turned his perfectly groomed head from one to the other.

"I'm Melanie Stewart." Melanie was so nervous her voice slipped out in a soft squeak that no one seemed to hear.

Finally the director hissed from his seat in the sound room. The words were audible over the whole stage. "Do something!"

"I'm sorry, folks," the announcer said slowly, "but there seems to be a bit of a mix-up here. Our winner of the Papa John's Peanut Butter contest is M. Stewart. Sir, may I have your full name, please?"

The handsome interloper gracefully inclined his head as he stated clearly, "Mitchel Edward Stewart." His glittering blue eyes dared Melanie to top that.

"And you, miss. Your name is?" The microphone was stuck in her face, and Melanie forced a tight rein on her temper as she answered.

"Melanie Clarice Stewart."

"Well, isn't this great. Are you two married?"

The stranger's dark head shook adamantly, his blue eyes hurling daggers at Melanie.

"I am not married and I have certainly never met Miss Stewart," he said, arrogantly dismissing Melanie's presence with a brush of his hand. "I was advised by telephone that I had won a contest and that I was obligated to be here today."

Melanie's simmering temper flashed to the surface. *Not so fast,* she thought, and tugged the rumpled letterhead from the pocket of her skirt, intent on wiping the smugly satisfied look from Mr. Mitchel Stewart's handsome countenance.

"I received this letter by special delivery," she said, waving the letter for all to see. Heat flooded her face as she stared into mocking blue eyes.

"I was to receive a phone call with further instructions, but—" She paused for effect. Her tone was acidic in the extreme. "Apparently, that went astray."

Mitchel Stewart looked stunned at her words. Obviously he thought she was faking. Anger rushed through her as Melanie remembered all the things 50,000 could provide for her friends. There was no way this man was going to do her out of what was rightfully hers. She couldn't afford to let Mr. Pushy M. Stewart push her out of the running. If his name really was Stewart!

Just then, Papa John stepped into the spotlight. Taking the mike from the dumbfounded announcer's hand, he spoke into it in the soft, musical drawl known throughout North America.

"Now, folks. It looks like there's been some sort of mix-up here today. According to my information, our winner, M. Stewart, lives at 300 Oak Street in Mossbank, North Dakota."

His weathered face studied the two. Melanie spoke up.

"Yes, well, I work at that address. It's a nursing home. Sunset Retirement Home."

Clearly, Mitchel Stewart was not to be outdone. He stepped forward.

"I am also employed at 300 Oak Street."

Her anger grew as she glared at him, her eyes narrowed and searching. How could he do this to her? He was lying. She knew it. She knew all the tenants in the home, and she knew the employees, as well. He wasn't one of them.

"I started two weeks ago." He said it triumphantly, as if this was a game of one-upmanship. Melanie fumed.

"This sure is a puzzler, folks." Papa John scratched his head, obviously considering the next step.

One of the most popular television stations in North Dakota was broadcasting a lot of dead air, which was certainly not good for business, but it seemed no one could think of anything to say. Finally, the announcer stepped forward and spoke directly to the camera.

"Ladies and gentlemen, you have watched a newsmaking event on WMIX tonight. We apparently have two winners in the Papa John's Peanut Butter contest, both named M. Stewart and both living in Mossbank and working at 300 Oak

Street." He smiled fatuously at both of them before glancing at the camera. "Keep tuned, and WMIX will keep you up to the minute with events as they happen."

As he gave the familiar station call letters, Melanie drooped with fatigue. Papa John moved to brush a gentle hand over hers.

"I'm real sorry about this, miss," he apologized. "I don't know what happened. There must have been some error. The selections were made by computer." Papa John grinned at her. "Couldn't have picked a better station, though, could I? WMIX. Mixed up, they should call it."

Melanie smiled weakly.

They both turned at the throat-clearing sound from Mitchel Stewart. The dark-haired man had absolutely no manners, Melanie decided grimly. He stood peering down at both of them, eavesdropping on their conversation without any compunction. She turned her back to him deliberately as Papa John spoke again.

"I'm sorry about you, too, Mr. Stewart. I promise you that I will get this straightened out and let you know as soon as I can. Thank you both for making time to come down." The old man reached into his shirt pocket for a scrap of paper and a pen.

"Where can I reach you during the day, Miss Stewart?"

Melanie shuffled through her purse for a business card. She tried to ignore the tall man directly behind her.

"I am the director of care at Sunset," she told him, keeping her voice quiet.

"That's the one attached to the hospital," Papa John said, scribbling in odd, unreadable ink strokes. "I know about it from friends."

"Here's my address," Mitchel Stewart announced gruffly, unasked. "I'm often at the hospital, but I'll give you my card with office numbers." Trust him to butt in, Melanie thought.

A lean, muscular hand proffered a crisp white business card. His fingers were long and well cared for. The hands of a surgeon, Melanie guessed. Surgeons were usually arrogant. She turned to leave the two men.

"I have to get back to work," she murmured. "Nice to meet you, Papa John." Melanie glanced at the interloper, nodding dismissively.

As she strode out of the building, she wondered what would happen next when strong fingers closed about her arm.

"I'll walk with you," that firm, bossy voice declared. "If you don't mind, that is. It seems we have something in common besides our names." He smiled that thousand-watt grin that made her pulse flutter. "I didn't realize you worked at Sunset. Guess I didn't notice you."

Egotistical male, Melanie decided and tossed her gleaming curls. Her normally clear skin flushed with irritation in the bright sunlight. That was just what every woman wanted to hear—that she had been overlooked.

"Oh, no, I don't mind at all," she said with a touch of sarcasm. "Please feel free to tag along."

She was not a small woman, but Mitchel Stewart seemed to tower over her. Even with three-inch heels, her five-foot-five-inch stature seemed small and ineffective beside his height. She felt as if she was losing the upper hand in every confrontation with him.

She glared at him, tugging her arm out of his grasp as she stepped back, her body language telling him clearly not to invade her personal space.

"I don't appreciate being accosted in broad daylight, Mr. Stewart," she said through clenched teeth.

"Oh. Sorry. Do you appreciate it more after dark?" he quipped, grinning. "It was a little joke," he said, his smile noticeably drooping.

"Very little." Melanie was not amused. "I expect surgeons are so used to getting what they want, they never think of anyone else's wishes." Her normally calm, even tones were scathing.

"I expect they are."

He was trying to mollify her. She could hear it in his voice.

"You admit it?" Her dark eyes opened wide in disbelief. His impudence galled her.

Mitchel wasn't sure exactly what was going on. He had been aware of her dislike. It emanated from every pore of her well-shaped body. But right now it was as if there was another conversation going on. One that he knew absolutely nothing about.

He studied her small, tilted nose. It fit perfectly with her high-and-mighty attitude. The original attraction he had felt onstage had not abated. For some reason her dislike drew him like a magnet. He wondered if she would consider… Well, why not forge ahead?

Turning quickly, Mitchel folded her arm in his and began striding toward the parking lot. Perforce the lady had to follow, although not happily.

"Will you stop dragging me about?" she demanded. As she tried to push his muscle-hardened body away, her heel caught in a metal grating. Mitchel caught her as she swayed.

"Now look what you've done," he said, smiling sympathetically. "All I wanted was to help you to your car and ask you out for dinner. I wasn't expecting you to fall into my arms."

Melanie pursed her lips and refused to rise to the bait. He was too infuriating. Instead she walked away.

"Where are you going?"

She pointed her finger at the tan beater parked haphazardly in a stall just six feet away. His black eyebrow arched quizzically.

"Vice-president, Communications?" Mitchel's gleaming dark eyes frowned at her. "I thought you said you worked at the retirement home." Clearly puzzled, he stared at her for several moments before his face darkened ominously.

"I get it," he announced, teeth bared. "It was all just a ruse, wasn't it? Just for the money. Well, I'm not going to be part of your little con game." His glittering sapphire eyes stared at the placard in front of her car. "Goodbye, N. Landt."

He turned on his heel and strode furiously away, shoulders stiff with anger.

Melanie sighed, resigned to her fate. "It has been a difficult week, Lord," she mused. "Today isn't going so well, either. And it doesn't look like things will be improving anytime soon. I know I can't understand everything You do, so could You just help me get through today?"

Sighing, she fished her key ring out of the leather shoulder bag and unlocked the car door. Gently she eased herself into the car, glumly grateful that she'd made it through this far. She would probably drive to the home, enjoy a cup of fresh coffee and get down to what she knew best.

A light tapping on her window roused Melanie from her thoughts. Turning, she saw a tall blond Adonis dressed in an elegant black three-piece pinstripe standing outside her car. She rolled down the window.

"Yes?"

"I'm terribly sorry," he apologized, flashing a movie-perfect smile, "but you are parked in my spot. I'm Neal Landt."

It was too much. Melanie burst into laughter, paroxysms of hilarity shaking her narrow shoulders.

"I'm very sorry," she apologized as concern etched itself on his worried face. Quickly she explained the reason for her visit. "I was so afraid I'd be late, I pulled into the first empty spot and rushed into the studio. I'll move right away," she promised.

Melanie flicked on the car's engine and waved at the bemused young man staring after her. When she glanced back, Neal Landt was scribbling furiously as he leaned against his silver-gray Jaguar.

"I'll probably get a ticket for parking in his spot, the way today is going," she muttered, and tried to ignore the pain pulsing through her puffy ankle.

"Once I get to work," she promised herself. "I'll be okay then. In fact," she muttered in frustration, "the whole day would have progressed very well if I had just ignored the stupid letter and gone straight to work in the first place."

There are no free lunches, she remembered Charity lecturing. *Whatever you get in this life is exactly what you've worked for, dear. There's no such thing as something for nothing.*

"As usual, you are always right, Mother," Melanie lamented sadly. "Especially today. But oh, what we could have done with that prize!"

It really was too bad the ill-humored Mitchel Stewart had not been able to see the funny side of this whole situation, Melanie thought, her lips tilting up as her mind replayed the scene. Humming loudly, she pulled into traffic and headed for Mossbank, confident that a return to routine would put her on track.

The mass of paperwork beckoned, and Melanie knew she would have to tackle it soon, but there was one duty she couldn't neglect in her daily ritual. Anyway, she didn't want to. She enjoyed it too much.

Quickly she slid out of the navy suit she had worn for her television debut and into the spare pink uniform she kept for just such occasions. She surveyed herself in the narrow mirror she had hung on the back of her door.

"Oh, lovely." She grimaced, noting the caked lines of eye-shadow and heavy red lipstick. "Wait till the candy stripers see you in this getup."

She grabbed a brush and tugged it through her dark russet curls, allowing them to fall to her shoulders. A few tissues and some cream took off the goop they had plastered on her at the studio, and she cleansed her skin well before applying a light touch of blush and a hint of mascara. She hated a lot of makeup, and anyway, she never remembered to renew it.

Satisfied, Melanie walked out the door and into the group of residents gathered outside.

"Mrs. Christie." She smiled, gathering the woman's blue-veined hands in her own. "I do believe it's a special day for you today."

The toothless old woman squeezed Melanie's hand tightly and nodded. Tears of happiness pooled at the corners of the weary, wrinkled eyes.

"My grandson is coming," she whispered as if afraid to say the words aloud. "He's bringing his fiancée. Isn't it wonderful?"

"Yes, it is." Melanie smiled at her. "And you look lovely," she told the elderly woman sincerely.

Each resident had something special to say to her, and Melanie allowed them to speak freely. It was so important to them, this time of sharing. Many felt neglected and alone, and they needed someone to listen. It mattered not that she had heard these same stories a hundred times before. What was important was the telling, recalling the happiness of the past. For many it was their only pleasant time in an otherwise bleak existence.

Except for Mrs. Rivers.

"Good morning, Nettie. You look lovely today. As usual."

The old lady sat silently staring out the window, her hands full of contest entries, which she shuffled from one hand to the other. She refused to answer any of the questions Melanie asked. Contrary to the administrator's evaluation, Melanie believed the older woman could understand everything that was said to her. It was merely a problem of finding the right subject or the right person to get her to talk. And heaven knew, Melanie had tried quite a few. Today nothing seemed to budge the woman out of her self-imposed silence.

"Well, Mrs. Rivers, I hope you have a good day today."

Because the stack of work still had to be dealt with, Melanie finally gave in. It was now or never. She returned to her desk, sat down and immersed herself in work, tuning out everything but the unfinished schedules and part-time applications that needed immediate attention.

A disturbance in the outside office alerted her to the possibility of trouble sometime later. Raised in anger, the voice barely carried through the strong metal door. Melanie dropped her pen to listen.

It was a man's voice, she decided. Rather low, but obviously furious. She grinned when Bridget attempted to intercept the flow of angry words with little success.

When her focus would not return, Melanie finally gave in to curiosity, grimacing as she stood. She would settle this and then it was back to the grindstone, she promised herself. No sidetracking.

As she opened the door, a familiar voice ranted at Bridget.

"It's a hospital, for heaven's sake. We can't have people wandering around in areas they shouldn't be, looking for lunch. Someone will get hurt. Don't you feed these people regularly?"

His tones were scathingly critical of her overworked staff, and Melanie surged forward, prepared to do battle.

"Dr. Stewart, we know exactly what we are doing in this facility. Perhaps if the medical staff in *your* hospital had enough sense to close the doors behind them, *our* residents would not wander into the hospital."

Mitchel Stewart whirled to face her, his jaw slack with astonishment. He was as good-looking as Melanie remembered. Still formally dressed in the dark suit jacket and matching slacks, he exuded the posh doctor persona.

Only the tie at the neck of his pristine white shirt was loosened and slightly askew. Curling dark hairs peeked out from his throat. He looked every inch a playboy with his rumpled black hair and twinkling azure eyes.

"You!" he gasped, clearly shocked. "What are you doing here?"

"As I told you before, Dr. Stewart, this is where I am employed. Supposedly you are, also, although I must have missed seeing you around." Melanie assumed a haughty look before demanding, "Is there anything else, Doctor?"

"I am not a doctor," he told her loudly. "And yes, there certainly is. May I speak with you privately?"

"Not Dr. Stewart?" Melanie stretched her lips thinly, faking outrage. "You lied deliberately, to try to cheat me out of that money, didn't you?" she accused, hands on her hips.

When a telltale flush of red covered his jutting cheekbones, Melanie felt deep satisfaction. Self-righteous and smug, she delivered the final blow.

"I don't think I want to be part of your charade any longer, whoever you are."

Turning, Melanie flounced into her office in high dudgeon, feeling a virtuous superiority. He had asked for it.

"We're not quite finished, are we?" His deep tones rumbled over her left shoulder.

"I've said everything I'm going to," she announced smugly and flopped into her desk chair.

"Good. Then *you* can hear *me* out."

Chapter Two

"Ms. Stewart, it seems there has been more than one mix-up today."

He had never before seen a woman so furious and yet so determined not to say a word, Mitch decided in amusement. He fully expected her to blow a gasket.

"What do you want?" Her low voice barely masked her frustration.

"Look, I came to say I'm sorry." She looked slightly mollified at his calm, contrite tone, but the glitter of suspicion returned to her eyes when Bridget walked into her office with Sam Sinclair shuffling alongside her. Mitch ignored them.

"*And* I came to make sure you keep those patients out of the hospital. They could get hurt." She had that look again.

"Ms. Stewart—Melanie—I'm very sorry I accused you wrongly earlier today. Please forgive me." Deliberately, Mitch made his tones sweet as honey.

"Fine. You're forgiven." Her voice was frosty, unwelcoming, with a tinge of bitterness. "Now, please, will you get out of my office. Bridget, would you do the honors?"

Leaning back in her chair, Melanie glared at him. He watched her huge green eyes flicker with something like suspicion as she studied him. Mitch decided the faint pink of her uniform was certainly her color.

Her almost round face, with its dainty nose tipped at that disdainful angle, dared him to try her patience. Her mouth straightened into a thin, disapproving line.

Deliberately Mitch tamped his growing interest and firmed his resolve. He wasn't here looking for a date. He was here to make restitution. Melanie Stewart was going to understand his concerns one way or another.

"Now, if we can discuss this rationally."

"Oh, buzz off—" She stopped short of saying whatever else was on her mind, and Mitch almost laughed at the childish phrase.

Melanie was fiery and determined and willful, but she had a streak of decency in her that forbade the use of cuss words. It was unusual in this day and age and something he admired, Mitch admitted. But he wouldn't tell her that just yet.

Stretching her long legs, Melanie deliberately ignored him. To Mitch, that was the final straw. He opened the door and ordered, "Look, just look.

"They're wandering all over the place," he told her, pointing toward one sprightly old gentleman dressed in an ancient green suit, which bore a striking resemblance to the apparel of a leprechaun. "This place is out of control."

He watched as she spluttered angrily. But as residents watched, Melanie Stewart refused to acknowledge his tenuous grip on her small hand. Smiling and friendly, she greeted each one, losing the smile immediately when they passed.

"The hospital cannot afford to have someone injured or worse, simply because you allow these people to wander around at large. It's my job to ensure we don't get embroiled in any frivolous law suits." He pulled her along behind him through the hallways, past the interested spectators gathered outside their rooms.

"You're a lawyer?" The way she said his profession, Mitch figured it rated pretty low on her scale.

It also brought on another tirade.

"Of all the silly, idiotic, lying tricks…"

Mitch let her rant until they came to a tiny woman sitting quietly on a bench in the hall. Bending his lips to her ear, Mitch teased her.

"If you scare these folks into thinking you're having a conniption fit, they are going to get worked up. Just relax, will you?" He breathed in the soft, light fragrance she wore, enjoying its teasing allure.

"Conniption fit? I haven't heard that phrase for years!" She frowned at him. "Anyway, Mrs. Rivers never says anything."

As they drew nearer, the little woman murmured something. Melanie stared in amazement. In two years, Mrs. Rivers had never been heard to utter more than one word. Suddenly, at the sight of this lawyer, she was speaking?

"I beg your pardon," Melanie said, hoping the old lady would repeat herself.

The woman's bright gray eyes were riveted on them, and she spoke louder.

"It's so romantic," she breathed. "Just like a knight in shining armor. Oh, Melanie, at last you have found your true love."

Mitch bowed as low as possible, a huge grin crinkling his smug face. "Thank you, ma'am."

Turning, he marched Melanie back through the office to her inner sanctum, then gently pressed her stiff, angry body onto the leather couch. As he moved to stand, Mitch gently drew his lips across her soft, angry ones.

"Maybe she's right, Melanie." He grinned cheekily before tossing his jacket across his arm and moving to the door. He slid his dark eyes over her once more before murmuring, "We'll see." The door closed softly on his laughing face.

Melanie hissed with frustration through tightly pursed lips. "No, Mr. Know-It-All Stewart, we definitely will not see."

Her hand swiped across her mouth as she tried without success to erase the feel of his seeking mouth. She clenched her fist as the pool of awareness in her middle refused to go away.

"Cad. Liar. Overbearing male. Rude. Pushy. Thief…oh!" There simply were not enough words, she decided.

"Talking to someone?" Shawna poked her head around the door. "I thought I heard someone calling names." She grinned, eyeing her friend's heightened color.

"Could be," Melanie answered, forcing a smile. "The way today's been going, anything might happen." She looked at her roomie curiously. "What are you doing here?"

Shawna unpinned her glistening hair and shook it free of her confining nurse's cap. She wasn't wearing scrubs, Melanie noticed.

"Not operating today?"

"Oh, Mal is late again. You know, it's getting so that the man never manages to arrive in the operating room until at least an hour after his scheduled time." Mal was her pet name for a doctor on staff she particularly despised. Short for malpractice.

"Doesn't that sort of throw things off?" Melanie knew enough about the tightly funded medical world to know that time is money, especially in an operating room.

"Oh, yeah," Shawna agreed. "And I can tell you that the other doctors are getting pretty tired of hanging around waiting for him to get his act together."

"Did you pick up your check?" Her eyes were big and round with excitement. "Can I see it? The money, I mean."

Melanie sighed deeply. "I didn't get the money." When Shawna's jaw dropped open, Melanie's hand went up, forestalling her comments. "It seems that two invitations went out, both of them to an M. Stewart. Unfortunately there were two M. Stewarts in attendance. One Melanie, one Mitchel. He just left."

The paging system interrupted her.

"I've gotta go. Mal must be here. Why now?" Shawna muttered in frustration. "I can't wait to hear more." Stuffing her long hair under the cap, the operating room nurse left in a flurry, looking model perfect.

It didn't matter how much she tried after that, Melanie could not concentrate on the job. Part of it was her own fault, she acknowledged bitterly. But most of it was due to a certain lawyer and she put in time without accomplishing much.

"I'm calling it a day, Bridget. Can you handle everything?" Melanie watched as Bridget nodded, her face lit with a huge grin. "Don't mention him," she ordered grimly. "This is all his fault!"

Melanie strode out the door, then turned.

"And don't call my mother," she ordered wrathfully. "All I need are the fearsome threesome hanging around trying to nurse me through this illness."

"Melanie! You know Faith and Hope and your mother only want to help. Why, I'm sure if they knew about that handsome man that just left, they'd be very pleased."

"Considering that they've been trying to marry me off for years, I suppose so." Melanie grimaced. "My mother was even trying to set me up with Judge Conroy's grandson the other day." She shook her head in dismay.

"Yes, but—"

"I have to go home, Bridget. My feet are killing me. See you tomorrow." Melanie left, winding through the maze of curious and grinning residents to the parking lot.

"Lawyers!" One last epithet and she was finished thinking about Mitchel Stewart, she decided.

* * *

"But they said he was dead! Killed in action." Hope stared at her two best friends in agony. "I pleaded and I begged them to check again and again, but they said they were sure."

"Hope, dear, God still works miracles," Faith murmured, patting the pale, smooth hand. "And He is the final authority. Just calm down and let us think this through."

Charity peered at the two women sitting in her living room and wondered if it was true. Had Hope's fiancé returned from the dead after nearly twenty-five years?

"How did you find all this out?" she asked. "Did someone from the government phone you, Hope?" She remembered the television clip from last evening. "I have heard that they are still finding some MIAs. Perhaps Jean was one of those?"

Hope shook her blond head, dazed.

"No, I don't think so. The lady who phoned said he'd been quite ill. Apparently, during a high fever, he mentioned my name. Lately someone's been searching for him. She asked me all kinds of questions, Faith. Strange questions."

"Questions? Oh, piffle!" Faith's normally sunny face was dark with foreboding. "What kind of questions?"

"Oh, if I was married now. And the year Jean disappeared. If I'd ever heard from him while he was in Vietnam. Things like that."

"There have been some private efforts to investigate claims about MIAs," Charity murmured, watching her friend's sad face. "Perhaps that's it. Maybe a family member?"

"Charity, he didn't have any family. And besides—" Hope winced "—Jean wasn't missing in action. They said he died!" Her voice was full of remembered pain. "How could they make a mistake like that?"

"We don't know, dear. Perhaps we never will. But God knows. And He will use this to bless you, you can be sure of that."

Hope's unlined face was haggard as she stared at her closest friends.

"I don't know what to do," she confessed wearily. "I don't know where to turn."

"Well, I do," Faith declared firmly. "First we turn to the Lord, and then I'm going to give Harry Conroy a call. He's got contacts in Washington. Maybe he can find out something."

"You don't have to phone him, Faith. He's coming over for dinner. And bringing his grandson." Charity smiled slyly. "Melanie's coming, too. Why don't you both stay? Maybe we can figure something out together."

"I can stay." Faith beamed happily, clapping her hands. "I just love fried chicken. And Arthur's away in Denver at that conference."

"Fried chicken," Hope murmured, a look of faint chagrin on her face. "Very well, I suppose one high-cholesterol meal won't hurt. Thank you, Charity. In fact, I'll help you. I can make a salad."

Charity peered at Faith with a look that asked the other woman for help.

"That's a good idea. A nice fresh green Caesar salad with croutons and cheese and lots of dressing. But first we pray," Faith ordered, and led off a heartfelt plea to her heavenly father.

After twenty-three laps, Melanie was definitely winded, but after thirty-two she was relaxed. The huge pool area was one of the apartment's perks she really enjoyed. Some people jogged, and some did aerobics. Melanie had always preferred swimming.

Slowly, she pulled herself out and walked the few steps to the whirling hot tub. She never could stand the overpowering temperature for very long, but it soothed and rejuvenated like no other remedy for stress. Eyes closed, she reclined and let the bubbling waters do their work.

"Miss Stewart, how nice to see you again."

Melanie blinked, almost believing the man standing in front of her was a dream. Goodness knows, he was certainly dream material. Tall and dark, clad in a black swimsuit, he exemplified male macho.

Melanie gulped as she moved her gaze from his strong, muscular legs to his lean hips and tapered waist, across the broad expanse of his golden chest covered in fine whorling black hairs to his sharply featured face. He was hunk material, all right, she told herself, trying to calm her thudding heart.

The time since their last meeting had not dulled her irrational attraction to him in the least.

"Mr. Stewart." It was a miracle anything emerged from her parched throat. For the life of her, Melanie couldn't think of a thing to say.

"Still mad, huh?"

Grinning, Mitchel Stewart walked to the edge of the pool and dove into its still waters. The ripples that spread seemed amazingly like those circles of excitement that rippled through her. She watched him swim with even strokes, broad shoulders and muscular arms cutting cleanly through the water.

Melanie gave herself a mental shake and turned her eager eyes from watching his graceful form. Instead she sank deeper into the hot water, hoping it would ease new tension. She closed her eyes and deliberately blanked out his presence.

"May I join you?" The question was perfunctory. Mitchel Stewart didn't bother to wait for an answer. He sank down beside her, his thigh brushing hers. Melanie edged away, giving him more room.

His dark eyes twinkled at her as he spoke.

"Okay, you win," he declared. "I think you have sufficiently paid me back with Mrs. Strange and her daughter." A rueful look passed over his face. "Some would even say you're points ahead."

Melanie burst out laughing. Agatha Strange was a lonely old soul whose fondest wish was to have her spinster daughter married before the old woman passed on, as she phrased it. When Mrs. Strange had come to her with a problem about her will, Melanie's plan had hatched. Who better to handle the old girl than attorney extraordinaire Mitchel Stewart? Gleefully, she had told the elderly woman about Mitchel, while managing to imply that he was single and desperately looking for love.

Throughout the week, bits and pieces of their exchanges had been relayed to Melanie until even she felt sorry for the man. Deidre Strange, the daughter, was at least twenty years older than Mitchel and about sixty pounds heavier. Truly, a perfect match.

His big blue eyes gazed woefully into hers.

"Could we please start again?" He sounded like a little boy trying to atone for stealing the last chocolate chip cookie. Melanie couldn't help it, she grinned. He thrust out one large, tanned hand.

"Mitchel Stewart. Mitch to my friends. Just moved into the building." He began to list his many attributes. "Single, good health, age thirty-two, six foot four, one hundred eighty-five pounds, legal counsel to corporate accounts." His bright eyes sparkled mischievously. "Same information I gave Mrs. Strange."

Giggling, Melanie shook his hand as she answered.

"Melanie Stewart, no age and definitely no weight."

"Okay." He dragged the word out. "So, Melanie, what's your favorite food?"

She joined in the game easily enough. Mitch appeared to hold no ill feelings, and she had more than paid him back for his high-handedness.

Besides, she was a little embarrassed at her behavior. Her temper had always been a sore spot. Whenever she lost it, she invariably regretted her lack of control. Maybe she could redeem herself. She focused on the conversation.

"Chinese, especially the vegetables. What's yours?"

Mitch lounged comfortably beside her, his long legs stretched out. Dark head tipped back, he thought for a few minutes before answering. "Food."

Melanie frowned. "Pardon?"

"I like just about everything as long as someone else cooks it." His mouth slanted mockingly as he leered at her. "I can make a mean raspberry punch, though."

"Oh. Well, good," Melanie answered lamely, refusing to acknowledge the spark of awareness that flew each time he brushed against her.

It was the heat, she told herself. She should never have remained in the Jacuzzi for so long. The reason she had, of course, was her swimsuit.

It had been a lapse in judgment. She knew that. Her bust was too full and her hips too round to wear something this defining. Nevertheless, the heat was unbearable, and she had to leave. Now!

"Excuse me, I have to get out." Melanie moved slowly and calmly up the stairs, aware of his eyes on her legs. Once out of the heat, she could draw cooling air into her lungs. She reached for her towel and quickly tugged it over her shoulders, trying to ignore him as he sat there watching her.

"Did I drive you out?" His eyebrows tipped downward.

"Oh, no." Melanie cinched her towel a little tighter across her shoulders. "I just can't take the heat." Her face flooded with pink. She rushed to correct herself.

"Of the pool. I mean, the Jacuzzi. After a few minutes, the heat really gets to me."

Mitch knew what she meant. The heat was getting to him, too. He could feel it frying his brain to mush as he admired the lovely Melanie.

He'd seen far skimpier suits on many of the local beaches, but nothing that looked as elegantly attractive as this. Mitch decided he much preferred it over the pink uniform she had worn the other day. Her long auburn hair was curling wildly around her shoulders and face, hugging the wide cheekbones and delicately arched brows.

Flushing brightly, Melanie turned her back to him to gather her belongings. As she did, her towel slipped to the floor.

What was wrong with the men in town, he wondered, watching her. The woman was gorgeous, and apparently had brains, too. Yet here she was, spending her evening alone. Idly, he wondered if there was someone special in her life.

Mitch watched her pull on a white terry covering that just grazed her thighs. When the heat began to addle his brain, he moved out of the swirling hot tub to tug on the baggy jogging pants he had tucked into his sports bag. Something was definitely going on between them, he decided, some spark of interest he'd noticed from the first. And despite his best intentions, he was going to investigate the fiery redhead.

"How about going to dinner with me?" The phrasing wasn't the greatest, he decided, but it was hard to make sense when your brain was the consistency of mashed potatoes.

She was slipping on shorts, and at his question, Melanie stood stock-still, perched like a startled flamingo on one leg. Her tousled hair tumbled around her face, huge green eyes questioning. She had a fresh, clean-scrubbed look he found very attractive.

"I don't—"

He cut her off before she could refuse.

"Please," he cajoled, tugging on a shirt. "You would really be doing me a favor." He tried to look forlorn and alone. "I just moved the last of my stuff in and I can't possibly do any more hard work today. I deserve a break. Please?"

She looked at him steadily, obviously gauging just how reliable he was. He was surprised himself at how anxious he was to get to know her better.

"All right," Melanie agreed finally. "But I think you'd better come with me. I agreed to have dinner with my mother tonight." If she thought she would turn him off by introducing her mother, she had been dead wrong.

"Is she a good cook?" Mitch asked warily, watching her gather her belongings.

"The best. You may need to do a few more laps when you're finished."

He looked affronted as he pulled on his clothes. One hand patted his washboard-flat stomach experimentally.

"I could stand to gain a few pounds. You think?" He cocked his head with that little-boy grace she was coming to recognize.

"No comment." Melanie giggled and went out. "I'll meet you downstairs in half an hour. Don't be late."

He wasn't late, but she was there before him, tapping one foot impatiently against the marble floor.

"I wondered if you'd changed your mind," she murmured, tossing her hair over her shoulders. Melanie stepped through the door and began to stride down the street. Mitch was forced to hurry to keep up with her.

"A woman who's on time," he muttered, huffing as he marched beside her. "Who would believe it?"

"Quite a few people, actually. It's just one of my failings."

"Why are we running when we could have taken the car?" Mitch panted, half-walking, half-jogging across the street.

"We're not running, we're walking. My mother lives only three blocks away. There's hardly any point in driving. Besides—" she grinned at him pointedly "—it's good exercise."

"I prefer swimming." He breathed, trying to look macho while his lungs burned. To his disgust, Melanie seemed totally unaffected by the speed race.

"Most out-of-shape people do prefer exercise that isn't weight bearing," she murmured without losing a step.

"Now just a minute! I am not—" Mitch felt himself collide with the pavement at the same moment his temperature hit boiling. There was a web of stabbing pain radiating from his left knee, and his pants were torn.

"Now look what you've done," he said furiously as he stood with some difficulty, pushing her helping hand away. "I'm not going out for dinner looking like this."

Her green eyes flashed with something he might have thought was sympathy. Except for her next words.

"Mm, lack of coordination, too. Don't ever take up jogging, Mr. Stewart. You're not the type."

"I don't think we have to worry about that," he said through clenched teeth as he brushed bits of gravel from his palms. "And I am not uncoordinated! If you didn't insist on making this the Indy 500..."

"Oh, now it's my fault! If that isn't just like a man! Blame it on me because I keep in shape and you don't. As if I or anyone else could make you exercise more. Men!" She spat the word with a telling glance that relegated him to one of the lower subspecies in the universe.

Mitch smiled grimly.

"I'm sorry," he muttered, limping at a pace that was still far too fast but considerably slower than her former fifty knots. "But I am a man. I wouldn't have come with you if I had known you hated men."

"I don't hate men," she said in exasperation. "I quite appreciate them." Her eyes flickered and he wondered if he could call that stretch of her lips a smile. "Some of you are even quite useful."

It was a put-down, sure as anything, and Mitch refused to let it pass.

"I think I understand why you're not, er, out tonight," he murmured under his breath. "You're a man-hater."

She stopped so quickly he crashed into her, the breath wheezing out of his chest at the contact. Melanie Stewart was mad. He could see it in her glinting green eyes. He could feel it in the tingle of electricity that pulsed through the air around them. But what really gave away her emotional state were the small, pointed fingernails buried in his arm.

"I am not stupid," she enunciated. "You think that if you make all these ridiculous accusations, I'll forget you're trying to swindle me out of that money, don't you? Well, Mr. Mitchel Stewart, or whatever your name is—" she snorted in pretended amusement "—it's not going to work."

Carefully, with extreme patience and not a little wincing, Mitch removed her talons from his shirtsleeve.

"I don't know why you keep saying that," he muttered fiercely. "My name *is* Mitchel Stewart. And I am not trying to swindle anyone out of anything." He peered at her, noting with interest the high spots of color on her cheeks. "Why is getting this money so important to you, anyway? Do you need cash that badly? I know the bank manager," he said, frowning at her rising color. "There's no need to be embarrassed about needing some help."

Melanie flushed more deeply. Her hands were balled into fists, but she raised her chin defiantly while her eyes hardened to cold intense chips of emerald.

"I don't want it for myself," she enunciated clearly. "I want to use it for some friends. They deserve to have some comfort in life, and this is my one chance to give it to them.

If you hadn't interfered, I would have the money by now and I'd be able to take care of them."

"I might have a perfectly good use for that money myself," he told her angrily. "Someone I care about very much could use that cash right about now."

"May the best woman or man win, then." Melanie snapped open a black wrought-iron gate with one hand and stepped through. "Well, are you coming or not?"

"Yes." He sighed. "I'm coming. And I still think you dislike men."

"No, she doesn't," a bright voice chirped. "Piffle! Melanie is just one of those modern career girls who put most of their energies into their work. When she gets married, she'll bury herself in that, too."

Mitch glanced up to see Faith Johnson's beaming face.

"Oh, hello. I didn't know you'd be here tonight." He grinned happily, pleased to see the beaming older woman. "Melanie didn't tell me."

"Melanie didn't know," his companion muttered. She glanced from one to the other. "Do I take it you two know each other?"

"Of course we know each other. I was here for dinner last week with my grandfather. Wait a minute!" He stared at her as the pieces began to fall into place. "You mean Mrs. Flowerday is your mother? But your names—"

"Are different because Melanie is adopted. My own very special daughter." Charity hugged the slim form to her ample bosom and patted Melanie's back. "I'm so glad you could come, darling. And you brought Harry's grandson! How marvelous. Do come in."

"Actually I'm her foster daughter. Harry's grand—" Melanie whirled to stare at Mitch, her eyes wide with dismay. "You mean you're Judge Conroy's grandson?"

Mitch bowed at the waist.

"The one and only."

"Oh, no."

No one else heard the softly breathed moan, Mitch was sure, but he did. And he didn't like it. The female of the species generally appreciated his company. But Melanie Stewart was looking at him as if he was a worm crawling out of the woodwork.

"You knew all about this, didn't you," she asked angrily. "You'd think you would know better than to fall in with the fearsome threesome's plans."

"I don't have a clue—"

"That's for sure," she said, her eyes shooting daggers at him. "Try to act normally. And if you don't make any waves, we may just get out of this early enough to nip their matchmaking in the bud."

She stomped away to talk to the two other women seated in Charity's living room. Mitch shook his head in confusion and headed for the nearest easy chair, only remembering as he sat that this particular chair had a bad spring.

"Oof!"

"Did you say something, boy?" His grandfather emerged from the kitchen chewing on a bit of meat.

"No, Gramps. Well, yes, actually, I said it was good to sit down." Mitch watched as everyone turned to face him. "I meant after the walk over. You know, in the heat and everything." Why were they all staring at him as if he had two heads?

His grandfather looked at him pityingly, eyeing the tear at his pants with some disfavor.

"Practice not doing too well, son?" He reached in his pocket, and Mitch cringed, remembering the habit from long ago. Before the older man could pull out his wallet, Mitch launched into speech.

"No, it's going really well. The hospital was a good start, and I've found a number of new clients this week."

Judge Conroy shook his head.

"Then why wear those things? Doesn't look too good for an up-and-coming young lawyer."

Melanie laughed her light, bubbly laugh, which Mitch hadn't heard for ages.

"He kissed the pavement on the way over here. Tore his pants and cut his knee." She grinned at the judge and winked. "Out of shape, I suspect."

"I am *not* out of shape." Mitch glared at her, gritting his teeth. "I tripped. It happens to lots of people."

"Oh, my dear! Let me see," Hope murmured, scurrying over to check the skin of his knee. "Come along, Mitchel. That needs cleaning."

The older woman had him firmly by the arm, and there was nothing Mitch could do but follow meekly. She plunked him on a chair and rolled up his pant leg efficiently.

"I remember this from my teaching days." Hope smiled. "How many Band-Aids did I use during those thirty years, I wonder? And the iodine!"

"I, er, I don't think I need iodine," Mitch murmured, trying not to remember his past and how that stuff stung. "Really, it's fine."

Hope looked at him with a knowing smile. "It's all right," she whispered, patting his hand. "Nowadays, the new stuff doesn't hurt nearly as much."

Mitch subsided, feeling a fool. He sat meekly as she dabbed and cleaned and bandaged him until he looked like a trussed-up turkey. His pant leg wouldn't go over the massive bandage she had applied, so Hope Langford carefully cut it off, leaving him with one short and one long leg.

He stared at his legs, aghast at the sight of his mutilated trousers. He had never been so thoroughly humiliated in his entire life, and the evening hadn't even begun yet.

"Well, you couldn't very well wear them to work with a

patch in the knee," Hope told him kindly, her blond head tipped. "This way you can get the other leg cut off and make shorts out of them." She waved the scissors thoughtfully. "Would you like me to do it?"

"No, thanks anyway," he said, backing out of the room. "You've done a wonderful job, though." Of ruining his only pair of designer pants, he added under his breath.

Mitch turned carefully to go to the living room and found Melanie in his path, her gaze wide with disbelief as she studied him. Her mouth tilted in a slash of amusement, and her eyes sparkled with delight.

"Don't say a word," he warned her menacingly. "And if there's anyone who'll be leaving early, it's going to be me."

"How the mighty are fallen." She giggled, walking behind him as he limped to his chair. Her face cracked up when he jerked upward as the metal prong stabbed him in the rear again. "Shall I call Aunt Hope for you, Mitch?" She chortled.

"Oh, go away," he told her miserably. His eyes moved to the seniors huddled over the pictures on the coffee table. "What's going on there?"

"Oh, that. Hope has just received word that the man she was engaged to years ago may not have died in the Vietnam war, as she was told. My mother wants Judge Conroy to help them check into it." Melanie's face was sad. "I feel bad because Hope never forgot Jean."

"But where on earth has he been?"

"I don't know," Melanie told him. "Let's listen in and see what we can find out."

"But if he wasn't killed there, why did they think he was?" Hope demanded. "There must have been some proof of identity." She glanced at the judge for confirmation.

"I don't know, dear," the old man murmured, covering her hand with his tenderly. "But I'll do everything I can to help you find out." There was a silence while everyone considered the implications.

Moments later the two older ladies went with Melanie into the kitchen and Mitch, his grandfather and Hope sat in the living room. It seemed the other two had forgotten him completely, so Mitch listened to their conversation unashamedly.

"Do you still have feelings for this man, Hope?" his grandfather whispered, his salt-and-pepper head bent near hers.

"I don't know. I don't know what I feel anymore. Everything has changed, moved out of its familiar pattern. I just wish I knew for sure whether or not Jean was alive." She stared at the old pictures with tears in her eyes, her face a study in contrasts.

"All those years ago I just gave up," she whispered regretfully. "Maybe, if I had kept searching, Jean and I would have had a future together."

Judge Conroy patted the soft white hand with affection.

"It's in His hands," he murmured comfortingly. "Let's leave it there while we do what we can, my dear."

As he sat at the dinner table, munching on wonderful home-cooked fried chicken and the smoothest mashed potatoes he'd ever eaten, Mitch studied each person carefully.

His grandfather sat next to Hope, and he was paying an inordinate amount of attention to the woman, Mitch noted. They were laughing about the good times they'd shared and their plans for the seniors' retreat at Lucky Lake.

Hope Langford was a beautiful woman, with her smooth blond hair and clear blue eyes. She was quiet but thoughtful, replying to the comments only after she'd carefully considered her responses. Which was totally unlike her friend Faith, who seemed to bubble with excitement. Mitch knew that the older woman had recently been married, so perhaps that explained her effervescence.

Charity Flowerday sat next to him, insisting that he try seconds of everything and teasing him about his good appetite. But it was her arthritic hands that he noticed most. Although they were bent and worn, they expressed her tender concern in a thousand different ways. She ruffled his hair affectionately, offered a friendly pat to Faith's shoulder, soothed Hope's fears and pinched Melanie's ear. And all with those deformed hands.

And Melanie? Beautiful, remote Melanie sat silent in her chair, watching the other members of the group with love shining in her eyes. Mitch could see the pleasure she took in their company, the careful concerned way she rushed to help her mother, sparing her unnecessary labor.

And later, as they sat around singing old songs, it was Melanie who played for them. Tunes that Mitch recognized from his grandfather's era flowed easily through her fingers as they rippled lovingly over the notes, her voice blending in with a rich, deep harmony.

They're like her family, he thought. *That's why she works with old people. A big, happy family that cares and shares their lives with each other.*

It was something he'd never known and always thought he wanted. It was something he intended to find out more about, Mitch decided firmly.

With the help of Miss Melanie Stewart, of course.

Chapter Three

Once his knee had healed, the pain of embarrassment had passed and he'd purchased a new pair of pants, Mitch asked Melanie out for dinner. Chinese food. They sat across from one another in one of the local cafés without speaking as they waited for their meal of stir-fried Chinese vegetables and the deep-fried shrimp he'd insisted on. He figured Melanie could think of nothing to say—unlike their past encounter. Her fingers rolled the edge of her napkin. She took a sip of water.

"I like your dress." Mitch's low voice cut into her thoughts. His magnetic dark eyes gleamed in appreciation at the sweetheart neckline and fitted waist. "Green is certainly your color. That swimsuit was a knockout on you."

Blushing profusely, Melanie thanked him before hurrying to change the topic. "Have you heard anything from the contest people yet?" she asked.

Once more that wicked grin flashed at her, and once more her pulse started that rat-tatting that Mitchel Stewart always seemed to cause.

"Nope, not a word. Maybe they'll decide not to award it or to draw again. How did you enter?"

"I don't know." She laughed—that light, tinkling sound

he had come to associate with her. Shrugging, she confessed, "I don't even eat the stuff."

"What?" He gave an exaggerated gasp before he admitted, "Me, neither." His forehead was furrowed in thought. "How do you suppose they got our names, then?"

Melanie blushed again, and he wondered why. Gazing at her hands, she explained.

"A few months ago I was really down. One of our residents had died unexpectedly, and I…I was sort of depressed." Her green eyes were filled with sadness as she stared ahead. "Mrs. Peters was so lonely, you see. Her kids never came to see her except on a duty visit at Christmas that lasted all of five minutes. She needed to talk to them and feel that they still cared." Melanie heard her own voice harden.

"Apparently, all they needed was the check she always handed out. When she died, I phoned them and they were there in thirty minutes. Yet when she had been asking to see them only one week earlier, no one had the time to get away." Melanie waved across the table as she tried to help him understand.

"I remember the last thing she said to me. She wanted to buy a new dress," she told him sadly. Mitch's warm brown hand was wrapped around her clenched fingers. She glanced at him sadly. "She got her dress, but it was too late."

They sat there quietly eating the delicious food. Mitch had done nothing more than listen, but somehow his quiet strength helped, and after a minute or two she continued.

"Anyway, I was working with Mrs. Rivers by then and she was entering these contests. I thought, why not throw in a few of my own entries. Maybe a windfall of some kind could take some of the sting away and provide at least some of the essential equipment that so many need." She grinned self-deprecatingly. "That's been a hobbyhorse of mine for a while now."

"Why don't your pals just buy what they need? Surely some have money?"

Mitch's question was legitimate, and she tried to explain the ways of those greedy families she had become familiar with.

"Well, many of them do have some assets when they enter the residence and they do get the help they need, as well as visits from caring families. But some of these folks are not mobile, and it's difficult for them to do their banking. Usually the family takes it over, and when they see how expensive it is to look after Grandma or Grandpa, many begin to resent every dime they lose."

"But the money isn't theirs," Mitch protested indignantly.

"I know, but when you begin to think of something as part of your inheritance…" Her voice died away. "Mr. Harcourt is one of those fellows who is quite capable of operating a motorized cart. It would get him out of the residence and to coffee with his friends. He's not wealthy and his family think it's a silly, wasteful expenditure, and so he sits, day after day, gradually growing more depressed."

The conversation had become dull and gloomy, and Melanie suddenly felt guilty for dumping all her problems on him.

"I'm sorry. This isn't a very happy subject, and I tend to harp." She smiled at him, trying to lift the tension. "Exactly what kind of law do you practice?"

He knew she was trying to lighten the atmosphere, and he went along with it. "Corporate. Litigations are my preference, although I do agreements for sale, probate wills, boring stuff like that." He grinned that sexy smile again, and Melanie felt her spirits lift.

"Do you ever practice family law?" Her inquiry was innocent enough, but his reaction was totally unexpected.

"No." Curt and abrupt, his answer did not encourage speculation.

"I'm sorry. I didn't mean…"

His charming smile was once again in place, a facade he hid behind, Melanie suddenly realized.

"I hate that end of the business," he told her. "Men and women who swore to love each other suddenly become bitter enemies, each trying to outdo the other in nastiness. Pulling children's lives apart so they can hurt each other." He shook his dark head. "I won't be part of that."

Melanie heard the underlying hurt and suspected that Mitch had been a product of just such a scenario, perhaps as a small child. He wasn't talking about it.

"Don't you want to get married yourself? Have a family someday?" She studied him curiously, noting the flush on his high cheekbones.

"No. Well, yeah. Maybe. I'm not really the type." The words spilled out helter-skelter, and he frowned. "If I ever did, I'd go into it with a no-escape clause. So far I haven't found anyone I want to be tied up that tightly with. What about you?"

"I always thought love and marriage would just happen, but lately work takes up more and more of my time, and truthfully, I just don't know how I could fit a family in with that." She grimaced. "Those residents are important to me. I don't know if I could give them all up for a mere man." She grinned teasingly.

"We're not going into that man thing again, are we?" He groaned. "I already apologized three thousand times."

"And that's not nearly enough." She smiled.

"You should talk! You called me out of shape, remember?"

"And?" She raised one eyebrow meaningfully. "If the shoe fits…"

"Time to go," he muttered, shaking his head. "Before war breaks out."

Melanie gratefully picked up her purse and moved to the door. She felt like a liar, because she knew she'd give up her so-called career in a minute for a loving husband and the warmth and comfort of a family of her own.

As they strolled along the street, Mitch took her hand in his and drew it through his arm.

"I think we'll make good neighbors." He grinned at her. "The really neighborly thing to do would be to invite me in for coffee."

The hint was hard to miss, and surprisingly enough, she didn't want to bid Mitch good-night just yet.

"Well, since you did take me out for dinner, I suppose it is the least I can do." Melanie deliberately made the invitation as unappealing as possible, pretty sure he would jump at it. She didn't want to seem too eager, after all!

They sat among the flickering candles on her patio, sipping the rich Colombian brew Melanie favored. In the dark, it seemed easier to talk.

"My mother often let me stay up in the summer and have chocolate milk on the porch. This reminds me of those times." Her voice was soft and filled with memories, and Mitch seemed loath to break the spell of quiet contentment.

"She probably wished I'd go to bed, but she and Hope and Faith never tried to talk me out of my daydreams. I will always be thankful for their love and care. I guess that's why I choose to work where I do." She smiled happily. "Seniors have so much life and love and knowledge to contribute, if only someone would take the time to listen."

"You were lucky," he told her. That hard tone had frozen the emotion in his rumbly voice. "Some kids never get the chance to experience any of that."

"But you had your grandfather. Didn't you ever come visit?" Melanie searched her mind, trying to remember Mitch from some foggy distant encounter.

"Not very often. We lived too far away, and my parents couldn't afford it. Gramps came to visit us once or twice a year for a week or so, but that's all. After I was on my own, I'd come out as often as I could get away. We kind of developed a bond then."

Melanie could tell the subject was closed, but she longed to ask him about his childhood, his parents, his background. One minute he was so charming and friendly, and the next he had closed up like a clam, cold and hard.

Soft music flowed on the evening air as someone on another patio below them enjoyed the cool evening air.

"Do you dance?" he asked suddenly.

Melanie stuttered over her answer. "Not very well. I, well, it's been ages, and…"

Tall and dark in his denim shirt and pants, he stood before her. She tipped her head to look at him.

"Don't tell me you're uncoordinated, Melanie, or I will be forced to make some remark that will draw the battle lines between us. Again. May I have this dance?" he asked. His eyes glinted in the candlelight. "I have to get my exercise, you know." And then Mitch tugged her gently from her chair without waiting for a response. "Here, put your arms around me like this."

Melanie let Mitch push her bare arms around his neck and then stood silent while he wrapped his around her slender waist. She was nervous and sure he knew it.

"No fancy moves," he reassured her. "Just swaying to the music."

They swayed gently, moving slowly to the music. As he held, she was aware of his warmth and strength, the spicy scent of his cologne and the momentary brush of his beard-roughened cheek on her own. Her skirt swished around her legs as his foot grazed hers. It was wonderful and exciting, and yet they did nothing but move leisurely around the tiny terrace.

She was relaxed, Mitch knew as he inched one hand a fraction lower on her hip. It felt so good to hold her like this, close but not too close, her soft presence filling the night air. His chin fit perfectly on top of her head, and he could just catch the soft, intriguing scent of her perfume. Against his neck, her silky hair caressed and enticed him. He bent his head and pressed the tiniest kiss to the soft skin of her collarbone.

Melanie Stewart was every inch a woman, soft and curvy, yet caring and concerned. She interested him. No one had ever said the things she had and been allowed to get away with it, and yet this fiery woman continued to hold his attention.

"What did you think of Hope's problem?" he asked finally, not wanting to break the companionable silence but needing to bring some reality into the evening.

"I don't know what to think. I'm afraid for her."

"Afraid?" He frowned. "For heaven's sake, why?"

Her finger absently played with the hair that just touched his collar as she moved slowly with him. Her touch bothered him, sending electric currents through his blood.

"Melanie?"

"She's waited so long. She'd almost let herself forget him. Did you know Hope has gone out with your grandfather a few times?"

Mitch jerked backward, staring at her in surprise. Suddenly, the little scene at Charity's made sense.

"You mean she's falling in love with him?" He frowned.

"I don't know, but something was happening between them. She was finally beginning to let go of the past and consider the future." Melanie heaved a sigh. "And now this."

"Makes you wonder who's in control of the universe, doesn't it?" he laughed.

"Oh, I know that God's in control," she told him seriously.

"And whatever He has planned is more wonderful than anything we could ever imagine. It's just hard to understand right now."

"I never thought of God as personally interested in our lives," Mitch murmured. "I always think of Him as some far-off entity. In heaven, I guess." He shrugged.

Melanie smiled knowingly. "Well, I'm certain He's there, but He's also here with us, guiding us through our daily lives. I just have to keep praying that Hope won't be too badly hurt by all this."

She snuggled her head against his shoulder, and Mitch stared at the stars. Melanie Stewart made him think of all those things he wanted but could never have. Things like a wife, a home of his own, a family. Things he had no business dreaming about.

Pulling her a little closer, he guided her carefully across the patio as the music died away. His left hand settled on her waist, and he tortured himself with the dream of someday holding someone who was special to him in just this way. In his ear there was a soft whisper.

"What?" he asked, missing the soft words.

"You move that hand any lower and you are in trouble."

Privately, Mitch thought he was in trouble anyway, but he decided to change strategies. His mouth touched hers softly in a whisper of a kiss that was over before it began. When she kissed him back, he followed the curve of her jaw with a tiny, feather-light brush of his mouth. His nose nuzzled the sensitive spot under one ear. That brought a tiny sigh from her. Then she edged away, pressing her palms gently against his chest.

"Thank you for a very nice evening." Her soft voice was primly correct, and he almost burst out laughing.

Nice? Talk about a nonresponse.

"You're more than welcome. And thank you for coming

to dinner." He grinned at her, unabashed at the color flooding her face.

Bending, he pressed a kiss to her soft, pink mouth and one on a tiny freckle just below her eye. Then he whispered in her ear, "I enjoyed it. All of it."

When her face colored again, he grinned smugly. "You do blush a lot," he teased her. Then, lest he hurt her feelings, he told her the truth. "I like it on you."

They walked to the door side by side, saying nothing, both feeling the tension of the moment. At the door Mitch took her oval face in his hands and rubbed his thumb along her lips.

"Can we share dinner again?"

Waves of feeling swamped her, and Melanie was unable to think straight. A noncommittal answer, that was the best.

"Maybe," she temporized, unsure of anything but her surging heartbeat. "I don't know if I'll be able to afford it if I don't win that contest. You eat a lot."

He grinned. "Save your allowance then, because I'm going to hold you to it," he promised. Mitch pressed one last kiss to her mouth. Then, sighing, he dragged himself away.

"Good night," he whispered, and pulled the door closed behind his tall figure.

"Good night," Melanie answered to no one at all. One slim hand touched her lips in wonder.

In a trance she moved through her nightly rituals, half dazed. Mitchel Stewart didn't seem nearly as irritating as he had two weeks ago. Nor as angry.

What Melanie recalled was the way his bad-boy looks had made her heart thump. And the black lock of hair that tumbled across his forehead. And his lazy blue eyes with their hidden flames. And the soft, caring touch of his hands.

Yawning widely, Melanie plumped her pillow and promptly fell asleep dreaming of Mitchel Stewart.

* * *

"You think this fellow is this Jean guy? The same one that Hope Langford was engaged to?" Mitch stared at his grandfather in dismay.

"Not only do I think he is the one, I'm pretty sure he plans to marry someone else. I've had someone looking into things for me. On the Q.T. of course." Harry Conroy rubbed his hand wearily across his stubbled cheek. "I'm stumped, laddie. I dursn't tell Hope about this. She's got her heart set on a reunion, and if this guy is what he seems, that isn't going to happen."

"What's his name?" Mitch asked curiously, flipping through the reports covering his grandfather's desk. "And where's he been for the past thirty years? Why didn't he let her know he was alive so she could move on?"

"I don't know, son. Those are all good questions that I'd like to ask the man myself. You don't go abandoning a woman like Hope without a darned good reason. Leave those papers be!" Harry sounded furious, and Mitch studied him with new eyes.

"You're pretty fond of Miss Langford, aren't you, Gramps?" he asked quietly.

"Fond of her? I've spent longer than I care to think about trying to get close to the woman. But she has this barrier she always puts up. Won't let people get too close. Leastways, not me." He frowned.

Harry Conroy peered at his grandson. Over the years he'd gained a pretty good knowledge of human nature, and he used it to good advantage now.

"I think you're interested in Charity's daughter, too. Aren't you, boy?" The faded gray eyes sparkled with hidden knowledge. "I was afraid it would never happen," he declared happily.

"It hasn't," Mitch assured him quietly. "I'm not looking

to get married, Gramps. You know that. Neither is she. Sure, I like Melanie. She's sharp and witty."

"Not too hard to look at, either," his grandfather added.

"No, she isn't," Mitch agreed with a grin. "But she's dedicated to her career as much as I am to mine."

Harry snorted. "Hogwash," he bellowed with disgust. "You're still thinking about your parents, aren't you, Mitch?" He shook his head. "Those two didn't have a marriage, they had a battle zone. That's not the way it's supposed to work, boy."

"From what I saw at Mercer, Lloyd and Jones, that's the way it usually works," Mitch told him soberly.

"I knew you didn't like Chicago, Mitch, but I always thought you liked your work."

"I hated my work there," Mitch said hoarsely. "Bottom man on the pole wasn't the problem. I had to take whatever they assigned, and it was always family court." He shuddered at the memory. "I still see the looks in the kids' eyes, Gramps. So tired. And scared."

"Well, I'm proud of you for getting yourself out of there, son." Harry wiped a tear away. "It's a sad thing to see a family torn apart, that's for sure. But it doesn't have to happen to you. All marriages aren't bad. Your gran and I shared some pretty happy years." Harry stared across his desk, his eyes focused on some memory Mitch couldn't share.

"You never knew her, Mitch, but she was the kindest, gentlest woman God ever created."

"Sort of like Hope, you mean?" Mitch watched, stunned, as his grandfather's head reared back and his round belly shook with laughter.

"Good heavens, no! Hope is nothing like your grandmother. If she thinks I deserve it, she can tear a strip off me. Most times, it serves me right." He chuckled.

"Mom must have taken after your Anna, then." When Harry frowned, Mitch rushed to make his meaning clear. "You know what Dad was like, Gramps. He never had a decent word to say to anyone, Mom included. Most of the time he was screaming vile things at her. And she took it all without telling him off. Not once as long as I hung around can I remember a time when she would retaliate."

"No, she wouldn't have," Harry whispered sadly. "That was our fault. Anna and I knew your ma saw the court cases come and go, and we were afraid she would learn that retribution often paid. So we taught her that fighting back never solved anything." He stared at the picture of the young laughing girl on his desk. "I regret that now."

"There's no point in regrets, Gramps." Mitch smiled bitterly. "We can only learn from the past, and what I learned from my old man and his successors is that marriage tears people up."

"I'm sorry 'bout that, too, my boy," Harry whispered as the door slammed behind his grandson. "Because I think marriage is the best darn institution God ever invented."

He sat staring at his oak-lined office for a long moment before rousing himself to action.

"I wonder," he murmured, shrugging into his black robes for the last session of the day. He pressed the newfangled speed dial his secretary had shown him how to use.

"Hello, Hope? I need to talk to you about something." He waited for her response, a smile curving his lips. "I thought maybe we could go for a picnic. Haven't had one of those in years."

When she started to protest he cut her off.

"I'm due in court now, my dear. Let's just plan to leave around six. I'll pick you up. Wear pants." Harry hung up the phone with a huge smile on his round face.

Yes, siree, this was going to be an interesting date!

* * *

"Jessica, I cannot afford to reprimand you again. This is the last time." Melanie watched as the young woman's face turned sullen.

"But, Melanie, Mrs. Lindstrom was—"

"I cannot condone your actions regardless of what our residents do or say." She cut her trainee off. "Your treatment of Mrs. Lindstrom was callous and disrespectful, and we do not allow that here." She searched Jessica's pretty face for some sign of remorse. "Do you understand what I'm saying?"

"I guess so." The voice was petulant.

Melanie refused to allow herself any softening. The bullying tactics she had just witnessed were unforgivable.

"I'll make it perfectly clear, then, so that we both understand the way things go at Sunset." She waited until Jessica's sullen blue gaze met hers and then she laid down the law.

"This is your last warning, Jessica. Our residents are seniors, yes, and sometimes they need help. But force will not be used on anyone unless he or she is a danger to themselves or someone else. Okay?"

"But she was pulling my hair! Don't I have any rights?"

Melanie sighed, knowing the teenager would have to be relocated.

"Jessica, please. You were forcing her into the bath. She hates water. She's afraid."

"Well, how was I s'posed to know that?" The young woman had shifted from cranky to defiant, her lip curling with disgust. Suddenly, Melanie was tired of the whole thing.

"I guess you would actually have to talk to her, like a real person, and then let her talk back to find it out," she answered acidly, unwilling to go over the same material again.

Melanie knew she was venting some of her foul mood on the trainee, but Jessica deserved it. She would have dumped on Mitchel Stewart, too, if he had been around. He had been at the bottom of a lot of her problems lately!

She waved Jessica away tiredly as she raked a hand through her disheveled curls. Her secretary walked in with a cup of coffee and a commiserating smile.

"What happened to decency and courtesy, Bridget?" She sipped a mouthful of the refreshing brew and closed her eyes. When there was no response, Melanie opened them again. The woman just kept watching her. What now? she wondered.

"I'm sorry, Mel, but Mr. Northrup is slipping away fast. Hospital phoned to say you should come over if you want to talk to him once more."

Melanie got up immediately and moved to the door. Jonathan Northrup had been at Sunset even longer than she had. He had been her inspiration and hope for so long. It would be hard to say goodbye. The only consolation was that they both knew they'd meet again in heaven. Still, it would be tough. She straightened her backbone and strode down the hall, not really hearing Bridget's voice as she gathered her thoughts.

"Mel, there's some fellow from Papa John's Peanut Butter wants to see you immediately. He's at the front desk."

The last few words were hollered at Melanie's disappearing figure. She need not have bothered, Bridget thought. She knew Melanie Stewart had her priorities straight. And Jonathan Northrup was certainly more important than some silly contest!

Half an hour later, Melanie closed the big hospital door. He was gone. Serene to the end, Jonathan had given her his final bit of advice.

"You have to get out and live, my dear. Old folks are selfish and depressing sometimes, and much as we enjoy all your efforts, you have to look after yourself. One day you'll find a man who, if you let him, can give you so much." He had stopped for a painful, wheezing breath. "Make sure you have enough left of yourself to give back. That's all I ask." His frail, veined hand had clasped hers one last time.

"Enjoy your life, my dear. You've given me so much happiness. See you in heaven."

"Yes, in heaven." A tear rolled down her cheek, but Melanie dashed it away angrily. She would not cry. Jonathan wouldn't have wanted it.

A deep voice spoke from behind her left shoulder.

"Are you all right, Melanie?"

Turning, Melanie found Mitch's tall, elegantly dressed figure behind her. He looked very handsome in his navy blue pinstriped suit, but it was his eyes that drew her. Dark and searching, they probed deep within, sharing her sorrow.

"He was someone special, wasn't he?" he asked softly as his arm moved across her shoulder. His hand was gently soothing on her back, and suddenly Melanie gave way.

Turning into his arms, she put her head on his shoulder and bawled like a baby.

"Oh, Mitch. He was my best friend."

He let her cry out her loss and feelings without saying anything. And as she cried, Melanie felt the stress and sadness slowly drain away.

"Thanks," she murmured, accepting the snowy white handkerchief he pulled from his pocket to wipe her eyes. She knew she had smudged her mascara, and her eyes must look like a raccoon's, but Mitch never said a word. Gently, he took the fabric from her and completed the cleanup himself before stuffing the square into his pocket.

Then he tipped her face to look at his.

"Have you time for a coffee?" he asked. "I need to talk to you."

His voice was so serious that Melanie stared at him for a minute before nodding.

"I suppose I can. I'll just tell Bridget I'll be in the cafeteria."

"Actually, I thought maybe we could go outside for some privacy." He pointed to a carafe and two cups. "And she already knows."

Shrugging, Melanie accepted his outstretched hand and walked to the patio that nestled on a tiny bit of green lawn between the hospital and the nursing home. There were lounge chairs spread around, and she sank gratefully into one in the sun. She needed the warm sunshine and light to banish her gloomy feelings.

When Mitch handed her the steaming cup, his fingers brushed hers, and Melanie felt the sparks his touch always caused in her body. She watched as his intelligent blue eyes studied her face carefully before he sank into a chair.

"Okay," he began, dark eyes probing hers. "I know my timing stinks, but I guess the best way to tell you this is to just get it over with."

Melanie watched his chest expand as he sucked in a lungful of air. A wave of foreboding hung over her. What now, she wondered.

He began.

"A rep from Papa John's was in to the office to see me today." His blue eyes bored into her. "From what I understand, they were also here to see you," he told her sourly. "Apparently they have come to some decision regarding their grand prize." Mitch's face was flushed, and he fidgeted in his chair uncomfortably.

"Say it," she ordered, gripping the armrests. When he didn't speak, she answered for herself. "I don't win, do I?"

"Melanie, just listen to me for—"

She ignored his pleading. All her grand ideas, all her plans. She felt her dreams dissolving around her.

"I thought it was probably too good to be true. After all,

I don't even use their product. How could I possibly endorse it?" She turned to him, eyes glittering. "That's it, isn't it?"

"Melanie, can you be quiet for once?" The usually calm, deep voice was hard and strident. "Just let me speak, would you?"

Pursing her lips, Melanie leaned back and folded her arms across her chest. Her soft curls flopped across her cheek, but she was too angry to notice.

Mitch, however, noticed. He noticed only too well.

Thoughts of their evening together flooded his mind until he could almost feel her in his arms, feel her silky hair against his cheek, taste her soft mouth.

Shaking his head sharply, Mitch ignored the heat that was building in his brain and forced himself to concentrate on getting this right. It would not be easy.

"Melanie, they have both our entries now. And the home address you put on yours seems to be my apartment. Number 108. The winner lives at number 108." He waited for her to assimilate the information. When she said nothing, he tried again.

"I said—"

She stopped him immediately.

"I'm not a child, Mitch. I know what it means. It means I don't win, right?"

Her reddish gold head was tilted to the sun. As he watched, a single tear trickled from the corner of her eye.

"Not exactly," he told her.

She studied him curiously, intrigued by his mysterious manner. When he said nothing, she punched him lightly on the shoulder.

"Explain." She gave the command with all the imperious demands of royalty. He smiled at her dictatorial tone.

"I, er, I kind of told them that we lived in the same building. That, uh, we were roommates. Well, almost."

Mitchel Stewart had never seen anyone move that fast. In microseconds she was standing over him, hands on her hips as she glared at him.

"You…you fibber! You cheat! You liar!" Then she stopped. Her huge green eyes blinked twice before crinkling in puzzlement. "Why?"

"It seems that my contest entry has no apartment number on it. My name, however, is on the lease for apartment 108."

"And?" Melanie was completely puzzled by his strange attitude.

"Well, your name does not appear on any lease. Just Shawna's." He met her glittering gaze squarely. "And there is no phone number listed in your name."

"I know that. I only moved in after another of her roommates was married. We share the phone bill." It was clear to Mitch that Melanie didn't understand what he was telling her.

"But your entry says you live in my apartment. If you are not in fact living in apartment 108, your entry is null and void because you have misrepresented yourself."

He watched her absorb the information. Her small hands rested idly on his shoulders as she thought.

"How do you know this?" she demanded.

"I'm a lawyer, remember? Corporate law. Well," he said smugly, "I asked this rep guy for a copy of their contest rules."

He waited for her approval. In vain. Melanie merely glared at him. "And?"

"They must award the prize if we can both be shown to be living in apartment 108." As dismay flooded her beautiful face, Mitch quickly changed his wording. "That is, if you and I are both living in apartment 108."

He was triumphantly pleased with himself. Mitchel had made it his business to find out about Melanie Stewart in the past few days, and he could understand how badly she needed that money. Sunset Retirement Home was an under-funded, overworked nursing home that was following the patterns of business all over the world by cutting back.

Several of his golfing buddies had relayed horror stories about the place before Melanie had taken over, and Mitchel found out she was well respected in her field. The simple, humanitarian changes she had wrought in her tenure as director of care had resulted in Sunset becoming one of the choice locations for those requiring the services they provided.

At the same time, he had watched her surreptitiously with a number of her clients. Melanie was unfailingly polite and courteous with everyone, but her seniors seemed her closest friends. Even Mrs. Strange had spoken glowingly of Melanie's special interest in each resident's needs.

"Don't you see?" he demanded, anxious for her to under-stand his contribution in all this. "If you move some of your stuff to my spare room and stay there for a few nights, they'll know you're living there, and you'll get your share of the money."

She looked as if he had hit her with a Mack truck, Mitch decided. The color was coming back to her face, but he didn't think that was a good sign. Mostly due to the sharp finger-nails digging into his shoulder blades.

He lifted her hands away, careful to keep the lethal pink nails far from his eyes. She looked steamed, and with her temper, she would probably scratch his eyes out.

"Let go of me, you lecherous, manipulating, overbear-ing…" As the stream of vitriolic descriptives flowed from her soft peach lips, Mitch twisted her arms behind her back.

He disliked using force, but he wanted to preserve the skin on his face, as well. He let her blow off steam, but when she had not stopped a few moments later, his temper peaked.

Using the method he most favored, Mitch pulled her stiff,

unyielding body close and pressed his lips against hers, stemming the tide of outrage. And he kept kissing her even when she stopped fighting him. Only when she finally started kissing him back did he pull away.

Women! Why didn't he smarten up? Surely after Sam's dirty tricks, he should be prepared for the way they operated.

"Listen, Ms. Stewart. I don't need a roommate so badly that I would go to these extremes. I've told you before, I don't intend to get married. Not now. Maybe not ever."

Mitch let go of her arms and stood back, furious that he had allowed himself to become so involved in someone else's affairs. That's what he got for trying to help!

"You know," he added, upset with himself for the stupid idea that had streaked into his head an hour ago, "I can use twenty-five grand for a few little schemes of my own. You're not the only person who has things to do, people you want to help out. And if you back out now, they will redraw the names." Mitch's dark eyes glared at her accusingly. "I'll lose out altogether because of your mistake." He told himself to calm down. Useless.

"I know how much you want that money. So do I. And this is the only way I could think of for you to share in it." Turning, he strode away, stopping only to add, "Sorry I interfered in your life," before yanking the door open and walking through it.

Melanie sank into the deck chair, her knees rubbery. Shocked, confused, dazed. Life was a perplexing whirl, and she wasn't sure of anything anymore. He had been trying to help, in a strange, rather unusual way. He wanted her to have the money, or at least some of it. But there was no way she was moving in with the guy. Get real!

"You're still there, directing me, aren't You, Lord?" she murmured brokenly. "Please give a sign. You know how much we need that money."

Glancing at her watch, Melanie decided that nothing made sense anymore and got up to return to work. As she gathered the cups and thermos, she permitted a tiny smile to tilt the corners of her mouth. Actually, Mitchel Stewart was kind of sweet. In a bossy, rude sort of way.

"He invited her to move in with him?" Hope fumed. Her eyes were wide open. "What a horrible young man!"

"He's not horrible at all," Charity murmured, threading the wool through her knitting machine. "Dear Mitchel was just trying to help. In a bizarre, unorthodox sort of way." She slid the carriage back and forth a few times experimentally and then began an even, steady rhythm that soon produced a width of white lacy fabric.

"Melanie was so hurt when her mother abandoned her. It took ages, remember, to get her to open up. That terrible childhood should have toughened her up, but instead she became more withdrawn." Charity smiled in remembrance. "My Melanie was the child who always needed an extra hug or a few extra words of praise."

"I remember," Hope murmured. "She'd work so hard in school, doing far more than was necessary for any project I assigned." Her eyes stared into the past. "She was always the one who lent a helping hand, stuck up for the little kid being bullied."

Charity nodded. "It was almost as if she was too insecure and afraid to believe in the love that Peter and I offered. When he died, I think she felt it was her fault for leaning on him so much."

"Well, I want her to be happy," Hope added stoutly. "But I don't want her to be hurt. And Mitchel will do that. He's had a terrible childhood, you know. Harry told me some of it." She filled them in on the few details she knew. "Melanie needs someone strong with a solid background.

Someone she can lean on. Not somebody with problems of his own!"

"I don't know why you're so concerned, Hope." Charity smiled as she started another color. "Melanie is a good girl. She wouldn't allow anything untoward to happen. And they would only be sharing the kitchen."

Hopes eyes were huge with disbelief.

"You mean you *condone* this crazy idea?" She gasped. "But you're her mother."

"I know that, dear. And I'm not saying I condone anything. I have only her good at heart. But Melanie is too self-contained. She's always pushing everyone but her seniors away. She's missing out on the best parts of life, and I want her to find happiness with someone her own age." She shrugged. "Maybe if she and Mitch do share an apartment, she'll realize the world is full of more than grumpy old men. It does have two bedrooms, you know." Charity's warm brown eyes twinkled. She delighted in her friend's shocked look.

"Oh, my," Faith breathed, her emerald green eyes glowing with excitement. "And wouldn't it be romantic. Why, they could have a candlelight dinner without the whole town knowing about it." She stared into space, lost in a daydream.

"Well," Hope said, "I'm ashamed of you, Charity Flowerday. And there's no way I'm going to allow Melanie's good reputation to be soiled by such a tawdry situation. I'm going to do my duty by the girl." She picked up her purse and swept regally through the front door, the light of battle gleaming in the depths of her blue eyes. "We'll just see about this…arrangement," she muttered furiously.

When Judge Harry Conroy showed up promptly at six o'clock, Hope was ready for him. She wore a pair of navy slacks and a white blouse with a navy and white cardigan over her shoulders. She could barely control her temper as

A Hopeful Heart

she waited for Harry to open her car door and her greeting wasn't as welcoming as it could have been.

"Is something the matter, Hope?" he asked at last. He started the car and pulled away from her house, then glanced at her curiously. "I mean, have you heard more about Jean or something?"

"Good heavenly days, no," she snapped irritably. "I hadn't even thought about that. Don't have time." She turned to face him angrily. "Charity is set on sending her daughter traveling down the path of destruction, and I intend to see that she doesn't do it."

"Charity is?" the judge murmured, puzzled. "But I thought…well, never mind that. What's Charity done now?"

"It's all because of that awful grandson of yours," Hope complained. "He flies into town, all handsome and debonair, and sweeps the girl off her feet."

"So you think he's handsome, do you?" Judge Conroy's eyes twinkled.

"Of course he's handsome," Hope spluttered. "You know very well he takes after you, Harry, and you were a heartbreaker at that age. You still are."

"Do tell," Harry murmured with a smile of appreciation, allowing himself to preen.

"But you had some scruples. You would never have up and asked a woman to live with you so cold-bloodedly."

Judge Conroy absently turned down the dirt road that led to the park beside the river where he'd courted his wife years ago. It wasn't much of a river now, of course. And he wasn't as young as he once was. But oh, my, things did sound promising!

"Mitch has asked someone to live with him?" he repeated softly. "That's strange. I didn't think the boy had any intention of getting married."

"He doesn't," Hope shrieked in exasperation. "He wants her to live in sin with him."

The judge stared at her as if she'd lost her marbles, sending Hope's blood pressure soaring.

"I hardly think Mitch would suggest—"

"Oh, yes, he would," she contradicted him. "I was visiting Nettie Rivers. We were sitting in her room, right by the window, and I distinctly heard him ask Melanie to move in with him." She slammed the door of the car and stomped to a clearing beside a tiny waterfall. "Well, I'm not having it," she spluttered, sinking down onto the blanket Harry spread. "Do you hear me?"

"Yes, dear," he murmured, trying to understand. It didn't sound at all like Mitch, but then the boy did have a mind of his own. "I'll talk to him," he promised, patting her hand commiseratingly.

"It won't do any good," Hope murmured, squeezing his hand gently. "But thank you. No, Charity's determined to go along with it all. She thinks Melanie needs to see what she's missing, working with old people all the time."

"Perhaps she's right about that, Hope. She is the girl's mother, after all. Charity wants to see Melanie happily married with her own children. So do I, for that matter." He stared at her. "Let's pray about it, dear. God can do anything. He can certainly handle this."

They bowed their heads, and Judge Conroy murmured a short petition, asking for guidance and help for their friends and relatives.

"Do you feel better now, dear?" he asked, after they'd finished the low-fat potato salad, cold sliced chicken sandwiches with tomato, lettuce and spicy mustard. For dessert, there was fruit salad and hot, fragrant herbal tea.

"A little," Hope conceded. She stared into the woods. "I think I shall keep my eye on that situation. Perhaps I can be of help."

"But won't you be busy contacting the authorities about

Jean?" he asked softly, knowing it wouldn't hurt her to discuss her past love. To the judge's immense surprise, Hope shook her head.

"No," she told him firmly. "I've decided to turn that over to the Lord. Jean has been gone for a long time. It's very doubtful that he's survived at all, but if, for some strange reason, he turns up alive, I'll be happy and I'll learn to deal with it. Somehow."

"What are you going to do?" Harry asked with a frown.

"Exactly what I've been doing for the past twenty-five years," Hope told him with a smile. "Take each day as it comes and plan on making it the best yet."

"Good," he agreed after a moment. "And I'll be here to share them with you."

"You have been for a long time now," she murmured, staring at his bald head as if she hadn't noticed it before. "We've had some good times, haven't we, Harry? You and Anna and I. She was my very best friend, you know. I always felt as if she was my sister."

Harry frowned.

"Well, I don't feel like your brother," he muttered. To his delight she giggled, leaning nearer to kiss him on one cheek.

"You don't look like him, either," she assured him, laughing. She jumped to her feet and tugged his arm. "Come on, lazybones. I let you feed me all that delicious food. The least you can do is help me walk it off."

"All right," he agreed meekly. "But I carefully planned a low-fat meal, just as you prefer. You know that. As long as we just walk. I'm too old for anything else."

Hope's blue eyes twinkled with mischief.

"Really?" she asked. "That's too bad."

Harry let her lead him down the path, resisting an urge to kiss her then and there. But no, he decided. He'd bide his time. They were just beginning to get closer, and she was only starting to come to terms with the possibility of Jean's reappearance. Everything looked positive, but he'd keep mentioning things to the Lord, just the same. A little heavenly guidance couldn't hurt, he decided, hearing Hope's sudden burst of laughter.

Chapter Four

"Have a nice day, folks. Enjoy that sun."

Mitchel Edward Stewart was not having a *nice* day, despite the radio announcer's bland wish. He had risen with a splitting headache on his first day off in weeks. The coffeemaker had refused to cooperate, and his doughnut supply was tapped out.

It should have been simple. Everything was so carefully planned. He would pick up some supplies from downtown and then he was heading out for a day at the beach. Sun, sand and surf, that's what he needed. Maybe even a cold root beer.

Sighing, he stared balefully at his bright red sports car once more. Apparently, some things were not to be. The expensive engine refused to respond to his orders, and since anything under the hood of an automobile gave him hives, Mitch had called the shop.

"Nope, can't touch it today." The youngster's voice was less than helpful. At least he thought it was. You could barely hear over the crashing of some heavy metal band in the background.

"Pardon?"

"No can do, dude."

"And why is that?" Mitchel had forced a tight rein of control on his temper and prayed for strength. Impudent little brat!

"Mechanic's out sick. Have a good one!" With a click, the kid had hung up on him, leaving Mitchel to bite out a particularly choice epithet that divulged his irritation with the world in general.

"Something I said?"

He groaned, recognizing her voice immediately. Why now, why today? He turned to face Miss Melanie Stewart, a flush of red hinting at his turmoil.

"Hi." There. Let her make something of that.

"Car problems?"

His reply was curt and succinct. "Yeah."

"Can I look?"

He stared at her. "Why?"

Green eyes glared at him as she slapped her hands on her hips. "Gee, I don't know. I thought I could steal a few spark plugs or maybe even the air filter."

Whew, talk about cranky! Without a word Mitch popped the hood and watched Melanie lean over to peer inside. His stomach dropped as his gaze followed her long legs to the white cuffed shorts that covered her shapely bottom. A tiny bit of skin peeked out between her waistline and the cropped red T-shirt she wore. He couldn't stop staring.

"Hmm, distributor cap's shot." She turned her head to glance at him. "You need a mechanic."

"Thank you for your assistance, Miss Stewart," he said sarcastically. "I have already phoned one. He's out sick." Butter wouldn't melt in her mouth, he thought grumpily.

She shrugged and slammed the hood shut. Fortunately, she missed his knuckles by at least a millimeter.

"Okay, looks like you've got it covered."

He frowned. Was that supposed to mean something?

"Want a lift?" she offered, bending to pick up a large woven bag and a small cooler. "I'm going to the beach, but I could drop you somewhere."

Like in the river, he mused, well aware of her quick temper. Mitch decided he should not look a gift horse, or a gorgeous woman, in the mouth. Enough things had gone wrong today. Here was opportunity. Opportunity didn't knock that often. He shouldn't turn it down. Besides, she might invite him to share whatever was in that cooler, and he didn't want to miss out on a decent meal.

Mitch assembled his features into his best hangdog look and muttered, "Well, I was going there, too, but now, with no wheels..." He asked deferentially, "Are you sure it would be okay?"

To his delight, she burst out laughing, her green eyes glinting in the sunshine. Seconds later they were hidden behind huge round sunglasses.

"You don't do humble really well." She giggled. "In fact, it's downright pathetic." She waved. "But I'll take pity on you anyway. Come on. You can hitch with me for today."

Mitch watched the animation flood her features as she laughed at him and thought how pretty she was when she wasn't arguing with him. Of course, even then, with the light of battle turning her eyes that mossy color, Melanie still looked fantastic.

When she motioned to her old beater, his face dropped. Unfortunately, she noticed. Never missing a chance, Melanie poked fun at him.

"I know. It's a step down for you." She smirked. "But if you want to get to the beach today, this might be your only chance."

Embarrassed, Mitch got in while trying to come up with an appropriate apology. When nothing remotely suitable surfaced, he glued his lips shut and studied the dilapidated vehicle.

She read his silence correctly.

"Don't worry." She laughed. "Everybody thinks Bessie is gonna give up the ghost, but she always keeps going." Lovingly, Melanie patted the worn dashboard. "She's got the innards of a true champion."

"Champion what?" It wasn't nice, but she didn't take offence.

"She may not be pretty but at least she's running," she reminded him gently.

Mitchel tried not to stare as her shorts displayed those lovely long legs. He turned and stared straight ahead, trying not to ogle her. Sort of.

"Do you always go to the beach on Saturday?"

Good, Stewart, he congratulated himself. What a stimulating conversation!

"No, only in the summer, when I have time and it isn't raining." She laughed. "Other than that, I don't bother much."

Her curls were bound up in a ribbon on the top of her head. Mitch decided he'd like to undo that ribbon and run his fingers through the glowing silky mop.

"You are a smart aleck, you know that?" he muttered. His eyes opened wide as he caught sight of her feet. Her toenails were bright pink. Mitch suddenly realized they had an effect on his already racing pulse.

Gosh, he was in a bad way. It was just her toes, for goodness' sake. He forced himself to look out the window.

"Mitch?"

"Melanie?"

They spoke at the same time, each turning to stare at the other.

"You go first," he offered gallantly. The words he had wanted to say were stuck in his throat anyway.

"Well, as you know, I have sort of a temper." Mitch snorted at the obvious understatement, and Melanie had the grace to blush.

"Okay, I have a temper," she admitted.

"A terrible temper," Mitchel revised, tongue in cheek.

"Anyway…" She glared at him over her sunglasses. "I wanted to apologize for jumping to conclusions the other day. I know you were trying to help me, and I'm sorry I snapped at you."

Mitchel Stewart's mind had wandered to considering whether she would wear that swimsuit again. "Uh-huh," he muttered, lost in his daydream.

"If you are still offering, I would like to take you up on your offer of a residence. Just for a few weeks," she added quickly. And then, for his information, "No strings attached."

Privately grinning with glee, Mitch calmly asked, "What changed your mind?"

Her sea-colored eyes studied him suspiciously before she answered. "Well, I think I'm being evicted."

His head shot up in surprise. "For what?"

Melanie grinned. He could see that half-hidden little twitch that seemed to say "Gotcha!"

"Shawna eloped with her boyfriend last weekend, and now she wants her husband to move in with her." She grinned. "Not unreasonable, I suppose, but I think it's going to be just a little crowded with the three of us." Melanie shrugged nonchalantly. "Who am I to stand in the way of young love?"

He was getting to know her, and he recognized a put-on when he heard it from her pink glossy lips.

"Come on, Melanie!" Her big green eyes stared at him innocently. Mitch smirked. "What's the real reason? I know enough about that nurse to know she plans everything ahead. She'd no more elope than you would. And you would no more move in with a man than fly to the moon. I never expected that you'd go for my suggestion." He stared at her. "What's changed?"

Melanie sighed in defeat, and he knew she didn't really want to agree to his plan, at all.

"We got a notice that the owners want the top floor for their children, who will be going to school in the fall. They will pay us two months' rent if we vacate immediately so they can do some renovations before fall."

She shrugged her slim shoulders before continuing.

"I've been praying and praying that God would lead me in this contest thing. Then this came up. Right after you offered to let me stay there." Her sigh was not encouraging. "I guess God is trying to tell me something."

Mitch stared. "You think He wants you to have this money so badly He'd force you to move in with me? Wow!" He was teasing, but the laugh stopped in his throat as she turned those expressive eyes on him.

"I think He must be trying to tell me something," she said quietly. "I've been praying for ages and nothing happened. Now suddenly there's the contest and the opportunity to get some money for Sunset. I get evicted, and there you are offering to share your place." Her eyes were wide with amazement. "It's like a small miracle."

"I'm not sure…"

"Besides, there's nothing between us. Everyone knows that. And I work all kinds of hours. I just need somewhere as a base until I can find another apartment." Her head tilted toward him as she careened around a convertible full of rowdy teenagers. "So I gratefully accept your offer."

"You must know what it's like to find accommodation in this town." Mitch added that just to let her know how lucky she was and how magnanimous he was.

They talked terms and conditions all the way to the beach. Melanie could move in immediately. It would be every man for himself. No cooking, no cleaning, she told him. No garbage, no lewd propositions, he promised.

Eyebrows raised, Melanie asked what that meant.

"I only make proper propositions," he joked, eyeing her heightened color with interest.

Privately, Melanie wondered what the future would hold for them. Especially after an afternoon of Mitch's company. Her body hummed from the massaging action of his large hands as he obligingly applied sunscreen to her bare back. His big, strong fingers worked the oil into her skin, and she felt supple and exotic as the fragrance of coconuts wafted around them. Mitch had been insistent that she wear sunscreen.

"I've seen sun damage," was all he would say. "It's not pretty." She was aware of his appreciation of her swimsuit.

Melanie was flattered that he found her outfit every bit as interesting as before, but she regretted those extra ten pounds she had never shed. Not that they seemed to matter to Mitch. Shortly after rubbing in the oil, he had rushed away for a quick dip in the cold lake.

"Come on in," he had teased, dripping frigid drops of water on her toasty skin. He laughed when she shrieked, then razed her unmercifully about her squeamishness until Melanie could stand his teasing no longer.

"I knew you were a beach baby," he muttered. One dark blue eye had opened as he lazed on his towel. It traveled the course of her body, following the lines of her swimsuit. "I doubt if that thing even withstands more than a dip in the hot tub," he added, disgusted. "Afraid of a little natural water, probably."

When Melanie refused to answer, he continued the goading.

"You can't swim, can you? That bit at the apartment pool was all just a ruse to get my attention, wasn't it?"

Melanie *had* sat up at that, fury wrinkling her forehead as she glared at him.

"For your information, I don't need to attract anyone's attention." She straightened her spine in haughty disregard. "I would have you know I am an excellent swimmer. I simply refuse to subject myself to that frigid water in order to prove something to you." She arranged her beach chair more comfortably and leaned back, soaking up the sun's rays. "I merely wanted some free time away from the office. I would appreciate it if you could let me enjoy the day."

Melanie thought she had won their war of words until she heard him mutter something under his breath.

"Pardon?" she inquired superciliously.

"I said, you're chicken, just as I thought."

"You know," Melanie said, eyeing him severely, sunglasses pushed to the end of her nose, "if you ever win in court, it must be because of your bulldog tendencies."

She stretched out on her stomach, letting the warming heat of the sun penetrate her skin. There was blissful silence for about sixty seconds.

"What do you mean, bulldog tendencies?" His voice was strident. "Admit it, you are a chicken." Big blue eyes glimmered with excitement. "Bok, bok!" He flapped his arms.

Melanie was getting tired of his ridiculous juvenile games. She looked around the beach and found several pairs of interested eyes trained on them.

"Stop that," she ordered angrily. "Everyone is staring at you."

Mitch continued to chant louder and louder.

There was nothing else to do. He would not leave her alone, and she wouldn't get a moment's peace until she put an end to this stupidity.

Melanie stood gracefully and walked to the water's edge, dipping the end of one big toe into the water.

"Agh!" She sucked in her breath. It was freezing!

But when she turned around, Mitch was looming behind her. His eyes met hers, and he mouthed the word *chicken*.

Melanie sighed, resigned to her fate and fully aware that he would keep it up until she got wet. She strolled slowly into the water, getting a bit more of her heated skin wet with each step. She turned carefully, trying not to splash, and found Mitch directly behind her.

"I hope you're happy." She glared at him. "I have no feeling below my waist, and my hands are getting numb."

He grinned and dived into the smooth water beside her, splashing her hugely. When he stood up, streaming rivulets of chilly lake water running down his face, Melanie let him have it.

"You did that on purpose, you sadist. I'm soaked and I'm freezing. I do hope you feel better now."

She turned to go back to shore and found him blocking her way.

"I'm sorry, Melanie." His voice was deceptively soft as his chilly hand closed around her arm. Wide and innocent, his baby blues stared at her soulfully. "I really didn't know you couldn't swim."

"Of course I can swim, silly," Melanie told him, trying to stop her teeth from chattering. She wrapped her arms around her midriff, hugging herself for warmth.

Unfortunately the motion pushed her full breasts upward, accentuating the cleavage her suit displayed. She watched Mitch's blue eyes grow rounder in appreciation before she realized the reason. Her hands dropped to her sides in embarrassment.

His laughing gaze met hers. One black lock of hair dangled boyishly over his forehead. A wide smile slashed across his rugged, tanned face.

"You are just going to have to get in there and swim a few strokes to prove it," he whispered in her ear as his hands brushed up and down her arms to warm her.

Melanie glared at him even as her body recognized the

heat flowing from his body. She moved closer. Just to get warm, she told herself. When his arms wrapped around her and she was pressed against the heat of his chest, she groaned at the warmth that was beginning to penetrate her skin.

"Come on, Melanie, let's swim."

It was the last thing she heard before Mitch's arms tightened like steel bands and he pulled her under the water.

Icy cold waves slapped against her and left her with two options: move or freeze to death. Melanie moved.

Breaking his tight hold on her, Melanie surprised Mitch with a move she had learned long ago in lifesaving class. In a few seconds he was flat on his back and going under. With one last shove, Melanie pushed him to the sandy bottom before swimming furiously away in a speedy crawl that had won her numerous competitions in high school.

Of course, Mitch demanded retribution. She just had not expected it to be a kiss. And when his cold lips pressed against hers, Melanie found that the fire building between them could not be doused, even by the freezing lake water. She kissed him back, returning his warm embraces until her blood was singing in response.

Mitch was the first to pull away.

"Okay, you win," he teased. "You can swim, and kiss." He grinned that devilish grin at her. "And you do both very well, I might add." Turning, he ducked under the water, surfacing twenty yards away to call out his challenge.

"I'll race you to the buoys," he dared her. His strong arms made a swath through the water. "Loser supplies supper," he told her when she caught up.

And so it had gone for the rest of the day. Teasing, talking, touching each other, but never getting too serious.

The long, lazy afternoon on the crowded beach presented a perfect opportunity for getting to know each other, but regardless of the many ploys she tried, Melanie gained very little personal information about Mitchel. It was frustrating and she was finally forced to admit defeat.

He lost their swimming contest and she left him to arrange their late supper, especially since he'd long ago finished off the sandwiches and pop she'd packed.

Ever resourceful, he'd come up with the very ingenious and inventive idea of hot dogs and chips, with chilled cans of iced tea to drink. As they sat around a campfire, replete with their feast, Melanie sensed he was deliberately shutting her out, refusing to answer her innocent questions. She turned a marshmallow, letting the coals toast it golden brown before popping it into her mouth.

Oh, he hadn't been rude about it. His answers had been polite enough, but, somehow, the subject of family was a closed book with Mitchel Stewart. And although he freely discussed his work, Mitch only let her see bits and pieces of the real man.

Melanie knew that he hailed from the East, that he had gone to school there and come to Mossbank a few weeks ago. She had learned a little about his schoolboy antics and that he loved to swim but wasn't very good at it.

But that was it. Mitch had told her nothing of his family or his past. And she wanted to know.

She gazed into the fire. Maybe a direct approach was the best. Plunge in and take the consequences. Somehow, the enveloping darkness gave her courage.

"Mitch?"

He sat on a log, staring vacantly into the flickering flames. The huge fire he had built had died down to an orange-red bed of coals. Wind danced across it, licking up a flame here or there.

"Hmm," he asked, staring languidly.

"Please, don't think I'm being nosy," she began, knowing darn well that nosy was exactly what she was being. "It's just that I would like to know a little more about you if we are going to be rooming together."

When his dark head jerked, Melanie held up a defensive hand.

"I know your reputation from my friends at the hospital, but…" Melanie hesitated, searching. "I don't know you." Her voice was soft, plaintive, a call for understanding.

Mitch had pulled a pair of tattered blue jean shorts over his swimsuit. Below the frayed cuffs, his long, muscular legs crossed and uncrossed as he fidgeted on the huge log. Finally he stood, towering over her in the gloom. Melanie could feel his blue eyes studying her. When he spoke, his voice was quiet but firm.

"Look. I've offered half of the prize money and a place to stay to make sure you can collect your half. Can we leave the personal histories out of it?"

He squatted in front of her and stared directly into her face. His voice was half-laughing, half-serious, but there was an underlying tenseness that Melanie couldn't ignore.

"I give you my word I'm not an ax murderer, or a psychotic, or any of those other terrible things you've been imagining." His white teeth glittered in the dark. Melanie thought immediately of a wolf and then remonstrated with her overactive imagination, sitting quietly when he continued.

"You are welcome to stay at my place for as long as you need to. But that's it. You go your way and I go mine."

His fingers closed around the soft flesh of her upper arms, drawing her upward. And Melanie allowed herself to be coaxed to his heat. He was like fire, and she a moth, drawn irresistibly to his flame. He attracted her with his hidden secrets and mysterious smile. His past was another facet of a man who occasionally let her see his generosity. And she would probably get burned, but right now Melanie could only concentrate on his touch.

"Don't get me wrong," he muttered as his eyes brushed her body, admiring her figure. "You're a very beautiful woman and I enjoy the view as much as the next red-blooded male." His hands slid down her back to the indentation of her waist, and he urged her closer.

"But I don't play games, and I have no intention of getting married just because I allow you to stay in my apartment."

"I never said I wanted to get married! Mitchel Stewart, you are the most egotistical, pushy, rude, overbearing—"

"You have said all this before," he reminded her. His hands were stuck carelessly into his back pockets as he studied her. "Get to the point."

With every atom of control she possessed, Melanie forced herself to refrain from violence. Curling her fingers into her palms, she sucked in a lungful of air.

"Look, buddy," she told him, poking a finger into his very broad, very bare chest. It confused her, that tingling sensation, so Melanie put her hand down and concentrated on the words.

"I will move into your apartment because I do need that money for my friends."

"We've already agreed on that." He chuckled, then bent to stuff the remains of their meal into the tiny cooler before dousing the fire.

"Right." Melanie tried to focus on her speech. "So I will stay there. But that's it. Not for anything else."

She tried to emphasize the words, but somehow they had little effect on Mitch. He smiled that lazy, sexy smile and agreed with her quietly as he tugged her arm.

"Right, darlin'," he drawled as he pulled her along beside him through the warm sand. When they reached the car, he dropped everything on the pavement beside it and wrapped one lean brown hand around her neck.

"And nothin' anybody can say will change it," he drawled right before his grinning lips closed on hers.

Melanie knew his effusive charm was just a cover. Something that would draw her off course so Mitch would not have to answer any questions. And she would tell him that he couldn't just get away with this.

Soon.

With a sigh, Melanie decided she would tell him so right after she'd kissed him back. For a few delicious minutes she allowed herself to enjoy the feel of his lips tasting hers before she pulled away from his strong embrace and climbed dazedly into the car.

She knew there was something she wanted to say. But right now she couldn't remember what it was. Not on the long drive home, not when Mitch kissed her a very thorough good-night outside her apartment and not when she was lying in her soft bed much later.

"Thanks for the sign, Lord," she whispered. "I'm taking this to mean that I should proceed full steam ahead. Now, if You could just work on his attitude a little."

A smile curved her soft, full lips as she drifted off. Yes, he had a bad attitude, all right. Tomorrow, she decided. She would remember to tell him off tomorrow.

"Oh. Uh, hello. Miss Langford, isn't it?" Mitch stared at the older blond woman in the doorway of his apartment. "Is there something I can do for you?"

Hope pressed past him without a word, her face drawn tight, lips pursed as she motioned to the items scattered at her feet.

"Actually there's quite a lot. But for right now, would you mind bringing in my suitcases? I'll be sharing Melanie's room. You're not going to destroy my best friend's daughter's reputation as long as I can stop it!"

Mitch stared at her, his mind whirling. Was this what Gramps had meant this morning on the phone? What had he said? "Hope has her feathers ruffled." Was that it? Apparently she was angry with him. Mitch groaned at the thought of this straitlaced busybody and her obviously mistaken impression of his and Melanie's unusual arrangement.

"Miss Langford, I assure you that there's nothing like that going on. Melanie and I—"

"Will have a chaperone," she interrupted smartly, straightening the cushions thrown haphazardly on his sofa. Her eyebrows lifted disdainfully at the coffee rings covering the glass surface of the coffee table. "Melanie should be staying with her mother. And if it weren't for the missionaries Charity had already invited, I'm sure that's where she would be."

Mitch watched transfixed as Miss Langford picked up a half-eaten box of doughnuts and dumped the whole lot in the trash.

"Hey! That was my breakfast," he told her, frowning resentfully. He decided to make a show of bravado, even though his knees were shaking. There was something about this woman that brooked no nonsense.

"Now, look here, Miss Langford. I'm letting Melanie use the spare room so she can get her half of the money for that nursing home she's so wrapped up in. That's all there is to it."

"Fine." Hope Langford stared at the carpet, grimacing at the bits of lint and fluff. "And while she's here, I'm here," she told him firmly. "Please bring my things through to Melanie's room. I'd like to get settled in."

Mitch found himself obeying even though the last thing he wanted was this neatness freak in his apartment. Fortunately his spare room had two single beds. He watched transfixed as Hope removed perfectly pressed clothes from the satchels and hung them in the minuscule closet that already housed a few of Melanie's uniforms.

His original houseguest had planned on moving the rest of her stuff tonight. It was going to be a tight squeeze in this dinky apartment, he decided, leaving Hope to pour himself another cup of coffee and contemplate the doughnuts in their box in the garbage can.

A really tight squeeze, if she was going to insist on chucking out his food supply. But how did you throw out an older woman determined to save the reputation of someone who didn't need it?

"Coffee is very hard on your stomach lining," Hope said in a stern voice. "I make a wonderful protein drink with raw eggs and yogurt that would give you lasting energy."

Mitch set down his cup hastily and grabbed his briefcase. He had to get out of here. Quickly.

"Er, uh, no, thanks," he mumbled, grabbing the doorknob like a lifeline. "I have to get to work. Early appointment." *At the convenience store across the street,* he thought. He almost had the door safely closed behind him.

"Young man?"

"Yes, ma'am," he answered, debating the propriety of a salute.

"I will need a key to this residence. There are several matters to be taken care of today and I will need to let myself in and out."

"Oh. Yes, of course." He thought. "I made a spare for Melanie yesterday. I think it's in the kitchen. In the drawer beside the sink. I'll get another cut this afternoon." He watched her carefully to see if that was all right with her, and when she nodded, he turned to escape.

"Have a nice day," she told him cheerfully.

No doubt all that happiness came from her power drink. He shuddered and climbed into his red Camaro with relief. Thank goodness it was running properly, at last. At work, Mitch could hardly wait to dial Melanie's work number.

When she answered, he almost bellowed at her over the phone.

"Thanks a lot," he shouted angrily.

"Mitch? Is that you?"

"Of course it's me." He tried, really tried to control his temper. "I'm just calling to say thank you."

"You're welcome," she answered politely. A few seconds later her puzzled voice came on the line. "For what?"

"Don't pretend you don't know. She arrived this morning, bag and baggage. All prepared to settle in for the duration."

He waited for her excuse; her plea for understanding for her aunt. He was all ready to shoot her excuses down, one by one.

Instead he heard:

"Have another cup of coffee, Mitchel, and call me back when you're awake and in your right mind. Okay, okay. I'll settle for awake." The telephone line went dead.

"Of all the overbearing, pushy women," he began, stuffing another chocolate-covered doughnut into his mouth.

"Mitch, your nine-thirty is here. Shall I show him in?" His secretary's eyebrows rose as she watched him nod and shove the doughnuts out of view. Amanda chuckled appreciatively. "Pigging out, are we?"

"Just show him in, will you, Amanda?" he muttered in frustration, trying to hide the sticky evidence.

Clarence Palmer had been a private investigator for thirty-five years. If there was a secret to be unearthed, Clarence knew exactly how to go about it. Mitch had known him for years and used his services several times, once for himself, to find the father he'd hated for so long.

He grabbed the older man's hand and slapped the thin back with pleasure.

"Clarence! Gee, it's good to see you again. Come on, sit down. Want a doughnut?"

"Mitch." Clarence nodded, peering at the doughnuts as he carefully wiped his hand on his handkerchief. "You still addicted to these things?" His observant gaze scanned the package. "Must be a bad day." He chuckled.

"Why do you say that?"

"Chocolate ones are all gone." Clarence grinned. He helped himself to a sugared doughnut and settled back in the leather chair. "This a good time?" he asked quietly.

"Yep, perfect." Mitch poured them both a cup of coffee and then leaned back, pen and paper at the ready. "What have you got for me?"

With a swift economy of movement, Clarence whipped open his notepad and began.

"I got a lot of this stuff from your grandfather's contacts. Jean LeClerc. You want age, birthplace, all that?" He waited for Mitch's negative reply, then continued. "Okay. Vietnam vet, killed in action, or so they said. Actually, the other guy was pretty sure this Jean was wounded and kept in an enemy camp for years. The Viet Cong deliberately left some of his stuff to be found so he'd be presumed dead. You know the routine."

Mitch nodded grimly. He did know. Very well, as it happened. He'd worked on a few cases involving fathers who had died in Vietnam. It wasn't pretty.

"Okay. Good old Jean came back but minus a few facts— like who he was. Met a volunteer at the vet hospital and they married. She had money and he put it to good use building an empire. Ever heard of Papa John?" Clarence looked at him through his wire-rimmed glasses and saw Mitch's astonishment.

"This means something to you?"

"Yeah, it does." He stared at Clarence, seeing not him but the elderly white-haired man he'd met at the Bismarck television station. "Let me get this straight. The Papa John's Peanut Butter magnate is Hope Langford's Jean LeClerc?"

"One and the same, we think. Only I'm not sure if *he* knows it. Legally his name is John Lexington. A nurse at the hospital said they called him that when he couldn't remember his name. He apparently responded to John, and they adlibbed his last name." Clarence left half his doughnut on a napkin as he dug through his notes.

"Nurse Mary said he had lots of nightmares and kept mentioning the same words over and over. One of those words was *hope*. They didn't realize it could be a name until I offered it as an explanation. Apparently this guy was worried that someone would think he'd reneged on their deal. But whenever he woke up, he remembered nothing and couldn't tell them any more about what he was hoping for."

"And she waited," Mitch muttered to himself. "She held on until she was sure he was dead. All this time she's been mourning his loss, and he's alive and well and married to someone else." He thought. "Have he and his wife any children?"

"Clarence shook his head. The wife's dead. Six years ago. Cancer. Long, drawn out and very painful."

"And children?"

"One. A boy."

"Can we talk to him?" Mitch snatched his pen, prepared to write down the name and address.

"No. He's dead, too. Drive-by shooting. And it almost did the old man in last year. Some of my contacts in his company say he found solace in his loss with some woman. Don't have her name yet."

"Wow!" Mitch sighed, turning it all around and around in his mind, wondering what this new information would do to the prim and proper woman ensconced in his apartment.

"Want me to keep on digging?" Clarence asked diffidently, as if it was none of his business either way.

"Heavens, yes." Mitch exhaled heavily. "The more we

know, the better. I'd like to know who he's interested in and where she lives. I'd also like to know if he's remembered everything and is just too much of a coward to come and explain it all or if everything is still a blur."

"Do what I can," Clarence assured him, snapping his notebook closed and rising to his feet in one practiced motion. "I'll check in when I've got something. See you, Mitch." And with those words, Clarence disappeared as silently as he'd shown up.

Mitch snatched his phone and stabbed out his grandfather's number.

"This is Mitch," he told the guardian secretary. "Is he there?" He listened, frowning. "As soon as he gets out of court, have him call me. It's important, Dora." He slammed the phone down in irritation and stood up to pace around his tiny office.

"Oh, Lord, oh, Lord," he groaned. "I know You're omnipotent and in control of everything. And You can make good things happen from bad." This was all so new to him. Mitch tried desperately to remember how the minister had told him to talk to God.

"Like a son talking to his father," Pastor Dave had told him.

Well, he hadn't had the typical father-son relationship, and he wasn't too sure just what that included, but Mitch decided to give it a try anyway.

"Father, I think a lot of people could be hurt by this. Please show me what to do. And help all those involved. Amen." Satisfied that he'd laid it all before the One who could deal with it, he returned to his desk and sat down.

A moment later, his head was bowed once more.

"And help me in this situation with Melanie so that neither of us get hurt. Just friends, that's all I want. Thank You," he murmured quietly.

* * *

It had finally happened, Mitch decided three weeks later. He had begun to lose his sanity.

Thing was, he wasn't surprised. Not really. In fact, he'd half suspected she would be trouble. It had taken her just one week to move in and throw everything out of whack. Melanie Stewart had thoroughly upset his placid life, and now he was going nuts fantasizing about a woman he barely knew.

He tugged the pillow over his head, trying to drown out the sounds of Melanie in the shower. It was impossible. Jumping Jehoshaphat, those two women got up before dawn every blinking morning! And they didn't care who knew it, either.

Resigned, he placed the pillow behind his head and lay back, calmly accepting his fate. The way he figured it, he'd once done something really terrible and now it was payback time. Fine, he would take his punishment, but why did this torture have to begin so early?

It wasn't the panty hose hanging in the laundry room, slapping him in the face every night, that got to him. It wasn't that light but lingering scent she always wore that clung to everything in the apartment and refused to be doused by the strongest room deodorizer.

It wasn't even that she brought some of her residents to his apartment for a meal, a game of cards or just a night out—and more often than not, they conned him into playing crazy eights, too.

He could deal with all that, Mitch told himself firmly. He'd even managed to tolerate Hope's insistence on chaperoning every second of time they spent in the apartment.

But this daily trauma of pretending he wasn't aware when she showered, wasn't waiting for the faint hint of her lemony shampoo to carry to him, wasn't visualizing her rosy cheeks and that fresh-scrubbed look she wore so well—that's what was really getting to him.

"Blast it," he bellowed, without thinking, and then wished he had zipped his lip.

"Mitch?" she called quietly. "Are you okay?"

"I will be if I can ever get into the bathroom," he hollered, stubbing his toe on the nightstand as he reached for his shirt.

"I'm getting darned tired of taking cold showers," Mitch grumbled sourly twenty minutes later. Hope's short, economical showers after her early—emphasis on the early—walks would probably have left enough hot water for him.

But Melanie's extended steam baths left little but the most frigid of showers which were, of necessity, very short. He'd taken to shaving in his room because the mirrors in the bathroom were too steamed up to let him shave properly even if there had been room for his razor among the multicolored little bottles, vials and tubes. He couldn't figure it out. As far as he could tell, neither woman wore much makeup.

When at last Mitch sauntered into the kitchen, he was in no mood for pleasant conversation. He was desperately searching for a cup of coffee. Melanie did make good coffee, he'd give her that. That is, if he got any. More often than not, Hope would pour the "vile black drug" down the drain as soon as her niece was finished.

Today Melanie sat alone at the breakfast bar, staring vacantly out the window. In front of her was an empty cereal bowl testifying that she had already eaten. Bran flakes, no doubt. A shudder tickled Mitch's back.

"How can you eat that stuff?" he demanded.

Melanie stared at him for a moment before answering.

"It's very healthy," she murmured as she strolled with that long-legged grace to the counter to rinse her bowl before bending to place it in the dishwasher.

Her slim, efficient body was immaculately clothed in blush-pink nylon, and she exuded freshness. By contrast, Mitch felt drained, lifeless. And he was beginning to hate the color pink.

"Maybe, but it tastes like dog food," he said grumpily, stuffing one of the doughnuts he'd bought the night before into his mouth. He glanced around to make sure Hope hadn't seen his secret stash.

"I wouldn't know." Her clear gaze surveyed his tired face. "I have never tasted dog food." She smirked at him. "It's a treat I'll leave you to savor."

Mitch wanted to stick his tongue out, but he managed to control the urge. Barely.

"Boy, are you cranky. Something bothering you, Mitch?"

Butter wouldn't melt in her mouth. He scowled. Miss Perfect Stewart was no doubt well refreshed after her night on the town with pretty-boy Jeff, the blond doctor. No doubt they had gone out for a healthy meal of sushi, Mitch told himself jealously.

He was getting fed up with the parade of men who frequented his apartment. "Friends," she said, but Mitch wondered. Most of them phoned to ask her out for coffee, to take her for pizza or to a movie. A few even ended up in his living room getting advice about a birthday gift for their newest love. Young and old, they came to ask her advice about a new girlfriend. The kids took her to dinner, baseball games and all the church socials in town while they plied her with questions about the best way to handle their totally uncool parents. He never got a moment alone with her.

Mostly Mitch was really sick of the tall, ever-charming fellow from the television studio. Neal Landt was becoming a frequent visitor on the weekends. Charming and personable, he had openly admitted his interest in Melanie. The man had even asked Mitch for advice about her favorite meal!

"I want to make a good impression. You know how it is, old son. She's one very foxy lady."

Old son, indeed! Could the woman not see that Neal must

have bleached his hair and his teeth to get them that white? Mitch forced his mind back to reality. That same woman was now sitting in his kitchen. Alone. Waiting.

"I was going to tell you—"

He turned toward the counter just as Melanie's elbow connected with his cup. The hot, sweet coffee splashed down the pristine white of his shirt. It was just enough to ignite his already red-hot temper.

"Blast it, woman, can't you be careful? It's not enough that you take over my apartment, use up all the hot water, constantly invite your seniors over and expect me to entertain them *and* run your Dear Melanie Advice Service from my telephone, now you've ruined my best white shirt."

Mitch's dark eyes flew to her face in time to catch the cascade of red suffusing it. Her jade eyes glittered sparks at him. He watched, mesmerized, as her temper flared and then he waited for the explosion.

Melanie jabbed her pink-tipped fingernail into the air, her voice betraying a tiny wobble, which she quickly corrected.

"What, exactly, is your problem?" she demanded. Her foot moved as if to whack him in the shin. He jumped back. "You are the biggest dolt I've ever known. And the grumpiest. I'm terribly sorry I woke you, bear face. And I didn't intentionally ruin your shirt."

Mitch was pretty sure she wanted to stick her tongue out at him, but she didn't.

"Crawl back into your den till spring and sleep it off," she advised him angrily. "By then I'll be gone, thank goodness!" She rushed out the door.

Berating himself for his rotten attitude, Mitch moved after her. He hadn't really meant to say it. It was just…

"No, wait, Melanie." His voice was loud and strident, but she was gone. Only Mrs. Green from 106 stood in the hallway, frowning at him darkly.

"A den of iniquity, that's what it is," the elderly woman groused. "People coming and going at all hours. It's a good thing Hope Langford is watching out for that girl. Otherwise…" She shook her head doubtfully at Mitch's coffee-stained shirt and red face before returning to her apartment.

Slowly Mitch walked inside, pushing Melanie's strappy black heels out of his way. He remembered how great she had looked last night. Black stockings, black leather jacket and skirt, and these bits of leather on her feet. It had been a fifties car thing downtown, he remembered. She'd ridden with some punks in a convertible.

Mitchel kicked the heels away viciously. Didn't the woman pick anything up?

"Forget it, will you?" he ordered himself. "You're an idiot. A stupid, blithering idiot!"

His fist connected with the door frame in frustration as he realized he was thinking about her again and wishing he hadn't been so rude. When the throbbing pain finally translated itself to his brain, Mitchel Stewart decided it was time to do some serious regrouping. He stuffed another doughnut into his mouth and poured a fresh cup of coffee as he pondered his situation.

Okay, he admitted to his niggling conscience. He liked her brash attitude and quick comebacks. A lot. And he wanted to get to know her. But after this morning's little fiasco, he doubted she wanted much to do with him, prize money or not. And he was going to have to figure a way to get past the hordes of people that always seemed to be around her.

"It's gonna take a lot of sucking up, Stewart," he told himself, then grinned. He knew he was feeling the sugar doughnuts hit his bloodstream, but suddenly he felt happier than he had in days. He had a plan, by George, and he was going to put it into practice today.

Whistling merrily, Mitch removed his sodden, coffee-stained shirt and replaced it with another.

"Fine." He grinned cheekily at himself in the mirror. "If she wants polite and restrained, that's what I will be. Decent. Upstanding. I can do that." At least he thought he could.

Melanie wasn't going to goad him into doing anything that would put her beloved money in danger. And if she didn't get that blasted cash for her old friends, nobody would lay it at his door.

There was a tiny voice in the back of his mind demanding to be heard. Was it really for the money that he'd talked her into staying here?

Mitch ignored the question. He straightened his shoulders. He had to get this cleared up. If she was staying, and he wasn't too sure about that, then he had some serious apologizing to do.

A gift, that was it. He'd give her something. He remembered something she had said about pets and old people being a natural. They weren't allowed here, but maybe at Sunset… Maybe that was the answer.

"Prepare for battle," he muttered to that little voice before grabbing his overstuffed briefcase and stomping out the door. His fingers snicked up the last doughnut on the way.

"Bran flakes, indeed!"

Chapter Five

"Junk-food junkie," Melanie muttered through tightly clenched teeth. Her heart sank as she spied Hope standing on the corner, waving madly. "Just what I need to make a lousy morning really complete," she muttered, staring at the woman's smiling face.

"Hi, Hope. Boy, you're up early."

She tried to infuse some enthusiasm into her voice while swallowing the little prick of conscience that reminded her that Hope had risen at precisely four fifty-eight, a full half hour before her own alarm went off.

"Yes, I had some thinking to do," Hope murmured, buckling herself in carefully after arching one eyebrow, then daintily removing a chocolate-bar wrapper from the seat with two perfectly shaped oval nails. "Could you give me a lift to the home, Melanie? It's my day to volunteer and I thought I'd get an early start."

"Yes, of course." Melanie steered into what passed for rush hour traffic in Mossbank and drove furiously through town.

"What did you say, dear?"

"Oh, nothing, Hope," Melanie lied, knowing perfectly

well what she had said and hoping against all the odds that her former Sunday school teacher wouldn't call her on it.

"You said, 'The man is a neat freak,'" Hope repeated, her voice serious. "I take it you're talking about Mitchel?"

"Oh, yeah." Melanie breathed, trying to stall all the unlovely things that begged release. "He was nattering at me again this morning. I accidentally bumped his arm and spilled his coffee. He's so rude!"

There was no point in holding back and getting ulcers, Melanie decided finally. Might as well lay it on the line.

"If I so much as put my feet up on the edge of the coffee table, he's there with a cloth, cleaning up." Melanie flicked the signal with more power than necessary and winced at Bessie's protest.

"If I have a glass of water, he waits, suspended at my side, ready to pounce the moment I set it down. Then he marches into the kitchen to put the glass in the dishwasher. As if I have some contagious disease!"

"Yes, he's become quite particular about things lately." Hope nodded, smiling happily. "And you could take a lesson from that, dear."

"I'm not messy," Melanie protested, her face flushed and angry. "I just like to relax for a while after work. It's not my fault he stepped on my keys last night. I didn't deliberately put them on the floor."

"He didn't say you had! He just asked you to be more careful. With the three of us, it is rather crowded, and you do tend toward accidents, my dear."

"I do not!" Melanie refused to back down when Hope's raised eyebrows begged her to reconsider. "Like what?"

"You left the lid off the blender two days ago, dear. When you started it, that tomato sauce flew everywhere. It took a long time to clean up." Hope's face was pensive. "I'm not sure it will ever come off the ceiling. Stipple is so dreadfully hard to clean, isn't it?"

"All right! One little accident. You're making it sound like a whole string of problems."

"Well, there was that business with the can of whipped cream, dear."

"I was trying to fix it! I didn't know he'd try to use it before I'd got the top back on properly." Melanie giggled in remembrance. "At least now we know what he'll look like when he gets old."

"And the barbecue? I don't think he'll be able to use the balcony without having some repairs done, Melanie. He also fell on your wet floor after the soap bottle broke. I'm glad he didn't break anything." Hope ticked an item off on her fingers. "You washed that white silk shirt of his with your red vest and put his watch down the garbage disposal." Hope looked sad. "There have been several problems, Melanie."

"And not all of them are my fault," Melanie complained, pulling into a parking spot. "That pizza last night, for instance. I'm allergic to shrimp, and yet he got it loaded."

"He didn't know, dear." Hope gathered her purse and sweater before brushing one hand over her hair. "You two always seem to be at loggerheads, and yet, really, I think if you'd admit it, you like each other."

"He hangs around in clothes a bag lady would reject and eats those horrible doughnuts nonstop," Melanie seethed. "And if I had a dollar for every file he's left strewn on the coffee table, or a quarter for the number of times he left his half-full coffee cup on the dishwasher instead of inside it, I could retire quite happily."

"Well, yes, it does seem to be the perfect case of a bachelor in a rut," Hope murmured. "Are you sure this money really means that much to you, dear? I mean, sometimes we ask the Lord for a sign and then we misinterpret things to our own benefit."

"But Hope," Melanie protested. "I've prayed and prayed

about Sunset's needs, and every time I turn around, the answer is right there. Get that prize money and you can fill some of those needs." She stared at her friend. "Do you think I'm wrong?"

"I think you have to be very sure that this is God directing Melanie and not you misconstruing what might just be chance."

Melanie shook her head vehemently.

"I don't think that's what I'm doing, Hope. I've prayed so hard, and everything just seems to have fallen into place."

"Not quite," Hope murmured dryly. "I mean you two *are* only sharing the apartment to get the prize money, right?" She opened the door and got out, straightening her skirt carefully. "But I daresay all of that could all be corrected. In time."

Melanie wasn't sure whether to agree or not but was forestalled from answering by the simple expedient of Hope's departure. She strode toward the nursing home in long, determined steps. Sighing, Melanie gathered her briefcase and purse from the back seat, her mind replaying the scene in the apartment.

So he wanted to be alone, did he? Well, tough. He had asked her to stay and, nasty as he was, she wasn't moving until that check came. As she stared at her white fingers clenching the handle of her briefcase, Melanie just wished the money would come today. She released each finger, one by one.

Breathing deeply, she tried to view their situation from a distance. What was it about Mitch that made her so nervous? she asked herself.

Well, for one thing, his hands were constantly touching her, under her elbow, on her hand, brushing her waist. He made the blood flow hot and sweet through her body and then left her wanting more.

"But I detest him," she muttered, and knew that she lied. No man had ever made her feel so vulnerable. It scared her. In her world of old people, she was in control. Even her dates allowed her to set the tone of the evening. But when Mitch touched her, control moved out the window.

Control, she decided. That's what she really needed. An abundance of control. Unfortunately, it had never been her forte. She grimaced as the morning scene flashed through her mind.

No, she considered ruefully, there hadn't been much control there. She resolved to think happy thoughts. Mitch Stewart was not going to get under her skin again.

She hoped.

"I could use a little help with this decision, Lord," she murmured.

Once she entered the nursing home, Melanie tried to focus entirely on her clients. The shock came when she opened her office door after morning rounds with the doctors. Immediately her eyes began to water. She blew her nose several times before her senses cleared enough to spy the frail little woman seated on her sofa, cuddling a pure white angora kitten.

"Look, Melanie, a wonderful present arrived for you." Mrs. Rivers's soft voice was perfectly clear, and Melanie marveled at the sudden change in the woman.

The dim gray eyes were bright with excitement as Nettie stroked the cat's fur, cooing gently. Melanie wiped her eyes again, trying to stifle a sneeze.

"Just waid dere, Bissus Ribers. A'll be ride…achoo— bagk." Melanie hurried out the door to find Bridget. "Youb god to ged id oud ob here, Bwidget. I can'd bweade."

Melanie left her secretary to deal with the problem and strode quickly down the hall to the patio. Once in the fresh air, she sank into a chair, breathing deeply. Eventually, her nose began to drain and her eyes stopped watering.

It was there that Mitch found her ten minutes later.

"Taking a break?" he asked, eyeing her red eyes with curiosity. "What's the matter, Melanie? I'm sorry for what I said. I didn't mean to make you cry."

His voice was concerned, and Melanie was touched. After his angry diatribe earlier, she didn't expect him to be so solicitous. It made her feel even more guilty. He bent on his haunches, peering into her face, his long fingers brushing over her hand.

"You didn't," she muttered, trying to find that elusive control she had ordered herself to exert. "I'm fine, actually. It's just that somebody foolishly brought a cat into my office. I'm allergic to cats," she enlightened him, curious about the red stain that was flooding his face.

"It's too bad, too, because Mrs. Rivers is talking a mile a minute. That's something she's never done the whole time I've been here. Now I'll have to have the dratted thing taken away." She grimaced. "That'll set her back but good!"

Melanie was less than thrilled with having to handle such a touchy situation. The extra time and patience it would take to convince Mrs. Rivers of the unsuitability of the cat in a nursing home would probably not erase the loss she would feel when the animal went.

"Honestly! If people would only ask before they do something silly like this."

Mitch turned away to stare at the nearby flower bed. He seemed utterly absorbed in it, and Melanie wondered if he had heard a thing she had said. She was surprised when his low voice rumbled quietly.

"Maybe she could keep it in her room. You wouldn't have to go in there, and she would still have her companion."

Melanie stared at him.

"A cat in a nursing home?" she scoffed. "We're trying to keep a sterile atmosphere so our residents don't catch every bug that's going around. Do you know the diseases a cat carries?"

It was clearly not an option, Melanie decided, but Mitch pressed on, trying to convince her that he had a feasible solution to the problem.

"Maybe it's too sterile. Maybe those people would enjoy having someone else to be concerned about and care for." His dark eyes dared her to deny it.

It was a convincing argument, and Melanie knew it. The trade journals were full of articles about experiments involving pets in nursing homes that had been tried with excellent results. In fact, Sunset Home already had a parrot, exotic fish and a gerbil. But a cat?

"If it makes such a difference in her life, maybe it would help some of the other residents too," he coaxed, anxiously watching her face.

"I suppose it might work," Melanie conceded, considering options. "The litter box will have to stay in her room, though." She sneezed once more, shaking her head.

"There must still be some of those fibers on my clothes." She wiped her red nose and then leaned over to pluck one from Mitch's dark jacket. "Look, I've even spread them to you," she muttered in disgust.

Melanie sneezed one last time. "I only hope it doesn't cross my path again," she added grimly. Her wide green eyes perused Mitch's formally suited figure with a frown.

"What are you doing here, anyway?" she demanded, suddenly suspicious. Mitch held out a long white envelope.

"This came just after you left. By messenger. It's from Papa John," he told her, smiling sympathetically as she blew her nose in the fresh handkerchief he handed her.

"Well, what do they want now?" Melanie asked, tired of all the delays.

Her fingers tore open the envelope and she pulled out the

single sheet of paper. Her face lit up with pleasure, eyes sparkling and pink lips grinning.

"Finally. They're going to award the prizes within two weeks," she told Mitch. "We'll be given the final decision within two weeks." She couldn't believe it.

Melanie jumped to her feet and, grabbing Mitch's hands, whirled around him like a top, spinning crazily out of control.

"Twenty-five thousand dollars! It's more than I ever dreamed of." Melanie hugged him happily before dancing off.

"Melanie." Mitch's low voice broke into her fanciful musings. Wide and green, her hazel eyes turned to study him curiously. "Things might not turn out the way you hoped."

Mitch kept his voice lightly cautious, hoping she would see the possibilities the company had left open in their letter. In fact, his legal brain had been perturbed at the gaps in the information Papa John had conveyed, but he didn't want to be the one to burst her bubble of joy.

Her arched brows quirked upward as her eyes opened wide to stare at him. He could see the awareness in her eyes and knew she was feeling the current snapping between them. Her pupils were dilated, but still she focused on him, allowing him to see into her soul.

"But it says right here," she said, reading the letter once more. Her eyes flew upward. "Don't you believe them?"

"Yes, of course." He felt constrained to agree. "It's just that I'll feel better when it's all settled." *A lot better,* he thought.

"So will I," Melanie burst out excitedly. Her eyes were glowing.

Mitch felt his heart drop to his highly polished loafers. She was too trusting, he decided. Melanie counted on that prize money to help her friends. She couldn't imagine not receiving it after all this time.

He, on the other hand, was well aware of just how swiftly her fortune could be rescinded in light of the errors that appeared on her application. Mitch made his decision. He wasn't going to be the one to erase the joy from her glowing face. His heart began its thudding beat as he stared into her rapt gaze. She was so beautiful. And so far beyond his reach.

The paging system disturbed their self-analysis, jolting each back to reality.

"I have got to get moving," Melanie told him. Her voice seemed breathy. She slipped around him to edge inside the building but his long legs caught up to her immediately.

"I'll walk you there," he offered, still dumbfounded by the depth of emotion he had seen in those deep eyes.

In her office, Melanie turned to call Bridget, allowing Mitch just enough time to scoop up the card he had included with the cat. It would not do to let her know the truth, he decided. Stuffing it into his pocket, he turned and came face to face with a grinning Bridget. She flicked her bright red nail at his lapel.

"Not such a good idea," she teased, laughing. "Next time try flowers."

Mitch tried to look nonchalant when Melanie called his name.

"Yes?" he answered, his blue eyes thoughtfully studying her.

"Aren't you going to work?" Melanie's impatient voice was like a douse of cold water. Glancing at his watch, Mitch strode to the door.

"Lord, yes. I've got to be in court in ten minutes. Gramps will probably cite me for contempt," he admitted. "See you later." With a wave he was gone, leaving Melanie to stare curiously after him.

She wasn't sure what it was all about, or even why he'd come. But, somehow, she felt as if Mitch had seen into her soul. Which probably was not good, given that Melanie seemed constantly attracted to his lean good looks.

Sighing, she turned to smile at a hovering Bridget, who stood inside the door with a box of tissues and a small vacuum. Now, for the cat.

Eight hours later, Melanie wished the cat was the sum total of her problems. She forced herself to sit and listen to the angry man deriding her and her staff for their inconsiderate lack of attention to the plight of families who came to visit the residents.

"Yes, Mr. Johnson, I realize that everyone works nowadays, but our clients need to eat their meals at a regularly scheduled time each day. We encourage them to come to the dining rooms on time, to eat with the others and to limit their snack foods." She waited for the next onslaught.

The blustering man's whining voice grew louder.

"But surely when we have made the effort to get here to see our mother, you could adjust the dinner hour somewhat?" His soulful brown eyes drooped with sadness.

Melanie's temper was wearing thin after forty minutes of his griping. There was still so much to be done before her daily to-do list was even halfway complete. She decided to set him straight and make her point without any pussyfooting around.

"Mr. Johnson," she said, her soft voice firm. "You have been to see your mother, what?" She consulted the open book in front of her. "Two times in the past month."

The man had the grace to turn red, but Melanie was relentless.

"Your mother is here every day of every week, all year long. She is hypoglycemic, which means that she has to eat regularly to maintain her blood sugar levels." She gave him her most severe nurse look. "Please don't ask me to adjust the routine of your mother and the other eighty-six residents, thirty-odd staff and an entire kitchen just so you can drop in for a visit once in a blue moon." She closed the big binder with a thud and stood in dismissal.

"I'm sorry, but you will have to wait until Mrs. Johnson is finished her meal or return at another time." Her tone suggested that she didn't particularly care which.

Grumbling and complaining, the man took his leave. Melanie sank into her chair with a groan.

"I didn't know we kept track of the residents' visitors." Bridget smirked from the doorway.

Grinning, Melanie held up the accounts ledger for housekeeping. "We don't, but it worked, so don't knock it." They giggled together for a few moments before Bridget spoke.

"You still need to call Mr. Richards's family about his clothes," she chided, glancing at her watch. "Or should I say lack of!" Bridget's round face beamed with mirth. "And then get out of here. It's after seven." She clucked at Melanie like a mother hen guarding her chick.

Two and a half hours later, at the end of a killer fourteen-hour day, Melanie reluctantly dragged her aching body into the apartment she shared with Mitch and Hope. Tossing her purse and sweater on the sofa, Melanie sprawled on the soft, cool comfort of Mitch's leather sofa, dreaming of a bubble bath.

"That's all I want," she mumbled wearily. "That and someone to cook me a wonderful dinner," she elaborated, closing her eyes for just a moment.

"Melanie." A big hand was shaking her and Melanie wished it would go away. She pulled one eye open with the maximum effort and saw a pair of huge blue eyes peering into hers.

Not now, she prayed. She couldn't deal with a sexily rumpled corporate type right now. She shut her eye and resumed her fantasy.

"Oh, boy, you look bad." Mitch's deep voice rumbled beside her right ear, bringing her awake.

"I know, don't even say it," Melanie ordered halfheartedly. "I've been doing CPR on a resident." She glanced into his dark eyes. Tiredness caused the tears to course down her wan cheeks. "We lost him."

To his credit, Mitch never said a word. He just tugged her gently into his arms and let her bawl on his new blue shirt. When she was finished, he wiped her eyes gently and then sat on the sofa behind her, propping her up.

"Come on, lady." He urged her forward a little, his hands moving to her shoulders. "I'll give you a massage." His long, lean fingers kneaded the tensely knotted muscles in her shoulders. "You're dead on your feet."

Melanie was too tired to do anything but relax against him and let him do all the work.

"Mmm," she moaned, unable to move an inch. "I guess dreams really do come true." She tipped her head and peered at him from beneath lowered lids. "Did you bring dinner? Something yummy like chicken chop suey or moo goo gai pan?"

"You don't want much, do you?" he chuckled, squeezing the knots in her shoulder a little harder. "A masseuse, a meal. Can I get milady anything else?" His voice had assumed a butlerish English accent.

"That fifty thousand dollars would be nice," she muttered drowsily, arching as his strong thumbs found a particularly sensitive spot by her neck.

"I'm working on that," he told her, grinning. "But we need to talk first." He grunted as he probed the aching muscles of her upper arms.

"You are as strung out as a cat on a thin wire," Mitch muttered, kneading the tight knots of tension from her shoulders. "This is some stressful reaction coming from a nursing home."

Melanie wished he wouldn't mention cats, but she was too

tired to lecture him so she eased into the sofa and sighed deeply.

"Melanie, what happened today to cause all this?" Mitch's quiet voice demanded a reply.

"The list is endless," she muttered. "One of the residents shed his clothes and took a stroll out-of-doors." Melanie could feel his knuckles manipulating the vertebrae in her back, and she curled her spine accommodatingly. "Unfortunately, several old dears had just completed a tea party with some of their friends, and the friends, members of the board, actually, were leaving the premises at the time. He flashed them."

The calm, sensible way she told the tale had Mitch nodding in agreement until he absorbed what she had said.

"Flashed them? You mean…" She didn't know why, but he sounded shocked.

"Uh-huh," she replied, stretching a little. "Could you move a bit to the right? Yes, that's it. Oh."

Mitch, to his credit, kept on working the muscles in her back as he appreciated the view. It wasn't every day he got this close to Melanie and he was pretty sure she wasn't about to stop him now. Not when her eyes were closed like that and she was breathing so deeply.

He had been dreaming about her for weeks, and he had no desire to end this contact with her, even if she was half-asleep. He was enjoying bringing her relief, he decided, as his fingers kneaded and manipulated the knotted muscles in her shoulders. She didn't seem to be protesting. He leaned forward for a better look and grinned.

Melanie lay asleep on the sofa, hair sprawled across her shoulders and over her face. Carefully, hoping not to wake her, Mitch slipped the silky strands off her cheek. A slow, satisfied smile tipped the corners of her wide mouth as she breathed a deep sigh of satisfaction.

"Thanks for the massage," she murmured. "I feel so much better."

Her mouth touched a tiny caress to the side of his neck in appreciation before her slim arms fell to her side. Curling like a sensuous kitten, Melanie nudged her foot against the end of the sofa, finding a more comfortable spot, before her huge eyes blinked shut. Seconds later she was blissfully snoring.

Mitch decided he could spend the evening just sitting there and watching her. She looked so peaceful, and there were none of those biting little witticisms coming out of her full pink lips. She looked adorable with her hair all mussed and her makeup completely gone.

He was in the process of easing a blanket over her, when he heard the key in the door. With a groan Mitch recalled Hope and her ridiculous assumptions about this arrangement. He knew he was going to have to move fast.

Mitch pushed Melanie up and propped her against the end of the sofa while he rearranged the cushions and smoothed the blanket over her. He had just straightened when Hope breezed through the door, a casserole in her arms and his grandfather following close behind.

"Hello," she greeted him happily. "I made my special tofu surprise this afternoon and I thought perhaps we could all share it." She trundled to the kitchen with the bowl held high.

"I suppose she wants us to eat our Wheaties and will serve spinach with it, too?" Mitch complained, glaring at his grandfather. "I'm not eating that stuff."

"You don't have to," Harry murmured. "Just pretend you're enjoying it and smile. I need some time to explain about Jean, and I was hoping it would be tonight." He stared at Melanie's slumped figure speculatively. "Will she wake up anytime soon?"

"I don't know." Mitch grinned. "She was pretty out of it after I gave her that mass—she was pretty tired," he amended. But his grandfather's eyes were glowing, and Mitch knew the old man had caught the slip.

"A massage? How kind of you. Never knew you to be so concerned about someone before," Harry murmured slyly.

The doorbell rang, signaling the arrival of Faith and Charity, who immediately began fussing over a groggy Melanie.

"My goodness, Melanie, you do look tired," Faith chirped cheerfully. "You should try some of that new tonic Arthur just got in. Liver tonic, I think it is." She shuddered. "Tastes vile but really restores your energy."

"Baloney!" Charity's brisk, no-nonsense tones were neither hushed nor quiet. "She doesn't need a tonic. Just some fresh air and a decent meal. Wake up, dear." She shook her daughter's shoulder briskly.

"Oh, is Melanie awake now?" Hope asked brightly from the kitchen doorway. Her spotless white apron was just as immaculate as the dress she wore beneath it. "My casserole will be ready in about fifteen minutes. We can all enjoy it together."

"Piffle! I hate—"

Charity's firm voice cut off Faith's protests.

"Mitch is taking Melanie out for dinner, Hope. Then they're going for a walk in the park or something. And Faith and I have already eaten." Mitch grinned at the frown Melanie's mother gave Faith. "But you and Harry go ahead. We'll just sit with you and visit."

Mitch was sure only he heard the whispered complaints between the two old ladies.

"You lied, Charity! I didn't have dinner yet."

"I didn't say you had." Charity's voice was cool. "I merely said we'd already eaten. Didn't you have breakfast and lunch today?" She waited while Faith nodded. "Then you've already eaten."

"But, Charity, I'm hungry," Faith wailed. "I've been weeding in your garden all afternoon, and I want my dinner."

"Badly enough to swallow her tofu casserole?" Charity muttered grimly. As enlightenment spread across Faith's countenance, Charity patted her hand. "We'll stop at Burger Heaven on the way home."

"Can I have fries?" Faith asked slyly, her nose curling as a strange odor wafted through the apartment.

Mitch wheeled and whispered in Faith's ear. When she nodded, he pressed a twenty into her hand.

Surprisingly, it took Melanie about five minutes to shower and change into a pair of white slacks and a cool blue top. Her hair was wreathed around her head in a coronet style that left the air free to caress her long, slim neck. Mitch decided he liked that style almost as much as he liked it when she left it loose and long.

"What did you give Faith twenty dollars for?" she demanded as soon as they left the apartment, the good wishes of the three ladies ringing behind them.

"To get rid of any of that *stuff* that's left," he told her. "You may be some kind of health nut, but I am not, repeat not, eating tofu casserole."

Quick as a wink, Melanie whipped open her tan leather bag and pulled out a ten, which she handed to him with a grin.

"Good thinking." She laughed. "I can't stand tofu myself. Particularly not after wading through those awful poached chicken breasts last night. They had no taste."

"Tell me about it." He chuckled. "Well, what's it to be? Artery-clogging fried chicken? Thirty fat grams of pizza? Or Faith's favorite—Burger Heaven?"

When Melanie beamed at him like that, Mitch wondered if it wasn't just about time to renounce his long-held beliefs on marriage and his aversion to it. Just about.

"None of the above. Let's try some lean, healthful Chinese food."

"Good idea! Like sweet and sour ribs and deep-fried

chicken balls. Health food! Now that's my style." He pulled away from the curb with a roar and steered off down the street.

He couldn't help but join in her hoot of laughter. Nor could he avoid the sense of camaraderie that being with her brought. It was almost as if he belonged.

Chapter Six

"Please, God, just this once, don't let him be there."

Melanie prayed fervently but without much faith. Since that fateful day two weeks ago when her sane, orderly life had been traumatized by a back rub that had massaged away the aches but replaced them with desires that couldn't be fulfilled, Mitch Stewart had dominated her thoughts.

Lately, Mitch managed to be at their apartment whenever she was. Casually waiting, smiling that mysterious smile. As if he knew about the flicker of desire that curled in her stomach whenever she caught sight of his dark head.

And Melanie was more aware of him than any man she had known before. Regardless of what he thought, she did remember offering him a kiss as thanks for his help. She was pretty sure she'd seen desire in his eyes at that moment. And Melanie knew Mitch had wanted her as much as she had him.

She wanted permanence, someone to depend on, someone to build a future with. She had a sneaking suspicion Mitch might fill that bill very well, Melanie admitted. But Mitch had made it very clear that theirs was only a temporary arrangement. It would end, and they would go their separate ways.

A Hopeful Heart

When she left for work, his dark blue eyes stroked over her uniform, noting every detail. When she left on a date, his glance followed every curve and line of her outfit, mentally chiding her for leaving him alone with Hope. Oh, he never said a word, of course. But she was a master at reading that poor-little-me expression.

Of course, it's only for the money she was staying. At least, that's what she told herself.

Ruthlessly ignoring the tingle of electricity that jolted through her whenever his twinkling baby blues met hers, Melanie focused on work. She came in way too early and left later than ever and was still far behind in her work. She accepted every date she was offered, even though she spent most of the time sitting thinking about who Mitch was with while she listened to someone else's love life and their problems.

That's why Papa John's visit last night had been so unexpected. And so infuriating. Hope had gone out with Harry, leaving Melanie to tolerate the friendly arm Mitch placed around her shoulders just long enough to avert suspicion before she moved across the room, far away from his big hands. And when he sat right beside her on a sofa that could have easily held six, Melanie made an excuse to refill the tea, even though the pot was still more than half full.

"Oh, yes, we're great friends, Mel and I," he assured the old man, flashing that sexy smile guaranteed to weaken any woman's knees. "We share everything from breakfast cereals to our taste in music."

Mel had gaped at that. Mitch liked jazz while she preferred rock music from the past. And as far as she knew, he never ate breakfast. Unless you counted doughnuts.

The one thing they did share was their obvious lack of use of the old man's product. Melanie sincerely hoped he wouldn't ask for some, because she was positive there wasn't a jar of the stuff anywhere in the apartment. But then, as usual, Mitch was miles ahead. He proudly showed their half-empty jar of nutty peanut butter to a benignly smiling Papa John.

"This is great stuff, sir. I've enjoyed it every morning." Grinning ear to ear, Mitch proceeded to wax rhapsodic about peanut butter!

Melanie thought she would be sick.

"Did your children eat a lot of peanut butter when they were growing up?" Mitch had asked curiously.

When the elderly gentleman lost all his color, Melanie helped him sit down and offered him a cookie.

"I'm afraid my only son died," he whispered, his face chalk white with strain. "I have no other children."

"Oh, I'm so sorry," Melanie murmured, patting the blue-veined hand as she glared at Mitch. "It must be terrible to lose a child." To her disgust, Mitch continued on quite easily, as if nothing untoward had happened.

"Yes, I imagine it must be just like losing a parent," he said thoughtfully. "I used to know some people who lost a father in Vietnam. It was very sad."

Melanie didn't think it was possible, but the old man's color receded even further, leaving him pale and wan.

"I, er, I was in Vietnam, too," he murmured, his hand shaking as he sipped his tea. "I had an accident there."

"I'm so sorry." Melanie rushed to reassure him, wondering why Mitch kept probing at a subject that was obviously painful. She directed a glare in his general direction, but it did absolutely no good. Mitch kept right on asking questions that were none of his business.

"What kind of an accident?" he asked curiously. "Anything you can talk about?"

"I, er, that is, well, you see, I lost my memory." His eyes were distant, staring into the past. "I was hit with some flying

debris when a comrade in the army stepped on a land mine."
He peered at Mitch. "I still don't remember it all," he
murmured. "But a friend of mine has been helping me understand that what's in the past isn't important."

"But what if there was someone, some family member
maybe, that had been waiting for you to return all these
years?" Mitch's eyes were deeply intense as they studied
their visitor. "Wouldn't you want them to know you're alive
and okay?"

"Of course," Papa John murmured. He rubbed his chin
and tried to explain himself. "But I just can't piece it all
together. Not yet. Sometimes I get these pictures of someone,
a woman…" He shook his head tiredly. "It's no good. I can
never remember the dreams."

"Perhaps a hypnotist, or some specialist," Mitch offered
quietly but Papa John shook his head.

"No," he said firmly. "I can't sit around waiting anymore.
I made my wife wait too long before we were married,
hoping I'd remember something from the past, some clue to
who I was." His eyes filled with tears. "Because of that, we
had so little time together."

"I'm sorry, Papa John," Melanie murmured. "We have no
right pressing you like this." She frowned at Mitch. "This is obviously a painful subject and absolutely none of our business.
I apologize for my friend." She laid special emphasis on the last
word, warning Mitch silently that she wasn't finished with him.

"It's just that I'd like to help. If I could," Mitch added,
his cheeks flushed. "I mean, could I conduct a search or
something?"

Papa John smiled as he stood, towering over them.

"That's very kind," he said. "But you see there's almost
nothing to go on. I don't remember any names from that time
except John. I think that's mine. And a date," he added. "June
twenty-first. I have no idea of the significance of that. And

you young things don't want to be fussing about an old man like me. You've got too much living to do. I'd better get going."

Melanie ushered him to the door, murmuring a few polite words of farewell. The door flew open just as she grasped the handle, and an unusually flustered Hope came surging into the room, her hair wild and disorderly, her normally immaculate clothes rumpled and dirty.

"The nerve of that man," she sputtered, her voice full of dismay. "He actually asked me to marry him. At my age! Can you imagine it?"

Papa John observed Hope with a curious look, his eyes wide and questioning, obviously amazed that she found a marriage proposal so distasteful.

"He wants to get married right away! As if I would even countenance such a thing."

"But why not?" Mitch demanded. "Gramps and you make a fine couple, and I think you enjoy each other's company. Don't you?" His stare was speculative, his eyes narrowing as the older woman brushed aside a bright lock of hair.

"Of course I enjoy Harry's company," she burst out. "But I can't just suddenly decide to marry him. Not now, not with everything so up in the air."

"You know," Mitch told her seriously, his eyes fixed on the white-haired man in the doorway. "We were talking about that very thing and how a person shouldn't wait for something that might never happen. Isn't that right, sir?"

"Well, now, I'm not advising any rash decisions," the old man mumbled, staring at Hope's blond beauty, bushy eyebrows furrowed. "But there comes a time when you have to grasp opportunity with both hands and get on with your life. Before it's over."

Melanie suddenly noticed that Hope was staring at Papa John, her cheeks pale.

"Do I know you?" she whispered, peering into his eyes. "I feel somehow that I…"

"I'm sorry, Hope. I should have introduced you." Mitch was beaming at the two of them. "This is Papa John. You know, from the company awarding us the prize money." He turned to the man at the door. "This is our friend, Hope Langford."

They nodded at each other, but Hope had not lost that odd look of speculation, and Melanie wondered for the hundredth time what was going on.

"Papa John Lexington," he told her succinctly, offering a quick little bow. "Most folks call me Big John." He turned to Melanie, who was standing dumbfounded as Mitch's muscular arm wound itself around her shoulders, pressing her against his side in a pose reminiscent of two young lovers.

"Any word on that prize money?" Mitch asked, snuggling Melanie's firm, unyielding form against his.

"It should be released any day now," Papa John murmured, still staring at Hope. "Strange, though, the entry forms having only the one initial. We don't think they were signed in either of your handwritings, either. We checked against the disclaimer we had you fill out." He was almost to the elevator before Hope's shrill tone stopped him.

"Wait a minute! Did you used to live near here? In a place called Sherman Oaks? You remind me…"

But Papa John was stepping into the elevator, shaking his white head.

"No, I'm afraid the name doesn't sound familiar," he told her. His gaze lighted on Mitch and Melanie still standing entwined. "Thank you for the tea. You'll be hearing from my company soon, very soon."

When the elevator doors finally closed on their guest, Melanie ducked out from Mitch's snug embrace to chastise him roundly.

"How could you?" she gasped. "He thinks we are in love with each other. He thinks we eat peanut butter. He thinks we actually like each other!" Her voice was squeaking, and Melanie fought for control.

"We could be, I do eat it, and we do like each other," he answered quietly before moving to clear away the dishes they'd used.

"But…but—" Melanie spluttered, unable to believe what she had just heard. She floundered, searching for words. "I never—that is, if we…I mean, darn it, will you stand still for a minute?"

She was frustrated at Mitch's calm acceptance of the situation. What did he mean, they could be in love? She had never given him any reason to think such a thing! Had she?

He did stop. Putting the tray on the ceramic kitchen counter, he placed his hands behind him as he leaned back to study her flushed face and wringing hands. His knowing grin made her palms itch to slap it away. This was no laughing matter!

"You know that you're as interested in me as I am in you," he told her. "We think alike. But if you want to keep pretending that there's nothing there…" He shrugged. "Fine. That's life. But you're only fooling yourself."

"I have no clue as to where you got this information," she told him spitefully. "But let me assure you that it is false. I am not attracted to you. You're too pushy and too bossy and—"

His big smile beamed teasingly at her.

"It's okay, Melanie. I don't expect you to own up to it. You never do." His blue eyes licked fire at her as he followed her figure to the cinched waist of her silky slacks.

"You're weird," she muttered angrily. "I don't understand where you get the wild idea that we think alike. I couldn't possibly think in nearly such a convoluted form as you." She glared at him. "Besides, I always own up to everything."

"Like this need you have to create big happy families wherever you go? Even if it means burning yourself out in overtime at Sunset with the residents?" His voice was low and intimate. "You know as well as I that you want your own family, and this is your way of creating one."

"You're being ridiculous." She bristled, angry at him for bringing the subject up. "I have family. I have Charity, remember?" She gasped when he shook his dark head.

"Yes, but is that enough? Can you deny that what you really want is to put down some roots of your own?" He chucked a finger under her chin. "There's nothing wrong with that, Melanie. What is wrong is to pretend you don't."

"I'm not pretending anything," she sputtered, turning away. It was a lie. She'd dreamed of her own family for as long as she could remember, and it infuriated her to hear Mitch speak of it.

"Keep fooling yourself if you must," he murmured softly, pressing past her to move out of the tiny kitchen. "But you don't believe that lie any more than I do."

Melanie stood, transfixed. Was he right? Was she hiding behind the residents of Sunset, afraid to take a chance on her own dreams?

And even if she wanted to, Mitchel Stewart would hardly be her choice. He was more like a shark than the easygoing kind of man she preferred.

It was too touchy for discussion, she decided, and pursued his other claims, instead.

"You're a fine one to talk about denial," she complained. "You don't use their peanut butter!" She was furious at his temerity. He was going to jeopardize everything.

"Of course I do," Mitch countered, his voice smooth as silk. "It so happens that Papa John's peanut butter tastes really great on doughnuts." He pointed toward the half-empty container on the shelf. "That's my second jar."

Melanie gaped. She staggered to one of the kitchen chairs

and sank into it gratefully. The thought of peanut butter on doughnuts made her gag, so she focused on his lean, taut body lounging against the counter. His legs were covered in disreputable old denim with strategically placed tears that gaped across both knees.

Melanie had no doubt those tears were from wear. He put the jeans on every chance he got, which was often enough. And that ragged old sweatshirt, too! Tonight he was dressed more sloppily than his usual relaxed attire. Why, the shoulders were so baggy, his shirt exposed more than it covered, and even on straight, it didn't cover an awful lot of his hair-roughened, muscular chest.

Melanie decided right then and there that it wasn't politic to focus on anything but his face. Not where her heartbeat was concerned. She forced herself to meet his sardonic gaze without flinching.

Blue eyes met hers, sparkling with suppressed laughter. He raked a hand through his wavy jet-black hair, and one irrepressible lock fell over his forehead. He looked very attractive in a jaunty sort of way. She felt her heartbeat speed up. It was time to go. Melanie turned, heading for the door.

"I'm going out," she murmured, hoping he wouldn't hear the little catch in her voice.

"Dressed like that, I expected so," he murmured, following her to the front room. "What is it this time? A teenage crush or counseling a reprobate husband?"

Melanie had a ton of sarcastic phrases, but she didn't get the chance to utter even one of the words that flew to her lips. Hope's soft voice broke in.

"That man," Hope murmured into the silence. "I…I think I might know him."

Melanie whirled to stare at her disbelievingly.

"Know Papa John?" She frowned. "How would you know him?"

"I'm not sure. He looks familiar." The blue eyes stared into the past. "I think he might be Jean." Her face fell as tears rolled down the clear alabaster skin, her eyes begging for understanding.

"But that's..." Melanie's mouth fell open when Mitch's fingers closed around her upper arm.

"Gramps and I think so, too," he told Hope gently. "I've been doing a bit of research on my own, and from what I can determine, Papa John might just be the guy we've been searching for."

"But he was reported dead." Hope's voice was faint and bemused. "They found his dog tags." She rubbed a hand across her forehead. "I don't understand this."

"I don't have a lot of information yet," Mitch told her, sitting beside her and enfolding her slim white hand in his big brown paw. "But when he was talking today, I got the impression that Papa John lost his memory and has never regained it." He patted her shoulder consolingly. "Gramps didn't want you to know until we were positive."

"Harry's known about this all along?" she whispered in confusion. "And he didn't tell me?"

"He didn't want to get your hopes up until we're absolutely sure. Unfortunately, I don't know if we ever will be. The guy still only remembers the name John and a date." Mitch shook his head in frustration. "It was so long ago, and there's so little information to go on."

"What was the date?" Hope whispered, her eyes huge and full of unshed tears.

"June twenty-first," he told her.

Melanie watched as joy flooded the older woman's countenance.

"He remembered that." Hope smiled gently, her tear-filled eyes sparkling. "Even with everything, he remembered the date."

Melanie looked to Mitch for an explanation, but he shrugged in confusion. They sat silent, waiting for Hope to explain. But she was clearly lost in her own world and not at all aware of them.

Carefully Melanie touched the older woman's shoulder, and when the blue eyes turned toward her, they were full of bemusement.

"June twenty-first was the day we were engaged," Hope told them tearfully. "Jean asked me to marry him and gave me this ring on June twenty-first." She fingered the diamond solitaire she'd worn on her right hand for two and a half decades.

Mitch tried to catch Melanie's eye and jerked his head toward the kitchen. When she frowned at him, he mouthed the word *kitchen* at her. Finally she nodded and got up from the sofa. Her eyes searched Hope's face for some sign, but the woman was staring, as if in a trance, across the room.

"Will she be okay, do you think?" she asked him, frowning. "Maybe we should call your grandfather."

Mitch shook his head thoughtfully, watching the concern that filled her green eyes.

"I don't think she'll want to see Gramps right now," he murmured, setting the kettle on the stove to boil. "But she does need her friends around her. Could you call your mother?"

"Yes," Melanie agreed, and dialed. "The fearsome three-some can band together and support each other like no one else ever could. Hello, Mother?"

Mitch listened as she explained the situation.

"You can? Great! Yes, bring Faith, too. She'll cheer her up." Melanie listened, then tipped her head, twirling a lock of glossy dark hair as she considered her mother's words.

"Well, I've got a date but I think Mitch will be here. Oh, just a minute." She turned to glance at Mitch, who was tapping her on the shoulder. "What?"

"I've got a date, too," he told her.

Her eyes widened, but she dutifully relayed the information to her mother.

"Yes, a movie just might do the trick. Thanks, Mom." She replaced the telephone and turned to stare at him. "They'll be right over," she told him.

The doorbell rang, and Mitch muttered something under his breath as he welcomed their latest guest. It was good old Jeff. Again. Tall, playboy Dr. Jeff, who never stopped grinning. Mitch endured the playful slap on the back, smiling halfheartedly as he noticed Jeff's fashionable outfit. So this was a real date!

"Jeff," he said without inflection. Mitch swallowed the gall that surged in his mouth. "Where are you going tonight?"

"Um, there's a performance at the local arts center. Operatic. We're going to opening night."

Mitch gulped down the sarcastic words at the warning look on Melanie's face. Manners, he told himself. That's what she wanted. Common decency. Assuming a politeness he didn't feel, Mitch smiled heartily.

"How nice. The opera." His black eyebrows surged upward when he turned to grin cheekily at Melanie. He tossed a handful of the freshly buttered popcorn he'd just pulled out of the microwave into his open mouth.

"Nala and I are going to stay here and watch a movie. Mushy old Cary Grant thing. So romantic." He stuffed some more popcorn in his mouth at the look in Melanie's eyes.

She was frowning, her gleaming head tipped to one side as she studied his face.

"Who's Nala?" Her voice was suspiciously abrupt, but Mitch gave no sign that he noticed.

"Oh, she's with Mercer, Metcalfe and Martens," he told her, naming a Bismarck firm. "Very bright, very smart, very high profile."

Right on cue, the doorbell rang, and Mitch opened it immediately, grabbing the tiny woman who stood quietly in the doorway. He wrapped her in an enthusiastic hug.

"This is Nala," he announced unnecessarily, watching Melanie all the while. Mitch swallowed his disappointment when his roommate showed nothing other than her usual courteous manners, greeting his date with a smile and a handshake before moving toward the door.

"Well, we had better be off," she murmured in her low voice. Her arm was threaded through Jeff's tuxedoed one. Mitch watched Melanie lips stretch in a happy smile. "Have a good evening."

"Yeah, you, too," he muttered. All discussion ceased as the elevator doors flew open and two elderly ladies swooped into the apartment.

"Are you all right, dear?" Charity murmured as she checked Hope's wan face and sad eyes. "Remember who's in control. He's never failed us yet."

"I know." Hope hugged Faith and then grasped Charity's arthritic hand in hers. "It's just been rather a shock." She stared at her friends. "I mean, if it is him." She shook her head in amazement.

"Then you'll deal with that, too," Faith told her sternly. She eyed Melanie and Mitch with a frown. "I thought you two were going out somewhere?" she said.

"I am—" Melanie began, but Mitch cut her off. He didn't want these little old ladies thinking any more terrible thoughts about him.

"Melanie's going to the opera with Jeff, and Nala and I are going to watch a movie," he explained cheerfully.

Faith seemed upset by this.

"Oh, piffle! I thought surely you and Melanie would be together," she blurted. "Don't you like each other after all?"

"Like each other?" Hope's voice was full of scorn. "They

can't stop bickering for five minutes. He eats doughnuts nonstop, and she leaves her stuff lying around. He likes to make packaged soup using every pot in the place. She detests whatever he makes—even when she likes it!" Hope shook her head in disgust. "It reminds me of my days at the junior high when everyone got a case of puppy love. I sorted out more disputes in those days." Her eyes searched her friends' for understanding. "But nothing I dealt with there was as petty as these two."

Mitch heard Melanie's weak voice. "Jeff, I, er, think we'd better go now. Good night, everyone."

Oh, sure, he thought, *leave me to take the heat for this, why don't you? If that isn't typical!*

But it seemed the ladies weren't hanging around.

"You need a break, dear. That's the best thing in the world for the worries. Take your mind off your problems and enjoy a bit of rest and relaxation." Faith was busy straightening up the apartment as she considered the possibilities Mossbank offered.

Which didn't take long, Mitch noticed with amusement.

"Why don't we go out to Fleming's Creek for a swim?"

He gaped at the gray-haired woman, wondering if anything he'd heard about her addled state had been exaggerated. Somehow, he couldn't see the fearsome threesome, as Melanie called the ladies, swimming in a creek.

"For heaven's sake, Faith, there hasn't been water in Fleming's Creek for ten years or more." Charity rolled her eyes.

"I've got it!" Faith's countenance shone with excitement. "The stock car races are on tonight. Let's go watch them."

Hope burst out laughing.

"I don't think I want to sit in all that dust and watch cars smashing into one another, but thank you for thinking of it, dear." She patted the rounded shoulder with affection. "No, I really think I'd just like to…"

As Mitch watched, Charity whispered something in her ear. He saw Hope's gaze flick over him first, then Nala. Her eyes grew round with something he couldn't define. She jumped to her feet, tugging at her wrinkled clothing.

"That's a wonderful idea, Charity. I'd love to rent a movie with you. I'll just change first, and then we can go."

"Go? Why do we need to go?" Faith sounded perplexed as her long fingers picked up the rented Cary Grant movie. "I love this one."

Mitch watched, mesmerized, as Charity shook her head at Hope and shooed her into the bedroom to change. Gently she lifted the black video box out of Faith's hands and replaced it on the television.

"You've seen this hundred of times, dear," she murmured, drawing Faith toward the door.

"I know. I really like how he falls in love with that young girl." She sighed. "It's so romantic!"

Mitch couldn't hear much of the rest but he did hear the excitement in Faith's voice when she said, "The Trevi Fountain, you mean? Ooh! I love the Trevi."

Within minutes, the three bustling sprites had scurried to the elevator, chattering a mile a minute. Hope glanced back just once, fixing Mitch with her sternest teacher look.

"I'll be late," she told him seriously. "Don't wait up."

And then with a swoosh of doors they were gone.

Nala stared at him openmouthed, her eyes wide with wonder.

"Mitch?"

"Yes?" He leaned down to straighten the mat at the front door. When there was a prolonged silence, he straightened.

"What," she whispered, awestruck, "was that?"

Chapter Seven

Four and a half hours later, Mitch finally acknowledged the truth. He had not fooled anyone, except maybe himself, anyway, with this crazy good-guy charade. Nala had her own ideas.

"You are in love with her," she said firmly.

Shocked, Mitch stared at his oldest friend. In love? Hardly. He'd never loved anyone. Melanie Stewart was gorgeous and full of energy, and he enjoyed her company. But love? Naught.

"I know what I'm talking about," Nala insisted. "And you are. Your eyes follow her around constantly. When you're not with her, you go all dopey daydreaming about her." She looked at him, her gray eyes bright with satisfaction. "It couldn't have happened to a more deserving fellow." She laughed.

"Nala, you know me." Mitch had appealed to her good sense. "You know I can't love anybody. Okay, I admit that I'm interested in her." He grinned sardonically. "In certain ways."

Nala merely swatted at his shoulder, brushing his argument aside.

"But love her? No. I don't know how," he told her.

"Nonsense," she insisted. "Okay, you've had some problems. Who hasn't? That doesn't mean you can't move beyond them."

They had argued good-naturedly for a long time. Eventually, Nala threw up her hands in frustration.

"I'm going home, Mitch. Your mind isn't here with me, anyway." She zipped her jacket as she spoke. "Just remember, you can run but you can't hide." Her soft lips had pressed gently against his forehead.

It was funny, Mitch mused. He had known Nala for years. She had pushed him through the bar exam when he would have given up. She was gorgeous, and fun, and bright. And he felt nothing when she kissed him. Zilch. Nada.

But when Melanie walked into the room, he could feel the air zap with energy, and the hairs on his arms stood at attention. He shook his head in defeat, disgusted with himself. Mitchel Stewart was mooning over a woman who shared his apartment because she wanted money. How trite!

Unfortunately, she wanted next to nothing to do with him personally. If he wanted her, he was going to have to make the first move, Mitch decided. But he wasn't in love with her, he assured himself. He couldn't love anyone. Not with a family history like his. What he could do was seize the moment, make the best of his time with Melanie.

"God is all-powerful, son," he remembered his grandfather saying just days ago. "He can work in ways you don't even know about. I know it was tough for you, but you've put your life in His hands now. Let Him show you what He has in store for you."

"Well, God," Mitch murmured, terribly self-conscious. "I don't know what to do. I'm not the marrying type, you know that. And Melanie Stewart definitely is. All she talks about is families and children." He stared at his hands before closing his eyes.

"Is it wrong for me to go out with her, date her, knowing that there isn't any future in it?"

There wasn't any answer. No still, small voice urged him to stay away from Melanie, and no one boomed, "Go for it!" in the silence of his apartment. Was it really so wrong to want to share a special meal with her, to share an evening that wasn't filled with problems? No answers came.

Sighing, Mitch decided he would start tomorrow. He would ask her out to dinner. He would be charming and scintillating and all the other things men were supposed to be. He only hoped Melanie wouldn't hurt herself laughing too hard.

"What did you say?" Melanie asked, staring at him, her head tipped to one side, as she considered his mental status. There had to be some reason for this abrupt change of mind.

"You heard me," Mitch muttered. He stared straight at her with those turbulent blue eyes. "Will you have dinner with me tonight?"

"Why?" Melanie felt like a ship suddenly freed of its moorings. The only thing that remained calm in her crazy world was the steady regard of his inscrutable eyes, fastened intently on her face.

"Because I want us to." He reached past her for the coffeepot. He drank thirstily before daring to face her again.

Melanie moved skittishly away from Mitch. He seemed different this morning. Sort of doggedly determined. And out of sorts, as usual. She eyed his rumpled T-shirt and baggy jogging shorts. Another ragged outfit.

"I suppose I could," she temporized. Suddenly, suspicion moved in. "Is this about the money?" she demanded.

"Oh, for Pete's sake, I just asked you out for a simple dinner. Does Jeff have to go through all this to get a date?"

Melanie's mouth hung open in astonishment. She was

positive she hadn't understood correctly. "A date? You are asking me for a date?"

"Yeah, a date. I'd like to remind you that you have been on one before, as I've had cause to notice. And no, I don't want your advice to the lovelorn." He frowned. "What's so peculiar about going out with me?"

Mitch was affronted, Melanie could tell. And his patience was wearing thinner by the moment. Not that he appeared to have much tolerance for anyone or anything before nine o'clock, even on the best of days.

Well, why not? Melanie asked herself. She had wondered about him for long enough. Maybe they could talk civilly. Share a nice meal. Then he would open up about his past.

His dark hair glimmered in the shaft of sunlight falling through the kitchen window. Melanie noticed the way he leaned against the cupboard, tiredly rubbing the knot of tension in the back of his neck. She decided to help him out.

"Rough night?" she asked quietly, her fingers kneading the knot in his neck. She tugged on his arm. "Sit down. I can spare five minutes this morning."

Melanie let her fingers press and poke, hearing his quiet moan when she found a knot of tension.

It was utterly unexpected, this sudden change of heart. Why would Mitch want to have dinner with her? Was there some reason he wasn't telling her about?

Yeah, right, Melanie. Like he's totally in love with you forever and ever. Get real!

She stifled the mocking voice and decided to take the plunge. *You can't define every single move you make in this life,* she reprimanded her laughing subconscious.

"All right," she agreed, hoping this meant a truce in their ongoing warfare. "I will have dinner with you. Where?"

Her arched eyebrows shot up when he mentioned a very prestigious restaurant in a nearby city. It was famed for its haute cuisine. She pondered, wondering if she could find something semiformal on her lunch hour.

But the real issue haunted her. It wasn't like him. It wasn't like him at all. And that unnerved her more than anything. She stared at him suspiciously.

"What's really going on, Mitch?" The question was automatic. And Melanie wished she hadn't said a word when he pushed away from her and stood jerkily.

Mitch sloshed another cup of coffee into his mug before he glared at her. His eyes were an angry ice blue. He took one sip of the steaming black brew before thunking the coffee on the counter and crossing his arms.

"Nothing's going on. I thought perhaps we could have a calm, cordial meal together for once, without biting each other's heads off and without benefit of dear sweet Auntie Hope." He jerked his head toward the bedroom door, where Hope had just disappeared to change her clothes.

"Perhaps I was wrong. Perhaps we've gone as far as people like us can go." The words were a stinging assessment of their relationship's deterioration in the past few weeks.

Melanie felt guilty. Here he was trying to extend the olive branch, and she suspected his motives. She could at least meet him halfway, she decided.

"Well, I have a board meeting until around five, but I could be home shortly after that. Is that early enough to leave?" She tried to infuse warmth into her voice. Privately she wondered how they would survive the evening without scrapping through every course, but if he was willing to try, then so was she.

"If you're sure you can make it," Mitch answered brusquely, hitching up his jogging shorts before retrieving his coffee. "I think we should leave about six. I'll make reservations for seven-thirty. That should give us enough time. Okay?"

He glanced at her, and Melanie nodded. A little prick of awareness twigged her consciousness. Something was strange, she thought, but perhaps she should try to meet Mitch halfway. Who knows? Maybe they did have something in common.

Anyway, it was just dinner. Yeah, right, her mind mocked. Just dinner with the most attractive guy she'd met in years. A man who, incidentally, was sharing her apartment. Or vice versa.

Melanie shook her head. This was getting too complicated. It was just a friendly, casual meal out together. That was all. They would be friendly and civil to each other, and she wouldn't have to cook. Nothing more.

By six o'clock, Melanie was beginning to doubt her intelligence in agreeing. Here she was swathed in black silk, and Mitch hadn't even come home yet, let alone showered or changed. She flicked through the channels on his big-screen TV three times before tossing the remote onto the sofa.

By quarter after the appointed hour, Melanie had decided to change into jeans and a T-shirt and forget the whole thing. It was a mistake to court trouble. She knew what Mitch was like. Unreliable came to mind. As did pushy and stubborn.

It was just that he was the best kisser she had ever met. Unbidden, the images floated through her mind of the first time he had visited her apartment and the way that evening had ended. And then at work, she remembered his comforting arms and the gentle coaxing kiss that had caused such internal uproar.

Firmly, Melanie dislodged the picture. She had no defense when his lips touched hers. And defenses were what she would need. She wasn't going to be swayed into a relationship with the man simply because they shared an apartment. Even if he was inordinately handsome and had allowed Hope to stay without saying a word of reprimand.

There was a strong smell of roses, and Melanie sniffed. Opening her eyes, she found Mitch squatting in front of her, holding out a beautiful bouquet of barely opened yellow roses. Melanie reached out to take them, burying her face in their sweet fragrance.

"You," she breathed, looking into his electric blue eyes, "are late."

"And you are welcome." He grinned his seductive smile. "You could thank me properly," he teased, pulling her out of the chair and into his arms. His hands pressed into the curve of her waist, belted above her jeans. He glanced down and his blue eyes widened to indigo orbs of admiration.

"Wow." He whistled. "You look very, uh, nice."

Melanie burst out laughing. He was trying, she would give him that. She curtsied. "Thank you, sir."

When his eyes darkened appreciatively, Melanie avoided his eyes and moved away to pull the silk wrap across her bare arms. Carefully she slipped her feet into the black heels she had chosen especially for tonight. A tiny black bag completed her outfit. She turned to face Mitch.

"I'm ready if you are." Her voice was husky as she took in the mouthwatering view of Mitchel Stewart in a black tuxedo. Long, tall and lean, he suited it perfectly. Even the black cummerbund at his waist and the pristine bow tie suited him.

"I think I might whistle myself," she murmured, wrapping her arm through his. He flashed his white teeth in a smile guaranteed to knock her socks off before brushing the ever-present lock of dark hair off his forehead.

"When did you get home?" she demanded. His behavior made her reverse all those terrible convictions she'd been reciting.

"Oh, I've been around, waiting for you." He had the look of a fox about to pounce on a poor innocent little mouse, she decided, mesmerized by his electric eyes. "Shall we?" he asked and Melanie strolled with him through the door and down to his waiting car. She eyed it with distrust before sliding in.

"I don't have my tool kit. Are you sure we'll get there in this thing?" she asked, gingerly doing up her seat belt. "That's the problem with these cars. They're all looks and no stamina."

He frowned down at her.

"Just because there was one little problem with my car does not mean you have to—" He stopped abruptly when Melanie raised her hands.

"I surrender. White flag. Sorry." She grinned at him, winking. "Let's call a truce. Just for tonight. Battle lines resume tomorrow."

And they did manage to discuss a few personal topics during the evening without coming to blows.

The restaurant was a new one, and Melanie eyed its sumptuous interior with wide eyes. The huge room glowed romantically in the subtle lights, silverware gleaming and immaculate linen perfectly folded. Handsome young men stood waiting on the sidelines in their black suits with crisply pressed shirts. In the background, a pianist added to the general ambience.

Melanie sighed in satisfaction as she pushed away her plate much later.

"I will never eat again," she pledged solemnly. "The salmon was excellent. And those tiny potatoes. Mmm." She smiled across the table at Mitch. "Everything was perfect."

Her plate was whisked away. Seconds later Kramer, their waiter, returned with a dessert tray that swept away all her good intentions. Mitch immediately chose the French silk pie while Melanie took her time drooling over everything before deciding on the lemon pistachio cheesecake.

"Do you come here often?" she asked, closing her eyes as her taste buds reacted to the sensational flavor.

When there was no answer, she opened her eyes to find him staring at her. Melanie tried to fill the silence gaping between them.

"I can see why you swim if you drop in here frequently. There have to be about seven thousand calories in this sliver." She shrugged. "And it's worth every one."

"No, I've never been here before," Mitch answered. "And I know what you mean. I don't think thirty laps is going to kill off this pie." Suddenly he grinned. "We'll have to think of something else."

Melanie's face colored as she considered kissing those lips again. Not that she would, but it *was* an interesting thought. Still, she refused to be baited into voicing those very personal thoughts.

"You mean dancing?" she asked innocently.

Mitch kept grinning. That, of course, prompted thoughts of the two of them together as a couple. To her dismay, that wasn't such a terrible picture at all.

"You seem to have settled into the apartment okay," he said quietly.

"Do I?" She laughed nervously. "I have to tell you, I still feel strange. It's a bit like lying to get something and then watching everything you say and do so you don't trip yourself up. That's the part that keeps bothering me." She shifted uneasily. "If there was another way to get that money for Sunset, believe me, I'd take it. Besides, they did say we were winners and sent the letters out, so I'm not trying to swindle anyone." She sighed.

"It is strange, though. The entry form said Sunset's address for both of us. I can't imagine how I made such a mistake."

"It's baffling, all right, but then the whole thing has been downright bizarre from the very beginning." His voice was low and full of something. What was it? Humor?

They lingered over coffee, enjoying the hauntingly familiar music and the mellow flavor of perfectly roasted Colombian beans. Melanie sat gazing at the couples moving slowly around the shining parquet floor before Mitch finally asked the question she'd been waiting for.

"Would you like to dance?"

"Yes." She rose from her chair with alacrity. "Remember, though, I'm not very good at dancing. Still, it shouldn't be too difficult. Everyone is just swaying to the music." And holding their partner in their arms, her subconscious whispered.

"Not difficult at all," he murmured as he pulled her a little closer against his chest. Melanie drew in a breath of air and held it as his hand slid down her back.

They moved slowly around the dance floor, brushing occasionally against the other couples. For once Melanie allowed herself to relax and enjoy the sensation. After all, what could happen with all these people around?

Which was probably how she came to find herself cradled in Mitch's strong arms as they swayed together on the terrace. She could smell the fragrant lily of the valley blooming in the pots nearby. And the delicate scent of gypsophila in full flower, growing wild around the edge of the brick patio, carried its heavy perfume through the night air.

"Isn't it a beautiful night?" she whispered, gazing at the star-studded sky. "It's nights like this when it's difficult for me to believe that anyone would think God doesn't exist. You can see so much beauty in His creation."

She felt Mitch's hands in her hair.

"There's beautiful and then there is beautiful," he murmured, sliding the ebony combs that held the upswept curls in place. With a swish they fell in a cascade of russet, tumbling wildly around her bare shoulders. One fat ringlet curved against the end of his index finger and clung there.

"You have beautiful hair, Melanie. It's so soft and silky." He buried his face in the gleaming tresses as his hands raked through the curls. One finger gently lifted a lock, and he replaced it with his lips.

"Your skin is like satin," he murmured, trailing a path upward to the pulsing cord in her neck.

Melanie couldn't say a word. Her breath was trapped somewhere between her throat and her mouth as she stood silent under his tender caress.

When at last his lips covered hers, she answered his question with all her pent-up longings, holding him closely as she ran her fingers down his hard, smooth back.

"Ah, young lovers. How sweet."

The mocking tones of an elderly woman watching them from the terrace grated on her nerves, and Melanie pulled away from Mitch abruptly. His body shielded her from their visitors, and Melanie used the opportunity to gather her hair in some semblance of its earlier style. Her fingers shoved the combs in roughly, stabbing her scalp with their sharp points.

In an effort to break the tension crackling between them, Melanie glanced at her watch, searching for something mundane to say. She was stunned to see it was already eleven.

"Good gracious." Her voice sounded suddenly breathless. She wondered if he knew she had been daydreaming about them. "I've got to get in early tomorrow. Would you mind if we left now?"

Reluctantly, Mitch guided her to their table. He shoved his credit card into his wallet before lifting her shawl from the chair.

"How much earlier do you have to get up?" he asked dourly, obviously envisioning being awakened in the wee morning hours. "You're already up before the birds."

"Don't worry," she told him gaily as he wrapped her shawl about her shoulders. "I won't wake you."

"Yeah, right." It was very faint, but Melanie clearly heard the muttered response. She wisely left the remark alone.

They rode home silently, except for the soft jazz sounds playing on the car's CD. For once Melanie didn't mind the music, letting it flow around her like a blanket. As they neared the apartment block, Melanie turned toward Mitch.

"Thank you again for a lovely evening," she told him sincerely. "I think I understand that legal brain of yours a little better now after listening to some of those college stunts."

Mitch snorted derisively. His dark eyes widened as he grinned at her.

"Somehow, I think that is a dubious compliment from a woman who rigged a wheelchair to collapse while her instructor demonstrated its use."

Melanie shrugged, widening her eyes to stare innocently up at him.

"Can I help it if I'm mechanical?" Her tones were the sweet, honeyed ones she used in the boardroom. They hadn't gained her much sympathy there, either, she reflected as Mitch's derisive tones followed her.

"Poor little thing!"

Mitch unlocked the apartment door and ushered her inside. Hope was nowhere to be seen. Melanie slipped out of her heels and curled her toes in the plush carpet. Suddenly the silence between them gaped uncomfortably.

"Uh, well, good night. And thanks again." Even to herself, Melanie knew she sounded like an embarrassed schoolgirl.

"Melanie." Mitch's deep voice urged her to stay even as his hand on her arm stopped her flight. Dark and brooding, his eyes moved across her face.

"I enjoyed being with you, Melanie. I'm glad we could share tonight." His voice was softly sensuous in the quiet apartment. "I want you to know that I enjoy having you as my roommate."

Mitch slid his hands up her arms slowly. His voice continued to surround her like a thick, numbing fog.

"I'm sorry I've been such a bear to live with. Forgive me?" He bent his head low enough to press a tiny kiss to the rapidly pulsing cord along her neck.

Melanie gulped, searching for the right words. It was hard to think with Mitch's spicy after-shave tickling her nose, reminding her. She finally muttered, "I like you, too," but her voice was squeaky. Probably because his hands were tangling in her hair, massaging her tingling scalp in a way that made Melanie's knees go rubbery. That misty voice was covering her in a haze of longing that begged for more of his touch.

His soft lips pressed a tiny caress to the corner of her mouth as Melanie felt his arms go round her. Then he was kissing her harder. And she was kissing him back.

It was crazy, Melanie thought. She couldn't get involved with this man. She had things to do. A mission. She wrapped her arms around his neck and let herself relax just a bit. "This can't be so wrong, can it?" she asked herself.

"I have wanted to do this for so long," Mitch told her. His hands slipped over the smooth skin of her arms, transmitting little sparks all along the way. "You have beautiful hair," he breathed, his hands moving up to luxuriate in the strands he'd loosened.

"Oh, Melanie," he murmured, "I knew a date with you would be sheer torture." His lips took hers once more in a kiss that threatened to send Melanie to outer space.

And somewhere, in her deepest thoughts, she relayed a message heavenward. *Oh, Lord, if this is wrong; if You don't want this, please tell me now.*

Eons later—or was it only seconds—Melanie became

drowsily aware that Mitch had stopped the gentle, tender movements of his hands. She lifted her head when he moved away from her, chilled by the cool air of the apartment on her skin. Dimly she heard a buzzing sound, but her befuddled senses couldn't seem to identify the source.

Mitch pushed the shiny auburn strands off her shoulders and pressed a tiny kiss to the corner of her mouth.

"Someone has incredibly bad timing," he muttered, frowning. "I guess we should be thankful it wasn't Hope and that she didn't burst right in." Muttering dire predictions, he stalked to the door and swung it open, ready to lambaste the intruder. Instead his mouth hung open in amazement. Not a word left his lips.

Their visitor, on the other hand, suffered no such affliction. She wedged her tiny jeans-clad form through the narrow opening Mitch's body allowed and stood facing Melanie. Her gamine features were enhanced by the short, spiky black hair that framed her face. Deep blue eyes crinkled when she smiled, standing on tiptoes to kiss his chin.

Then she strode to Melanie and thrust out her hand.

"Hi," she greeted her brightly. "You must be Melanie. I'm Sara. Mitch's ex."

Chapter Eight

"Oh, Father, I need Your help."

Melanie prayed desperately for the floor to cave in. Since it didn't, she decided to brazen it out. If this was God's answer, it was a pretty clear one. She felt disoriented, confused. She'd been on cloud nine. Now she slammed into old terra firma with a vengeance. She should have known better than to expect someone who looked like Mitch to be free and available, and indisputably she should have known he wouldn't be interested in her, plain, boring Melanie.

Melanie felt exposed, her desire for this man revealed for this interloper to see. It was humiliating to realize how much she had wanted him to be Mr. Right, and now to see how little she obviously meant to him.

Although she knew her lips bore the imprint of his kisses, Melanie decided to leave the room with as much dignity as she could muster. She also decided to get out of her outfit. Maybe some of the embarrassment would fall away with a change of clothes.

"I'll leave you two alone, then," she murmured, moving toward her bedroom. "Good night." The quiet words took every ounce of pride she had left.

"Sara," Mitch exploded as soon as Melanie had closed the door. "What in the world are you doing here?" His tone was not welcoming.

"Breaking up a cozy little tête-à-tête, by the looks of it." Sara grinned unrepentantly. She shook one finger at him. "Living together? Mitchel Stewart, I am aghast and dismayed that you've dropped your standards."

Mitchel could have cheerfully strangled her, but he sighed deeply and decided instead to find out what had made this visit so necessary. Sara's surprises were well-known. But first things first, he resolved.

He'd watched Melanie's face when Sara had dropped her bombshell, and Mitch knew he would have to talk to her. He had no intention of letting Melanie go that easily. Why, he wasn't sure, but it was somehow important that she know he hadn't been lying to her, that she was the woman he'd wanted to be with this evening.

After settling Sara with a cup of coffee at the kitchen counter, he knocked loudly on Melanie's door and then, when he heard her tell him to go away, disobeyed and opened it.

She was standing in front of her closet arranging the black dress on a padded hanger. Her makeup had been removed, and her long hair hung in loose waves down her back. He noticed she was swathed head to toe in flannelette. The sight had a ridiculously unsettling effect on him. It was her face that caught his attention, however. It was pinched and white. Her huge green eyes stared at him, pools of color in her wan complexion.

"I don't think this is a good idea—"

He cut her off. "Well, tough, because I do." In two strides he reached her. Gently he fastened a hand around her arm. "Sit down for a minute, Melanie. I want to talk to you about Sara."

"None of this is any of my business," she murmured, trying to pull away.

Mitch wasn't having any. He would blasted well nip this in the bud. He grimaced. Then maybe they could go back to where they were before Sara had thrown a wrench into things. Much as he hated disclosing his personal life, Sara's arrival had left him little choice.

"Melanie, Sara isn't my ex-wife, she's my ex-sister. Sort of." He could see disbelief cloud the clear green of her eyes, and he rushed to explain.

"My mother was married to Sara's father when we were kids. They got a divorce before they killed each other, thank heavens. But when each of them got married again and we were split up, Sara was heartbroken." He took a deep breath. It was still painful seventeen years later.

"She always had this family thing," he told her, as if he didn't. "Sara was only ten at the time, and she needed a friend. The only way I could console her was by telling her we would still be related, and she clung to the relationship. She still uses it whenever she needs a hand, or a shoulder to cry on."

Mitch brushed the soft curls on her shoulder. One curling tendril fastened itself around his finger.

"If she's here, it must mean something has happened. She wouldn't come to me unless she had nowhere else to go."

He tipped her rounded chin up, forcing her sad eyes to meet his. He smiled gently and brushed a feather-light kiss on the corner of her mouth. The sizzle was still there, he mused, pulling his mouth from hers with difficulty.

"I promised I'd be here if she ever needed me, Melanie, and I can't renege. Can you understand that?" He deliberately held her wide-eyed gaze with his, letting her see into his soul. He hoped somehow that she would understand, but he held his breath just in case.

The bedside clock ticked loudly in the silence of the room while Melanie watched him. Finally, her soft hand closed around his as it cupped her chin.

"Go," was all she said, but it was enough.

Mitch leaned down to press one more kiss on her full, inviting lips.

"Thank you," he whispered. When she kissed him back, he was drawn into a maelstrom of heat that burned in its intensity. Finally, he forced his head up. Getting off the bed, he straightened his backbone and walked resolutely to the door. Before he pulled it open, Mitch stopped and turned to face her.

"We are not finished our earlier discussion," he said quietly. "Not by a long shot. And one of these days we are going to finish what we start." Then he turned and walked through the door, pulling it softly closed behind himself.

Two hours later Mitch decided that life couldn't get much more complicated. He had given Sara his bedroom and now he searched for some comfortable spot on the sofa. He was beginning to realize comfort was not one of the assets built into this piece of furniture.

But worse, he kept seeing Melanie sitting on her bed, wearing her pyjamas, her face full of something he didn't want to define. A picture of Hope's astonished look when she'd let herself in an hour ago and found yet another female in residence was more than enough to scare away what little sleep he thought he might gather.

Enough!

Mitch rolled over and decided to focus on the previous evening and the conversation he and Melanie had shared. He'd been impressed with her plans for the nursing home. The money from Papa John's ridiculous contest would go a long way toward her dream of installing those new bed monitors she had described.

Mitch had been appalled when Melanie described how some patients were restrained from injuring themselves and others.

"That's inhumane," he told her, outraged at the idea of anyone being restrained in a chair or bed.

"Yes, it is," she agreed. "That's why I'm trying to change the way we deal with residents. But the monitors are new and very expensive." She'd studied her hands.

"There is a lift that I've requested from the board several times, which lifts the resident out of the bathtub without endangering him. And a special type of whirlpool for those with arthritis." She ticked the items off on her fingers. "And it sure would be nice to get a stock of those new bed linens that would replace our present five layers of cotton. All that washing means we need a large laundry staff, and our bills are horrendous."

To Mitch, the list was unending.

"Is the place that far behind?" His question had irked her.

"I haven't even told you about the van I want, to take residents on excursions to the park or whatever." She smiled. "And we need a big-screen television that the visually impaired can see without squinting." Melanie had enlightened him with several more plans, her hair shimmering red sparks in the low light of the restaurant.

"Mitchel, there is a terrific need to update old machinery everywhere, including the special care homes. More and more, we are trying to keep seniors in their homes for as long as possible, with the help of visiting nurses and live-in care, but our population is aging, and the costs keep soaring."

He had seen Melanie's green eyes flash fire with the intensity of her feelings. He watched her face, fascinated by its mobility as she described the home.

"But it's more than monetary needs. It's also a perception of the way we treat senior citizens." Her long fingers had pleated and folded the pale green napkin carefully as she spoke.

"So many people today think that older people have lost their ability to hear and see and feel. They are rude and condescending to people who were once someone's boyfriend, lover, coworker or friend. They have dehumanized our parents and grandparents into statistics. That's something I won't tolerate."

Her tone had been fierce, and Mitch was amazed at the amount of feeling Melanie had shown. It was clear that each resident was an individual to her, important in his or her own way. He had seen it well enough in the visitors she invited to the apartment, or had taken on long drives through the countryside. Just yesterday he'd watched her feed ice cream to a man who drooled continually. Melanie simply wiped his chin matter-of-factly and kept right on feeding him, talking all the while.

Mitch sympathized with her opinions. In his own work, Mitch had watched as some of his clients tried to bully their parents into choices they clearly didn't desire. All for the sake of money. It was a poor excuse, he knew that from firsthand experience.

He was seriously attracted to her, Mitch decided, thunking his pillow once more. He had known that for a long time but had refused to acknowledge their growing chemistry because there was a part of him that steadfastly resisted becoming involved in a serious relationship. He had been involved with his heart once before.

When the one person he had really trusted had walked away without a backward glance, Mitch had been stuck with pain unlike anything he'd ever known. But this thing with Melanie was different somehow. Wasn't it? She would never do what Sam had done. But no matter how he phrased it, his mind stubbornly resisted and told Mitch exactly what happened when you got involved. You got hurt.

And no doubt that little voice was right. He had watched his mother's marriages go down the tubes for most of his childhood. He had experienced the pain and destruction that went along with it, all in the name of love. His father's brutality had convinced him that love was not to be desired. No way would he do that to another person.

Life didn't come with guarantees, and there was no way he would subject another human being to the feeling of loss and abandonment he had known. He would enjoy Melanie's companionship, yes, but his heart would remain untouched. He repeated it, just to make sure his subconscious absorbed all that.

And yet as he lay there rolling the pictures through his mind, an inner voice questioned his truthfulness. Wasn't it possible that he was already losing his detachment?

Unbidden, the tape in his mind showed a giggling Melanie as she had tossed a laughing little boy in the air. Mitch had come home to find her baby-sitting her friend's child one evening last week. He'd felt a funny tremor in his throat, a sort of tightening as he watched the two of them romp together. Her face had been alive with pleasure as she enjoyed the little boy's hug. Her eyes lit with an inner light before she set him down to continue their game.

For a moment, he'd almost thought that child was himself, years ago. It was exactly the scene he had always wanted to remember from his own youth and never would. Somehow that expression of love and devotion signified the kind of caring he had ached to have someone show him, but never had.

He tossed the thought aside grimly.

Don't get sentimental, buddy, he told himself. *Your life was about as far from her picture-perfect world as it got. And it isn't going to change just because you've gone all syrupy over one beautiful nurse.*

Mitch turned over on the uncomfortable sofa, refusing to examine more closely what he felt. He hit the pillow one last time, deciding to get some sleep. Which wouldn't be easy considering the way the sofa cushions separated under his ribs.

"Lord, You know how I feel about this. And You know what's inside of me, creating this ache for someone to be close to. Please help me to know the right road."

At three-thirty Mitch switched everything end for end, then lay down on the puffy unstable cushions once more. He still had Sara's problem to deal with, he reminded himself. It would be a long day before he got that little issue settled to everyone's satisfaction.

It was probably going to be even longer before he got another chance to be alone with the woman in the next room. Mitch decided to forget everything but the picture he had in his mind of Melanie in that black fluffy outfit she had worn tonight. A smile curved his lips.

Yes, sirree, that was quite a woman.

"Melanie, Thomas McCabe peed in his juice glass again!" Bridget was not amused.

Melanie faced Bridget, thinking out loud. "I have always deplored using diapers on adults just because it's not convenient for the staff members to be kept constantly running to assist them." Her face tightened. "But in Thomas's case, I might be persuaded to reconsider. At least the dishes would be safe."

Melanie heard Bridget's laughter bubble out behind her as she reluctantly left the applications she was perusing to deal with the recalcitrant Mr. McCabe.

Of course, she didn't get back to work immediately because, for the tenth time that day, one of their most uncooperative residents refused to lay off the buzzer beside his bed.

She sucked in a deep breath, ready to lay it on the line, when the piercing shriek of a door alarm went off. Since she was nearest, Melanie headed for the exit at top speed, warily checking left and right to see who had activated it.

She used her master key to silence the bell before heading out the door. She came face to face with Mitch. He was red with embarrassment as his sapphire blue eyes guiltily met hers. He shuffled from one foot to the other, jiggling his black leather briefcase impatiently.

"Melanie." His low, husky greeting caused a flare of excitement within her, which she forced herself to ignore.

"What, exactly, are you doing?" she demanded, fixing him with her fiercest glare. When a worried RN stuck her head out the door, Melanie assured her that everything was fine. "Mr. Stewart merely lost his way," she said. "Please leave the door unlocked. I'll set it when I go back in."

Melanie planted her hands on her hips. "Well?"

"Yes, well, uh, Mrs. Rivers, um, do you see her?" He was peering into the shrubbery like Inspector Clousseau.

Melanie was not amused. She thought of those interviews that needed doing if she wasn't to spend another weekend covering several part-time shifts on the floor. Not to mention the reports due two weeks ago. And she hadn't even started charting the med orders that awaited processing after this morning's rounds.

"Time is of the essence here, Mitch. Exactly what do you want?"

He looked over his shoulder to be sure no one was listening. "Mrs. Rivers phoned my office, asking me to be here at two-thirty sharp. She said it was urgent and a secret. She left specific directions to meet her here." He looked around the courtyard again. A small frown pleated his forehead. "At least I think it was here," he mused.

Melanie burst out laughing.

"Nettie Rivers suffers from memory loss, Mitch. She may very well have made an appointment, but chances are she's totally forgotten what it was about." Something clicked in Melanie's mind. "Did you activate the alarm or was it already going?" Her voice was sharp with anxiety.

Mitch grinned self-consciously, brushing a hand through his black locks. Melanie privately thought he looked even cuter all mussed up.

"I guess I set it off," he admitted. "That means she couldn't be out here, right?"

"Right." Melanie tugged on his wool-suited arm. "Come on, Mitch, time to move on. Nettie is probably on her way to the dining room or already drinking her afternoon coffee as we speak."

She pulled him through the door and set the alarm. Brushing the fall of hair off her neck, she sighed.

"I could do with a cup myself." As Melanie strode energetically down the hall, Mitch moved to catch up.

"Where's her room?" he asked. "I'm curious to see if it has all been a hoax. My secretary said the old girl sounded pretty impatient."

Melanie stared at him. "Nettie's room is down this corridor, then turn right." She turned to speak to one of the special care aides, and when she turned back, Mitch had disappeared down the hall. Shrugging, she moved wearily toward the dining room. She had just poured herself a cup of coffee when he returned.

"Can I join you?" he asked warily, noticing the lines of tiredness around her eyes.

"Help yourself," she told him, waving toward the trolley nearby. She was absolutely not going to wait on him. Not today, when her feet felt like lead.

As they drank their coffee, Mitch told her more about the unusual phone call.

"My secretary said she was whispering. I'm afraid I couldn't get here when she wanted, so she said this afternoon would be fine." His blue eyes, wide open and boyishly touching, stared into hers.

Melanie told herself not to get mushy. There was a roomful of residents and staff surrounding her. Most of them had their eyes fixed on Mitch. She could imagine their thoughts.

"I just thought of something." Melanie motioned to one of the activities aides. "Didn't Nettie Rivers go out this afternoon?" she asked curiously.

The woman nodded, a grin creasing her full cheeks.

"A limo picked her up right after lunch. Very fancy. She won't be back till five or so. Your mother was with them."

"My mother?" Melanie frowned. Charity seldom went out with anyone but Faith and Hope, and certainly never in a limo. "And who is *them?*"

But the aide had no more information. She hurried away to rescue her bingo game. Melanie looked at Mitch, shrugging.

"I don't know what they're up to," she said thoughtfully. "But if the fearsome threesome are involved, it's liable to be complicated. Guess you got the times mixed up or misunderstood her."

"No," he told her seriously, "I know she specifically said two-thirty." He shrugged. "I'll come back at five," he told her. "Maybe she'll be back by then."

They sat talking for the rest of her break. Melanie asked him questions about Sara, to which he relayed the barest information. He refused to give any details, and after a while Melanie gave up.

By the time she arrived home, Melanie's curiosity about the strange afternoon had soared. She made herself sit and talk amiably with Sara until Mitch came home, but the minute he was through the door she nabbed him.

"Did you find Nettie? What did she want?" But Mitch wasn't giving.

"Sorry, Mel, but it's client confidentiality. Can't discuss it." His eyes twinkled as he undid his flashy tie.

Melanie flushed with embarrassment. He was enjoying this, darn the man. Okay, she could play, too. Turning to Sara, she asked innocently, "What was it you were telling me about Mitch's girlfriends, Sara?" She grinned, satisfied when she saw his head whirl. Melanie winked at Sara, who caught on immediately.

"Well, they're all so cerebral, if you know what I mean. Brainy without an ounce of human kindness. There was this one…" Her voice trailed away as Mitch's bedroom door slammed shut. The conspirators looked at each other and burst out laughing.

Sara was a good sport, Melanie decided. Maybe his sister would help her try to understand what made Mitch tick, why he was so negative when it came to family and commitment.

"Sara, please don't think I'm trying to pry." Melanie began slowly, feeling her way. "But why is it that Mitch is so closed off, self-contained? What's his problem?"

Sara studied her, her dark head tilted to one side.

"I have a pact with him," she told Melanie in soft undertones. "I don't break his privacy, and he reciprocates. But in your case…" Her blue eyes searched Melanie's. "In your case I'm going to make an exception." She took a deep breath and began the story.

"Mitch has been a loner for as long as I've known him," she told Melanie. "I suppose he's told you that we are not really related?"

Melanie nodded.

"Well, Mitch and I were so happy when our parents got together. We thought we would be a family, you see. He wanted that so badly for his mother." Her huge blue eyes were sparkling with unshed tears.

Melanie thought about what Mitch had told her of Sara's need for family. Now she knew Mitch had needed one, too.

Sara dashed her tears away and continued.

"As it turned out, there couldn't have been a worse move for our folks. They couldn't agree on anything. And they fought continuously. About everything." The younger woman was lost in thought.

"Can you tell me any more, Sara?" Melanie hesitated to ask, but any information she could add to her cache of knowledge about Mitch could help her understand him better. She leaned back in the hard kitchen chair as Sara resumed speaking. In her mind she began building a picture of a vulnerable little boy.

"I was ten and Mitch was fifteen. He was so happy to have a father who didn't beat his brains out. Problem was, he couldn't seem to relate to my dad." Sara brushed her short hair off her flushed face. "Not that I blame him. I had a little trouble there myself." Sara grinned that self-deprecating smile.

"Anyway, things between them went from bad to worse. Add to that our parents' total unhappiness with each other, and it's not a pretty story." Sadness flooded across her pretty face.

"Finally, of course, they divorced. Mitch was furious when his mother married again just one year after she got the papers. He came to see me once in a while, and I got the gist of his life at home. It was pretty bad."

Melanie watched with pity and sadness as disgust and loathing distorted Sara's face.

"It was her sixth marriage, and although she seemed to have finally found happiness, Mitch couldn't adjust. He and his stepfather argued continually. The guy was pretty straight and very tough, insisting that Mitch tow the mark one hundred percent. Mitch's mother sided with her husband. When she wasn't strung out on tranquilizers or booze, that is."

Melanie put her hand on Sara's shoulder in consolation. It was obvious that Sara had felt Mitch's pain deeply. Still did.

"I suppose you knew that's why he doesn't drink?" Her eyes were bright with curiosity as she watched Melanie. "Mitch always said his mother did enough for both of them, and he won't touch the stuff. He won't even take an aspirin without being in severe pain."

"I'm afraid I didn't notice," Melanie told her. "All I have seen is this cold, hard side of him that he's convinced can't be changed. If you push too hard, he shuts you out."

"Yes, that's exactly how he's always survived," Sara told her, a wistful smile on her face. "I guess it's better than not surviving at all," she added. "Fortunately, Mitch excelled at school, so his mother decided to send him to boarding school. Paid for by his stepfather. His mother was pregnant and sobering up by then, and they wanted him out of the way while she dealt with her problems." Sara's face was grim.

"You couldn't blame them for that. The woman needed help. But pretty soon a pattern began to develop. Every time he returned for holidays or school breaks, there was a child around whom his mother and stepfather doted on, and no place for him—or at least Mitch didn't think so. Eventually he didn't even try to fit in. He wasn't so hardheaded then, though." Sara's voice died away.

"That happened when Samantha Jones arrived."

Melanie thought back on the few statements Mitch had made about himself. She didn't remember anyone named Jones.

"Who?" Melanie tried to keep her curiosity under control.

"She was someone he fell for in law school. And he fell hard. Samantha had him wound around her little finger." Sara's voice was filled with disgust. "Anything Sammy wanted, Sammy got. Mitch had to hold down two jobs just to get himself through law school, never mind provide the little baubles she constantly demanded. And don't forget he was studying all hours, as well."

"I imagine it must have been difficult," Melanie said sympathetically.

"Difficult? It was darn near impossible. But he did it—until Samantha got him cutting back on his study time." Sara's eyes glittered angrily. "Poor little rich girl needed a date to Daddy's dinners!"

"Oh." Melanie cringed at Sara's sarcasm. "But couldn't he have refused?" she asked curiously.

"He did, at first. But Samantha wasn't giving up. And little by little, she took over his life. He was so totally besotted, Mitch never knew what hit him until he got his marks. He flunked the year." Sara moved to pour a glass of water. She drank slowly, her eyes deep pools of bitterness.

"Well?" Melanie demanded, finally getting an insight into what made Mitchel Stewart tick. "Go on."

"Mitch knew it was make-or-break time. No way was he going back to his stepfather. And by then his grandfather was encouraging him to buckle down. Mitch got his professors to agree to let him repeat the year, but he lost the funding that paid for his tuition."

"But couldn't Samantha help with that?" Melanie asked curiously. "Make him a loan or something?"

Sara snorted. "She had a new boy toy by then, Melanie. She had never been interested in Mitch other than his abilities as an escort to parties or showing her off on the dance floor. He was a hunk who could ferry her around. He wouldn't stay at her wild parties, so she dropped him. She finally told him to his face exactly how little she thought of him." Sara shook her head sadly.

"But for Mitch, it was the final straw," she explained. "He had tried for years to be the son his mother wanted and never quite made the grade. Now a woman he thought really cared for him, someone he had based his future on, wanted him to be something he wasn't. When he wouldn't even pretend to do as she asked, Sammy turned her back on him." Sara's voice overflowed with disgust.

"In fact, she left him for his best friend. And Mitch was left to pull his life together. Alone." Sara wrapped her arms around herself as her big eyes fixed on Melanie.

"Well, he pulled out of it, passed the bar and went into practice. I was there the day he got his degree. He told me he was finished trying to find love. He cut himself off from his mother and stepfather, got his own life and never talked to any of them—except his grandfather, as far as I know."

"You mean his parents are still married?" Melanie asked curiously, caught up in the story of such a sad family.

"Oh, yes. His mother finally found a man she loved. Unfortunately, she lost her son." Her eyes were sad with regret.

"But Mitch…" Sara shook her head. "He's convinced himself that he can be totally enclosed. Because he lost the ability to trust his own feelings, he will not believe in anyone else's. He's frozen that side of his life. Now he doesn't make any commitments." She shook her head. "And so he is never disappointed."

Sara rubbed her tears away.

"I have got to get going. I'm going to buy a house here, and as soon as I do, the kids are coming. We're supposed to put the down payment on one I really like today and then we can move some stuff in. Mitch said he could help. See you later." Sara drummed her fingers on Mitch's door. "Come on, bro. You've got a heap of lifting to do today."

They left shortly after that, insulting each other with good-natured gibes.

Melanie sat on the hard kitchen stool and contemplated the little boy who had never received the affection he craved. Was all that male macho and freewheeling debonairness just a facade? She remembered his remarks about trust and knowing who you were and she cried for that needy child and the man he'd become. She could still hear his pain.

"You were lucky," he had said about her mother and the adoption. "Some kids never get to experience any of that."

Kids like him, she thought sadly. Kids who needed a hug so badly they ached. Bitterness welled within her at the child-hood of pain that still clung to him.

Suddenly, the anger and frustration Melanie felt toward Mitch mellowed as she perceived his attitudes through a different light. Trust would come hard. And loving? Well, that would be very difficult. If it ever happened.

She knew there was something between them. It was there when he had wrapped his big arms around her last night. His kiss had not been cold and calculated. Instead he had touched her with sensitivity, gently nullifying all the inhibitions she had so carefully held. And he had asked for as much as he gave. Somewhere under that immaculate facade was a man who had a lot to give the world, if he would only let go. Then, later, he had asked for her trust.

Well, then, she would trust him, Melanie decided. She would explore the building relationship between them as far as he would let her. And if the time came when he no longer wanted her around, well, Melanie would deal with that, too.

Finally, she acknowledged what she had known for days. She loved him.

And the emotion scared her to death. He'd been hurt, badly. And she had no experience in dealing with men like him. It had always been she who had been in control in the relationship. Now, suddenly, there was no control. Melanie felt as if her life was in free fall.

It was hopeless. It was wonderful. It was crazy. And Melanie had no idea how to act. She was living with a man who refused to discuss his past. They shared his apartment, rubbed shoulders daily. And they waited for prize money he would help her acquire. Meanwhile, he aided a stepsister who needed his help.

Melanie was convinced that Mitch had fooled himself. He was a man who had a lot of love to give, he just didn't know how. Somehow he needed to see that.

"Oh, there you are, dear. Had a good day?" Hope scurried in the door, her usual immaculate, efficient self. She was carrying several shopping bags but didn't offer to show the contents.

"Interesting," Melanie replied, with an astute glance at the parcels. "And you? I heard you were at Sunset today." She watched for a reaction and was rewarded when Hope's eyes widened in surprise.

"Oh, well, yes. The girls and I decided to go visiting."

"Did you? How nice. How long did you have Nettie out for?" she asked solicitously.

"Oh, well, you know how these tea things go. A couple of hours." Hope's normally pale skin was suffused with color.

"I see. Did you go in your car?"

"Oh, dear me, no," Hope said. "That is, we didn't need to. Papa John was there, and he took us all for a ride in his limousine. We went to the malt shop."

Melanie stared, her brain striving to assimilate the unlikely picture of the four older women and a silver haired, pot-bellied man daring to breach the sanctity of the teenagers' local haunt.

"Papa John was at Sunset?" Melanie frowned. "I never heard a word."

"Oh, my dear, he's been visiting Nettie for simply ages. They're quite good friends, you know. And he's ever so kind and gentle with her. Nettie speaks so freely when she's with him."

"But doesn't that bother you? I mean, Mitch told me he might be your Jean."

Hope shook her head. "Oh, he's not my Jean," she said softly. "I think my Jean died a long time ago. Papa John doesn't have Jean's French accent and doesn't express himself the same way at all."

"So you don't think…" Melanie hated to say the words.

"Do I still think he bears a resemblance to Jean?" Hope murmured thoughtfully. "Oh, he definitely does. But that's not exactly what I meant. You see—" She fiddled with a strand of hair. "Jean was that special person in my life all those years ago. We shared our hopes and dreams and there was nothing we didn't discuss."

"And Papa John isn't like that?" Melanie tried to understand.

"Yes, he's like that all the time. But with Nettie. He really cares for her. And whatever he may or may not have once felt for me, I wouldn't dream of destroying the happiness they seem to have found." Hope looked up, tears rimming her eyes.

"Whatever Jean and I might once have had is past and buried. It hurts something fierce to say that, but it's true. I'm just beginning to realize that all these years I've been waiting for a fairy tale that couldn't possibly come true." She wiped away the tears with her hand in a most indelicate fashion.

"Maybe it could come true," Melanie persisted. "Maybe if he could just remember that you and he were once engaged…"

"Oh, you mustn't encourage that, dear. It would only make him feel sorry for me, obligated somehow. And he's not. Not anymore. No one is. All these years everyone has been so sympathetic." She glanced at the ring on her right hand thoughtfully.

"No, my Jean is gone, and I think it's time I removed this and started living in the present. That's what Papa John had to do when he returned from the war. He didn't have a past. And maybe that's for the best. Sometimes people get bogged down in the past.

"Don't you think the same might be true for you?" the older woman murmured.

"I, uh, don't know what you mean," Melanie insisted. "I'm not dreaming any fairy tales."

Hope shook her head regretfully. Her voice was very gentle when she spoke. "Oh, Melanie, do you really think I don't remember how much you wanted a family? Why, you always used to dream up games about happy families with fathers and mothers and perfect children." She wiped away a tear. "Your mother, Faith and I used to pray that you would find your dream someday." She fixed Melanie with a stern glance that reminded Melanie of days spent in her class.

"Don't you think perhaps that time has come? With Mitch?"

"You mean you think I should ask him to marry me?" Melanie tried to fob off the question with a laugh. "He's told me numerous times that he's not the marrying type, Hope. And, truth to tell, I'm not sure I am, either. At least not to someone like him."

"What's wrong with him? He's as handsome as a movie star, established in his law practice. He's even trying to help you get half that prize money, although I confess I wish that aspect would disappear." She chuckled. "A real prince, I'd say."

"Maybe." Shrugging, Melanie got up to fill her coffee cup. "But he's also got a lot of baggage from the past."

"We all carry baggage from the past, Melanie. Some of us just hang on to it longer than others."

"Maybe," she said again. "But even though he is handsome, Hope, I still don't think Mitch is the type of man I need." Melanie wanted to nip this particular matchmaking idea in the bud.

"I want someone who is solid and dependable. I have enough bad history to deal with. Those kids I used to dream about…" She paused, staring at the light fixture. "The truth is, they're a long way from my own childhood reality. I wouldn't know how to raise a child. Not properly. I have no history to draw on. And I won't be responsible for wrecking a child's life."

Hope's soft, smooth hand covered hers and squeezed gently.

"I'm no expert, of course," she murmured. "But I've watched children and their families for years. And my conclusion is that nobody knows exactly the right way to raise a child. And every child is different from every other child, so there is no magic formula."

"But that's precisely what—"

"God gave us this as a plan," Hope told her seriously, picking up her Bible from a nearby table. "The only formula we have is to ask for God's help, search His word and then apply some good common sense." She spread her hands wide. "And that's it. Except for loving them, of course. And that's usually not too hard for a new mother."

"Maybe," Melanie murmured doubtfully. "But it seems awfully risky to embark on such a thing with a person you barely know."

"Sometimes you have to take a leap of faith," Hope told her sternly. "And it's not really so frightening if you have God behind you, is it?"

"It's very frightening! How can I know that something is God's will and not just my own wants or needs?"

"You ask Him," Hope told her simply. "And then when He opens a way, you take it. Slowly. And trust that He will direct your footsteps through life." She glanced at her watch and stood. "I have to get going. I told your mother I'd have dinner with her." She patted Melanie's hand. "Think about it, Melanie. And pray for His will to guide you. God gives us desires for a reason and He wants to fill those secret wanting places more than we can imagine." Hope tugged on a sweater and moved toward the door.

"Don't waste the present, my dear. Trust me, it's not worth the pain when you find that life has moved on and left you standing alone in your ivory castle, waiting for some fantasy while the real thing walks right past."

Melanie sat for a long time, considering Hope's words. They whirled around her brain until she couldn't make sense of them anymore. Wearily, she set about making supper for Mitch, his sister and herself.

"Is he the one, Lord?" she asked. "But we're so different!" She closed her eyes. "I'm scared, Lord. Scared of getting hurt so badly that I won't be able to pick up the pieces. Please help me to know the right way."

Chapter Nine

"Well, girls, I have some news for you." Hope's voice was brimming with excitement as she burst through the door at Charity's cozy home. She glanced from Faith to Charity and sank into a nearby chair. "You two have been my dearest friends for so long now, I wanted you to be the first to know."

"Go on, then, tell us." Faith beamed, green eyes wide with excitement. "I just love surprises!"

"Yes, dear. Share it with us."

"I'm getting married!" Charity lost three stitches when her knitting needles fell to the floor, and Faith's mouth opened and closed like a fish gulping for air.

"Then it is Jean. I knew he'd come back." Into the shocked stillness, Faith's voice rang with joy. "Praise the Lord!"

"I don't know that Jean has come back, Faith, but I am going to marry Harry. In three weeks."

"Harry Conroy?" Charity squeaked, her brown eyes huge.

"Of course, Harry Conroy," Hope told her, frowning. "He's been asking me for years. Why are you surprised?"

"Because he's been asking you for years. What's suddenly changed that makes Harry so acceptable as a husband now and not ten years ago?" Charity's expression was full of suspicion. "It's not because you're afraid this Papa John fellow is getting really fond of Nettie Rivers, is it? Hope, are you afraid you'll be left out?"

"Of course not! Charity Flowerday, have you ever known me to act so foolishly?" Hope murmured in disgust.

"I have," Faith said, smiling with a delight. "Remember, it was when we had that new preacher. The one before Pastor Dave. He was so interested in you, Hope, making all those lovey-dovey eyes. And you wouldn't even give him the time of day." She twiddled her finger at Hope's reddening face. "He was so handsome—a real hunk."

"Faith! Wherever did you learn such disgusting terminology?" Hope asked indignantly. "And for your information, I had no desire whatsoever to become a minister's wife. I'm too outspoken for that. Besides," she mumbled, wringing her hands in exasperation, "he ate far too many sweets."

"So does Harry," Charity reminded her friend with a knowing smile.

"Well, it's just different, that's all," Hope told them with a shrug. "Harry's been my friend for so long, he feels warm and kind. He doesn't care about my little foibles."

"Just like my Arthur," Faith crowed proudly. She swept Hope into a tight, suffocating hug that wrinkled her best blouse. "I'm so happy for you, dear. Can I help with the wedding?"

"That's what I wanted to talk to you both about." Hope smiled, hugging Faith back. "I have a little plan in mind and I want you to help me carry it out."

Faith jumped to her feet, clapping in excitement.

"I do so love your plans, Hope." She beamed happily. "You're always so organized and efficient. What shall I do, Hope, dear?"

"I think perhaps you'd better explain this plan first, Hope. I have a feeling it involves more than you and the judge. Am

I correct?" Charity waited for Hope's nod. "I daresay you have some notion of involving my daughter in it."

Charity rose from her easy chair and stood frowning at her best friend.

"I do not want Melanie involved in one of your schemes, Hope. Something might go wrong, and my daughter would be very hurt. She knows what she wants out of life, she just hasn't found it yet."

"Oh, yes, she has," Hope murmured. She brushed a soothing hand over Charity's bent shoulder. "I'm not suggesting anything nasty. Just a little helping hand. That's all, I promise."

"And I'll give a helping hand, too," Faith offered. "After all, I did a pretty fair job of it with Gillian and Jeremy, didn't I?" She beamed with satisfaction.

"You did a wonderful job, Faith. And they make a very nice couple. Those two truly love each other." Hope's voice brimmed with tenderness as she smiled at her friend. "I couldn't have wished for a better man for my niece than your nephew."

"Good heavens." Charity breathed in astonishment. "You don't mean to say that you're trying to match up my daughter with Harry's grandson?" She shook her head. "Oh, Hope. I don't think it's a good idea at all. Melanie doesn't even *like* the man. It could all go so wrong and then everyone will be miserable."

"It's not going to go wrong," Hope said firmly. "Now, here's my plan. I intend to ask Melanie and Mitch to help us with our wedding." She detailed the arrangements carefully, and when she had finished all three women were smiling broadly.

"I knew you'd have a wonderful plan," Faith cheered. "You always do."

"And with a lot of help and several minor miracles from above," Charity added dourly, "you just might get it to work."

If she hoped to dampen the spirits of her friends, Charity acknowledged that it wasn't working.

"Well, then, let's ask for that help right now," Hope urged them. "You might remember, Charity," she chided her friend. "God can do anything." And reverently they bowed their heads to ask their heavenly Father's help in carrying out Hope's wonderful plan.

Hello, Mother. I stopped by to ask you if I might move in with you for a while. Just until I can find another place."

Charity stared at her daughter standing drenched and glum-faced in the sudden downpour, still clad in her pink uniform.

"Darling, of course you can. You know that! Come in."

She urged her inside and waited while Melanie tried to dry herself off. "But I thought you had to stay at Mitch's until they awarded the prize money?"

"Originally that was the plan. But now his sister is here, and the house she bought isn't ready for her or the kids, and I think it's only fitting that Sara stay with her brother." She swooped her damp hair into a knot on the top of her head. "There's just not enough room."

Charity stared. "But I thought Hope was moving out?"

"She did. This morning. That's another reason I think I should leave. It doesn't seem right for me to be staying there now. And Sara and the kids need my room." Melanie peered at her mother suspiciously. "Is there some reason you don't want me to come home, Mother?"

"Of course not! The very idea!" Charity led the way into the same living room Melanie had spent her teen years, without notable success, to decorate to resemble the pictures in several fashionable magazines. "You know that you're welcome anytime."

"Thank you, Mother." Melanie hugged the thin shoulders

gratefully. "I was hoping you'd say that, because I've got my stuff in the car outside."

She raced out to the car and returned with two huge suitcases and a paper sack that broke as she came in the door. Melanie blushed as her mother's eyes roved over the bits of tulle, tiny plastic cupids and packages of mints splayed across her floor.

"What in the world?" Charity's eyes were huge with amazement as she spotted white ribbon embossed with bells and tiny golden rings.

"They're for the reception. Hope wanted something for every guest. And the rings go around a little scroll that tells about the custom of marriage. It's really quite lovely."

"But the woman hasn't even chosen her invitations yet," Charity gasped. "Shouldn't that be first on the list?"

"I asked her the same thing," Melanie said, stretching to reach the last ring under the heavy oak bureau in the dining room. "She said, and I quote, 'It's being handled.'"

Melanie plopped into the badly sprung easy chair, edging carefully away from its protruding spring, and frowned at her adoptive parent.

"Mother, what do you really think of it all?"

"Darling, Hope is my very best friend." Charity smiled as she flicked a speck of dust off her coffee table. "I want her to be happy, so naturally I'm very pleased she's found someone to brighten her life."

"Yes, of course," Melanie agreed absently. "But why now? Why all of a sudden like this?"

"Melanie," Charity reprimanded her in a tone of voice Melanie was very familiar with. "Hope and Harry Conroy have been dating on and off for nearly fifteen years. I hardly think this is a *quick* decision. Besides, maybe she's begun to realize that each person only has a finite amount of days available to him."

"I think it has more to do with Jean and Papa John," Melanie murmured slyly, peering up between her lashes.

Charity frowned. "Why would they matter?"

"Hope thinks Papa John is Jean. And Papa John is attracted to Mrs. Rivers. He's always coming to visit her, brings her flowers, takes her for a drive. They even have long, involved conversations."

"Melanie!" Her mother scolded her with her eyes. "They are adults, entitled to their privacy. I thought you encouraged that at Sunset."

"Of course I encourage it," Melanie told her defensively. "But I can't help noticing, can I? Besides, what on earth do they have to discuss? They've hardly known each other long enough."

"Oh, darling." Charity laughed. "When you find your heart's mate, you discuss everything under the sun. You and Mitchel seem to have some of those same discussions," she said offhandedly.

To her disgust, Melanie felt her face color. She frowned. "We've only been discussing the wedding," she claimed stoutly. "For some reason, Judge Conroy has asked Mitch to help out with the wedding. Although what that lawyer knows about weddings could probably fit into a thimble with room left over for your finger."

The doorbell rang, preventing Charity from chastising her youngest child.

"Why, Mitchel! Do come in. How are you this evening, dear?"

Melanie straightened and whirled to face her nemesis, filled with foreboding. To her surprise he had a smile on his face.

"Hi, Mrs. Flowerday. I'm fine, thanks. I wondered if I could speak to Melanie for a moment. I happened to notice her car out front."

"Of course, dear. Come in and have a seat. I'm just going to pick up a loaf of bread from the grocery store. I never baked any today, you see." She glanced from one to the other of the young people. Realizing that they were paying her absolutely no mind whatsoever, she grasped her purse and headed out the door.

"Are they in there?" Hope whispered as soon as Charity had negotiated the stairs. "They're not fighting, are they?" she demanded in the next breath.

Charity wrapped her hand around Hope's thin elbow and drew her along the sidewalk.

"Now, Hope," she chastised in a smiling voice. "You were left to manage your own love life. Let's give them the same opportunity."

"Ha!" Hope's lips turned down in disgust. "I stayed with them for weeks in that apartment, and as far as I can tell, their minds never got close enough to *consider* marriage, let alone view the other as marriage material!"

"Perhaps, my dear Miss Busybody Hopeless," Charity said, using an old childhood nickname, "perhaps you don't see as clearly as you once did."

Melanie, meanwhile, was having trouble with her breathing. Instead of his usual grungy after-hours attire, Mitch was handsomely turned out in a pair of pressed white cuffed shorts and a shirt the exact shade of his cobalt blue eyes. He had on brand-new runners with white—*pristine* white—socks. His hair was tousled as though someone had just run a hand through it, and for the tiniest moment Melanie felt jealous.

"Hi," he murmured, his eyes moving over her wrinkled, still soggy uniform and the scraggly wad of hair pinned to the top of her head. "Have another rough day?"

"No," she informed him abruptly. "I got caught in the rain." She sucked in a deep breath of courage and then let it out in a whoosh. "I'm moving into my mother's for the next little while. You and Sara need the extra room, especially with the kids here now, too."

"I see." He looked almost sad, she decided. "It's a good thing I came over then, isn't it? Otherwise I might not have known." She would have started explaining, but he cut her off.

"Anyway, thanks for thinking of them. This house thing is going to take a little longer than either of us had realized." His eyes studied her carefully. "What's really behind your decision, Melanie?"

"I just didn't feel right about living there anymore," she told him softly. "Not after last Sunday's sermon about living a lie. And anyway, my mother's guests have left now. I always said I'd leave when I found another place." She refused to meet his glance.

"Could we talk as I unpack the car? I have a ton of things to do for this wedding, and one of my best nurses just went on maternity leave. I may have to go back in."

"Sure. Come on, I'll help you." And he did. Stoically, without complaint, he carted in box after box, ignoring the dust and mud spots on his clothes. "This isn't all of it, is it?" he asked after lugging the last box up the narrow stairs to her old bedroom.

"No, but I couldn't manage any more in one trip."

"Well, let's go get the rest of it, then. If you're anything like Sara, you can't do without even one of your possessions!"

It sounded like a good opening to an argument, but after his willing help, Melanie didn't have the heart to take him up on it. Besides, she was so hot and tired, she wanted to save every ounce of energy for lifting.

"Okay," she agreed. "Might as well get it over with."

"Might as well." Mitch spoke in a voice that Melanie wished was a little less enthusiastic. Did he want to be rid of her that badly?

Sara had just finished laying the table when they arrived. Melanie could hear the boisterous voices of children giggling and laughing in the other room. Since the children had only arrived that morning, Melanie hadn't had the chance to meet them yet. She moved curiously through the front door, wiping her hands on the seat of her pants. There were two of them, one boy and one girl. They were playing some type of tag, racing around and around the apartment, each trying to avoid the other.

"Becky and Ben," Sara sternly said. "This is an apartment, not the playground."

The two looked suitably chastened. Their black hair and wide blue eyes were identical. Sara spotted Melanie and grinned.

"These two are mine," she told her proudly. "Kids, this is Uncle Mitch's roommate, Melanie."

Mitch's mouth twitched at her words, but neither he nor Melanie had any opportunity to remonstrate with Sara as one of the twins spoke.

"Are you Uncle Mitch's girlfriend?" Becky asked, her head tilted.

Melanie's cheeks flushed a dark red, but as she opened her mouth, the other child spoke.

"We always like Uncle Mitch's girlfriends. Are you getting married?"

Mitch's blue gaze met Melanie's head on. In his eyes, she could read the message clearly—*fat chance.* He chastised the children for their rudeness and then explained their situation.

"Melanie is a friend of mine. She was staying here until she could find her own place, but then you guys arrived and she decided to move out to give you more room. You be nice," he added sternly.

Both shrugged. "Okay," they agreed happily before moving to turn on the television.

Sara went to shower while the casserole cooked. Melanie was in the kitchen when she felt a long finger under her chin as Mitch tipped it up to look into her bright eyes.

"Sorry about that," he murmured, his hand cupping the curve of her jaw. "They tend to talk first and think later." His eyes twinkled at her. "You have to admit, though, they only asked what a lot of people in this town already think."

Melanie couldn't control the surge of red that colored her face.

"It's a good thing I'm going, then," she managed to say. "Maybe my departure will settle all the gossip down."

Mitch laughed at her embarrassment as his hand tugged her thickly curling hair. The caress was softly intimate, and Melanie felt the familiar thud of her heart as it pressed to jump out of her body.

"They'd worry even more if they knew about this."

She felt his gentle touch on her neck before his lips closed over hers. It was a softly questioning kiss, seeking an answer from her. Melanie kissed him back, then delicately pressed her lips against his stubbled cheek.

"Fortunately for your reputation, I don't kiss and tell." He dipped his head again, seeking the touch of her mouth. They would have continued but for the giggles that erupted.

"I told you she was his girlfriend," one knowledgeable voice whispered. "That's why they're kissing."

"Is not," the other said. "It's 'cause she's got a boo-boo. Uncle Mitch is making it all better." Nodding, the two continued their investigation of the apartment by returning to the living room.

Melanie tried to break away, but Mitch wouldn't let her. He tightened his arms around her waist.

"Do you have a boo-boo?" he asked quietly, his eyes dark and serious. "Tell me where it hurts."

Melanie considered his offer and then tapped a finger to

her cheek. Her mother hadn't raised any fools, and if this was to be her last opportunity to be close to Mitch, she was grabbing it with both hands.

"Right here," she murmured. His lips pressed gently there. "And here," she added, and waited for his touch on her temple. "And here." Daringly she pressed a hand to her mouth, waiting with bated breath.

His eyes watched her, deep fathomless pools of blue, until finally his hand slid across her shoulder and his mouth brushed across her lips in a tender caress that made her heart ache.

"You're asking for trouble, Melanie Stewart," he murmured.

"No," she whispered. "Just a kiss. To make it all better."

He kissed her with more passion than she had dreamed possible. Melanie would have crumpled to the floor if his strong arms hadn't held her against the counter. When he finally moved his mouth, she tipped her head, giving him free access to the sensitive skin of her neck. And Mitch took advantage until the buzzing timer and loud voices drew him out of his lethargy.

"I'm not crazy about your timing," he muttered in her ear as they listened to the high-pitched squeals in the next room. "But I am crazy about your…boo-boos." He grinned saucily, stepping away from her when she would have retaliated.

They could hear Sara chastising the children a few feet away. Reluctantly, Melanie turned off the timer and lifted out the steaming dish as her mind protested the end of their embrace.

"Later," he whispered in her ear, before his sister walked into the room.

Mitch raved about the Spanish rice dish, and the children ate everything on their plates, including the little bit of salad they were served and had deemed yucky. There was a great deal of frivolity during the meal, and Melanie felt Mitch's gaze on her warm face more than once. She was glad when they could resume carrying boxes. At least he couldn't stare at her all the time!

"You didn't have to do this," Sara murmured as she packed in the last of Melanie's knickknacks. "The kids and I could have gone to a hotel. Especially when it means you might lose the prize money."

"Don't be silly! Of course I'll stay with Mother for a little while. You guys need the room. I probably should have moved there in the first place," she muttered, getting in behind the wheel. "Missionaries or not."

"What! And spared me Hope's tofu casserole and your early, early morning rising?" Mitch teased, getting in beside her. "Not to mention bran flakes and all the odious comments about my health."

"Why are you in my car?" Melanie asked, frowning as his knee brushed hers. "You live here, remember?"

He bowed. "Yes, thank you. I do remember. Senility does not run in my family." He arched an assessing look at her. "But my car is at your mother's. Besides, I need to talk to you about something."

"Oh. I forgot." Melanie put Bessie into gear, waved goodbye to Sara and pulled away from the curb. She kept her lips closed and her eyes on the road ahead. But it was totally impossible to ignore the grinning giant next to her.

"What is that noise?" he asked at last, shifting gingerly in the narrow confines of his seat. "Is it going to blow up?"

"Not yet," Melanie said, refusing to rise to the bait. "Bessie needs her carb cleaned. I just haven't had time."

The car backfired, jolting Mitch out of his seat with a jerk.

"It needs to be retired," he muttered, casting her a baleful look. "I hadn't realized your love of seniors ran to cars."

"What did you want to talk about?" Melanie asked,

ignoring the bait and changing the subject adroitly. "I left your key and half of next month's rent on the hall table."

"I don't want your money," he spluttered. As her eyebrows rose, he swallowed. Melanie watched his Adam's apple bob up and down several times before he cleared his throat and began again.

"I have the wedding invitations for Gramps and Hope," he told her. "I just wanted you to look them over. Hope said you would need to know the color scheme to order the flowers and stuff."

"*You* chose the colors? *And* the wedding invitations? Why?" Melanie couldn't absorb the idea of Mitch Stewart entering a bridal shop to pick out such a thing.

"Why?" He sounded indignant. "Because she asked me to, that's why. She's too busy trying to find a dress and bridesmaid dresses and deciding on a place for them to live. The invitations have to go out fairly quickly, you know." Mitch preened. "I picked out the most suitable and had them printed up by special order. I've also chosen a lot of the hall decorations."

Melanie pulled in beside his bright red sports car with a jerk and turned to stare at him.

"But I thought I was supposed to do all that," she protested weakly, unable to envision him choosing wedding decorations.

"No, you're supposed to do the church, the table favors, the caterer and the emcee. Forget the groomsmen, though. Gramps already has everything picked out. And he won't change his mind."

Stunned, Melanie carried box after box into the house, glad that for once her mother wasn't home. She could never have explained this crazy situation. When they were finished, Mitch went out to his car and returned with yet another box. He carefully slit the tape and opened it, lifting out a smaller white box.

"Now, proof this and tell me if everything is okay."

Melanie stared at the pale green announcement with amazement. It was embossed with two pearlized calla lilies and elegant script, which invited the recipient to "Please Join Us."

She slid apart the two lilies and opened the heavy bond paper to see what syrupy sentiment Mitch had chosen. To her surprise, the invitation was beautifully worded.

"Miss Hope Langford and Judge Harry Conroy invite you to join them as they pledge their marriage vows to one another on August third at eleven o'clock a.m. in the sanctuary of Third Avenue Church. A buffet luncheon will be served in the community hall immediately following the ceremony. Your presence will be your gift to us."

Two embossed Hs were linked at the bottom.

"It's, uh, very nice," Melanie sputtered, astonished at this new image of Mitchel Stewart, wedding consultant.

"It did come out well, didn't it," he agreed happily. "I didn't want it to sound sappy or anything. I mean, they do have their dignity. And this is an important occasion for them. I want everything to be just right."

"So do I," Melanie told him, shaking herself mentally. "But I thought everything was scheduled for three in the afternoon. Who changed it?"

"Gramps." Mitch grinned that wide, alluring smile. "He wants to take Hope on a honeymoon trip to Paris. The plane leaves at three."

Melanie gaped. "Paris," she whispered, her mouth sagging. "Lucky Hope."

"Well, she doesn't know yet, so don't tell her, okay? Gramps wants it to be a surprise, and he'll tear a strip off me if she finds out."

"All right." Melanie could barely say the words. Nothing was sane in the world anymore!

"The thing is, I've got their lists, and the invitations need to go out right away. I wondered if you'd help me address them all. I could help you wrap those candy things later if you want." He looked like a little boy begging, and Melanie couldn't help the smile that curved her lips.

"All right," she agreed. "I'll help you for a while tonight, but first I've got to set up Mom's VCR. There's a program on that I want to tape for Mr. Harper. He just loves Westerns, and there aren't that many on anymore." She set the controls and then poured a cup of coffee for each of them.

Melanie could feel his eyes following her, watching her every move.

"You really care about those people, don't you?"

Melanie didn't understand why he seemed so surprised. "They're my friends," she told him. "Of course I care about them." She began writing out names and addresses with the thin-tipped gold fountain pen Mitch had given her. They worked companionably together for several minutes before Mitch spoke again.

"We got a letter today." He waited expectantly, and Melanie's eyes flew to his. "Here, let me read it. 'Dear Miss and Mr. Stewart, Papa John's Peanut Butter has come to a decision regarding the prize money of fifty thousand dollars that was to be awarded in regard to our recent peanut butter contest. Our client has requested your presence at our office on Friday next to discuss the resolution of this issue. Should this time be unsuitable, please feel free to contact us as soon as possible.'"

"But that's the day after tomorrow," Melanie said.

"I know," he admitted. "Can you make it?"

"You bet I'm going to make it," Melanie told him firmly. "Twenty-five thousand dollars is a lot of money, and I need every dime of it for Sunset. And, believe me, I intend to collect every cent."

"Melanie, it might not be that easy," Mitch cautioned. His voice had dropped.

Melanie stared at him. "What do you mean?"

"Well," he began reluctantly. "If they're going to award the money, why didn't they just send the checks? Why make us go in there and discuss a 'possible resolution'?" He shook his head. "It just sounds odd to me."

"Oh, you worry too much," she teased. "I know that God has sent that money just when we needed it most. He'd hardly take it all away now." Her thoughts meandered. "I can hardly wait to start improving the place. They've waited for so long."

Mitch said nothing, but she could tell he was still thinking about the letter. An hour later he stamped the invitations they'd addressed and carefully packed away the rest, folding the lid closed just as Charity walked through the door.

"Thanks for the help," he murmured, walking beside Melanie to his car. "I sure appreciate it."

"Oh, you're welcome." She smiled. "I want everything to go off without a hitch for those two. Goodness knows, they've waited long enough."

He stood staring at her until Melanie flushed a dark red.

"What are you staring at?" she demanded at last.

"A very beautiful woman," he whispered. "One who isn't afraid to give to other people and just keeps on giving, no matter what." He leaned forward and kissed her, his arms tight and compelling around her. Then, in a movement so quick she had no time to protest, he was in his car.

"Good night, sweet Melanie," he murmured before shifting gears and pulling away.

He disappeared down the street and around the corner, his car softly purring in the stillness. It wasn't until another car passed that Melanie realized she was still standing on the street, staring.

"Good night," she whispered, brushing a finger over her tingling lips.

Chapter Ten

"Today's the big day, Mother. You'd better pray extra hard this morning. Sunset needs that money now more than ever."

Having thus ensured that someone would be talking to the Lord about her problems, Melanie glugged down her coffee. She wanted to be on the road as early as possible. Since Mitch had neither offered her a ride nor asked to come with her, she felt free to leave when she wanted. Why wasn't that a pleasant thought?

Charity's hand on her arm was the only thing holding her back.

"My dearest girl," she murmured with a smile. "If God wants those folks to have things, they don't have to depend on Papa John's beneficence. God will make His own way."

"I know, Mom. The Lord will provide." They grinned at each other as she recited their favorite saying from years gone by. "But He already has, otherwise I wouldn't have won."

"You don't actually have that money yet, Melanie. Please let God work this out in His own way." Charity's usually smiling face was sober.

Melanie kissed the smooth parchment cheek and hopped

into her car, waving one hand. Just down the street she could see Faith and Hope striding toward her. Their faces were strained, and Hope seemed to be crying.

"Bye," Melanie called and drove away, wondering what the problem was. *Why doesn't life ever seem to go smoothly?* Unfortunately, the answer evaded her.

At WMIX, Mitch had already arrived and was seated in one of the comfortable leather chairs. His blue gaze swept over her quickly before he looked into her eyes. She couldn't read his. They were closed off, shuttered.

"You made it," was all he said as Papa John's lawyer offered her a seat.

"Of course I made it." She stared at his elegantly suited figure. "How come you're here so early?"

"Business," he told her. "Melanie, I need to talk to you. Privately."

His face was white with strain, and he looked distant. This tall, cool man who sat across from her was suddenly a stranger. And it hurt. Oh, he treated her with courtesy and respect, but there was no sign of the man whose big hands had rubbed suntan oil onto her back, who had massaged her tired shoulders when she had been depressed and beaten, who had held her when she'd lost Jonathan. Melanie searched his blue eyes, looking desperately for the man she had come to know over the past few months. But he wasn't there.

"But not now. Now we'll settle this prize thing. If you're ready?" the chilly-voiced stranger inquired coolly.

"Yes, go ahead." She tried to pretend his cool civility didn't hurt.

Papa John sauntered in, grinning brightly from ear to ear.

"Ah, my two prospective winners," he bellowed in that down-home voice he assumed for official duties. "Let's chat, shall we?" With a flick of his wrist he motioned the corporate exec types out of the room.

Melanie was confused. Chat? Weren't they supposed to award the prize now? And what was this *prospective* business? She glanced at Mitch for confirmation, but he shrugged, unable or unwilling to shed light on the situation.

"I wanted to speak to you two alone for a few minutes," the old man began, glancing from one stiff figure to the other. "I foresee several problems that never occurred to me before and I wanted your input. You, Mitch, will know all the legal implications of this."

Melanie frowned. She didn't like the sound of this. Not at all.

"The thing is, folks…" Papa John's voice was solemn. "I have shareholders, lots of them. The board is made up of some of the most crotchety old codgers you've ever seen." He smiled faintly as if just realizing that he was one of those codgers.

Melanie stared at Mitch, trying to assess what she was hearing. But Mitch's face was a frowning mask that told her only that he, too, was dismayed.

"Cut to the chase, Papa John," he muttered, interrupting the old man's flow of words. "What, exactly, are you trying to say?"

The old man scratched his whiskered chin with one lean, manicured hand.

"Well," he began cautiously, "the board feels that the company's image with our loyal public is based on wholesomeness. If you know what I mean."

Melanie disregarded the wink he cast Mitch's way. Why didn't he get down to business?

"What is the problem?" she blurted. If he didn't soon enlighten them, Melanie was going to reach out and yank on that beard. Hard.

"We can't award the prize money to two people who are living together in sin."

The baldness of his statement shocked her. Never mind that the sentiment was hopelessly mawkish and very dated. Papa John was insinuating that she and Mitch…that they were…

Her face blushed a deep, dark red as she considered how it must look. If not for Hope's insistence… She burst into speech.

"But we're not. I mean I moved out a few days ago. Anyway, nothing happened. You can ask—"

"Shut up." Mitch's voice cut her off midstream. She stared at him. He glared at her, daring her to say another word. "I'll do the talking here." He turned to face Papa John.

"You had two winners to your contest. Us." He pointed to Melanie and himself. "The conditions have been met, correct?"

Papa John bumbled around, but Mitch refused to let him off the hook.

"Do we, or do we not, get the prize money?"

"Well, young fella, there's no need to git all uppity. If you'll just hold yer horses…"

Melanie could feel the sizzle of anger that radiated off Mitch from her perch six feet away.

"Cut the hillbilly lingo, John. It's a put-on, and so is this bluff you're trying to pull on us here." Mitch slid his hands into his pockets and leaned against the door frame lazily. He looked like a shark deciding where to bite first. "Do we or do we not get the fifty grand?"

"Not." The word entered the room like a jolt of electricity. Melanie stood up from her chair.

"What? But I thought—"

Mitch's big hand pressed firmly on her shoulder. His voice was frigid.

"Sit down and be quiet."

She did both.

"Either you award that money to Miss Stewart and myself or we'll sue."

As she studied the rugged lines of his face, Melanie decided she would not like to face Mr. Mitchel Stewart in court. He would be a skilled opponent—razor sharp and tough as steel. For once she was glad he could hide his emotions so readily.

Papa John shook his head while his thumb snapped one suspender placidly against his rounded belly.

"No grounds," he responded sedately. Melanie could hear the ping of the metal as it hit a button. "The agreement was to award the money to M. Stewart, once we got the address problem straightened out. Miss Stewart here claimed to be the person living at apartment 108, when in fact your name is on the lease and hers appears nowhere on it. Doesn't seem to have a phone in her name, either."

Melanie noted Mitch's frustration by the clench of his hand, flexing in and out.

Papa John continued. "She didn't even move in until well after the contest drawing, did she?"

Melanie felt her cheeks burn with the implication in those beady old eyes. So this was what a harlot must have felt like. She tried to explain the situation.

"But I was just—"

"If you don't be quiet, I'm leaving," Mitch barked at her. "This is a legal issue. Papa John is legally bound to hand over that money to us. We have the reassurances of our prizewinner status on official Papa John's Peanut Butter stationery," His blue eyes penetrated her green ones, daring her to deny the facts.

But Melanie couldn't think of a word to say for, truth to tell, she didn't have that letter. Hadn't a clue where it was. Without it, she doubted they would award her anything but a jar of peanut butter. She sealed her lips tightly. Whatever

Mitch could salvage out of this terrible day was the most she could hope for.

"Go ahead," she told him quietly.

"Well?" Mitch's voice was pure ice as he glared at the owner of Papa John's.

"Miss Stewart has no claim."

Melanie sucked in a breath of air, ready to defend herself as Mitch shifted those eyes to her. She subsided without a sound.

Mitch turned his attention to the older man. He let that statement go to counter with one of his own.

"And me? Why can't you award the total to me?"

Papa John stoked his chin thoughtfully. "Well, you see, there's the rub. Actually you were not an employee at Sunset, nor a resident at the apartment, at the time of the drawing. In fact, you began your job after we made the drawing, and you took possession of the apartment two weeks later."

"Nope." Mitch smiled that cat-that-got-the-bird smile and leaned backward on his wing tips. Melanie saw the satisfaction curve his hard mouth. "I was there at the television station, remember. That was two weeks after I'd arranged for residence. You haven't got a hope."

Melanie thought the old fellow looked downright smug and self-satisfied.

"Sorry, son." He smirked, tapping his toe on the soft, thick broadloom. "The draw date was twenty-eight days before the show. That was the first date WMIX could give us the time slot we wanted. And we had to inform the *prospective* winners."

Melanie heard the subtle emphasis on the word and turned to study Mitch's face. Disgust and frustration creased his forehead as he glared at the old man.

"So it was all just a game," he rasped. "A total waste of our time?"

"Good Lord, no." the old man exploded, erupting from his chair with a bound. "I wanted to award that money to you folks. Still do. But I'm not taking any heat from the board or unfavorable publicity from the public to do it." He studied them with intense scrutiny.

"What exactly do you want from us?" Mitch's low voice sounded like ice on a hot pan as it sizzled across the room. "What's the catch?"

Papa John ambled over to sink his plump body into the big leather chair behind the mahogany desk. He folded his hands calmly as he met Mitch's furious glare.

"No catch, son." He leaned back and studied the ceiling for several moments. Then he straightened and fixed them with his watery eyes. "The only way my board will let me award that money is if the two of you are married."

"*What?*" Melanie jumped from her chair, glancing from one male to the other. "Get married? For money?" Silence reverberated through the room until Mitch's soft voice whispered in her ear.

"You were willing to live together for it. Why not marriage?"

Melanie stared. She couldn't help it. She gaped like a goldfish gulping air. "Do you mean you're going along with this? Are you crazy?"

Mitch smiled sardonically. "Oh, no," he muttered, shaking his head. "I'm not going along with it at all. I just thought it was interesting to see where you draw the line at getting that money." He swiveled to face the man behind the desk.

"Your board is going to have a little more to worry about, Papa," he said with anger. "Especially when I launch a campaign that challenges the trust your customers place in your product." He grinned at the older man sardonically.

"It's pretty bad when you can't depend on a company as big as Papa John's to deliver on its word," he continued. "I wonder what the public will think when they learn that you're not exactly who you say you are."

Melanie wondered why she had ever thought Mitch's eyes were warm. They had hardened to chips of glacial ice.

"Your lawyers will hear from us," he announced with a diamond-hard look. She felt his strong hand under her elbow. "Come on, Melanie. We're leaving."

"But…but—"

"No sense suing, son. Even if you did win, the money would all get spent on lawyers and court costs. Or else defending a libel suit. No, sirree." He shook his white head sadly. "Only thing left for you two to do is to get married."

As Melanie stumbled through the door to the hall, she heard Papa John's last words dimly.

"You let me know the date, kids. I'll be there."

"I'll just bet you would." Mitch's voice raged softly in her ear. "Can't you walk any faster?"

"Oh, suddenly you're a speed walker?" she asked furiously. He ignored the comment and whisked her out of the building and into the car before she could say anything else. It was only when she was straightening her skirt over her knees that Melanie realized they were sitting in his car.

"My car's over there," she told him, pointing across the lot. He glared at her.

"Don't you understand what's going on here? You could lose everything because of some narrow-minded old cronies." He smiled at her grimly. "The old coot's done his homework. We haven't got a chance of winning anything out of this fiasco."

"But I thought you said…" Melanie frowned at him.

"It was just a bluff. We haven't got the kind of cash it would take to start a smear campaign even if we could get away with it." His hand smacked the steering wheel. "Don't you get it? It's gone, all of it. You're not going to see a dime of that money."

It took a few minutes to absorb it, but when she did, Melanie felt the dam burst. She covered him with her fiery words.

"Yes, I'm quite well aware of that, thank you very much." Frustration clouded her judgment, and Melanie spewed out words she immediately wished unsaid.

"And I'll lose it all because of you. Come into my parlor, you said. I'll help you get the money, just move in. You—you spider!" Her green eyes snapped at him as the frustration of the past weeks poured out. "You're the one who insisted I give false information about my address. It's all your fault!"

The enormity of losing twenty-five thousand dollars hit her, then and Melanie did the only thing she could to relieve her frustration.

"Ow, ow, ow! Ooh, that hurts!" She sucked on the knuckles of her hand where it had made contact with the rock-hard dash. It had been a puerile thing to do, and she didn't feel one whit better. Her turbulent sea-foam eyes glared at Mitch.

"You're blaming this on me?" he bellowed incredulously. "This is my fault?" He looked astounded. "The only reason I ever got involved in your little Save Our Seniors campaign was because you wanted that money so badly." He shook his head in pretended amusement, but his lips were pursed tightly.

"I don't believe this. You try to help someone and all you do is get knocked down. So much for brotherly love." He thrust his hands in the air. "That's it. I give up. I quit. Do whatever you want, just don't involve me in any more of your harebrained schemes."

"Brotherly love? Ha!" Melanie yanked the door open and stumbled out. "There's nothing like that involved! Stick your head in the sand and give up, then. See if I care!"

She slammed the door of his car as hard as she could and stomped across the parking lot in red patent shoes that pinched her toes with every click the four-inch heels made against the pavement.

And all the way, Mitch could hear her castigating the male of the species. One in particular. They were nasty words that didn't explain his motives at all. And they were totally untrue!

With an angry flick of his wrist, he shifted into gear and floored the gas pedal, screeching out of the parking lot as his new tires laid their expensive tread on the asphalt. He ground his way into second, ignoring the car's protesting sounds. And to think God actually thought men *needed* women!

Seconds later, Melanie followed, honking angrily at an elderly white-haired gentleman who almost backed into her as she took the corner on two wheels.

The old fellow smiled fondly. Kids these days. So excitable. Wait till he told Nettie about this latest development.

"Mitch, I know you said you didn't want to see anyone, but I think you'd better see this fellow. He says it's urgent."

Mitch groaned, thrusting away the salad he'd picked up at the store. Salad, for Pete's sake, when he really wanted a burger and fries! Or a doughnut.

Clarence Palmer's opinion was the same as he loped through the door.

"You sick?" he asked curiously, eyeing the three kinds of lettuce, chopped celery and radishes that filled the black plastic bowl. "Got a heart condition or something?"

Ha! Now that was appropriate. Melanie Stewart definitely affected his digestion, but his heart?

"Might be," he told Clarence sullenly. "Just might be." He dumped the last of the ranch dressing into the bowl and took another mouthful. "What's so all-fired important?"

"Thought you'd want to know right away." Clarence

beamed. "I don't think this Papa John fellow is the lady's old beau, after all."

"What!" Mitch jerked straight up in his chair. "But I thought you were so sure. What's changed?"

"For one thing, I got hold of some medical records. From what I know, your Papa fellow has his bones intact. Our Jean had broken his left ankle once and the right arm just below the elbow. The surgeon I talked to says he thinks he'd be able to see evidence of that on the X ray."

"After this long?" Mitch was skeptical.

"There is no sign of a break on this John guy's arm, according to his personal physician. A few other minor things seem to indicate that this LeClerc fellow is not the same as your Papa John. I've put it all in my report so, unless you have some new information, I'm closing this file."

Mitch scratched his chin in disbelief. "You're sure about this?" he demanded.

"As sure as I can be, which isn't much given the few facts in the case." Clarence eyed him appreciatively. "This one something important to you?"

"I was hoping for something that would give me a hold on the guy, yes. He's trying to do a friend of mine out of fifty thousand dollars, so I guess that does give me some interest in good old Papa John."

"So she's not getting a dime?" Faith looked aghast at the news. "But how could he do that to them?"

"He apparently wants them to get married so his shareholders don't feel that they are condoning some illicit relationship." Hope stared at her hands. "And truth to tell," she murmured, "I don't thing it's such a bad idea. Nettie seems very encouraged in their interest in each other. She says Mitch has been to the home a number of times to help out with some function or another."

"They did seem rather interested in each other after the Sunday school picnic," Charity mused. "He deliberately didn't tag her when she got that base hit, remember? That was nice."

"He also pitched it straight to her so she could hit the thing," Hope sputtered in sheer disgust. "That run cost our side the game. Love makes people so silly." The words were enunciated with disgust.

"Oh, Hope, dear, I think it's affected even you." Faith chuckled. "You were out walking in the rain last night, you and Harry. Arthur saw you," she added when it seemed Hope would deny it. "Didn't it bother you to get your hair all wet?"

Charity watched as Hope's clear, pale skin flushed a dark red. She decided to get the conversation back on track.

"The thing is, girls," she said firmly, "Melanie really likes him, I'm sure she does. And it's all so new. She's just a bit afraid of admitting it." She glanced at her friends' bemused faces. "Now what are we going to do about it?"

"I think we need to give them some time alone," Faith murmured. "I mean, Hope chaperoned them nicely in the apartment, but young folks need time together."

"So do older people," Hope sniped. "And they don't need Peeping Toms watching out the window when they go for a walk!"

"*I* wasn't peeping," Faith grumbled. "Arthur saw you on his way home from work. If you're ashamed to be seen in public—"

"I am not ashamed!" Hope's quiet voice was rising steadily.

"Girls!" Charity was firm. "How are we going to get Mitch and Melanie together again?"

"I've had them both over for dinner twice this week," Faith mused, staring into space. "I can't very well ask them again or they'll know something's up."

"And I've pulled all the little problems with the wedding that I can think of," Hope said mournfully. "They're both so efficient that they run right over all my complications and dilemmas without being deterred and without asking each other's help."

"If I ask him over here too much more," Charity said, "Melanie's going to know I'm up to something."

The three ladies sat stewing over their plans, trying desperately to come up with something new. The phone rang as Melanie walked through the front door.

"I'll get it," she called.

Unashamedly, the threesome sat listening to the one-sided conversation, their faces broadening with satisfied grins as they did.

"Oh, hi, Mitch. You are? Well, I don't think *I* took it, but I can look if you like. No, thanks. I don't really *need* any help, Mitchel."

Faith nodded at Hope, who raised a thumbs-up sign at Charity.

"Actually, I just got in the door. No, I haven't eaten but I imagine Mom's—"

"I'm going out, dear," Charity interrupted. "Special meeting of the ladies' group." She shook her head at Faith's wide-eyed dismay. "Why don't you eat out at that new Mexican restaurant tonight?"

"Sorry, Mitch. Mom was just telling me something. Oh, you heard. Yes, I suppose that would be okay. Around seven-thirty? All right. Bye."

Before Melanie could hang the receiver up, there was a flurry of action in the living room. Hope grasped her purse and her scarf and flung her sweater over her shoulders before helping Faith find her pocketbook and the list of baking she was doing for the reception. Charity struggled to slip her tired feet into the orthopedic shoes. She finished tying the laces at the same moment her daughter breezed into the room.

"I didn't know there was a ladies' meeting tonight, Mom. That's three times this week. What's going on?"

"Planning a wedding shower," her mother whispered, eyes rolling in Hope's direction.

"Oh, well, if she's going to be alone, maybe Hope would like to have dinner with me?"

"Isn't Mitch coming over?" Charity's question drew her attention from the pair by the door, so Melanie missed seeing Faith's elbow imbed itself in Hope's side.

"Well, yes, but—"

"Thank you anyway, dear," Hope murmured, her eyes watering. "But Harry and I are going to go over some reno-vation plans tonight. And I've just time to change my clothes." She glanced at her watch before grasping Faith's arm firmly. "Come along, Faith. I want to make sure you get home safely," she said sweetly.

As they moved through the door, Faith's light voice carried back.

"Hope, your fingernails are too long. They're digging into my arm."

"I have to rush off, too," her mother told her. "I've got so many things to do before this wedding." She was almost out the door before Melanie's voice stopped her.

"When and where is the shower, Mother? I'd like to go, if I can."

"Uh, we're just going to decide that tonight," Charity murmured, scurrying out the door. "See you later."

Melanie stared at the empty living room.

"You certainly know how to clear a room," she muttered fatalistically. Then her thoughts turned to Mitch and his offer.

She hadn't wanted to let the fearsome threesome know, but she was glad he'd invited her to go for a swim. She des-perately needed to work off some of this stress, and besides, it would keep her from thinking about his ridiculous marriage proposal. After changing into a bright yellow T-shirt and dark blue shorts, Melanie sat down to view a stack of videos.

"It just wouldn't do to lose the punching bout of the century," she reminded herself. She got caught up in a rerun of the "Little House on the Prairies" series, and her eyes were full of tears when the doorbell rang. Brushing her hand across her cheeks, she hurried to answer it.

"Hi," she said brusquely, sniffing. "Come on in."

"Gee." He stared at her grimly. "I don't think I ever had this effect on one of my dates before. And we haven't even left yet." He followed her into the living room and rolled his eyes when he saw what she'd been watching.

"You've seen this thing ten times," he muttered, hitting the rewind button. "And you still bawl. Why do you watch it if it makes you so sad?"

"It doesn't make me sad," she retorted in watery tones. "It's makes me feel wonderful to be alive." She blew her nose loudly.

It was obvious that Mitch didn't share her pleasure in watching a family make it by pulling together through the tough times. And how could she tell him that the show symbolized everything she wanted in her life? He would call her a maudlin sentimentalist.

"Yeah." He grimaced, swiping at one of the tears on her cheeks. "I can tell you're feeling really great right now." Mitch sifted through the tapes scattered across the floor, his fingers plucking one from the mess. "Ah, here it is. I think." He thrust the cartridge into the VCR and waited.

"What in the world!" His eyes were huge blue puddles of disbelief as the start of a boxing match was quickly overridden by a diminutive woman with silver curls and a red-lipsticked mouth who stood on a platform.

"Men are not like women," the woman doctor was explaining. "They do not think of love in the same terms as we do. The males of our species take things literally, so if you want something from them, you have to come right out and ask for it. Don't assume anything, because men tend to think with their—"

Mitch hit the stop button as fast as he could, his face beet red.

"What happened to my boxing?" he demanded, looming over her. "Is the whole tape ruined by that—that ridiculous woman?"

"She's not ridiculous. She's a well-respected therapist. Thousands of people pay huge amounts of money to get her advice."

"Thousands of people paid huge amounts of money to see that fight," he said. "And I paid a fair bit to obtain a taped copy of it."

"Sorry! I must have grabbed that one by mistake and taped right over your show. I didn't mean to!" Melanie glared at him, preparing herself for the battle that was sure to follow.

But Mitch didn't look angry. He looked, well, resigned. He closed his eyes and mouthed the numbers from one to ten. When he opened those big baby blues, his grin tipped wryly to one side. He squatted in front of her and took her hands.

"Never mind. I'll get another one made," he told her quietly.

"I really am sorry, Mitch. I taped it for one of my residents. You remember Jonathan Northrup. That doctor is his sister." Her voice dropped. "He died before I got it to him."

"Oh, yes. I understand completely. Anything for the home and the people there." His blue eyes moved over her like a warm, snug blanket covering her with care, his voice was smooth.

"He's the fellow who told you to try moving into today's world, isn't he? And he's right, Melanie. You can't hide out at Sunset forever."

"Move into what? Murders, bombings, people full of hate and bitterness? That's not the type of world I want to live in, Mitch." Her voice was sour as she remembered the things she'd had to do today.

"What's wrong, Mel?" he asked, sitting beside her and wrapping his arm around her shoulders. "I mean really wrong."

"I'm cranky," she admitted at last, luxuriating in the feel of his big hand on her hair, soothing and gentle. "I had to order bed restraints on two residents today."

"Hmm," he sympathized, tugging her head onto his shoulder companionably. "I know how much you hate that."

"Yeah, I do. But there was one good thing. I at last managed to locate a motorized cart for Mr. Harcourt." She grimaced. "There's no way the administrator will okay an expenditure of four thousand dollars for one patient, though."

She felt his chin rest on her head as his chest wobbled under her cheek.

"What is it your mother always says?" he asked, chuckling.

"The Lord will provide." Melanie answered dully. "But I want it right now!"

"You remind me of Sara's Ben. Come on." Mitch chuckled, tugging her to her feet. "You need to get out of here and get some fresh air. I have just the thing."

"I thought we were going for a swim and then dinner." She frowned.

"We are. Now come on."

So Melanie went, noticing the soft luxury of his bucket seats and the feel of the fresh breeze playing with her hair.

"Where are we going?" she asked finally, only beginning to notice that they were on their way out of town.

"We're going for a swim. In the river. That friend of yours, Jeff? He told me about this place. Said it was quiet." Mitch parked beside a grassy spot that edged the river.

"Would madame care to sample the speciality of the day, compliments of Enjoy Gardens?"

Her eyes widened as she took in the assorted boxes and bowls he was removing from the trunk and laying out on an old quilt he'd spread on the ground. There were all manner of succulent odors emanating from the tinfoil dishes. A tiny smile curved its way across her face hesitantly. She glanced up at him.

"What's all this?"

Mitch's face was serious as he replied. "I'm tired of fighting, Melanie. I was hoping we could share dinner and discuss the situation rationally, without running away or verbally slaughtering each other." His eyes glinted with mirth. "And just for the record, that woman on the tape was only partially right. I can understand most things without having them spelled out for me in black and white."

Melanie flushed as she remembered Dr. Lana's advice. It was a good thing he hadn't heard any more than he had. Mitch had made the first move. She was a big enough person to accept it.

"Thank you. I love Chinese food." She sank onto a tattered cushion with the old-world elegance of a Victorian maiden.

"I know. Health food," he murmured, his eyes glinting. "It's one of the things I like most about you. The other is your sense of humor."

Melanie raised an eyebrow. Her fingers peeled back the lid on a container and she breathed in the fresh, sesame-scented air. As she spooned a large helping onto her plate, she looked at him through her lashes.

"What *exactly* are you doing this for, Mitch? What is it you want to talk about so badly?" Her eyes noted the light flush on his cheekbones. Melanie's curiosity grew.

"Mitch? What is all this really in aid of?" she queried,

noting the candles flickering on the quilt and the paper-towel napkins he had folded into little tents. "What do you want?"

Mitch slapped a hand to his chest in affront. "I'm insulted. How can you ask such a thing?"

She grinned cheekily.

"I can ask because I'm beginning to know you." She studied him. "And I know you want something right now. That tic at the side of your mouth gives it away. What is it?"

She watched knowingly as his hand searched for the non-existent tic and smiled when he glared at her. Nothing could have prepared her for his answer.

"What I really want is for you to marry me."

She sat there with the grass tickling her ankles, a plate of her favorite food on her lap, and wondered if she'd inhaled too much fresh air. A surfeit of oxygen was supposed to be lethal, wasn't it?

"Melanie?" His big hand was shaking her shoulder none too gently. "Say something?"

"Hello." She smiled stupidly, wondering what in the world he expected her to say to such a strange proposal. His blue eyes narrowed.

"What is the matter with you?" he asked, worried. His fingers twitched water from her water glass onto her face. It was cold, and she veered away.

"Hey! Quit that."

"Well?"

"Well, what?" Melanie made herself meet his probing glance.

"What do you think?"

She grabbed the opportunity. "I think you may be allergic to shellfish, too," she told him seriously. She watched the pulse throbbing rhythmically at the side of his temple for a few seconds before picking up her fork. "Mm, this broccoli is perfect."

He leaned back on his cushion and glared at her.

"Okay, I'll bite. Why do you think I suffer from this malady?"

"Surely it's obvious. Something has made you lose your mind." Her forehead wrinkled. "Or else it's me."

"Now that I might go along with," Mitch muttered.

Melanie frowned. He wasn't going to start *that* again, was he?

"Look. Are you or are you not going to marry me?"

Melanie strove for control. Here he was joking about the one thing she wanted more than anything. Well, she wouldn't fall into the trap. She knew better. He was baiting her, trying to trap her into saying something she would regret.

She laid her fork down and crossed her legs, hands folded carefully in her lap.

"Gee, this is so sudden." She smiled sweetly. "Why, exactly, would we be getting married, honey?"

"Well, I thought… I mean, well… The money…it's the only way." Mitch stumbled through the speech, obviously nonplussed by her attitude.

He probably thought she would jump at the opportunity. After all, at her advanced age and everything. Ooh!

"I see." She recrossed her legs calmly, biting down the sarcastic remarks that begged to be uttered. "So you want to marry me for my money, is that it?"

"Well, yes. Sort of." He glared at her. "No."

"That's clear! Okay, and then what?"

"Excuse me?" Mitch was staring at her as if she had turned into one of those vile reptilian forms he seemed so fond of. "What do you mean, then what? We'll get them to award the money and you can get what you've always wanted."

"And then what?" She repeated the phrase, hoping he would say the only three words she wanted to hear.

Mitch stared at her. "Huh?"

"It's a simple question, Mitch. You can figure it out. What happens after we get the money?"

"I guess we could learn to live together, or whatever."

"I'm just a little leery of the whatever," she murmured. "Thank you very much, but no thanks." She slipped a spear of celery into her mouth with more aplomb than she felt.

He was dumbfounded, Melanie could see that easily enough. His mouth pursed. That meant he was close to losing control. Good! She was pretty close to the edge herself.

"What do you mean, no? Are you going to throw away all that money just because you don't like the idea of getting married? It's ridiculous. You could do all the things you had planned and more."

Melanie stopped him right there.

"Oh, I like the idea of getting married, all right. But I like the idea of staying married even more. I want a husband who wants me, not my money. I want kids and a home and a life that all that money couldn't buy." She glared at him. "I am not marrying anyone for money, least of all you. The whole thing has gone too far."

"But what about your residents, that guy who needs the cart and the new sound units?"

Melanie felt frustration well up, but she shoved it away, hardening her heart against the guilt waiting to crowd in.

"They will just have to find another way. And maybe I'll have to find another job."

Mitch was aghast. Did he repel her so much she was willing to quit her job, a job she loved doing, just to get away from him? He thought about Sara's advice.

"You've got to back her into a corner, honey. She's the type that won't give in without you saying the words. Don't give her any platitudes or grandiose schemes. Just tell her the truth."

Maybe it was worth a try. God knew he didn't think he was

anything like the type for home and family, but he was darned good at making things happen. He would blasted well make sure she got that money! And in the process, he would gain the one thing he really wanted out of all this—Melanie Stewart.

"Listen to me, Melanie. I know it sounds crazy. I know we argue almost all the time. I know you think I'm just offering you a way to get the cash." He swallowed. Hard.

"But I'm not. I want to marry you. I, er, that is, I think I'm in love with you." He gulped a drink of water and wondered if he had really finally admitted it. But one look at her gaping face made him continue.

"I like it when you tell me about your day and the folks at Sunset. I like feeling your hair when it's loose and curling at the ends like that. I like the way you go all out for something you believe in." He grinned. "I like kissing you, too. And I think you like kissing me."

"Mitch, marriage is a whole lot more of a commitment than that!"

She sounded stunned, Mitch decided. Good. Now maybe he'd have a chance to get the words said.

"I know that. And I'm ready to make that commitment to you." He knelt in front of her. "I don't know much about marriage, Melanie. I never had much of an example except Gramps. But I do know that it takes two people and a special spark. I think we've got that."

He slid his hand under the heavy fall of her hair and circled her neck, leaning in to press his lips against hers. When Melanie immediately responded, he felt a rush of warmth. No matter what she said, Melanie Stewart was not immune to him!

"You can feel it, too, can't you?" he whispered in her ear, his arms drawing her closer.

"Yes," she said, her arms sliding around his neck. Her eyes were dark in the dusky light. "But, Mitch, it's going to take a lot more than attraction to make a marriage work. What about the money?"

He felt the grim chill of reality, and suddenly wished he had never heard of Papa John's Peanut Butter.

"Melanie, the money doesn't have anything to do with this. It's just a byproduct of us getting married, it's not the main reason."

But Mitch could tell she wasn't listening. She had withdrawn into that shell that protected her from pain.

"I can't get married because of some prize money," she whispered. "Marriage is a serious commitment between two people and God. It's what I've believed all my life, and I can't just forget my principles because there's money involved."

"But money isn't the reason I'm asking you," he told her. "I care for you. Really."

"Do you?" She looked skeptical, at best. She was placing the covers on various containers. "I think we'd better go now," she murmured. "I've got several loose ends to tie up before the wedding next week."

There was nothing to do but follow her lead for now, Mitch decided grimly. But she'd come around. She had to.

"You'd better pay attention to all those details," he told her on the drive back. "You're going to need to remember them when our day rolls around."

"Don't start on that again," she pleaded. "Please?"

"You are going to marry me, Melanie. Sooner or later you'll realize that. So make up your mind to it because there's no way you can talk me out of it."

"I'm not marrying you, Mitchel. No way. So don't think you're going to bully me into it." Melanie got out of the car and stomped up the front steps. "I'm not getting involved with you for the money."

"No," he agreed. "We're not getting married for money. Not at all."

He pulled her against him and covered her mouth with his. Within seconds her arms wound round his neck and she was kissing him back.

He grinned. She did want to marry him. She was just too stubborn to admit it. Now they needed to get down to business. And he knew exactly how to do it.

He grinned as Melanie flew into the house, to the safety of her private space. He waited about ten seconds and drove off, content that Melanie wasn't immune to him, despite what she claimed. Not at all immune, if that kiss was anything to go by.

As he drove toward his apartment, Mitch thought of Nettie Rivers's words to him at their last meeting.

"If there's anything I can do to help you and Melanie, Mitch, you only have to ask." She had smiled a coy little grin. "After all, I do have some influence, you know."

He hadn't been exactly sure what she'd meant then, but maybe it was time to find out. He could use all the help he could get.

Chapter Eleven

"It's just a ceremony, Melanie. It's not condemning yourself to death." Charity looked at her daughter in amusement. "It's a promise for the future."

"It sounds like a death sentence. Why does Hope want all these silly things in her vows, anyway? Is there something wrong with the good old-fashioned kind?"

"Maybe she wants to express her feelings especially to Gramps," Mitch murmured from his position opposite her. His big fingers struggled with the narrow ribbon as he fluffed and tied a tiny bow around the mint satchels they were making. "Every couple experiences things differently. And they have waited a long time. I'm sure she just wants everything to be wonderful."

Melanie sighed tiredly. Mitch was like a dog with a bone. He would not give up this marriage idea. Whenever she refused to consider it, he started kissing her. Then her knees turned to mush and her brain blew a fuse and she couldn't understand what he was saying for ages afterward.

"Just think about what you're going to say to me at that altar," he whispered in a voice loud enough that neither Charity nor Faith could fail to hear.

"Oh, I am," she assured him grimly. "I'm thinking of a lot of things that I'm going to say to you. But mostly in private."

Mitch had tricked her into blood tests by requesting, through official administration channels, of course, that she have a full range of blood work to update her files and make sure her insurance coverage was up to date. It had been so skillfully done that Melanie hadn't even seen his hand in the thing until he'd presented her with their license.

"Blood tests all done," he'd crowed, waving the papers in her face Sunday morning before church. Thankfully, she'd hushed him up, although it had meant sitting next to him all through the long service. Melanie had been fully aware of the speculative looks, the press of his knee against her leg and the warmth of his hand when he'd clasped hers so tightly.

"I need some encouragement," he'd whispered when she had tried to tug away. "After all, as you pointed out, marriage is a big responsibility for a man."

And his hand had stayed under her arm, under her elbow, holding hers until he'd walked her to her mother's. He seemed totally unperturbed when Melanie threatened to dump her entire glass of iced tea into his lap just after lunch. He merely coaxed her into sitting on the patio.

"I've told you a hundred times," she said, "I am not getting married. Not to you, anyway."

Mitch leaned across and kissed the tip of her nose.

"Yes, dearest Melanie," he insisted, "we are. Sooner or later."

Melanie shook her head firmly. "I won't be there."

"Oh, yes, you will. Shawna and Sara will be there. Your mother and her friends, too. I think it would be nice if Gramps walked you down the aisle, don't you?" He smiled fatuously. "What do you think of autumn colors for the invitations?"

"Invitations?" Melanie tried to remember discussing that,

but her mind drew a blank. He had told her so many things she couldn't keep track anymore. It was like being pestered by a whirling dervish. He was constantly on the go, planning something or other.

"These are some of the people I want to invite," he told her seriously. She unfolded the piece of paper to find a wedding invitation inside with a long list attached. "Unless you'd rather elope? I'm all for that." He kissed her again.

"How could you choose invitations when you don't have anyone to marry you?" She deliberately avoided his arms.

His blue eyes peered into hers. "Don't I?" he whispered softly into her ear. Seconds later she forgot what they had been talking about as his mouth teased hers in mindless abandon.

"You did say your favorite color was green," he whispered, tickling her earlobe. "I thought maybe a dark spruce tone would be nice."

Melanie burst out laughing. She just couldn't imagine him walking into a bridal shop and demanding to see their spruce-colored wedding invitations. The man had nerve, she admitted. Lots of it.

"I didn't realize you were into sweetheart roses," Melanie murmured, struggling out of his arms. She agreed the invitation was very nice, and he accepted the issue as settled, which it wasn't but she wasn't risking another one of those sock-stealing kisses. It was hard enough to keep away from the man.

"I'm going to see Nettie now," he murmured two hours later when the mints were all wrapped. "She has something to discuss with me, she said."

"You two seem to spend a lot of time together," Melanie said grumpily, knowing he wouldn't tell her the subject of their discussion. "If you two are so thick, why don't you ask her to marry you?"

She grinned triumphantly, but Mitch wasn't in the least put off.

"She's already involved with someone," he told her, pressing a kiss on the end of her nose. "Besides, she thinks we belong together. I'm Prince Charming, remember?" He grinned smugly. "Bye, Charity. Thanks for a wonderful lunch." He pressed a flyaway kiss to her mother's cheek and proceeded down the line to encompass Faith and finally Hope in his magnificence. "Just four more days, Gramps," he chided, smiling. "Can you wait that long?"

"That boy sure is pleased about something," Faith said when the door closed. "Why, his spirits have just lifted to the skies. Melanie?"

"Yes, Faith?"

"Do you have any idea what Mitch is so happy about?" Melanie caught the knowing glance her mother exchanged with the other members of the fearsome threesome.

"Not a clue," she lied airily. "He lives a fantasy life most of the time. Hope can tell you about that. She saw it as well as I did." Melanie glanced at the other woman for confirmation and instead found Hope shaking her head.

"I always thought he was very down-to-earth and sure of himself," Hope murmured. "Didn't you, Harry?"

"He certainly is now." Harry chortled. "And I think the thing he's decided on is Miss Me—" His booming voice died away in a sudden coughing spurt.

"I've got to get those thank-you notes from that shower finished this afternoon." Hope broke the silence. "Come along, Harry. You can help me. See you later, girls."

They were gone, soon followed by Charity and Faith, who were picked up by Arthur for a drive in the country.

With nothing left to do and no one to talk to, Melanie found herself glancing through the bridal magazines Hope had left behind. She laughed outright at several of the most improbable pictures, but stopped at the center section.

"It's perfect," she whispered.

The dress was long and elegant with not a flounce to be found. The sweetheart neckline draped gracefully over the model's shoulders, ending at the opalescent sheer sleeves that formed a delicate point at the wrist.

Melanie could almost feel the heavy silk caress her skin as she studied the tiny row of buttons up the back and the beautiful full train that trailed behind.

"Her hair's wrong," she murmured, imagining a soft upsweep that would emphasize the tiny Juliet cap with its delicate pearls and fluff of netting.

"Yes, you're right," a voice whispered in her ear. "This is definitely your style. I can see you coming down the aisle carrying palest peach roses."

Melanie came awake with a jerk as Mitch's mouth nibbled on the corner of hers.

"What are you doing here?" she demanded, startled and embarrassed. "I thought you had an important engagement."

"I did." Mitch grinned his lazy well-fed-cat smile, his fingers wrapping around one tendril of her hair. "And then I came back to you. Miss me?" His eyes sparkled like blue diamonds in the sun.

"Of course not," Melanie muttered, shutting the magazine with a thud. "I'm just going out for a walk."

"Wonderful idea," he agreed. "A little exercise with my bride-to-be. Just what I need."

She smiled, remembering his last venture in walking.

"It's everybody at their own risk," she warned, bending to tie her shoes. "I've got a very stressful week to prepare for."

To her dismay, Mitch beamed with delight.

"Perfect! I can hardly wait."

Melanie deliberately started out at a far faster pace than was good for her, hoping he'd drop out and leave her alone. To her amazement, Mitch kept up, jogging, even talking to her as they went. And all without a sign of breathlessness when she could hardly draw in a lungful of air for the pain in her chest.

She asked Sara about it later.

"How's it going with you and Mitch?" Melanie asked tentatively with just the right note of compassion. "Any problems?"

"Problems? With Mitchel?" Sara had repeated. "No, since you left he's been a model host. He's up before dawn to jog for forty-five minutes, has his shower, eats his Wheaties and then he's off, whistling, for work!"

"Wheaties?" Melanie stared at the phone. "Mitch only eats doughnuts for breakfast." And lunch and dinner, she repeated to herself. "And he hates jogging."

"Not anymore, Melanie. He says he's turned over a new leaf, and I believe it. The kids don't get their usual junk food treats from him anymore, you know. Now he brings home apples and grapes and popcorn. *Popcorn,*" she repeated with amazement.

"Well, I, for one, don't believe it," Melanie murmured. "What's wrong with him, anyway?"

"I don't know," Sara told her seriously. "All he's saying is that I'll know when he makes the big announcement."

"What announcement?"

"Beats me, Mel, but I can tell you there's a lot of fishy stuff going on here." Sara's voice grew faint as she called to her children. "Yesterday, for example. Just as I was leaving, a little old lady showed up here. Said she had an important meeting with Mitch. It was weird, I can tell you."

"At least that explains this afternoon." She quickly described her jogging and Mitch's unexpected ability to keep up. "He's up to something," Melanie asserted. "I can feel it."

"Well, whatever it is," Sara said, "I like it." She went on to tell Melanie about her husband's imminent return from his peacekeeping duties overseas. "The kids and I will be so glad once we move in to our own place. Not that we don't feel welcome here, but after all, it isn't home."

That night as she lay in bed, Melanie dared to ask God once more for direction.

"I love him, Lord. But I'm just not sure that he loves me. At least not enough to spend the rest of our lives together. Please, could You help me with this? Send me some little sign?"

It was rather providential that a dozen red roses arrived the next morning at work, addressed to her. Tucked inside was a card. *Marry Me!* it ordered in bold print, underlined for effect.

"That's not exactly the kind of sign I meant," she said. Melanie stuffed the card into her purse and refused to answer the questions with which her staff bombarded her. Mrs. Rivers strolled past her office in the afternoon and, sighting the roses, buried her face in their fragrant petals.

"Oh, Melanie, I knew Mitch was your true love," the old woman told her softly. "I just knew the two of you were meant to be together. God let me see it so clearly."

Melanie stared. With vivid accuracy, she remembered the day she'd met Mitch, when Mrs. Rivers had said those exact words. She tried to laugh it off.

"Oh, Nettie, I don't think he's my true anything."

The old face crinkled with dismay. "But he loves you, dear. Very much." Nettie nodded. "I've seen it."

Melanie excused the old woman's silliness. After all, she suffered from dementia. Nettie Rivers could afford to indulge in fairy tales, Melanie thought. She needed to focus on the duties of the day.

The next afternoon, right after lunch, Melanie returned to her office to find someone had delivered chocolates, a monstrous box of the expensive Belgian kind she especially adored and seldom bought. The card inside was identical to the one that had come with the flowers. *Marry me,* the card insisted. She filed it away in her purse with the first.

Melanie hated to do it, but she didn't want any reminders of him around to poke and probe at her conscience, so she passed the delicacies around to her staff, watching sadly as, one by one, the delicious tidbits were eaten.

Mitch showed up for an afternoon coffee break that day, full of bouncing good humor. Melanie found herself envying his sparkling eyes and obvious good health. She hadn't slept at all well for days.

"Anything interesting going on?" he asked cheerfully, flopping down in the chair next to hers after he'd brushed her cheek with his lips.

"I wish you wouldn't do that in public," she told him angrily. "Now the entire staff will be talking about us."

"They will anyway, once our engagement becomes public." He grinned affably.

"For once and for all, we are not engaged. You've mixed yourself up with your grandfather."

He ignored her cranky words and pulled two huge red apples from his pocket.

"Here, eat this," he ordered her smoothly. "Your blood sugar must be slipping. Did you eat a proper breakfast?"

"Oh, that's rich." Melanie glared at him. "The king of junk food asking me about my eating habits!"

Mitch sipped his black unsweetened coffee without reacting to her gibe. He bit into his apple with those sharp, even teeth, blue eyes twinkling.

"Maybe your problem is too much sugar in that coffee," he offered kindly. "Why don't you switch to juice?"

"Ooh! Why don't you go jump in the lake?" Melanie advised crankily. "And stop sending me things," she ordered. "You can't make me marry you." She stomped from the room. To her dismay he followed her into her office.

"I'm not trying to *make* you do anything," Mitch murmured, his hands closing around her shoulders. "And we will be married, as soon as you come to your senses."

She had a number of things to reply to that, but her mouth never got to say them because suddenly he was kissing her and she had wanted that for so long, she couldn't help wrapping her arms around his neck and enjoying every moment of it.

"I knew I was right!"

Melanie heard the words through a fog and turned to see Nettie Rivers standing in the doorway, her faded eyes bright.

"What do you mean?" Melanie unwrapped her arms and moved away from Mitch.

"My dear, you're only fooling yourself. You and Mitchel are meant to be together." She turned slowly and moved through the door. "I must go tell…" Melanie didn't hear the remainder.

"Now look what you've done," she said to a grinning Mitch. "She'll tell the whole world that you were in here kissing me, and everyone will be staring at me!"

She could have screamed when he smiled before using a tissue to wipe a smear of pale pink lipstick from his mouth.

"I think the kissing was mutual." He snorted in amusement. "And as wonderful as that was, I did come here for a purpose." He straightened his tie and flicked back the errant lock of hair that seemed perpetually out of place. "I wanted to ask if you'd come to my place tonight."

"Are you kidding?" she asked. "I'm up to my ears with this wedding tomorrow. I'm certainly not going to open myself up to any more of your silly tricks."

"Okay." He shrugged agreeably. "I'll just have it delivered to you and come to your place." And with a grin and a wave he was gone.

"Of all the rude, pushy, overbearing…"

"I like rude and overbearing men." Bridget giggled from the doorway. "Especially if they're also tall, dark and handsome." She eyed the flush on Melanie's cheeks and the agitated motion of her hands. "Give in, my dear, and admit you're head over heels in love with the guy."

"I am not," Melanie muttered, snatching the schedules from Bridget's hand. When the older woman simply smiled, Melanie glared. "Don't you have anything to do?"

Bridget shrugged.

"Grumpy and out of sorts. Refuses to admit the truth. Yep, you're in deep, Melanie, my girl." And whistling "Here Comes the Bride," she strolled out of the office.

That afternoon a package arrived for the Director of Care, Sunset Nursing Home. Melanie eyed it warily, suspecting Mitch of some trickery. But the plain, brown-wrapped package looked innocent enough, so she signed for it and tore away the paper. Three CDs were nestled inside the box, all of them wedding music.

Melanie stuffed the items into her purse before anyone saw. The enclosed card with its peremptory edict she filed with the others. The day dragged after that, and Melanie found herself scurrying home, wondering what he was up to.

By seven-thirty it looked as if there might be some respite. She checked through her list three times, organized the bows, bells and other fripperies and generally piddled around until the doorbell rang. It was a delivery man. Or rather, a delivery boy.

"Hi," the young voice greeted her. "I'm to deliver this into your hands." The youngster thrust a large, plain white box into her hands before loping off down the street. Melanie pushed the door closed with her foot as she tried to peer into the box. The thing was huge and weighed a ton, but the box was securely fastened, and she had to set it down on the dining room table before she could free the sides.

She gaped at the contents.

"Oh, my, now he's really done it," she muttered.

A square one-layer wedding cake sat nestled inside covered with a thick white frosting. Misty green tulle curled in soft gathers around the bottom. The cake had a trellis pattern on the sides. On top a tiny bride and groom stood below an arch with the tiny scripted gold letters PJPB on it. Across the top in pale green script were inscribed the words "Melanie and Mitchel."

She let him have it when he came through the door.

"Are you crazy?" she squealed. "You're going around planning a wedding and you don't have a bride! This wedding cake must have cost a fortune. It's custom-made, you know, and they're not cheap." When he kept on smiling, she tried reasoning. "You're going to be very embarrassed when you end up standing at the altar all by yourself."

Mitch studied her seriously while Melanie wondered about the odds in a marriage where only one half of the couple, the bride, for example, was in love. But, in the end, she refused to dwell on it. She prepared to do battle instead.

"I do have somebody to marry," he told her seriously. "And I don't want anybody but you." He looked at the cake. "They've obviously mixed up the orders. I'll call them first thing tomorrow morning. Hope's cake is much more elaborate than this." He picked up on her sigh of relief.

"Don't get any notions about trying to keep this a secret, Melanie," he told her sternly. "I've already asked your administrator if you can have two weeks off after the wedding." He added the kicker with a smirk. "I also told her the reason why."

Melanie studied him with a thoughtful frown. What reason? she wondered curiously. Had she missed something here? Why was everything spinning so wildly out of control?

"Are you going in for a lobotomy?" she demanded irately.

Honestly, if the office people at Sunset knew about this wedding, then not only Sunset but the whole town would soon know. "What reason?" she asked, dazed.

"Our honeymoon, of course," he announced, obviously pleased with himself.

Melanie desperately wished she could have slapped that grin off his smug face. But there didn't seem to be much point. The whole world had apparently been informed of their blissful status. Sighing loudly, she rested her head on her folded arms atop the table, wondering if he would let her sleep through it all. Maybe she would wake up to find it had all been a dream, a very bad dream.

Instead, Mitch tugged her into his arms. He flashed his brilliant smile at her. Perhaps it could work, she considered. Perhaps, one day, Mitch would come to love her.

But then reality intervened and she remembered the PJPB on the cake. He was still thinking about that money! She floated to earth with a thud, to an engagement that wasn't and a wedding that would never be.

"By the way," she asked, "where is this grand occasion supposed to take place? You've done all this planning, and I'm certain you have not forgotten that tiny detail." Her tone was only half joking.

"Uh, actually, I don't have it all arranged yet," he told her, clearing his throat. "Once I get the order in to the florist, I'll look after the place and the time."

Melanie knew he would not tell her until he was ready, so she gave up, wisely deciding to focus her attention elsewhere.

"What kind of flowers are you ordering?" When he stared, Melanie flushed. "Not that I care, since I *will not* be there. I was just curious."

"I know." The big oaf was grinning like a fool. "And you do know what happens to cats that are curious?"

"Yeah," she replied pertly. "They die." She shook the curls off her face and smirked. "They don't get married."

His lip turned down. "That's not nice, Melanie. I'm doing this all for you."

"Then stop." Melanie whooshed out a puff of air in exasperation. "I am not marrying you for money. I'm not even getting married. Period."

Nothing disconcerted Mitch. He sat down with his gargantuan list and began studying brochures. Although she asked questions constantly, Melanie got very little satisfaction from his vague answers.

She knew he was planning a reception, but she didn't know where. She knew he had planned on a honeymoon, but Mitch wouldn't say where they were going. She knew he had chosen someone to give her away, but he refused to tell her who. And on and on.

"Why don't you just plan everything? I'll just show up when you tell me to," she muttered in frustration.

"Exactly what I'm doing," he told her smugly.

Despair filled her as Melanie realized she had fallen into his fantasy trip. She jumped up from the table in frustration, wishing bleakly that her topsy-turvy world would right itself.

"I am not, not, *not* marrying you."

Mitchel Stewart barely glanced up from the funeral wreath he was studying with interest. Melanie shuddered at the glistening black roses entwined with baby's breath. She could only hope he wouldn't go for that! Nobody deserved black roses. Not even for this peculiar marriage.

"I think you're protesting too much." He leered. "I think you like me a lot, too."

"Mitchel Stewart," she snarled. "Sometimes I don't like you at all."

Ignoring his smug grin, she turned away. It was only with the firmest resolve that Melanie got herself away from that room and into Charity's office. He was going to have a rude awakening, she told herself. And it would be all his own fault because he didn't or wouldn't understand that she had absolutely no intention of marrying him.

Half an hour later his knuckles rapped on the door just before his head peered round the corner.

"I'm starving." He grinned. "Want to go out for supper?"

Melanie shrugged. Why not? It would be nice to get out of the house and away from all these stupid wedding plans, she decided. Besides, there were a few things that needed to be discussed about the real wedding tomorrow.

"Okay. Where?"

"Why don't we go out for dinner and dancing," he asked her softly. His blue eyes shone in the dimmed light. "We'll celebrate." With a wink, he disappeared, leaving her to stare after his retreating figure.

"Oh, no, you don't," she muttered. "You can buy me dinner and dance with me, but that's all that is going to happen here. I'm not getting involved any deeper in this hallucination of yours. Just keep a level head, my girl," she told herself over and over. "And watch out for those lips."

She needed this break, Melanie told herself later, studying her new aqua outfit. An evening of fun dressed to the nines was just the thing to take her mind off that elaborate overdone wedding cake sitting on her mother's dining room table.

Mitch whistled when he saw her, his eyes moving from the tousled curls on top of her head to the slim, straight lines of her dinner dress.

"You look very, er, nice," he stammered, his eyes slipping over the shimmery silk as it hugged every curve.

"Thank you." Melanie giggled, enjoying the rise of red in his face. "What kind of dancing do you like?"

"Close ones!" His comeback was quick, and he drew her into his arms. "Ones where I can hold my partner and do this." He brushed his mouth over her cheek, stopping just short of kissing her.

Melanie moved back slowly. She wanted to remember tonight, savor it for all the dull, lifeless future days without him. Tonight would be the last time she had anything to do with him, she decided. She was determined to put an end to this foolish dream of his if she had to camp out at the nursing home to do it. The whole thing had already gone far enough.

"Ready?" he whispered in her ear, and Melanie nodded.

"Lead on, MacDuff."

Where he led her was to the restaurant they'd visited the night Sara had appeared. A pianist was again the featured artist. The decor was slightly different if still rigidly formal and very posh, but good old Kramer was there, waiting to take their order.

"Welcome back, Mr. Stewart, Miss Stewart," he murmured softly. His stern face creased into a smile. "Are we celebrating tonight?"

"No."

"Yes," Mitch overrode her. "Miss Stewart and I are getting married soon. We're here to escape all the madness for a few short hours."

"Congratulations." Kramer bowed. "Champagne?" He said it with a French accent that made it sound exotic, and Melanie fell into a daydream about Paris and young lovers, which only reminded her of her current predicament.

"You shouldn't have told him we're getting married, Mitch. This is getting way out of hand."

Mitch grinned, holding up his crossed fingers. "Oh, ye of little faith," he murmured. "Relax, Melanie. That's what tonight is all about, relaxing and enjoying the calm before the storm. And don't make any mistake—we are getting married."

Melanie peered at him, trying to read the dark flashes in

his expressive eyes. Calm before the storm? Was she missing something here? If that's how he regarded marriage, why was he so determined to go through with it?

Kramer ended up bringing a lovely nonalcoholic champagne that was every bit as delightful as the real thing. Melanie sipped it, enjoying the tickles of the bubbles against her nose.

"I'm having a steak," Mitch told her, eyes wide with innocence. "I have a feeling I'm going to need all the energy I can get tonight."

She frowned. "For what?"

He winked, and it only added to the worry that was settling around her. He was up to something. And that wasn't good!

"For whatever comes along. Like dancing," he added, obviously noting the suspicion crossing her brow.

"Oh, right. Dancing." She stared at the menu while her pulse drilled. "I guess I'll have the pheasant," she decided at last. "And those potatoes I had last time," she added, glancing at Kramer. "They were excellent."

"Oui, madame."

"Oh, she's not madame yet, but she soon will be!"

Melanie pursed her lips at Mitch's boisterous voice but refused to take the bait.

The salads arrived almost immediately, and they munched away in silence. To her surprise, Melanie found she was hungry. Kramer kept filling their glasses with the bubbly concoction, and Melanie was glad it wasn't alcoholic. She would be under the table by now, she considered, recognizing the signs of nervousness as she took yet another sip.

As usual, the meal was exquisitely prepared. They ate silently, enjoying the Chopin flowing from the nearby baby grand. The evocative notes made her introspective, and she drifted off into a dreamworld where everything was wonderful. Slowly the music changed, flowing into a slow, dreamy number that released all kinds of wonderful thoughts in her brain.

"Come on, let's dance." Mitch's deep voice was suddenly behind her. She turned to find him holding her chair.

"Oh, thanks for asking," she muttered as he escorted her to the floor. "Don't mind if I do." She glowered at him. "Do you ever ask before you steamroll everyone into doing your will?"

"Sometimes. But only when I know I'll get the answer I want. Tonight you're cranky, and I wasn't sure."

He sounded funny, Melanie decided. Like he was choking or something. She pulled her head from his comfortable black shoulder and squinted into his face. It looked like the face of a smugly satisfied male, she concluded.

"Well, you should try it more often. Asking, I mean."

With a whirl, Mitch steered her onto the patio. The brick terrace was surrounded by flowers that gave a soft, welcoming perfume to the chilly night air. She wondered absently how they kept the blooms from freezing during these autumn nights.

"I'm glad you feel that way," he was saying. "Because I wanted to ask you something quite important."

She waited timeless moments for him to continue until the fear and nervousness in her unruly stomach could not be quashed any longer.

"Well, ask then," she ordered peremptorily, fed up with all this silly suspense.

Melanie's eyes grew huge with astonishment when Mitch pulled the brilliant diamond solitaire that sat perched on a wide gold band from his shirt pocket. She stared at it stupidly, watching the light reflect off its many facets. He pushed the golden circlet onto her finger. It was a perfect fit.

"I really am very fond of you, Melanie. And I want to marry you. Will you please say you'll be there, ready to walk

down the aisle? If you don't, I'm going to be terribly embarrassed."

That hangdog expression was the pièce de résistance, she
decided. He looked so woebegone that she stifled her hys-
terics and tried to speak rationally.

"I've told you, Mitch. I don't want to be married just so
I can collect twenty-five thousand dollars." *Please say that's
not why,* she begged silently. *Please tell me you love me.*

"What if it were the full fifty thousand?"

Melanie yanked her hand out of his, pulled off his lovely
ring and thrust it into his hand. She hurried into the restaurant, her heart breaking. Moving swiftly, she gathered her
handbag, picked up her stole and swept outside. Mitch
followed minutes later.

"Melanie? Where are you going?"

"I'm going home. Either you can take me or I'll get a cab,"
she said sadly. "But whichever way it turns out, I am not,
repeat *not* marrying you. Not even if it involves a hundred
thousand dollars. I am not marrying anyone for money."

Fortunately, a car pulled up to the entrance just then and
Melanie's friend Jeff came loping down the stairs to accept
the key from the valet. She hurried across the damp
pavement, calling his name. "I need a ride, Jeff. Can I tag
along?"

"Mellie? What are you doing here?" Jeff stared at her.

"I'll take you home, Melanie. You don't have to go with
him." Mitch sounded frustrated, but Melanie ignored the
plaintive tones, rounding on him fiercely as she swallowed
her pain. She couldn't deal with this. Not now.

"You're right, for once, Mitchel Stewart. I don't have to
do anything. Including marry you. And I am not going to!"
Whirling, Melanie flung herself into the front seat of Jeff's
car, oblivious to everything but the need to get out of
there. Now!

But as Jeff drove her home Melanie didn't feel victorious or smug. What she felt was a sharp, stabbing pain in the middle of her heart. She was alone. Again.

One little four-letter word was all it would have taken, she thought. *Just one tiny word. And he couldn't say it.*

At home she avoided the fearsome threesome in the living room and scurried up to bed. But she lay for a long time before her eyes closed, and when they did, all she could dream of was Mitch and the things that would never be.

Chapter Twelve

"He's besotted with her." Faith giggled enthusiastically. "I've seen him watching her, and I'm positive Mitch loves our Melanie every bit as much as she loves him."

"That may be," Charity muttered, fastening Hope's beautiful pale peach dress with difficulty. "But she hasn't told him, and if I know my daughter, she probably hasn't even admitted it to herself. And I'm positive that he certainly hasn't told her any such thing."

"I'm so happy myself, I can hardly imagine anyone being sad." Hope smiled sympathetically. "I just wish there was something I could do."

"You can pray, dear. We all can. The Lord will make a way through this mess. He is in control."

"Faith's right," Charity murmured. "And this is your special day. Don't let anything or anyone spoil it for you, Hope. Not when you've waited so long."

There was a pounding on the door, which sent all three ladies scurrying.

"Who is it?" Charity called out just before Faith opened the door. They all gaped at Mitch's grim countenance and Melanie's white face as they stood together in the doorway.

"Uh, I'm sorry to bother you, Hope. Really, I wish this could wait, but it can't. I have to talk to you right now." Mitch's voice was low and husky.

Charity advanced like a mother hen protecting her chick, but Melanie forestalled her. "Leave them, Mother. This has to be said."

Mitch led Hope to a seat and knelt in front of her.

"I'm so sorry to do this, Hope," he murmured, holding her small, fine-boned hand between his brown paws. "I've had a private investigator checking into Papa John. He assured me a week ago that Papa John and Jean LeClerc were two different men, but today I received a phone call that seems to prove the two are one and the same."

Hope's face grew white and still. Faith scurried up to support her with a comforting arm around the shoulders while Charity rushed to get a glass of water.

"But I thought that wasn't possible," Hope whispered. "I understood there were records or something that totally disproved that hypothesis?" She stared at Mitch in confusion.

"So did I," Mitch murmured. His eyes were dark with sympathy, and Melanie was glad he was there to help her deal with it. "But Clarence just phoned me with information about fingerprints. Apparently an old set was found from long ago, in France, and they match Papa John's."

"And John?" she asked quietly. "What does he say?"

"He says he's very sorry," John murmured from just outside the door. His white head was bowed, his eyes full of sadness. "I would explain it if I could, Miss Langford, but I simply don't remember. Not you, not our plans, not the war. I have only confused fragments of the time in hospital, a date and the name John."

Hope stood, a slim, delicate figure in the bright afternoon sunlight.

"And Harry," she murmured in confusion.

"I'm right here, Hope." Harry Conroy moved forward to enclose her in a hug that crushed her dress and made Charity frown.

"All these men in the bride's room." She fussed, straightening a pillow with a surfeit of energy. "It's just not fitting."

Harry pressed Hope onto a nearby sofa and sat down beside her, gathering her hands in his.

"My darling Hope, I'm still here. I always will be. If you want to call this shindig off and think about things, we can do that. I know it will take a while to assimilate everything."

"You're so dear, Harry," Hope whispered, cupping his cheeks in her palms. "Such a dear, wonderful friend when I've caused you so much…"

"Happiness," Harry finished for her. "Nothing has changed, my dear. I still love you as much as I always have. All I want is for you to be happy and content. If it means that you have to talk to this fellow, think things over, then that's what we'll do."

Melanie watched as a thousand different emotions flitted across Hope's face. Hope glanced from John to Harry and then back to John as if she couldn't quite grasp this latest development. Then she moved forward to grasp John's arm.

"I'm so glad you're alive," she whispered. "So glad. If only I'd known sooner…" Her voice died away. Harry stood, walked to the door and silently pulled it open.

"Where are you going, Harry?" Hope asked, her voice stronger.

"You'll need some time to discuss this, absorb what it means to you. I'll just go to the church and tell everyone to go home." The judge's tones were quiet.

Charity gasped in surprise while Faith issued a wail of dismay. But Hope stared at her fiancé.

"Are you backing out on me, Harry Conroy?" she demanded.

"No, of course not, but—"

"Yes, you are," she told him severely. Then her face creased in a smile. "That's an awful thing to do to a woman who's waited until her late fifties to get married," she teased. "And I'm not letting you get away with it." Hope held up her ringed finger in front of his face and spoke in a sure, steady voice.

"I loved Jean once, Harry. And when he never came back, I locked my feelings away and decided that love wouldn't be a part of my life. I thought that if I were stoic enough, God would give him back." She shook her head.

"But after Anna died, and you and I got involved in the seniors' center and the choir at church, I realized that Jean had left my heart. Yes, I remembered him fondly, but I wanted something real, someone alive in my life. And finally—" she kissed his cheek "—finally I realized that I loved you."

Harry's face was a beaming circle of happiness as he hugged Hope.

"I'm not waiting any longer, Harry. It's now or never for me."

"Then it's now," Harry boomed, and led her from the room.

Those in the room heard two voices whispering outside, then Hope scurried into the room to stop in front of Papa John.

"I'm very glad that you're safe and alive and have gone on with your life," she told him sincerely. "And while things might have been different, God has led me down a new path." She stood on her tip toes to kiss his cheek.

"Be happy, Jean. Make your life as full and rich as you can. And don't worry about me. I'm going to be very happy." And smiling through her tears, she glanced around the room at her friends.

"Are you going to miss my wedding, girls?" she chided, giggling like a schoolgirl.

Charity bustled forward and scooted the men from the room.

"No, we're not," she said firmly. "But everything must be done decently and in order. Mitch, you get your grandfather to the church right away."

It was Faith who led Papa John from the room. Melanie tried to listen in on their conversation but all she heard was Faith's quiet voice inviting the elderly man to the festivities.

"And bring your lady friend," she encouraged brightly. "Hope will be glad to know you have someone special in your life, too."

Melanie drove to the church and checked the pew bows, the flower arrangements and the bridal bouquet, but she couldn't help repeatedly seeking out Mitch's tall, dark-suited frame.

"It seems that everyone has someone special in their lives," she murmured to herself as the organ music started and her mother led the procession down the aisle leaning heavily on Frank Bellows's muscular arm.

"Everyone, that is, except me."

Life should have settled down in Mossbank, back to its usual boring routine of work, eat and sleep, but Melanie couldn't truthfully say that she got much of the latter. Not since Mitch had cornered her after the reception, saying it was urgent that he talk to her.

"I have something extremely important to say to you," he said.

But his important business had to take second place. A telephone call demanded her immediate attention at the nursing home, and not wanting to spoil the festivities, Melanie kissed Mr. and Mrs. Harry Conroy, gave them her best wishes and hurried away, Mitch trailing behind.

"Why is it that whenever I want to talk to you, you take off?" he demanded, grabbing her by the arm. "What's so important this time?"

"Sunset's on fire," she told him grimly. "I've got to go." When he insisted on coming, Melanie didn't argue. She couldn't seem to find her car keys, and he was as efficient as she might have wished for.

Melanie was doubly glad he had come when she saw the red flames licking up the south wing. And he was a bulwark of strength, propping up her shaky body when she saw the damage.

"It's okay," he muttered, brushing his hands over her hair gently. "Everyone got out, the fireman says. They have it almost under control."

Melanie stared past him unseeingly, her mind fixed on the blackened, ragged edges of Sunset and on her residents. As each of the clients came to mind, Melanie finally broke free of the stupor holding her inactive.

"I've got to see them," she whispered, hurrying toward the wing of the hospital nearest the home. "Please God, let them be okay."

"He'll have them safe, honey. Don't worry."

Mitch was right behind her, and he stayed close as they worked to organize the residents, calming and settling as they went. Nettie Rivers was white and pinched with fear as she sat clutching the cat she spoke to constantly.

As Melanie watched, Mitch coaxed the elderly woman out of her chair and to her room, tucking the covers around her carefully after she had swallowed her medication.

"Please stay with me until John comes," the old woman whispered in a thready voice. Mitch sank onto the chair beside her bed, still holding the blue-veined hand. "Someone phoned him, and he promised he'd be right here."

"I'm not going anywhere, Mrs. Rivers." Mitch patted her

shoulder reassuringly. "I'll sit with you until Papa John comes. After all, you are my biggest client."

Melanie frowned as Nettie patted Mitch's shadowed cheek. Client? What was that about, anyway?

"You're such a dear boy," she told him. "The most suitable mate for our Melanie. I know you don't think I should have done it, but I was so sure that you two would be the perfect foil for each other. All of us did."

"None of that matters now, Nettie," Mitch murmured, helping her to lie back. He tossed a sideways look at Melanie and shrugged. "Just rest."

The paper-thin lids closed as Nettie breathed out a sigh.

"Melanie needs a man who will challenge her," she whispered. "Someone who's not afraid to dare her to take a chance. She's buried herself here for so long, seeing to our needs. I just knew God would send someone very special. If only…" The words died away as Nettie drew a deep breath and slept. Melanie stared at Mitch.

"What was all that about?" she demanded softly. "You'd think she had some hand in our meeting." His skin flushed a deep pink. "Never mind," she murmured. "I've got to go check on the rest. This sure would be a good time for Papa John to hand over that money."

The pained look on Mitch's face drew her immediate suspicions. "What now?"

"That's what I was trying to tell you earlier, Melanie. I have notified him and his company that we have no further interest in them or their prize money."

"What?" Too late Melanie remembered to keep her voice down, but Nettie seemed undisturbed. "Why in the world did you do that?" she asked angrily.

"Because you said you thought I only wanted to marry you because of the money," he told her softly. "I was trying to prove to you that it simply isn't true." Mitch's deep blue eyes blazed with something Melanie couldn't or wouldn't define.

"I don't have time to deal with this right now," she told him furiously. "I'm in the middle of a crisis here."

"I know. We can talk about it later. I've got some more ideas for the wedding, anyway." He smiled that heart-stopping grin that shook her to the core.

"We are *not* getting married," she enunciated clearly, whirling from the room. "And you have just made doubly certain of that by ending what little chance I had to improve Sunset. Now if you don't mind, I'd like to get on with my job."

And so she did. She worked steadily using a matron's office to phone families and friends of those who had been displaced by the fire. Miraculously, there were only a few.

When Melanie and the fire chief toured the building, it seemed that most of the home was undamaged. Smoke and water had rendered the southern end unusable. This was the area Melanie had been trying to convince the board to replace. The task of erecting temporary walls was made much easier.

Her staff had handled the situation with the quick-thinking aplomb of troupers, and Melanie made it a point to congratulate them on their speedy solutions. Doggedly, Melanie continued on, refusing to give in to the ache of tiredness that edged its tentacles toward her body. There was too much to do. Besides, she didn't want to think about what might have been.

By seven in the morning the seniors had all returned safely to their rooms. Tired and discouraged, many had agreed to go to bed and rest a little, while a stalwart few demanded breakfast.

Melanie sighed as she pushed the heavy fall of hair off her face and took a deep breath. She sank into her plush chair with a sigh as Bridget carried in a tray of coffee and toast.

"You had better sit and eat this before you fall down," the older woman chided her. Bright gray eyes studied her thoughtfully. "You can't do it all yourself, Melanie. We can manage. Faith and Charity are coming over, and they'll give us a hand settling everyone down. Go home. Get some rest. Then you can pitch in again when you're feeling better."

"You know, Bridget," Melanie said with a sigh, leaning her head back thankfully, "this is one time when I'll welcome the fearsome threesome's presence. Even if they are minus one." She grinned. "They'll be a ray of sunshine here."

"Yes, they will," Mitch said quietly from the doorway. "Come on, I'm taking you home."

"I have a lot to do," Melanie said tiredly, not wanting to face him and his pressure tactics. "I should probably—"

"Come with me." He grinned, tugging her from the chair. "That's what I said, and I meant it."

"And I agree with him," her mother said from the doorway.

"We both do," Faith added, grinning from ear to ear as she set a bouquet of flowers on Melanie's desk. "And these are from Hope and Harry. They'll be back in a few days to help, but they send their love and thanks."

"Oh." It was the only thing she could think of with everyone standing there staring at her.

"Now do I have to get the wheelchair?" Mitch teased, with a glint in his eye as he rolled up his dingy, smoke-crusted sleeves. "Or are you going to come willingly?"

"Yes, I'll go," Melanie acquiesced at last, yawning widely. "I could use a few hours' sleep."

Mitch ushered her down the hall and out the door, steering her away from Nettie Rivers and her companion, Papa John.

"It's going to be more than a couple of hours," Mitch ordered in a no-nonsense tone. "And when you wake up, after you've showered and eaten, you and I are going to talk.

Without interruption." He stared at her soberly. "I have something to say to you, Melanie, and I have no intention of letting this go on any longer."

He wheeled his sports car in front of her mother's house, helped her out and ushered her inside without pausing.

"Where did you get a key?" Melanie demanded crossly. "I suppose you've wrapped my mother around your finger just like you've done with Nettie."

"Your mother and I had a...discussion," he murmured. "And she is perfectly satisfied with my intentions. So is Nettie."

"Your—" Melanie yawned "—intentions?" She stared at him, bleary-eyed. "You didn't start that marriage nonsense again, did you?" She saw his lips curve, but Mitch merely steered her toward the stairs and gave a slight push.

"Go to sleep, honey. We'll talk later."

She stepped slowly, heavily, up the carpeted stairs.

"I wish you'd stop saying that," she mumbled, tiredness tugging on every limb. "We both know it isn't true." She thought she heard him say something, but couldn't be bothered to do more than undo her once pretty party dress and crawl between the sheets.

"Please help me, Father," she whispered. "I'm so terribly confused."

Seconds later her eyes flopped closed as her body relaxed and images of a tall, dark-haired groom whirled through her unconscious mind.

Mitchel Edward Stewart was scared spitless. He'd rehearsed the lines over at least seven hundred times in his head, and still nothing sounded just right.

"I want to marry you, Melanie Stewart." No, he'd already said that. And a fat lot of good it had done him, too.

"You wouldn't have to change your name." Too frivolous.

"Why don't you just admit you love me?"

Ha! Good question. And if she came back with the same one, he was in deep trouble. By the time his grandfather and Hope stopped by, glowing with happiness, Mitch's palms were itchy with sweat.

"Just on our way to Sunset, boy. Hope and I want to check on things there. Might be able to help out." His grandfather frowned, noting the lines of tiredness creasing his grandson's handsome face. "Something wrong, son?"

"No. I'm just a bit worn out from the fire and things." Mitch stared at them both. "Wasn't Paris supposed to be in your plans somewhere?" he asked grimly.

"Still is. There's just a few things around here need straightening up," Gramps muttered with a sly look at Hope.

"Yes, Harry had one or two things that just couldn't wait," she murmured in agreement. Her fingers flipped a stray lock of hair off his forehead. "You do look worn to a frazzle, Mitch."

"Reckon you'll feel better once you get your hands on half that money." Judge Conroy chortled. "I should think twenty-five thousand dollars would put a smile on that face."

"I'm not getting the money, Gramps. Neither is Melanie." Mitch hated saying those awful words. He knew how much she'd wanted her half of the prize to buy equipment for her friends. Now, because of him, she would never get it.

"But I thought—" The judge's booming voice was interrupted by his wife's softer but firmer one. Mitch had to smile at the meek look on Harry's face.

"This isn't the time, Harry. Look at him. He's dead on his feet." Hope whirled around and glared at her new husband. "He's tired out and needs to be left alone."

"Yes, dear," Harry agreed, patting her hand gently.

Hope lifted Mitch's unshaven chin until her faint blue eyes met his darker ones.

"You go to your grandfather's, Mitch. There's no one there, and you'll be able to rest. Your grandfather and I will stay here and make sure Melanie isn't disturbed."

"No." Mitch shook his tired head, his hair flopping forward onto his face. "Thanks, anyway, Hope. But I have to be here when Melanie wakes up. I need to talk to her."

Mitch studied the two of them for a time, wondering how much he should say. But he was tired of carrying this burden around by himself for so long. What would it hurt to share it with these two? It wasn't as if they could do anything about it. He'd have to settle that himself.

"You see, Papa John actually did agree to give us the money. But only if we get married."

"What? I didn't know that." Hope frowned. "Why must you get married?"

"He says it has something to do with his company's image and moral standards. Besides, we don't have a leg to stand on. I think Nettie Rivers entered my name in their stupid contest. And I took possession too late for qualifying." He shook his head tiredly. "It's all rather complicated and confusing, but the bottom line is we have to get married to get the money, and Melanie blames me for the whole fiasco." He grimaced.

"I wanted her to get that money. She has so many plans for those residents, and I knew how much it meant to her. I figured if I helped her out everybody would benefit. I'd get twenty-five grand myself, she would get her bed alarms and new sheets and stuff, and everybody would be happy."

"That was a perfectly generous thing to do." His grandfather nodded benignly. "I knew he'd turn out all right," Harry muttered to Hope. "And I was right."

"You see, when things started getting complicated, I did tell her she might have a better chance if she moved into my apartment. I thought I was helping her." Mitch sighed. "And now that's the stumbling stone. 'Living in sin,' he called it, and now Melanie thinks I've ruined her reputation completely, even though I offered to get married."

The newlyweds stood staring at him as if he'd grown purple horns from his ears, and Mitch couldn't blame them. The whole crazy thing sounded ridiculous, especially the way he'd just phrased it. He wasn't even sure Melanie had entered that crazy contest, either. What was it Papa John had said? Something about the handwriting? When you added that up with Nettie Rivers's strange comments, well…

"It's not just the money, though, is it, Mitch? There's something more to your proposal now, am I right?" Hope's face was a study in thought, but her eyes were bright and curious as she waited for Mitch to return to reality. At his nod, she smiled. It transformed her stern face.

"I thought so," she burst out, hugging him tightly. "I've wondered for weeks when you'd finally admit it. You're in love with Melanie, aren't you?"

"What?" Harry stared at both of them as if they'd lost their minds. "In love? Mitch? He's not in love. Doesn't believe in it."

"Honey?" Hope's voice was quiet. But there was a thread of compelling determination in it. Harry stopped speaking and stared at her. "I'm not finished."

"But you said…" Harry took a second look at his new wife's face and then swiveled to stare at Mitch. Finally he sank into the nearest armchair, shaking his head in amazement. "I never thought I'd see the day," he mumbled.

Hope ignored him and concentrated on Mitch, who could feel her steady gaze penetrating his tiredness.

"You can't talk to her now, Mitch," she murmured at last. "You're far too tired to explain this properly. Go and rest and when you've shaved and showered and eaten something, you can talk to Melanie and get the whole thing straightened out."

It was tempting, and Mitch almost gave in.

"No," he muttered finally. "I should be the one to show her this." He tugged the rumpled letter from his pocket. "It's from the peanut butter company, accepting our notification that we are dropping all claims to their prize money."

"You renounced all your legal rights?" Harry bellowed, starting up in his chair. "Haven't you learned anything, boy?"

Hope whirled, her hands on her hips.

"I'm sorry to have to say this to you, Harry," She spoke firmly. "But it needs to be said. Hush, will you? This is not your courtroom."

Harry's face flushed as Mitch stared at Hope with a glint of admiration.

"But the boy doesn't understand—"

"He understands more than you think." Hope smiled, pressing a kiss on top of the balding head. "Now just hush while I sort this out."

Justice Harry Conroy, Esquire, hushed.

"Now you go to your grandfather's, Mitchel, and you get some rest. The time will come for you to talk to Melanie. But that time isn't right now. She's got a whole lot of work to do to get things on an even keel, and I expect she's running on empty right now." Hope led him out the door and down the steps.

"You rest and relax. If you really want to do something about this situation," she advised firmly, "you start praying. God will provide a way for things to happen according to His will." She opened the car door and stood waiting for him to climb inside.

Instead Mitch wrapped his big arms around that slim, immaculate form and hugged for all he was worth.

"Hope Langford Conroy, I think Gramps knew exactly what he was doing when he married you." He laughed, kissing her smooth, flushed cheek. "You're a martinet, but I mean that in the nicest possible way. Welcome to the family."

"Thank you." She blushed. "Now go and rest. I'll see if I can recruit a few prayer warriors for you, and we'll talk to the Lord about this."

Mitch drove toward his grandfather's old bungalow with a heavy heart. She meant well. And no doubt Faith and Charity would be called in to help out with the heavenly petitions. But Mitch was pretty sure that even the fearsome threesome couldn't work miracles in the iron-hard rock of Melanie Stewart's heart.

"I guess it's all up to You," he prayed tiredly, as his head sank against the crisp cool sheets. "I guess it always was." He turned and stared out the window at the bright, sunny day.

"Please show me the right way," he whispered. "There has to be something I can say, something I can do that will show her how much I love her."

But whatever it was, it eluded him. At last his eyes closed, and he allowed the blanket of sleep to override his aching body and whirling mind.

"Charity, I'm telling you that we have to do something. They've broken things off, and Mitch is desolate. I don't think he's going to keep asking her. Your daughter has rejected that boy once too often." Hope listened to her friend's voice for a long time, nodding and murmuring from time to time, until finally her face cleared and her lips smiled.

"Are you sure this will work?" she demanded finally. "I still want to go on my honeymoon, you know."

Again there was a reply that made her smile.

"All right. I'll handle that. You and Faith go see Nettie. And keep praying. Hard!"

"Hope, dear." Harry came up behind his wife and tapped her on the shoulder. "I was just feeling a bit peckish," he murmured apologetically.

"Harry Conroy," Hope burst out, grasping his lapels, "you

help me with this and I'll buy you the best steak dinner you've ever eaten."

"Done," he agreed, kissing her cheek. "Now, what's up?"

Chapter Thirteen

Melanie rolled over and squinted at the bedside clock. Her room was lit by a few golden rays of sunshine, and while a little breeze blew through the curtains, the room wasn't hot. She wondered what had woken her and realized the phone in the hall was pealing a summons. Rubbing her eyes, Melanie padded out to pick it up, praying there hadn't been another incident at Sunset.

"'Lo," she mumbled, yawning widely.

"Melanie, darling, it's Mother. How are you feeling, dear?"

"Tired. I just woke up."

"That's good, dear. You don't want to sleep too long after these things. Best to get up and get back into the scheme of things."

It was the last thing Melanie wanted to do, but she agreed anyway. "Yes, Mother. I'm far too tired to go anywhere, though. Where are you?"

"I'm with the girls. We're having a little coffee party." Charity's voice changed, lowered to a whisper. "Faith wants to come over and see you, dear. She has something she wants to say."

"Oh, Mom! I'm not fit to receive visitors." Melanie grimaced at her tousled reflection in the hall mirror. "Whatever Faith wants, can't it wait?"

"Why, no, dear," Charity murmured. "I don't think it can." There was a pause and some whispering before she came back on the line. "She'll be over in fifteen minutes. Okay?"

"I suppose," Melanie mumbled ungraciously. "It's not as if I have any choice about it, is it?" But Charity had hung up and Melanie was talking to herself. "It figures," she complained. "That's the first sign."

With a lot of effort and only by resolutely ignoring the bunch of fresh-picked daisies standing on her dresser with a card that carried Mitch's scribbled signature, Melanie managed to shower and dress in fifteen minutes. As she did, snatches of the last evening she'd spent with him returned.

He'd refused the prize money!

The thought shocked her into stillness. Just when she had him figured out, he went and did a silly thing like that, throwing all her preconceived notions out the window.

But why? That was the question. It wasn't because he didn't need the money. Nobody in their right mind refused twenty-five thousand dollars. Of course, if you believed he wasn't in his right mind... No, she wouldn't go there.

Melanie was still puzzling when Faith breezed through the front door, her arms loaded with fresh-baked cinnamon buns.

"Hello, dear." She beamed happily. "I thought perhaps some calories might make you feel better." Quick as a wink, the older woman had made coffee, whisked out two of the steaming, dripping concoctions and set places for them both.

"Oh, Faith." Melanie breathed, closing her eyes as she inhaled the fresh cinnamon scent. "You didn't have to go to all this trouble. I didn't need a lot of fuss. I could have had a piece of toast." She slipped a bit of cream cheese topping into her mouth and smiled. "But this tastes much better."

"Oh, piffle! Of course I wanted to fuss over you," Faith said sternly. Her blue eyes were narrowed. "People want a chance to fuss over you, Melanie. You're always doing something for someone else, and we just want a chance to pay you back."

"I didn't do anything special," Melanie said. "I was just doing my job to make sure everything was settled down after the fire."

"You always do your job. That and more," Faith murmured. "It's almost as if you're afraid to stop and let us love you."

Melanie jerked in her chair as she stared at her mother's dearest friend. There was something different about Faith today. Some strange look in her eye.

"It's not that," Melanie denied softly. "It's just that I feel it's my…" She couldn't express it exactly.

"Your duty," Faith added steadily. "Melanie, do you think that we could love you any more or any less just because of what you do or don't do for people?"

"Of course not!" Melanie burst out, red flags of embarrassment warming her cheeks.

"No, we couldn't, but my dear, you spend so much time going the second mile that you never let anybody minister to you," Faith murmured softly. Her hand affectionately stroked Melanie's loose auburn waves.

"I'm sorry," Melanie said stiffly. "I never realized that I was bothering anyone. Someone should have said something."

"That's not what I'm saying at all, dear," Faith told her firmly. "And I think you know it." She waited, watching carefully for the grudging nod of admission. "We love you, Melanie. All of us. Your mother, Hope, me, your friends at the nursing home, the people you always have time to give an ear to. We all think you're a very special person, and we are very grateful for the many things you've done for us all."

"You don't have to say this," Melanie blustered, feeling insecure and slightly childish, as well. "I'm only doing what I should. 'It is more blessed to give than to receive,'" she quoted staunchly.

"Piffle," Faith exploded, standing. "That is the most misquoted piece of scripture I have ever heard. And it's never referred to by the people who need it most."

"I, uh, don't know what you mean." Melanie frowned, pouring herself another cup of coffee. "What people?"

"Greedy souls who can never see another person's need." Faith's usually sweet voice was harsh. "No." She held up a hand. "Don't get me started on that or I'll get sidetracked and never say what I came to say."

Melanie blinked several times, trying to focus on the conversation.

"What did you come to say?" she urged quietly. Her nerves felt taut, stretched.

"Melanie, do you love Mitchel?" Faith demanded outright.

"I, er, that is, well…" She looked into Faith's green eyes. "I don't know."

"Yes, you do. If you look deep inside yourself, you'll know whether or not Mitch is the man you want to wake up to in the mornings. If the thought of him makes your skin crawl, then you'll know he's not the one."

Melanie blushed at the straightforward words, assessing the older woman with a different perspective.

"He doesn't make my skin crawl," she admitted, looking at her tightly knit fingers. In fact, the thought of kissing Mitch and having him kiss her back made her skin react in an entirely different way altogether, Melanie acknowledged privately.

"No, I suspect he makes your heart beat faster and your breathing quicken whenever he's around, doesn't he?" The older woman nodded wisely. "And when something interesting happens at work, or you hear some special bit of news, you want to share it with him first, don't you?"

Melanie didn't answer. She couldn't. She was busy remembering those special moments for herself.

Faith let her think for several moments before her worn, tired hand with its sparkling gold band slid over Melanie's.

"Why won't you admit that Mitchel Stewart is the one and only man for you?" she demanded quietly.

"Because he's not," Melanie told her, dashing the stream of tears from her eyes. "I've prayed and prayed about it, and whenever I ask for some guidance, another obstacle comes up. God doesn't want me to get married. He wants me to continue with the work I'm doing and be content with my life."

"So now you know the mind of God?" Faith snapped her fingers in disgust.

"But, Faith, it's true. I've prayed and prayed."

"So there were a few problems. So what?" Faith sank into a chair across the table and stared straight into Melanie's eyes until the younger woman was sure Faith could see clear through to her heart.

"Darling Melanie," she began, shaking her head in dismay. "I believe you love Mitch far more than you've even admitted to yourself, but you think you're not worth loving, or some such silly nonsense. You think that you need to earn love when love is freely given, whether you will accept it or not." She smiled sadly. "Let me ask you something, Melanie. What did Mitch have to do to earn a place in your heart? Did he have to invite you to stay in his apartment? Did he have to take you out to dinner so many times or spend a certain amount on flowers?" Faith's voice rose. "Was it important that he be a lawyer and have a good job so he could buy you things or drive you places in that flashy new car? What list did he have to fill to be worthy of your love?"

"I don't have any list of criteria for men," Melanie spluttered, aghast at the thought. "There wasn't anything specific that he did. It's just who he is." She was getting frustrated.

"So it wasn't because he was tall, dark and handsome," Faith offered. "He earned your affection because he was willing to help you get that money?"

"He didn't earn it," Melanie almost yelled. Her chagrin with the deliberately vague woman overflowed. "I fell in love with him just because of who he was."

As soon as the words had left her mouth, Melanie's eyes widened. She clapped a hand over her mouth in dismay but Faith was beaming from ear to ear.

"Exactly." Faith's countenance glowed with satisfaction. "And who do you think put that love in your heart and let it bloom and grow if it wasn't your very own personal God?"

Melanie stared at her.

"Do you know the scripture that tells us to ask God for the desires of our hearts because He wants to give us them more than we know?"

Melanie frowned. "But that's being greedy and concerned about ourselves, isn't it?"

"No, dear. That's admitting that we're human and we like company through our life." Faith closed her eyes and leaned back in her chair. "You know," she reminisced, "I recall the way you used to play, years ago. You were always so intent on playing family. It didn't matter what the other kids wanted, you always returned to your favorite game of a mommy and a daddy and their children." She sat up and grinned.

"I used to think it was because you hadn't had a really good home life and wanted that for yourself. But you know, Melanie, I believe that even then, God was working in you, creating and building on the desire for a family because that's what He intended for you to have. Do you think that

He would ask you to forget about what He's specially planted in you?"

"But I don't know how to be a mother." Melanie grasped at the only straw she could think of. "Or a wife, for that matter. I never had very good role models. Charity's been wonderful, of course, but she had already raised her children when I arrived. She knew what she was doing. I haven't got a clue what to expect. What if I mess up?"

Faith burst out laughing.

"Oh, my darling girl," she gasped. "If you only knew how many phone calls Charity made to us asking if we thought she was being too soft or too strict, if we thought you should be allowed to go out with the Whalen boy or not, if we would pray for you when Charity's husband died and you blamed yourself." She wiped the tears away.

"My dear girl, if you mess up in life, you clean up the mess and move on!" She grinned. "It's time for you to take a break and relax, Melanie. Have a day off. Contemplate your navel."

"I don't know about that," Melanie whispered in a gurgle of tears and laughter. "It sounds hedonistic."

"Maybe a little hedonism is what you need right now." Faith giggled. "Nobody knows the future, Melanie. All we can know is that we can trust in God because He thinks we're worthy of it. After all, He paid the same price for all of us."

"Yes, but this isn't the same thing," Melanie wailed. "Mitch doesn't love me. He keeps insisting on this proposal because he wants the money. I want someone who wants me for myself."

"Proposal?" Faith's birdlike glance lighted on Melanie for a moment while she digested this. "What exactly did he say, dear?"

Groaning at her slip, Melanie gave her a shortened version of Mitch's tactics, ending up with tears rolling down her face. Angrily, she dashed them away.

"He just wants the money," she reiterated. "And he'll do anything to get it. He's rude and pushy and overbearing and bossy and—and—" She stopped to sniff.

"And wonderful and handsome and the man you love more than anything," Faith finished with a smile. "And he doesn't want to marry you for the money. Of that I'm sure."

"Why?" Melanie demanded. "What has he said?"

"To me, nothing. But think, my dear. Think of the childhood he's had and his attitude toward marriage. I don't think money could motivate him that strongly when his old girlfriend with the rich father didn't stop him from finishing school, do you?"

Melanie stared.

"How do you know about…" She stopped and shrugged. Some things were just unexplainable, and the fearsome threesome's knowledge of everyone and their history was one of those things.

"Furthermore, Mitch is a legal eagle. If he intended to marry you simply for the money, I'm sure he would have drawn up a prenuptial agreement that would set you both free without any unnecessary encumbrances." She raked a hand through her white curls, sending them every which way.

"Besides all that, he isn't getting the money, is he? He's told Papa John that neither you nor he will accept it. That's because he wants to start on the fresh, firm foundation of something much stronger than money. Love." She crowed triumphantly.

"And that's another thing," Melanie grumbled. "How can he just up and tell them to stuff their money without talking to me? I wanted that cash."

"I know." Faith nodded. "For Sunset." She studied Melanie. "I wonder," she murmured.

"Faith? Yoohoo!" Melanie waved her hand. "What were you thinking?" she asked when the green eyes finally focused once more.

"Oh, I'm just wondering if you weren't just a little too wrapped up in that money and God needed to get your attention. It's possible, you know, that Mitch wanted that money out of the way so he would know you wanted to marry him for himself and not because you'd get some cash."

Melanie thought about that for a long time, tossing the idea into the air and then discarding it as her own wants and not fact. But then, according to Faith, she didn't know which end was up anymore. And, strangely enough, right now Melanie would have agreed with that assessment!

"In a way, you're right, Faith," she admitted at last. "All this time, and I've really only fooled myself into believing money was the most important thing. And it wasn't." She smiled grimly. "I wanted that money so badly that I forgot to let God handle it. I thought I could force things, get what I wanted my way." Melanie grimaced in remembrance. "I wanted to matter to someone so much that I even thought I could fake living with Mitch if it meant I'd get that money and be the lifesaver for Sunset." She shrugged miserably. "I forgot who's really in charge."

"We all do from time to time, dear," Faith said encouragingly. "Then the Lord has to catch our attention. Now that you're listening again, you can ask Him for more directions."

Melanie sat thinking about those words of wisdom.

"I must go," Faith said, staring at her watch. "Arthur's coming home tonight, and I want to make myself look good." She preened in front of Charity's kitchen mirror. "He likes me in autumn colors, you know." Her voice held the girlish giggle of a young woman meeting her beau. She turned to Melanie and patted her hand.

"Think over what I've said, my dear. Relax, enjoy a day off. Go to the park and take a walk to clear your head while someone else takes over at Sunset." She smiled hugely. "It's time for you to let others enjoy the gift of giving while you learn the fine art of receiving. Open up your heart and let the sunshine in. Ta, ta." And with a whirl and a swish, Faith was off down the steps and into the street, whistling merrily as she skipped along.

"Learn the art of receiving," Melanie repeated. "It makes sense. In a strange, weird kind of way." She cleared the dishes away, wrapped the cinnamon buns in plastic wrap and wiped off the table before grabbing her jacket from the closet.

"Maybe a walk is the best thing," she told herself as she strode down the street. "Maybe I do need to go out and see the world differently. The truth of the matter is," she lectured herself, "I've been trying to *get* for a long time now. I don't need that money. Sunset will manage just fine. The important thing is that I'm doing the job I was put here to do—with whatever God gives me to do it with."

So intent was she on her voyage that Melanie failed to notice the three pairs of interested eyes peering out the sheer curtains at Hope's. Nor did she pay particular attention when a white-bearded gent stopped in front of a house across the street and escorted an elderly woman up the front walk. But the arrival of the couple set off a flurry of activity that Melanie would have done well to pay attention to.

Chapter Fourteen

Melanie tipped her face up and enjoyed the warmth of the sun as it shone down brightly, lighting the trees from above. The dark green leaves were fading and would soon take on their autumnal reds and yellows.

No children played on the sidewalks and streets since school was back in session, and the luxuriant park grass was empty except for a busy squirrel who chattered madly when Melanie passed too near his cache of nuts.

She took a path and followed it around through the underbrush, between the picnic sites and far beyond the playground. On and on she went, across the ball diamonds and past the pond where she sat staring into the still, reflective waters for a long time. Now and then a trout jumped to catch a mosquito, making her glance around the peaceful enclosure again.

But no matter how hard she prayed, how diligently she stormed heaven's doors, Faith's words kept rolling around her brain.

"You love him, Melanie. Give him a chance. Find out if this is a gift to you from God. You'll be sorry if you deny yourself the love of a lifetime because you're too stubborn to give in."

"Okay, Lord," she whispered at last, rising to her feet and studying the bright, clear sky. "You're in charge here. You direct events. I sent him away once and I don't think he'll be back, but that's up to You. I'll do my best to listen for Your direction. And if You give me another chance, I'm grabbing it with both hands."

Peace, calming and steady, flowed through her mind as she walked up the roadway from the lake. It wouldn't be easy, but she would wait until God showed her the next step.

Melanie reached the small grove of evergreens before she saw him. He was unmistakable, even in brand-new, immaculate jeans and a brilliant blue shirt. He was crouched in front of a pit, building a fire.

"That's the most pathetic fire I have ever seen," she told Mitch truthfully, peering in at two fat logs that sat atop a piece of crumpled and barely smoking newspaper. "Weren't you ever a Boy Scout?"

"Melanie!" His face lit up, his eyes a bright blue, only to dim seconds later. "I wasn't sure you'd come."

"Since I didn't know I was coming myself, that would have been difficult to predict," she admitted acerbically. "What are you doing here?"

"But I thought—that is, they said…" His voice drifted away as he stood staring at her. Finally he shrugged. "That doesn't matter, I guess. I want to talk to you, Melanie."

She was nervous and sort of frightened, and her palms were sweaty, but Melanie was determined none of that would deter her from hearing him out.

Still, she needed to do something, so she bent and with a few swift strokes of his ax, built a pile of kindling. Pushing his nonburning creation to one side, she built a fire from a piece of his newspaper, added several tiny wood chips and then coaxed the flames upward with ever larger bits of wood. When it was blazing nicely, she pushed the big log on top, dusted off her hands and stood straight and tall before him.

"Talk about what?" she asked calmly.

"About you and me. Us. The future, Papa John, everything." He frowned. "Are you okay? You look tired."

"Let's just skip the compliments and get to the heart of the matter," she muttered, annoyed. "I understand you told the peanut butter man to stuff his fifty thousand dollars. Fine. It's done. What more is there to say?"

"I had to," he said simply. "It was getting in the way."

"In the way of what?"

If the Lord was directing her down this path, Mitchel Stewart was going to have to spell it out good and clear, Melanie decided. She wasn't taking any more chances.

"In the way of us." He moved to stand in front of her, his face pale in the bright afternoon sun. She noticed that the daredevil look had disappeared from his face. Mitch looked completely serious. And more vulnerable that she'd ever seen him.

"I know I haven't handled this very well. I never explained anything or gave you an acceptable basis for my actions," he admitted softly. "But I had a good reason for it."

"You did?" she asked, gulping when his hands came out to clasp hers.

"Well, I thought it was pretty good at the time," he murmured. "Now, after listening to some good advice on the subject, I guess I was just scared."

He was rambling, babbling about some advice he'd gotten, when all Melanie wanted to hear was the reason he was scared. *Say the words, Mitch,* she ordered subconsciously. *Just say the words.*

"Aren't you going to say anything?" His harsh voice finally penetrated her thoughts.

"Say anything about what?" she asked, blinking in confusion.

Right before her eyes, Mitch's chest puffed out like a bantam rooster's and his face turned several shades of angry, frustrated red.

"I just thought that when a man tells you he's in love with you, you might possibly have something to say," he said in a wounded tone. "Is that asking too much?"

There were several comments she wanted to make, but something in his face, some tiny spark of worry that flickered in his eyes, made her relent.

"No, not at all," Melanie murmured at last, grinning from ear to ear. "The only thing is, I didn't hear you talking about love. Would you mind repeating it? Please," she added as an afterthought.

His grin reappeared, wide and white and full of that bad-boy sparkle that never failed to tug at her heartstrings. He walked slowly to where she was standing and deliberately wrapped his arms around her.

"I said, I love you, Melanie Stewart. More than any money or peanut butter could ever make up for. I love you so much, I want to marry you. That's why I had to get it over with, this whole fiasco with the prize money. The money doesn't mean anything. We can earn our own money. And we'll find some way to get that stuff for Sunset."

He was talking ninety miles an hour and only stopped because Melanie placed her index finger over his lips. He arched one eyebrow.

"What?"

"Do you know you talk too much?" she told him firmly.

"You asked me!" He looked offended. "Besides, I was only explaining." He stopped explaining immediately when Melanie's lips touched his, and he didn't bother to begin again until a long time later.

"I love you, Mitch," she whispered when she could get her mouth free. "I have for a long time. But I didn't want to face it because I thought love like this couldn't possibly be meant for me."

"Why in the world would you think that?" he asked, his lips nipping at her earlobe. "Someone as lovely as you should have been snapped up long ago."

Melanie drew in a deep breath and let out all the worry and fear that had been trapped inside for so long.

"I thought I wasn't good enough," she told him clearly. "I thought God wanted me to continue the way I was going, single and alone, because I wasn't worth loving. That's why I've spent so much time working, I guess, pouring myself into the home and its needs. I was trying to avoid my own desires."

She stared at him, grimacing.

"Then you came along and that windfall of money clouded my judgment. Whenever I prayed for guidance, another problem would come up. I took it to mean that God didn't want us to be together. That I was trying to have something that I didn't deserve, wasn't worthy of."

Mitch set her gently away so he could stare deeply into her eyes.

"You can't earn love, my dearest Melanie. Of all people, I know that the best." He smiled grimly and turned away. "I have to tell you something, Melanie, and you can't stop me until I'm finished. Is it a deal?"

She frowned, worried by the dull gray look in his wonderfully sensitive eyes.

"It's all right," he murmured, brushing a hand over her head gently. "It's nothing for you to worry about. I just need to say it."

"Say it, then," she agreed finally, but her fingers curled around his for comfort.

"You know about my mother from Sara, don't you?" he asked, and watched her nod. Mitch felt the prick of pain he always experienced whenever the subject came up, but he damped it down.

"Okay. Well, suffice it to say that I had a rather awful childhood. My mother couldn't stand up for herself or me, and the alcohol was her escape route." He swallowed hard and continued. "My father used to beat her up and she'd never say a word to us except that he was our father and we should obey him. We owed him that, she said." Mitch frowned. "I didn't owe him anything and I hated him with everything in me. Eventually he got tired of us and moved on and I was glad. My mother drank some more. She was in and out of three marriages in about as many years, and each one was worse than the last."

"Oh, Mitch." Melanie squeezed his hand. "You don't have to tell me all this."

"No interrupting." He grinned crookedly. "Anyway, in all that turmoil, there never seemed to be a place for me to fit in. I tried everything I could think of to earn a little bit of her love, but I never really felt like she cared." He stared at their entwined fingers.

"Even after I went away to school, I'd come home and be the odd man out, trying to fit in where I didn't belong. By then I was cold and cynical and I looked for a fight with everybody. I usually found it with my stepfathers."

He breathed a little easier when Melanie wrapped her arms around his waist and snuggled her head on his shoulder.

"I made up my mind that never, not ever, would I be a soft, easy target like my mother. Nobody was going to hurt me like that. I was pretty sure I could get through life without loving anyone, but underneath the fear wouldn't go away." He smiled grimly.

"I coasted through college and got into law school without any commitments. Until Samantha."

"Mitch, I know about Samantha," she whispered. "You don't have to say it."

He was grateful for that. "Well, anyway, after Samantha dumped me, I was humiliated and ashamed. It was just as usual, I had let myself be conned by love, and in so doing, lost my scholarship, a year at school and my standing at the top of the class. I resolved not to ever get my heart involved again."

He bent and kissed the top of her head.

"And then you came along. Somehow nothing was ever cold or calculated with you around. Here I was just learning about God and His care for me and there you were, insisting you get that money for Sunset." He chuckled at her dismayed look.

"I told myself to keep it cool. I'd help you out, make sure you got that cash, listen to you talk about your seniors, but I wasn't going to get involved." He snorted. "Ha! I was up to my neck in involvement! I had you and Hope in my apartment and an assortment of people coming and going. I watched you with them, Melanie. And envied them."

"Envied them? Why?"

"Because they belonged. You belonged. Even Gramps belonged. But the closer I tried to get to you, the more I realized that I didn't belong. Again. You weren't the type to tolerate my no-commitment rule. You talked about families until I realized that that was what I wanted, too, underneath it all." Mitch's voice was soft. "The thing is—" he hesitated, looking at her "—I don't think I'm a family man, Melanie. I don't know how to be." He stopped speaking, his face drawn and white.

"Do you know what my father said once when he was finished punching the daylights out of my mother?" Melanie shook her head. "He said, 'You hate me, Mitch, but one day you'll be just like me.'" His face was pinched. "I can't let that happen, Melanie. Not ever. I won't."

"Mitch, you're nothing like that! You're you, and you would never do that to a woman or a child." The assurance was heartfelt, and Mitch stared at her, trying to believe.

"But I don't know anything about raising children, how

to be a proper father." He looked utterly shocked when she started laughing. "What's so funny?"

"I said almost exactly the same thing to Faith this afternoon," she admitted. "And thank goodness, she made me see how silly I was being." Melanie wrapped her arms around his neck and pulled his head to hers.

"We'll pray and learn about it together," she told him seriously. "After all, we've got the Creator for a teacher. We'll start with Him as the head of our family."

Mitch was distracted. He wanted to tell her the rest of it, but he also wanted her to keep on kissing him. Still, there was something niggling at his brain.

"Faith?" he asked a moment later. "But she was over at my place. She's the one who suggested I come to the park this afternoon."

"No doubt about it." Melanie grinned. "The fearsome threesome have been busy today. For once, I don't mind their meddling. They've been at me to get married for so long that I'm looking forward to telling them I'm taking their advice. They can be grandmothers for our kids. I'm sure they'll tell us exactly what it is we're doing wrong!" She only stopped speaking because he put his hand over her mouth.

"Melanie," Mitch complained dryly. "Dearest, darling Melanie. I hadn't finished, you know. I haven't even proposed yet, and you're discussing our children!"

"You've said all I want to hear right now, Mitchel Stewart." Bright and teasing green eyes glittered at him. "You love me and I love you and we both love God. That's all we need to start out with." She kissed his chin. "And you did propose, Mitch. Remember? Several times." She grinned teasingly. "I'm just a little delayed in my answer." She reached up and wrapped her arms around his neck.

"Yes, please. I will marry you. Because I love you and trust you and want you for my husband."

There was a large gap in the conversation while Melanie convinced him that she was serious about becoming his wife. Mitch's head was reeling when she finally stepped away. He glanced down bemusedly when her pointed nail tapped him on the chest.

"What?" he asked, noticing the brightness of her eyes and the glow on her face.

"Could I have my beautiful ring back please, dearest fiancé?" she pleaded softly. Her eyes grew wide and anxious when he continued to stare at her. "Mitch?"

"Only if you promise one thing," he told her seriously.

"What's that?" she demanded, sensing he needed to hear her say the words.

"That you promise to love me for as long as I love you and never, ever doubt that love again." He watched her steadily.

"Yes! I remember you once telling me that if and when you got—tied up was your phrase, I believe—you would only consider it under conditions of a very secure lifetime commitment." Melanie chuckled. Her face teased him as she watched him in the deepening gloom.

"And I have no problem with those stipulations, counselor. Where do you want me to sign?" she asked archly.

But Mitch was ready for her shenanigans, and he scooped her up in his arms to settle onto one of the log seats by the fire.

"Right here," he ordered, tipping his head down and pointing to his mouth. "In triplicate."

"No problem. I love you, Mitch."

"I love you, Melanie. Now hurry up and kiss me before your fire goes out and I don't get my dinner."

Melanie stopped to glance at the cooler on the picnic table.

"What's in it?" she demanded warily.

Mitch shook his head. "First things first," he told her.

Between kisses Melanie heard him whisper delightfully teasing words like hot dogs and potato salad and marshmallows. It all sounded divine to her. But nothing was as wonderful as the feel of Mitch's arms holding her tight.

Chapter Fifteen

"I've always dreamed of an autumn wedding," Melanie said, staring at her mother's garden. "Thank you, Lord, for another prayer answered."

The sun shone down warmly as a tiny breeze danced, releasing the last few red and gold leaves. Bright and blue, the sky promised a fine start to her new life together with Mitch.

"Melanie? Come down here." It was her husband-to-be. His face was wreathed in a grin as big as all get out. "I've got something to show you."

"No way. You're not even supposed to be here this morning. It's bad luck." Her mouth tilted as he roared with laughter.

"As if any silly old superstition could keep us apart. Now come on. I've got things to do today, you know. For one thing, I'm supposed to be at a wedding at two."

"Yes, I remember." She got lost thinking about it until he whistled. "I'll be right there," she called, and scurried down the stairs to find the fearsome threesome arguing.

"He shouldn't be here," Hope was saying. "He'll spoil everything. I'm going to have Harry speak to that boy."

"Oh, piffle," Faith argued. "You saw Harry on your

wedding day before the ceremony, Hope, and it hasn't hurt you two any. Leave the children alone." A dreamy look wafted across her face as she noticed Melanie standing on the bottom step, her hair in big fat rollers and covered head to toe in a thick gray terry robe. "Such a beautiful bride." She sighed.

"It must be something important," Charity said, peering out between her lace curtains. "Otherwise why would he have come so early?"

"Relax, all of you," Melanie ordered calmly. "This is my wedding day, and nothing is going to spoil it." She kissed each one lightly and hurried to the door. "Back in five," she called.

Mitch was waiting by the chrysanthemums, and he scooped her up into his arms, kissing her soundly before he set her down.

"I come bearing news." He grinned. From his breast pocket he pulled a small piece of paper.

"What's that?"

"A check, my dear. Made out to Mr. and Mrs. Mitchel Stewart and dated for tomorrow. In the amount of fifty thousand dollars." Mitch waited for her cry of surprise, clearly worried when it didn't come. Instead, she was frowning fiercely. "What's the matter?"

"Not again," she told him firmly, shaking her head. "I'm not going through all that again. I thought you told them to keep it."

"I did!"

"Well, then, send it back. I'm finished with Papa John and his peanut butter money." She watched his face with a tinge of worry. He was up to something. She knew that look. It always spelled trouble. "Mitch? What are you thinking about?"

"How much fifty thousand dollars can buy."

Melanie's heart sank. Then she slapped him on the shoulder.

"That's not funny."

"No," he murmured. "I mean it. Buzzers, bed linens, those mechanical carts. Think of it, Mel. We could get a good start on outfitting Sunset." He stared at her with a question in his glittering blue eyes. "What do you think? Shall we make it out to Sunset and let your board of directors deal with it?"

It took her thirty seconds to decide, and then Melanie flung her arms around his neck and hung on for dear life, hugging him tightly.

"I love you, Mitchel Stewart," she whispered, tears running down her cheeks. From his response, the three onlookers assumed that he loved her, too.

"Now, children," Charity murmured, patting Melanie's shoulder. "You'll have lots of time for this later. Right now we need to get on with your wedding preparations."

Somehow the three of them managed to get Mitch on his way and Melanie upstairs. Shawna and Sara arrived moments later to help Melanie dress in Charity's beautiful silk wedding gown and while they did, the fearsome threesome stood around babbling.

"Melanie, dear," Hope murmured, flicking a nonexistent piece of lint off her dress. "I…that is, er, the three of us want to say something."

"Are we going to tell her about the prize now?" Faith demanded.

"I already know." Melanie grinned. "And everything's wonderful."

"You know about Nettie sending in the contest entry?" Charity frowned. "That she arranged it all from the beginning? That Faith and Hope and I only helped a little at the end?"

"So that's how our names got in there," Melanie exclaimed. "I knew something was odd about the whole thing. I might have known. How did she know Mitch?"

"That's the strange part, dear. She didn't. Hadn't ever met the boy." Charity rubbed her earlobe thoughtfully. "It really was the oddest thing that your phone call went to him."

"With God all things are possible." Faith smiled serenely. "Hadn't we better get you ready for that wedding?"

"My dearest daughter." Charity sighed and hugged her gently. "You look so beautiful, and I'm so very happy to give you to Mitch. He loves you, dear. Never doubt it."

"I won't," Melanie whispered.

"Turn around now, dear," Hope ordered, fastening the last of the tiny buttons down the back. "This rich ivory suits your skin so well. And the fit is fantastic. Faith's done a wonderful job altering it."

"Piffle," Faith blustered proudly. "You can't go wrong when you've got such quality material to work with. Charity bought the best way back then."

The dress left Melanie's shoulders and neck covered only by a film of sheer silk while the strapless bodice lovingly molded Melanie's full curves, dipping out to a billowy tulle skirt below her hips. A short veil fell to shoulder length, held in place by a row of delicate, fragrant lily of the valley.

In her arms she carried a cascade of glowing yellow roses, a gift from Mitch. He'd insisted on choosing the bridal bouquet himself and surprising her.

"I picked out the invitations and the cake," he'd asserted proudly. "I can do this, too." Melanie had finally acquiesced, praying desperately that his taste didn't run to the black roses she'd seen him studying.

There was a tiny card attached to the green ribbons, and Melanie laughed when she read the words. "Marry Me Today!" it ordered. In small letters on the bottom Mitch had printed, "I Love You."

In the deepest recesses of her mind, Melanie knew she would never doubt his love again, but she tucked the card into her dresser drawer to remind her in the future. Then she slipped on the silky blue garter Sara held out.

"Something old, Mother's dress. Something new, my shoes. Something borrowed, my veil. Something blue, the garter." She grinned at her friends. "I guess I'm ready," she told them.

When the limo came to pick the bridal party up, Melanie was eager to go. Shawna and Sara spent a few moments preening before the mirror in billowy sea foam dresses that matched. Sara's children were beautiful in their tiny wedding outfits. Ben wore a minuscule black tux, complete with cummerbund and bow tie that made him certain he was one of the big guys. Becky was the picture of daintiness. The women carried a parasol of golden mums and white daisies, while Ben gingerly held two gold wedding rings on a satin cushion.

"Mitch picked these," Melanie told them proudly when Shawna commented on the flowers. Sara grinned.

"My ex! He is pretty special." She giggled, enjoying Melanie's grin.

The car was full, with Faith and Hope taking turns fussing over her dress while Charity tried to remain calm. When they drove up to the Sunset Retirement Home, Melanie's mouth formed a perfect Oh of astonishment.

"We agreed that we should be married here," she whispered to her mother. "But I never expected this."

Pots of bronze, gold and pale yellow chrysanthemums nestled along the edges of a white carpet, which guided her to the privacy of the courtyard. Through the doors, Melanie could see the rest of the wedding party waiting.

Smiling gently, she kissed her mother's cheek and watched Charity hobble down the aisle on the arm of Sara's husband. When Charity was seated, Sara drifted forward slowly, followed by Shawna. The birds sang happily overhead as a wedding march played softly in the background. Then Melanie urged the children forward, surprised to see them scattering rose petals as they went.

"Thank you, God," she whispered.

As Melanie moved forward, she felt an arm grasp hers. Glancing down, she stared into Nettie Rivers's happy face. The delicate, petite figure was covered in gracefully elegant autumn hues that enhanced her parchment skin as it glowed in the afternoon sun.

"I am going to give you away, my dear," she told Melanie shyly, her white-gloved hands slipping under Melanie's arm. "After all," she whispered, beaming from ear to ear, "it's due to me, and John, that you two are together. With the Lord's help."

There was no time for Melanie to puzzle it out. It was time to go. Slowly, carefully, she walked beside the tiny woman, moving over the white carpet toward Mitch.

He looked elegant and heart-stoppingly handsome in his black tuxedo. Clear and deep, his blue eyes met hers and telegraphed a message that left her blushing. Melanie turned her head to identify an older man standing at Mitch's side. Amazed, she recognized the features of Papa John, who was resplendent in a black suit and white bow tie. Well, he certainly was a best man, she supposed. Today, nothing surprised her.

At the front, Mrs. Rivers placed Melanie's hand in Mitch's and nodded to Judge Conroy, who stood in his official robes waiting to marry them. Then the two seniors moved to the side, to take their place beside Faith, Hope and Charity.

Melanie focused on Mitch. Even through the filmy clouds of her veil she could feel his love shining through. His big hand squeezed hers as they turned toward the minister to repeat their vows before the God they had entrusted their future to.

Oblivious to the crowd of residents watching from the chairs crowding the lawn, unmindful of the beautiful piano solo Sara was playing, Melanie and Mitch focused on each other. They repeated their vows, exchanged rings and smiled all through the hearty congratulations. They were far too busy enjoying the good wishes of their friends to hear Hope whisper to the man at her side.

"Bless you, Jean. That was a wonderful wedding present for them. Thank you for all you've done." She patted Mrs. Rivers's hand with a friendly touch. "I know the two of you will be very happy together."

"God has given me the desire of my heart by giving me John," Mrs. Rivers murmured softly, beaming at the man by her side. "Just as Melanie has hers."

The fearsome threesome turned and stared openly at the tender kiss the handsome bridegroom placed on his pretty new wife's smiling lips.

"That's another success to our credit." Faith giggled, her face wide with satisfaction.

"Yes, it is." Charity beamed with motherly satisfaction as the bride laughingly tossed her bouquet over her shoulder. "An inspiration to us all. Now, about that nurse you mentioned…"

* * * * *

Dear Reader,

Thank you for picking up book two of my
FAITH, HOPE & CHARITY series. I hope you enjoy
Melanie and Mitch's love story. When I was writing
A Hopeful Heart, my husband's father had to move into
a nursing home. Although so much of this proud man's
long-held freedom was lost, he still took great pleasure
in the little things of life: the tart, greenish taste of a
crabapple, the fresh, clean scent of a pine needle and
the childish giggles of his grandchildren. He reminded
me of my grandfather during his stay, years earlier.
Both of them loved to go for a car ride with the sun
beating down through the windshield as they studied
the crops and named them one by one. It was a small
thing, yes, but it gave so much pleasure.

The Bible says that if God only gives us a cup of cold
water, then we are to use that to help another. We have
so much in our lives and so little time, it seems. Will
we regret, in ten, twenty or thirty years, that we didn't
exert that extra effort, go that second mile, take that
extra time to make someone's days on this earth a little
bit better? I believe God has given each of us just one
life to live and that He intends that life to count for
something eternally worthwhile.

My wish for you is a generous life, lived to the max
and brimming with His love.

A HOME, A HEART,
A HUSBAND

Trust in the Lord with all your heart and lean not on your own understanding. In all your ways acknowledge Him and He will make your paths straight.

—*Proverbs* 3:5-6

To Connie,
who persists in following her own path despite
the barriers life and other stubborn people present.
Live long and prosper!

Chapter One

"She's doing it again!" Katy McCarthy whistled.

"Who's doing what?" Her nine-year-old twin sister refused to move her eyes from the computer screen.

"Mom. Getting all gussied up. That's what Grandpa calls it."

"Hmm." Keeley kept her eyes glued to the monitor and refused to be drawn by her sister's ramblings.

"I don't know why anybody would wear such an outfit," Katy muttered, peering through the grate once more. "Dresses are silly."

With a sigh of resignation, Keeley left her computer and knelt on the floor beside her sister to peer through the old-fashioned floor grate into their mother's bedroom below.

"It's that Brian guy again," Keeley whispered knowingly as she watched her mother spritz on a bit of perfume and fluff her hair around her shoulders. "She always dresses fancy whenever she goes out with him. She says she feels special then. They're in love."

Katy jumped to her feet. "Are not," she yelled, her face red with anger. Her hands were clenched on her hips. "He's…old. She wouldn't be in love with somebody that old."

"She is," Keeley assured her with the knowledge that

came from being born eight minutes earlier than her sister. "Our mother is looking for a husband, and Grandma and I think Brian is the one." She flicked her blond curls behind her shoulders just like she'd seen the stars do on TV.

"But he lives in Calgary," Katy protested, moving to sit on the bed. "He wouldn't want to drive this far every day."

"Well, duh!" Keeley grimaced at the dirt Katy had just deposited on her bedspread. "Get your feet off, Katy. You're wrecking my bed!"

Obediently Katy swung her sneakers to the floor, her mouth puffed out as she considered her sister's words. "Well, how could he live here then, Keeley, huh?" she demanded in a superior tone of voice. "Married people live together, in case you didn't know."

She watched Keeley rearrange her "cosmetics" on the little table their grandfather had made for Christmas last year. Katy knew that Keeley was waiting for her to ask the question again. Well, she wasn't going to do it! She'd sit here until her sister answered, and if that wasn't pretty soon, she was going to mess up this bed *really* good.

"I think," Keeley began quietly, twirling a shiny fat curl around one finger. "I think that if they got married, we would all live with Brian."

"In the city?" Katy shrieked, pink gum dropping out of her mouth, which now hung open. "But what about the farm? We can't leave it!" She stared out the window, aghast at this possibility.

"They'll probably sell it," Keeley said. She swallowed the lump in her throat. She didn't want to leave, either, but not for anything would she let Katy see that. Someone had to be the grown-up around here and think of her mother's feelings.

"No!" Katy's wail and stamping feet penetrated to their mother's room below and seconds later Keeley groaned as she heard the warning knock on the wall.

"Now you've done it," she rasped angrily. "And just when Mom is all set to go out, too."

"Girls! I don't want to hear any of that going on tonight. You know that Mrs. Pettigrew has very bad nerves. She simply can't take all the bickering that the two of you indulge in," Maggie McCarthy called as she left her room to climb the stairs to her daughter's room.

Both girls knew their mother had put in a grueling day today, especially when Billy Wolf, their always-dependable farmhand, hadn't shown up for work.

In fact, it had been a hard week. Seeding time was always tough when you lived on a farm. That was partly why Keeley wanted her mother to go out tonight. Maybe then she'd feel better, laugh more. Mom never laughed much anymore. And she never seemed to have time to dress up really pretty, not unless Brian was coming.

"Wow! You look beautiful, Mom." Katy raced over, baseball glove dangling from one hand, to give their mother a hug. "Where are you going?"

"Brian has invited me to dinner and the opera," Maggie told her daughter. "And for once I'm going to accept the invitation. That section by the bay is too wet to work tonight anyway. It needs a little longer to dry."

"What's the op-era?"

Keeley groaned. Katy was always full of questions.

"Singing. There's a story and the singers tell it in music." Maggie brushed the golden tumble of curls off Katy's red face and shook her head at the pink bubble. "Get rid of the gum, Katy. You know it's hard on your braces."

"I hate braces," Katy complained as she tossed the wad into a nearby garbage can. "But I like music. Still, it's a funny name. Sounds like operate." She considered that for a moment and then whirled around. "Hey, maybe I could go with you guys to this op-era?"

"Uh, I don't think so, Katy." Keeley grinned at her mother. "You wouldn't like it. It sounds like screeching and screaming to me. Worse than cows bawling."

"Yes, but *I* might like it." Katy sniffed haughtily.

Keeley felt like bopping her sister on the head. Couldn't the child see that her mother and Brian needed time together? Just then the doorbell rang. That would be Brian, and Keeley knew he hated waiting.

"Go and have a good time, Mom. Just relax and enjoy yourself." Keeley could see the questions forming on Katy's face and decided to get her mother out of there. Quick. Before her sister blew it. "Forget about the farm tonight and enjoy the opera. We'll be fine, won't we, Katy?" She hustled her mother toward the stairs.

"Yes, well, all right. Thank you, dear. Good night, girls." Maggie looked a little puzzled but she paused just long enough to kiss each of them tenderly. "Get to sleep early, will you, Keeley? And you too, Twenty Questions. We've got lots to do tomorrow."

"Aw, Mom. It's Friday night!" Katy groaned.

"We'll go straight to bed, Mom. Don't worry. Just have fun." Keeley motioned for her sister to be quiet as they waited for their mother to leave.

Shaking her head, Maggie finally slipped downstairs to greet her date. Keeley managed to keep Katy quiet until they heard Brian's low voice reply and the sound of the front door closing.

"Come on," Keeley ordered, heaving a sigh of relief. She dragged Katy over to the window and told her to wave as Maggie looked up. At last the couple drove away in Brian's brand-new silver-gray Mercedes and Keeley could relax. Only then did she meet her sister's frown with a smile.

"Maybe he'll propose tonight," Keeley whispered softly. "If they got married, Mom could take it easy for a while. Brian's got lots of money and a nice place in Calgary."

"So what?" Katy yelled, fists clenching by her side. "I don't care what you say—I am not leaving this farm. Ever!" She hiccuped down a sob. "Somehow we've got to come up with a way for us all to stay here." With an angry glare at everything in the frilly pink-and-white bedroom, Katy stomped out and raced across the hall to her own sanctuary, loud sobs punctuating her flight.

Keeley ignored it. She had to. There were important things to focus on right now. Later on, when her twin had calmed down, she'd collect Katy and go to the barn with her. A few minutes among the horses and her sister would listen to reason. They needed to stick together now more than ever if they were going to find a way to make her mother happy.

Of course, staying on the farm *would* be nice, but it wasn't necessary. Not if leaving meant that Mom could smile more often and worry less. She and Katy could manage—they'd have to!

"But, oh God, please don't make us have *him* for our daddy," Keeley prayed. "In fact, we don't even really need a daddy. Maybe you could just get my mom a big strong man who could be our new farmhand? That would be good enough."

Grady O'Toole steered carefully around the series of potholes that littered the gravel road. Two flats on the camper in one afternoon and now a cracked windshield. What next?

"Why did I ask that?" he groaned, slamming on his brakes as he rounded the bend. Big, friendly, black-and-white cows stood placidly here and there, munching on the fresh spring grass.

He tried to shoo them off the road, but evidently the juicy green shoots were just too good to give up because the animals completely ignored both him *and* the truck horn.

A rambling old farmhouse sat shining in the twilight of

the evening. Grady figured that decrepit monstrosity was about a quarter of a mile away and since it looked like his only option, he decided to go for it. Grabbing his jacket and locking the truck, he headed off down the rough road, his snakeskin-booted feet protesting at yet another trek into the unknown.

A little girl answered the door. She was a bit of a thing with ruffled blond hair and the biggest blue eyes Grady had ever seen.

"Is your daddy home?" he asked, smiling even as he wondered who such a dirty kid belonged to. She didn't look unkempt, just as if no one bothered to wash her face lately. Surely she couldn't be alone.

Of course, Grady reminded himself dourly, he was in the boonies. It was likely that no one in this backwoods ever locked their door, and it would be easy to let a kid run free and wild instead of fencing everything in.

"My dad?" She shook her head decisively. "No. He's gone."

"Well, how about your mother?" Grady sincerely hoped the mother was one of those big, capable types who would take five minutes to corral the animals and let him get on his way to the nearest campsite. He was beat.

"Mom's out. On a date with Brian."

Grady jerked backward, staring at the child in stunned amazement. "I beg your pardon?"

"She went on a date," the little girl enunciated. "In Calgary. Someplace where they do lots of singing—really loud singing. Mom had on her special clothes, you know?"

Grady grasped at straws, wondering vaguely if he should have stayed with the cows. "Uh, maybe I—I could talk to someone else at home?" he stammered.

"My sister's home. Yeah, I guess you can talk to her. I have to get her though. She's on the Internet. Again. Keeley!"

The sudden bellow nearly deafened him and Grady stepped backward only to find the little girl's fingers clutching his sleeve.

"Come on," she invited. "Don't let the mosquitoes in. Hey, do you know where mosquitoes go when it rains?" She was studying him seriously.

Grady frowned and then shook his head stupidly. "Sorry."

"I didn't think so," the little girl muttered in disgust. "Nobody knows that one." She sighed heavily. "Wait here. I'll have to go upstairs and get her. When she gets on that computer, Keeley doesn't hear *anything*."

She whirled away and was gone in a flash, leaving Grady standing there wishing he'd taken the four-lane highway back to Calgary instead of rambling down some back road. The whole scene reminded him too much of a future he'd never have, and memories of that loss were the last thing he needed today.

"Did you want to see me?"

He glanced down to find the little girl back in front of him, with a carbon copy standing curiously beside her. So much for the older sister. Grady glanced from one to the other in amazement.

"Boy, you two really look alike. Hi, Keeley, I'm Grady." He held out his hand and engulfed hers in it. "And your name is?"

"Katy," muttered the one who had opened the door. "But how could you tell us apart? No one ever can."

"Really?" Grady said, raising his eyebrows. "It's quite easy, actually. You're not really alike at all."

"Of course we are." Katy frowned. "We're identical twins."

"Yes, of course." He grinned. "But I meant that inside you're different. For instance, Keeley likes computers but you like baseball, right?" Katy stared at him in amazement and Grady smiled. "And I'll bet that Keeley likes blue ribbons in her hair and you don't like any."

"How did you know that?" Keeley asked openmouthed, twirling a blond curl with one finger as she studied him.

"Oh, I just know. Are you two here alone?" He glanced behind them searching for an adult. Surely no one would leave two small children alone at night, in the country.

"Just for a few minutes," Keeley told him solemnly. "Our grandmother is on her way over. Mrs. Pettigrew had to leave. Her husband was hurt on the tractor. Farm accidents take a high toll on those who make their liveli…on people who live on 'em," she told him in a rush, clearly relieved at remembering most of the phrase. "They always say that on TV. Do you like TV, Mr….what was your name?"

"Grady," he reminded her, smiling and holding out one big paw. "Grady Shawn O'Toole, at your service."

"Wow!" Keeley breathed in a sigh, her eyes huge. "I never thought you'd get here so fast."

"Pardon me?" Grady frowned. He'd been on the road for weeks, eating his own cooking and bathing whenever he'd been close to water. No one knew where he was or how to find him, let alone expected him, so just what was going on here?

"You were expecting me?" he asked in a strangled tone.

"It's a miracle," she told him solemnly. "God sure does work fast."

"Uh, nobody sent me," Grady told her, flushing at the intense scrutiny of those big eyes. "Not exactly. I'm just passing through. Or I was." He shook his head, trying to remember what had brought him to the door of this strange house. Oh, yeah.

"There are cows blocking the road over there," he informed her sternly, pointing to the west where his truck and camper sat waiting. "I couldn't get through."

To his amazement, the two little girls merely nodded.

"Walton's," the tomboy said. "They're always having problems." Again the girls looked at each other and shrugged, as if he should have known.

"I'll phone them right away," Keeley told him. Clearly she was the one in charge. "Come on in. You don't have to stand in the porch."

Grady had to admit it was nice to step inside a place where his head didn't bang on the ceiling and he could stretch out on a chair without hitting something on the other side. The trailer was great but it wasn't home. Of course, he didn't have a home anymore, did he?

He scraped his boots on the braided mat, sniffed the scent of fresh-cut lilacs mixed with furniture polish and followed them through to the kitchen.

"Walton's number is busy. Have a seat."

He sank down onto the kitchen chair with relief and took a cookie from each of the blue-eyed sprites hovering on either side of him.

"So how long till your grandparents get here?" he asked, munching on the homemade chocolate-chip cookie. "Where do they live?"

"In Willow Bunch," Keeley told him, grinning. "That's about five miles away. They used to live here when my mom was a little girl. Katy's got Mom's old room."

"Didn't you come here on purpose then?" That was Katy, snapping her suspender to a beat he couldn't hear. "It's kind of far away from everything."

Grady smiled. No kidding, he felt like crowing. Just one short year ago this would have been the back of beyond.

"Actually, I left my truck and camper on that road over there." He jerked his thumb over his shoulder. "Just until the cows decide to move on. Then I can get going."

"Going? Going where?" Keeley asked anxiously. Grady

felt a twinge of discomfort as her clear-eyed glance studied him. "I thought you were looking for work?"

His eyes opened wide and he stared at the two elfin-featured girls. He was prevented from answering by the rush of activity at the door. A tiny woman with bluish tinted hair cut in a fashionable chin-length bob swept through, her arms wide in welcome.

"Hello, darlings! I've come as quickly as I could. There's someone camping on the old Kelsey trail, did you know?" She embraced the girls in a hearty hug and then turned to face him.

Grady shifted to his feet with alacrity, noticing the piercing quality of deep blue eyes that exactly matched those of the girls.

"I'm Kayleen Davis," she told him, firmly squeezing his hand with her tiny fingers. "My, you're tall. Who are you?"

"I'm Grady O'Toole…."

"He's the new handyman, Gran. And he's not camping there. He had to stop because the cows were out again." Keeley kept her hand folded in her grandmother's, as if she expected the older woman to flit away somewhere at any moment.

Mrs. Davis waved them back to their seats and dropped into one herself. "Those Waltons," she muttered, picking up a cookie from the plate and dunking it in the huge glass of milk Katy poured for her. "Thirty years I lived here and never a week went by that somebody didn't have to round up those cows."

"Uh, I'm not really…" Grady gave up trying to break into the fast-paced conversation between the children and their grandparent.

"Mom's gone with Brian, Gran. Again. Keeley says they're gonna get married and then we'll have to sell the farm," Katy accused, tears rolling down her cheeks as she clung to her grandmother's blue-veined hand.

"Well, they are," Keeley began self-righteously. "Mom's working herself to death out here. I heard Mrs. Enns say so at church last Sunday. And Mom's always tired. Mrs. Enns said if we moved to the city, our mother would have all the pretty clothes and fun times that other young women have." Grady hid a smile. She was clearly quoting the conversation verbatim. Grady watched as Mrs. Davis tenderly brushed the tomboy's disheveled curls off her tear-stained face and patted Keeley's rigid shoulder comfortingly.

"Your mother does work hard," she murmured. "Very hard. And she does need a little fun in her life. Now that Grady is here, perhaps she'll have more time to spend with you two." She smiled a warm, endearing smile that stopped Katy's weeping. "Now, then, Mr. O'Toole."

The miniature whirl of energy turned that electric blue gaze on him and Grady straightened self-consciously from his slouching position.

"We rise early around here, but I'm sure you're well used to that being a handyman and all. If you want to drive your rig over by that weeping birch, you can park there and we'll run a cord out to it. Maggie, my daughter, will fill you in on the particulars in the morning." She waved her arm and the children pushed away from the table obediently, brushing her cheek with a kiss.

"Right now, however, my granddaughters need to get their sleep. I know Maggie has a list of chores planned out for them tomorrow. Away you go, girls."

And they did, Grady noticed in surprise. In about twenty seconds, they had pressed smothering kisses on their grandmother's porcelain skin and flown up the stairs.

"Mrs. Davis, I really don't think…"

"No, young man." She smiled. "You probably don't. I've noticed that about a lot of young men these days. But there is no point discussing this any further tonight. It's almost time for the news and I always watch that at ten." She waved her tiny birdlike hands toward the door.

"Away with you now. I'll try the Waltons' again. We'll have those cows moved in a jiffy. Get your rig into position and get yourself bedded down for the night. Maggie will deal with you in the morning."

Shrugging, Grady did exactly as he was told, amused at the way everyone assumed he was here looking for work. Well, it wouldn't hurt to camp here for one night, although he couldn't help thinking that Maggie would probably be less than interested in taking on a hired hand after her evening on the town. He doubted she'd be much of a boss anyway. Too interested in having fun, no doubt.

Which was a good thing, he decided later, lying in his trailer and staring out into the barely dark sky. He wasn't looking for a job anyway. Not now. What he really wanted to do was get back to Calgary and find out what was happening with his company. But of course, that was impossible. He was going to have to do as old Reverend Holden had advised him and wait on God to show him the next step.

"Stand on the promises of God, son," the older gent had advised, his hand firm on Grady's shoulder. "You've had a tough time of it but there is a reason behind it all. You've got to steer a steady course now and concentrate on letting go of the stress. Worry never produces anything but fear."

The advice was sound and Grady had been glad of the past few months and the income that had let him travel where and when he wanted. How many times had he sat beside an isolated brook or mountain stream and reveled in the wonder of God's creation? But lately he'd chafed at the long hours of being alone. Maybe God wanted to use him in this little backwater. Who knew? He'd just have to trust that, sooner or later, the plan would become clear.

"It would sure be nice if it was sooner," he muttered,

grinning to himself. He needed to set his mind on something, to get involved in a project. Was this it?

A little after one-thirty, Grady's wide-open eyes riveted on the expensive gray car as it rolled into the yard. A man got out and moved out around to the other side to escort a slim, light-haired woman in a fitted blue dress to the door. In the yellow glow of the yard light, Grady watched unashamedly as the man tugged the woman into his arms.

She seemed to teeter for a few seconds on ridiculously high heels before falling forward. Grady could see the man's large hands slide down the woman's back and stop at her waist.

Grady grimaced as he watched her press her hands against the man's chest and pull back from the embrace. The guy really must be a creep if he could stand there, in front of the kids' windows, acting like some lovesick teenager.

And what kind of a woman would allow a man to touch her in view of her children? So what if they were asleep? They might wake up. Where was the woman's discretion? He turned on his side in disgust and ignored the pair. It reminded him too much of a past he only wanted to forget and of the woman who had taken everything he had to give and left him with nothing.

This might be a good place to camp out after all. He could check on things in Calgary. There was no point in showing up too soon and tipping his hand. Not when he was this close to getting back what Fiona had so nearly destroyed.

Okay, maybe he'd wait it out and play the part of farmhand. For now.

Chapter Two

"Remember, kiddo? It's supposed to be *heavenly* sunshine," Maggie McCarthy muttered softly to herself as she forced her eyes open in the bright sunlight. She made her bed, hung up her one and only good dress and tiptoed into the kitchen to make a pot of coffee. While it dripped she popped two pieces of bread into the toaster and got out the cream.

Her eyes fell on the note her mother had left taped to the cupboard, and she grimaced as she reread the word *accident*. Kayleen was even now in the spare room upstairs and Maggie rolled her eyes as she envisioned the grilling ahead of her.

Snatching up her toast and coffee, Maggie headed out to sit on the porch and enjoy the cool breeze of the morning. Her favorite willow chair was there, right where it had been ever since her father had given it to her almost eleven years ago on her wedding day.

"What could be better than sipping your coffee on a sunny spring morning with the birds singing in the bushes?" she asked herself, drawing a breath of fresh spring air into her lungs.

A thousand answers popped into her mind, but she ignored them all. She wasn't going to think about seed bills or broken machinery right now. She sure wasn't going to think about the bank and mortgage payments that were due and past due, let alone dwell on her hope for a bumper crop. She wasn't even going to think about Brian's proposal last night. She was just going to enjoy this brand-new day and concentrate on God's promise from Psalms.

"I will bless her with abundant provisions; her poor will I satisfy with food." Maggie closed her eyes, allowing the words to sink in to her brain.

"Good morning."

"Aaagh." Maggie swallowed the burning hot liquid and felt the stinging tears fill her eyes, obscuring the design of gray snakeskin boots standing on the porch in front of her. She let her eyes slide up blue-jean-clad calves and thighs to a wide leather belt. Then, more slowly now, over the wrinkled chambray shirt to the lean craggy good looks of a perfect stranger who stood leaning against her peeling white balustrade.

"Good morning," she croaked, staring.

"I don't suppose you'd be willing to share some of that coffee?" he asked, tilting one eyebrow questioningly. "I forgot to buy some fresh beans yesterday and I'm all out."

"I…I suppose." For the life of her, Maggie couldn't think of a word to say. She watched his dark brown head tilt to one side as he grinned at her mockingly.

"Not a morning person, huh? That's okay. Of course, it might be easier if you quit partying all night and got to bed a little earlier, Mrs. McCarthy."

She sat openmouthed as he breezed into her kitchen, poured himself a coffee and returned, carrying it in her very favorite black whale mug. Nobody used that mug but her, and then only on special occasions. When he folded himself onto the porch swing, Maggie could restrain herself no longer.

"Who are you?" she demanded furiously, glaring at him as he swung his feet up on the railing. Her railing. "And what are you doing on my land?"

"I'm the new handyman. Hired on last night." His warm brown eyes would have melted butter. "I can start anytime now, ma'am. I've been up since five."

"Five? As in a.m.?" She groaned, sinking her head into her hands and letting the heavy curtain of hair obscure her face. "Don't tell me about it. Seven-thirty is quite early enough."

Wait a minute! Handyman, she asked herself, frowning. What handyman? "Who hired you?" she demanded, wishing she could go back to the night before and refuse that last cup of cappuccino Brian had ordered for her. What imp of perversity had made her drink even more coffee?

Of course, she hadn't been able to sleep after *that,* which made getting up more difficult than it usually was, and let's face it, morning was *not* her finest hour. Maybe her mind would clear a little faster with a plain old regular-type coffee fix, she reasoned, swallowing another mouthful and wincing as it burned down her throat.

"Three little ladies who figured you were too busy partying to spend much time running this place." He tapped at a loose spindle with one foot as if for emphasis. "Appears to me they were right."

"Partying?" Maggie gave a derisive hoot of laughter at his description of the previous evening, and then grabbed her aching head as pain shafted through it. "I hardly think you can call the opera 'partying.'" She straightened and took another sip of coffee with the faint hope that it would help her withstand the scrutiny from his melting chocolate eyes.

"Opera? Yeah, right." He sounded like her father, pandering to her irrationality, Maggie fumed.

"Yes," she retorted. "The opera. A Verdi one. I can't

remember which. I do remember that it was long. And it was loud. Very, *very* loud."

"Not an aficionado, then, I take it." His tone was openly mocking.

"I really don't care if you take it or leave it," she muttered angrily.

"But you would like to leave the opera behind?" he questioned. His husky voice was rich with laughter as she shook her head slightly to clear it.

"That and the cappuccinos I drank when I knew I'd already had enough of them," she grated. "My head feels like little lead bullets are pounding into it." She rubbed her thumbs against her forehead. "I can't afford to be sick," she whispered in despair. "There's too much to do."

"Like what?" he asked, leaning forward, elbows on his knees.

Maggie really wished he hadn't done that. For one thing, he was too close. For another, those crinkling brown eyes were right in front of her face and she could see the tiny lines radiating from his eyes and mouth. It wasn't exactly a handsome face, more like rugged looking. Full of personality. His eyes stared back at her with discernment. As if he, too, had seen the rough sides of life, Maggie decided.

Maggie jerked her head back and straightened the slipping line of her housecoat. "Who, exactly, are you?" she demanded huskily, and wished her foolish voice would act its age. "Why are you here looking for work?"

"Why not?" He smiled lazily, sipping his coffee. "This is a pretty place. You certainly need a handyman. I need a job."

"Sure you do," Maggie agreed, glancing across the yard at the shiny black truck and fairly new-looking trailer. "I can see that you haven't got a dime. Must have blown it all on the club cab over there. Or maybe the trailer. Those things don't come cheap. Self-contained, isn't it?"

"You're right," he agreed, brown eyes narrowing assessingly. "I saved up for a long time for that rig. And I've toured it around the southern states for the past few months. It's been a good investment."

Maggie stood up. There was no point in looking a gift horse in the mouth. If he wanted to work, she'd work him. He'd probably leave after the first hour. But that was okay, wasn't it? Then maybe she could get some peace and quiet to decide about Brian, the farm, the twins and her future. Or the lack of it!

"Fine," she told him abruptly, tightening her belt. "You can start with the horses. They need to be let out and their stalls cleaned." She filled him in on the going rate, days off and his job description. "If that's agreeable to you, you can start right away."

He nodded. "It's fine. There's just one thing. I need to take next Friday off. Personal reasons. I'll work Sunday if you want."

Personal reasons, she mused, staring at his implacable face once more. He was hiding something, something important. But what?

"I suppose that's okay, but we don't work Sundays. That's the Lord's day, and we go to church in the morning. The rest of the day is your own. If you need more time, just let me know." Maggie studied his lean body with a frown. "There's a lot to do around here, you know. It won't be easy work." As she turned to move into the house, Maggie barely caught the softly breathed words.

"Maybe if you pitched in," he muttered, "things would get done a little faster around here."

She threw him a frosty look and kept moving, swallowing the short succinct phrases that would have explained exactly how long she had pitched in and how tired she was of being the one responsible for everyone and everything.

Maggie showered and dressed while her mind roved over the newcomer once more. Where had he come from? she asked herself again. No farmhand she had ever known wore snakeskin boots. And his hands were clean and well cared for, as if he'd had more than one manicure in his lifetime.

Hours later Maggie had more questions than answers about one Grady O'Toole. She snuck a look over her shoulder, watching as he patiently showed another knot to Katy. He was good with kids, that's for sure!

And not bad with barns, either. The horses had been curried as if by a professional, and their stables were fresh and clean. He'd repaired two fence posts and moved some bales into the barn. Maggie had also noticed the filled water troughs for the chickens and seed scattered in their yard.

Katy's high-pitched giggles forced Maggie's stare away from Grady and toward the front of the house where Kayleen sat sipping ice tea in the shade. Her mother had a smug look of satisfaction on her face that sent prickles of worry up Maggie's backbone.

"Bother," she muttered, rubbing her grazed knuckles as she tossed the wrench to the ground where it couldn't do any more damage. "Why won't the thing start?"

"Problems?"

She jumped, banging her head on the metal hood as she whirled around to glare at Grady, who stood grinning behind her.

"I wish you wouldn't creep up behind people," she gritted, sucking on her throbbing, grease-stained knuckle. "And yes, you could say there's trouble. I need to finish seeding and this stupid tractor refuses to move."

"Let me look," he said, smiling, edging her aside.

"Why?" Maggie demanded. "Do you know something about farm machinery that I don't?"

He grinned that breathtaking smile that made her knees

weak. "Oh, is that what this is? Farm machinery." He flicked a strand of hair out of her eyes. "I thought it was something off the ark. Like maybe an ossified woolly mammoth." He took another look at the decrepit piece of metal. "Or maybe a dinosaur."

Maggie slapped her hands on her hips, rapidly losing patience with his amused derision. "Which only goes to prove you know nothing, absolutely nothing about farming," she grated. "It isn't that old."

"Listen, lady—" he grinned, bending to pick up the wrench "—I grew up on a farm and I've fixed more machinery than you've ever seen. And nothing—" his brown eyes flicked derisively over the tractor "—nothing was ever this antiquated."

"Well, it's all I can afford right now," she told him defensively, hunching down on the grass to wait as he tinkered. "New tractors are expensive. They don't grow on trees."

"There are all kinds of programs available for farming operations to purchase equipment," Grady informed her softly. He half turned to peer down at her quizzically. "Why don't you apply for one?"

Maggie snorted. Ha! A lot he knew. "Don't think I haven't," she muttered, thumping her sneaker against the ground with force. "I've filled out more forms than I ever want to see again in this lifetime. Even the tax department doesn't have that much information on this place."

"And?" He crooked one eyebrow at her. "Where's the new tractor?"

She hung her head, resting it on her knees as the sun beamed down on them. Maggie hated telling him. Hated saying the words that denigrated her and her family, especially after she'd spent the last five years slaving over this farm.

"We're too debt heavy," she murmured. "I'm carrying some pretty big loans already."

She didn't mention that most of those loans stemmed from her husband's last purchase before his death. If they had a good year, Roger spent every dime. And the last dime he'd spent had been a doozy. All to acquire a piece of land that she didn't want, couldn't sell and hadn't the resources to farm. Inevitably she had ended up digging in deeper and deeper to cover more and more debts.

"If you factor in the transient nature of my staff and the accidents they've had around here lately…" She tilted her mouth down in wry self-mocking. "Well, I suppose no one in their right mind would lend money to this operation. I'm just not a very good risk."

"But surely your parents…"

"They help as much as they can," she told him quietly. "But my dad had triple bypass surgery in February. He's still recovering and in no condition to come back to the farm. Even if the doctors would okay it. Which they won't." She shrugged, glaring at him angrily. "Anyway, this is my job and my problem—not theirs."

He studied her intensely for several long, drawn-out moments before turning away. "We'll just have to pray that this thing works then," he murmured.

"It needs more than prayer," she told him.

"There *is* nothing more than prayer," he answered quietly, and then buried himself under the hood.

Maggie thought about that bit of theological wisdom while Grady worked silently for the next few minutes, grunting as he twisted the wrench several more turns. His hands flew over the engine, touching this and tapping that until everything seemed to meet his approval.

"You broke off some wires," he said, grinning from ear to ear. "I think I've got it. At least for now. Go ahead and try."

Maggie raised her eyebrows, well aware that no two-minute diddling with this engine was going to start it. Shaking her head, she jumped up into the seat anyway and turned the ignition. To her surprise, it coughed wildly for a moment and then caught, sputtering away. Loudly, it was true. But still running.

"I don't believe it." She exhaled, swiping a hand across her cheek to push away the strand of hair that clung. "Bessie's almost purring."

"'You will pray to Him and He will hear you,'" Grady quoted, winking. "You just need a little faith, Mrs. McCarthy."

"Faith. Right." Maggie didn't want to think about faith right now. Faith was the evidence of things hoped for. She wanted to see a little evidence that her faith was working! "Yes, well," she mumbled as she put the machinery into gear and eased up on the clutch, checking once over her shoulder to make sure the seeder was following properly behind, "I'll remember that. You can tackle some of the odd jobs around here. I'm going to do some more seeding," she called. "See you later."

"Yeah, later," Grady muttered, watching as she bounced along in the old metal seat. He rubbed his hands on the oily rag with little success. "Bessie? Whoever would call that hunk of junk a pet name?"

"My daughter would," Kayleen answered, chuckling behind him. He turned to find those intense blue eyes fixed on him. "Maggie is usually able to find joy in the smallest thing. Which is good, I suppose, given that she hasn't had much happiness lately." Her eyes brightened. "I'm just so thankful that you came along, Grady. You picked the best possible time."

"I didn't exactly plan to come out here," Grady muttered, staring down at the tiny woman.

"Of course you didn't." She chuckled again, wrapping her arm in his and leading him toward the house. "But God works in mysterious ways, don't you think?"

"Yes, ma'am, I guess He does," Grady agreed dazedly, wondering if he should blame God for his stupid decision to hang around this run-down, dilapidated place.

"Now, you've just time for a cup of coffee and some of my fresh blueberry pie before you'll need to gas up the truck and drive it out to the field," Kayleen told him briskly. "Maggie will need more seed by then. Nobody's idle when it's seeding time. Come and sit down, boy."

Grady sat, although he couldn't remember the last time someone had called him "boy". Not that it mattered; he rather liked it. Made him feel as if he belonged. He glanced around, wondering suddenly what the twins were up to.

Keeley was busy vacuuming; he could see her pushing the machine back and forth across the worn living room carpet. But Katy wasn't anywhere nearby.

"You'll be needing to take the old three-quarter-ton out to Maggie," Mrs. Davis informed him, one finger tapping against her chin as she considered that. "It's already loaded, I think. Probably yesterday. Katy'll go with you and show the way. I'll send a bite along for Maggie. And her sun hat." She shook her now-silver head. "She won't stop till the field's done. Not if she can help it. And she'll be burned to a crisp by noon. She has the fairest skin of all my children."

Grady politely inquired after the rest of the family and learned that the Davis family had four daughters. The rest seemed to have left home for high-powered careers well away from the bucolic life of the farm.

"Maggie never went to college. She married Roger two days after she graduated from high school. And when Roger wanted to farm, Dad and I decided it was time to let the younguns take over. They got a loan and bought us out and we moved to town. Roger's parents died three years ago. Car accident."

"What happened to Roger?" Grady mumbled, his mouth full of pie.

"He's gone now."

That was the second time someone had spoken of Mr. McCarthy as missing, Grady noted. Curiosity tweaked his tongue.

"Gone where?" His eyes widened. "Do you mean he ran off and left a woman with two daughters to run the place?"

"Didn't exactly run off." Kayleen smiled sadly. "He died. Five years ago. Heart attack." She carefully pleated the red-checked cotton of her skirt with fingers that were rough and worn from hard work.

"Sorry." Grady murmured the word perfunctorily as the pieces of the story fell into place.

"Yes, it was a sorry situation. Particularly when Maggie found out he'd cashed in his life-insurance policy. There was no money. Nothing. She scraped herself up and moved on, just as we knew she would." Kayleen's eyes were filled with tears. "She hugged and kissed her babies and then got on with her life, but it's been rough."

"But what did he do with the money?" Grady asked softly as he patted her thin shoulder awkwardly. "Whatever he bought, couldn't she return it?"

Kayleen jumped to her feet and dashed the tears from her eyes, shaking her head while her eyes avoided his. "Here I am gabbing, and Maggie is probably waiting for you to bring some more seed. She'd be furious if she knew I'd told you all this. She likes to keep her affairs private." Kayleen's voice dropped to a whisper Grady could barely hear. "Only, lately, I think it's gotten to be just a little too much. She's young and pretty and this place is wearing her into the ground. She's almost desperate to get away. Oh, I'm so afraid she'll make another mistake."

The tiny woman was lost in her private thoughts, her mind miles away, and Grady left the kitchen without speaking. It wasn't that he didn't want to know about Maggie McCarthy's personal life; he did. But some things were too private to share with another. If anyone could understand that, it was Grady.

He spent the next thirty minutes finding the truck and making sure it was loaded and ready to go. If he was lucky, the clutch would hold until he got it back here.

"Katy! Come and help me out." He stood in the yard and bellowed for all he was worth. A few seconds later the little girl appeared in the door of the barn.

"Come on," Grady called out. "You're going to show me the way to the field your mother's working in."

Katy dusted off her hands agreeably and climbed in to the rickety old truck. "What's she seeding?" Katy asked, her chin jutting out as she studied him.

"Canola. At least, I think it is." When he'd checked inside the seeder earlier today, Grady had recognized the tiny black seeds that were crushed to make margarine and oil. The same stuff was in the back of this truck. "Ready?"

"Uh-huh." Katy peered out the window like a wise little man until they came to the first corner. "Turn right here. We go about a mile west."

Grady nodded, shifting the noisy gear into third as they bounced along the rutted track. "What were you doing in the barn?" he asked, risking a look away from the road to her shining face.

"Cleaning the sheep's pen. I think the babies are coming pretty soon. The mother is huge. Her name is Bettina." She grinned happily, one arm wrapped around her middle. "I love animals. You can always ask them all the questions you want and they don't care. Not like adults."

Grady smiled at the sourness she inflected on the word *adults.* "What do you want to ask adults?" He kept his eyes on the road ahead and let her think it over.

"Tons of stuff. Like, do viruses get sick?" She twisted her

fingers together and stared at the configuration. "And why is it called a paramecium if there's only a single organism? It shouldn't be a *pair* of anything."

"Okay." Grady nodded, hiding his smile. "That's logical, I suppose. What else?"

"Well, I was wondering…" Katy murmured, frowning as she tilted her mussed blond head upward. "If you turn the monitor off on the computer, does the screen saver still work?"

Grady couldn't help it; he burst out laughing. "I'm sorry, Katy. I don't know. But I think so. It's a program built into the computer that tells it if the keyboard has been inactive for a certain time. If it has, it signals the screen saver to come on. Even if you turned it off, the keyboard would still be inactive, so it should still work." Grady puffed up his shoulders, proud of his response. "I think," he muttered after several minutes of intense scrutiny from those deep blue eyes.

"I have so many questions." Katy sighed. "Keeley says I drive everyone crazy with them and Mom calls me 'Twenty Questions' when I ask too many. But sometimes I just hafta know. Ya know?" She peered up at him questioningly.

"Well, why don't you ask your mom? I'm sure she could help." Grady decided the second thing he'd repair on this truck would be the shocks, if vehicles had shocks back when they made this wreck. His backside ached something furious.

"Mom's usually too tired when she gets done working on the farm. Once she fell asleep when I was reading to her about El Salvador." Katy grinned, her happy state restored once more.

"That was my social project at school," she told him seriously, her eyes glittering with excitement. Grady watched the way her head tipped back proudly. "I got an A."

"Wow!" He gave her a thumbs-up with a grin. "A's are

pretty cool. I don't know anything about your dad, and not much about El Salvador, either, but you can still talk to me." In fact, Grady told himself, he enjoyed his discussions with the girls very much. They were articulate and very well informed, but like all kids, they had boundless curiosity.

"My dad's been gone for a while. I don't remember him very well, but I bet he loved us." Katy's voice was tiny, her face begging him for reassurance.

"Of course he loved you," Grady replied, wondering why he'd started this. "Fathers are like our Heavenly Father. They always love their daughters. That's because girls are made of sugar and spice and everything nice."

Katy stuck out her tongue. "Yuck! That's Keeley. I'd much rather be made of snips and snails and puppy dog tails," she told him. "That's more interesting. And babies. I like to learn about babies of all kinds. Don't you? Hey, we're going in the ditch!"

Grady straightened the wheel with difficulty as he tried to quiet his ragged breathing and pounding heart.

"Er, where do you learn about babies, Katy?" Grady asked the question, thinking of Keeley's hours on the computer and the various information that was available on the Internet.

"In the barn, of course." She sounded disgusted. "You can't believe the storks bring babies if you live on a farm. Besides, we don't have any storks in Alberta! I've already seen two calves and eight kittens being born this year. And Nettie—that's Keeley's horse—is going to have a foal pretty soon." She peered up at him in concern. "You see, what happens is..."

"Uh, Katy, we're here." Grady heaved a sigh of relief, praying that she'd abandon the topic now.

His relief was short-lived as the little girl bounded from the truck and raced over to her mother who sat in the tall grass at the edge of the field, a long green stem between her teeth.

"About time you got here," Maggie muttered, getting up to dust off her jeans. "I called Mom on the radio ten minutes ago. I want to get back to work."

Grady saw the tiredness etch her pretty face and tugged out Kayleen's care package. "Here. This is lunch from your mom. Why don't you relax with it and your coffee while I fill the seeder?" When she would have objected, he held up one hand. "I've done it before. Don't worry."

"Mom, Grady and I were talking about where babies come from."

Grady heard a startled cough from Maggie interrupt Katy's high-pitched voice. He wheeled to find Maggie's bright eyes staring right at him. He could feel the heat rising to his cheeks and would have looked away but she wouldn't release his gaze.

"You talked about what?" Maggie asked, her voice husky from the coughing. She took another sip of the steaming coffee.

"Babies. I 'splained it all to him," Katy told her mother.

"I see," she murmured. As he watched, Grady saw a wicked gleam of teasing fill her eyes. "Didn't he know about babies, then?"

"Nope." Katy fiddled with her mother's hair for a moment. "Why don't you have more babies, Mom?" Katy stopped suddenly, her eyes narrowing speculatively. "Unless you're too old?" she quizzed.

"Katy," her mother protested, face bright with color.

Maggie continued in a soft tone. "Honey, I have two daughters and I'm very happy with them. If that's all God gives me, then I'm thankful." She hugged her daughter tightly, brushed a kiss against the dirt-smudged cheek.

"I'll load the seeder," Grady muttered, turning away. "You can finish lunch."

She jumped up the moment he shut off the auger, and shoved the containers back into the bag her mother had sent.

"I've got to get back to work now." Maggie dragged herself back up on the seat of the tractor and shifted gears with only a slight grinding. "Tell Granny I'll be done about six," she yelled, gathering her hair in a bunch and stuffing it under the hat he had given her. "You could fix up that broken screen on the back door, couldn't you, Grady? And the gate by the back pasture?" Her eyes were cool and formal as she gave him a list of chores for the afternoon.

Grady could see where the sun had burned the tip of her nose. At least she'd had sense enough to wear long sleeves. As he watched her drive away, Grady felt a sadness creep up on him. Maggie McCarthy was earthy and natural and very, very beautiful. In addition to her physical attributes, she was warm and caring. Exactly what he'd hoped for when... He cut the thought off before it could go any further. There wasn't much point dwelling on a future that would never be.

Grady wheeled around to pick up the sack and thermos of half-drunk coffee that Maggie had left behind. She'd eaten the pie voraciously, he remembered. As if she hadn't had breakfast.

"Come on, Katy, me girl," he called in his best Irish accent. "Time to get home. We're going to fix those front steps this afternoon."

"Can I help?" The child gazed up at him eagerly, her fingers slipping into his. "I like building things."

"Good." He grinned, holding her door open. "You can measure for me. I can't see a thing without my glasses."

"Why don't you wear them, then?" she demanded, frowning.

He grinned, enjoying the child and her quick repartee. "Because I hate glasses," he told her succinctly. "Probably the same way you hate braces."

She quirked an eyebrow at him, studying his face for a while as she snapped her bubble gum in loud annoying clicks.

"Maybe," she agreed, nodding. "But at least you can take them off. I'll never get rid of these things!"

"Never is a long time," he murmured, trying to remember back to his own childhood. "It only seems like things will never end, Katy. But everything does." He should know. Not that long ago his life had come to a complete and utter standstill, and he didn't know yet if he would ever get it back.

"Granny told me the Bible says there's a time for everything." Katy sighed, slipping off the seat as he pulled to a stop by the side of the house. "I wish the time would come when we'd stop being poor." Her voice dropped to a murmur as she bent to pet the big collie nudging at her leg. "Then maybe I could stop worrying."

Grady stopped and waited for her to continue. But when Katy kept her eyes downcast, staring at the ground, he brushed a hand over her mussed-up hair and asked the question straight out.

"What have you got to worry about, Katy McCarthy?" he whispered gently as she kicked the hard dry ground with one foot. "Can't you tell me?"

She looked up at him and Grady was astonished to see huge tears in her eyes, poised at the ends of her golden lashes. "If I tell you, you can't say anything. Not to anybody. Promise?"

Grady held his hand over his heart and nodded.

"My mom's gonna sell our farm," Katy whispered loudly. "And when we move to Calgary, I won't be able to have my horse or Bettina and her babies or even Laddie." She threw her arms around the dog and hugged it desperately. "And I don't *want* Brian for my new daddy. I don't want a new daddy. I just want to stay here forever and ever."

"I know it's hard, little one," he murmured, brushing the tears off her freckled cheeks. "But whenever I get really scared and I don't know where to turn next, do you know what I do?"

Katy shook her head, blond strands flying everywhere.

"I pray about it," he told her quietly. "The Bible says that God cares even about those little brown sparrows over there and that He knows just when they need something. So I figure, if He knows what they need, He must know what I need, too. And if He knows, He'll figure out how to get it to me at just the right time. So I ask Him to help me not worry about it anymore.

"Do you think you can do that, sweetie?" He watched the bright blue eyes start to glow.

"Yes." She nodded at last. "I think so. And my Sunday school teacher said that if we really believe in something and ask God for it, and work as hard as we can, God will help us get our heart's desire." She suddenly bounded up the stairs. "I gotta go do somethin', Grady. I'll be back to help you in a while." And with one final bound through the door, Katy had gone.

Chapter Three

Tired and sore, Maggie stood in the doorway and marveled at the two children seated on the living room floor. The two best things in her life sat watching the television. They were identical twins, the doctors had assured her nine years ago. Alike in every way.

Huh! A lot they knew. Keeley and Katy were as different as night and day. Always had been. Keeley was quiet, thoughtful; slow to react and very stubborn. She liked to spend time thinking about things. Katy, on the other hand, favored her father. Roger had never been one to stifle his opinion, and Maggie had learned early on in their marriage to do things his way first, regardless of her own opinions.

"Now that was a nasty thought," she chided herself. "'Love hopeth all things, believeth all things, endureth all things.' Remember that." She slipped her shoes off and started up the stairs to take a shower, ignoring the stiffness in her arms and legs just as she ignored the grumbling complaints and hissed warnings coming from the two on the floor.

"Girls," she murmured, peering over the balustrade. "No arguing. Not tonight. I'm just too tired."

"Yes, Mother," they recited together, and Maggie smiled as she moved upstairs, knowing that Keeley would soon have Katy involved in some computer project. Either that, or they would both end up out in the barn, waiting for the new little lamb to appear. "And peace will reign," she told herself. "For a little while, at least."

"Did you get finished?" Kayleen asked from the bedroom after Maggie had showered.

"Yes, it's done at last," she muttered, entering her room and towel-drying her wet hair. "Now maybe we'll get a little break before we have to start the spraying. If I can find the money for it."

"You've still got some of that flax to sell," her mother reminded her, sorting out the piles of laundry onto the bed.

"Yes, but that's about all that's left. Then I'm tapped." Maggie changed into a cotton chambray sundress that was faded and worn but extremely comfortable. Then she gathered her hair into two tortoiseshell combs, letting the thick strands curve and coil as they wanted. "And it isn't going to be long before we have to start haying." She groaned, slipping one hand to her back at the thought of it.

"Count your blessings, dear. At least you've got Grady. By the way, Glynis Logan called this afternoon from Banff. She's sold two more of your quilts." Kayleen's eyes were sparkling with some pent-up secret and Maggie's eyes widened at her excitement.

"Okay, give," she demanded. "How much?"

"She sold the one you did of the mountains for fourteen hundred dollars," Kayleen said jubilantly. "*And* they've commissioned a smaller one, too."

"Fourteen…oh, my word," Maggie breathed, grabbing her mother's hands and squeezing. "Maybe the kids can go to camp this summer, after all. Of course, I have to pay for those parts first, and then there's the feed store bill. Where in the world…?" Her voice trailed away and she wiped away a tear of relief. "I'm just glad the Lord found a buyer. That store has been a godsend for me."

"Do you have anything else that could go? Glynis said she's had a real run on your quilts with the big influx of tourists this year." Kayleen studied the pair of well-mended cutoffs in her hand. "Which one owns these?"

"Katy." Maggie grinned, whisking her own underthings into a drawer and smoothing the quilt she'd fashioned for herself years ago. "The knees were gone anyway, so I cut them off. That child goes through clothes faster than I use sunscreen."

"Mom! Grady's here," Katy bellowed up the stairs.

Maggie rolled her eyes expressively at her mother before slipping on her sandals, walking out of the room and downstairs. "You don't have to bawl like a calf, Katy. I have perfectly sound hearing. Besides, it's not polite." She smiled guardedly, her eyes whisking over Grady's dusty clothes. "Nice job of the steps," she murmured. "I'd been meaning to get to them."

"I thought somebody already had." He grinned mischievously. "There were about five pounds of nails in those short stubby pieces. And every one of them was bent."

"Yes, well—" Maggie strode toward the kitchen to hide her red face "—I'm afraid carpentry is not my forte." She heard him mutter something. "I beg your pardon?"

"He said 'That's for sure,'" Katy told her innocently, glancing up from the television show she and her sister were watching.

Maggie glared at her tall and lean hired help and watched his teeth flash in a grin that wasn't in the least apologetic.

"Sorry." He shrugged. "Did you get the seeding finished?"

"Yes." She sighed, pouring out two cups of coffee and cutting two huge wedges of the triple-layer chocolate cake her mother had baked that afternoon. "Finally." She motioned him to a chair and sank into one across from him, slicing into her cake with abandon. "Man, I'm hungry."

"You missed supper," he murmured, sipping his coffee as he watched her. "I could have done the seeding, you know. You're not all that strong. Missing meals probably isn't a good idea."

"I'm a lot tougher than I look," she told him defensively. Her shoulders lifted proudly. "I have to be. Besides, I like to finish what I start."

Maggie saw the frown that marred his craggy good looks and stopped eating her cake.

"Why don't you let me carry some of the harder jobs for a while?" he asked, his voice low and thoughtful. "I think you and your kids need to spend some time together, too."

"I spend as much time with them as I can." Maggie glared at him. "It isn't enough but it's the best I can do right now." She snapped the fork onto the plate with a decisive click.

"I'm not criticizing, Mrs. McCarthy. I just thought since school would be out soon, maybe you could ease up a bit. I'm perfectly willing to take on the heavier stuff as part of my duties."

Maggie automatically picked up one of his hands and noticed the blisters and welt that screamed redly across his palms. Regret twigged at her conscience.

"I don't know if that's such a good idea," she murmured, brushing a thumb across the largest blister. "You're obviously not used to this kind of work."

His eyes were glowing with a kind of inner light that she didn't understand. When he finally pulled his hand away, Maggie could feel the loss right down to her toes. Silly to feel so strongly about him injuring himself, she told herself. She paid him to work.

"I haven't done it for a while," he agreed softly. "But I'll toughen up fast. I don't have this delicate white skin to watch out for." Seconds later his hand touched her arm. "What have you done to yourself?"

"Oh, that." Maggie shrugged, looking down at the long angry welt on her upper arm. "I scraped myself on something a couple of days ago. It's fine now."

"It doesn't look *fine*," he spat out harshly. "It looks like it could have used some stitches."

Maggie felt funny, watching the way his eyes flashed when he looked at her like that. Quickly she moved to the sink and rinsed out her cup before placing it and the other dishes in the dishwasher.

"It's fine," she told him hurriedly. "I'm no beauty anyway, so what's another little scratch? We farm girls get used to that stuff." She turned back to the table, striving to look him in the eye.

"You're kidding, right? You could give several well-known movie stars a pretty good run for their money."

Maggie shifted uncomfortably under his intense scrutiny. "I'm sure," she mocked, her face heating. "Anyway, I appreciate all the repairs you've made around here, Grady. It's nice to have the screen door fixed at last, and Mom said you managed to get the stove working again." She wiped off the table and flung the dishcloth into the sink.

"Tomorrow's Sunday so we'll all be going to church. We'd like you to join us, if you want. We usually leave around nine."

Grady nodded and Maggie took the matter as settled. She opened the door to her workroom and switched on the lights then turned back as she suddenly remembered something.

"Oh, by the way," she added, stopping when she realized that he'd followed her, had almost run into her from behind. "Sorry." She stepped backward automatically and kept going when she realized how close he was. "Uh, Grady?" His big brown eyes flew from the quilting frame to her face. "This is my private work area." She waited until he absorbed that. "I don't let anybody else in here."

"I want to check out the window," he told her quietly, staring with interest at the bright array of colors laid out on the makeshift cutting table. "What do you do in here?" he asked, staring at the clutter that covered every available surface.

"Oh, I do a little quilting," she told him offhandedly. "Right now I'm doing a seascape in various colors and textures." She frowned, laying a bit of rippled, sand-colored cotton against the pale aqua, lost in the colors. "It's not quite right yet."

The tension grew between her shoulder blades as Grady stared at the finished works that lay against the wall. She felt open, exposed. As if he had seen right inside her to her most private thoughts.

"I know it doesn't seem like me." She made a face. "No one, least of all me, expected that someone as clumsy as I could actually make something turn out. But they sell and that's what counts."

"Stop doing that!" His order was quiet but fierce, and Maggie's eyes opened wide.

"I beg your pardon?"

"You're always denigrating yourself. As if you're some kind of country bumpkin instead of a beautiful woman who has managed to provide for her family as best she can. There's nothing wrong with being a farmer, for heaven's sake!"

He sounded exasperated, Maggie thought privately. Couldn't he see that this kind of a life didn't begin to compare with what could have been?

"This is beautiful work and it shows a very powerful creative spirit." His brown eyes blazed into hers. "I strongly suspect that it's that same spirit that's gotten you through the past few years after your husband's death."

"Well, I couldn't very well give up, now could I?" she spat out furiously. "I had the girls to think of." She dared him to comment on that.

"Yes, you did," he answered right back, his eyes shaded by the shadows in the room. It was clear Maggie's position as his boss didn't intimidate him in the least. "But a lot of women would have refused to break their nails on a relic like that tractor, never mind muck out animals and repair broken steps." He looked up then and Maggie could see the admiration on his face. For some reason it angered her and she slapped her hands on her hips in a snit of fury.

"Don't make me out to be a saint just yet, Grady," she told him harshly. "I hate grunging around on this farm, looking like a beggar and owing every shop in town. I like silk as much as the next woman you know," she answered snippily, watching his face. "If someone offered to buy this place and give me a job in the city that would provide for my kids and their needs, I'd jump so fast you wouldn't see me for the dust."

Maggie knew her face was red and she couldn't help the sharp tone of her voice. "You come here in your fancy clothes and brand-new vehicles offering to do a bit of charity work for us, and then you think you have permission to draw conclusions about our lives. Well, you don't," she snapped, angrily dashing away the tears that welled up in her eyes. "You don't know how much I'd love to work in a nice quiet office where you put everything away at five and don't worry about it again till the next morning." She sucked in a breath and continued.

"Just once I'd like to be able to buy myself some decent clothes instead of having to sew up my own stuff. I'd like to take the girls on a real vacation and let them see how the other half lives. And once, just once," she retorted on the last breath of air still pent up inside, "I'd like to have long smooth nails that weren't torn down to the quick or blackened and filthy from greasy, dirty old farm machinery!"

She turned her back on him as the whole miserable weight forced her shoulders to droop in despair. It was hopeless; she should know that by now. She would never climb out from the mountain of debt that had accumulated around her.

"I'm sorry," she murmured at last, keeping her hands up by her face as she sat at the old oak desk. "I'm just tired. I shouldn't have dumped all that on you."

"You're probably very hot, too," Grady muttered, striding over to push and shove at the window with several loud grunts of exertion, until it finally flew open and a fresh evening breeze wafted in. In just a few minutes the room temperature had dropped several degrees.

"Thanks," she whispered, ashamed of her outburst.

"I suppose it must be difficult to keep it all together," he mused, running one fingertip along the edge of her cutting table. "And then to have to work on these, too." His eyebrows met in a grimace. "That's a lot of pressure."

"Oh, this isn't work," Maggie assured him, brightening as she gazed at the arrangement of fabric before her. "This is what I look forward to at the end of the day. I guess I should be thankful that I have a paying hobby." She glanced up apologetically and found his eyes strangely glittering as they focused on her face.

"You should be thankful for a lot more than that," he growled, moving toward the door. He stopped a moment and then turned toward her as if he just had to say the words that were bottled up inside. "You should be very thankful, Maggie McCarthy. You have a place to call your own. A place full of memories and history. You have your parents to lend a hand when you need it." His almost black gaze bored straight into hers.

"You've known the love of a man and you have two wonderful daughters who think you're the best mother around. They are happy, well-adjusted girls who live comfortably. That's far more than most people ever get in this lifetime." A second later Grady had disappeared through the door and Maggie was left wondering what was behind the stark raw pain she'd seen in those eyes.

"I'm sorry, Father," she whispered, getting up to stare out the window at the lowering gloom. "All I really need is You and You are always there. Help me to keep on keeping on. Amen."

Then with a resolute determination, Maggie picked up her large shears and began cutting out the pieces she intended to use for seashells, completely losing herself in her work until the old cuckoo clock chimed nine and she rushed out to send the girls to bed.

Grady O'Toole perched on a folding chair on a patch of lush green lawn and stared at the big old farmhouse.

"Why me, God?" he demanded. "Why did You give me everything I thought I wanted and then yank it all away? What have I done wrong?"

The girlish giggles coming from inside the house pricked at his mind until he could tolerate it no more. With a grunt of dismay he stood and began walking toward the thick grove of trees behind the house.

In his mind's eye he could see Fiona—beautiful, elegant Fiona who thought you could deal with the problems life handed you by buying someone off. He remembered the night he'd proposed and the way she'd cooly accepted his kiss on her cheek.

Funny, he thought to himself. *I hadn't remembered that*

cool, chilly kiss until today. He sifted through the memories and his mind zeroed in on another. *She hated the ring I chose.* The thought was traitorous, but try as he would, he couldn't ignore it. *She wanted something more showy, something that would be suited to her position in the firm. She hadn't cared that his diamond had been nearly flawless. Size and one-up-manship, that's what Fiona was all about.*

"I shall expect to travel, Gradin," she'd told him that evening, straightening the red silk dress with her polished fingernails after he'd tried to hug her. "And I think we'd better start looking at houses soon. You can afford better than this." Her piercing glance tore apart the small apartment and its under-stated furnishings. "After all, we shall want to entertain."

Grady approved wholeheartedly of entertaining. He'd gone along with her plans quite happily until he'd discovered that Fiona had no intention of including anyone in the invitation who didn't have substantial power or influence in the business community. Her choice of guests was strictly limited to those people she could use to get ahead.

And still he hadn't seen through her.

Grady walked slowly through the bush, only half hearing the twitter of birds in the treetops. The land sloped down here and he followed it gladly, thankful for the energy it required to find a way through the thick undergrowth. If only it were so easy to take away the words in his head.

The engagement party had been a disaster that no one could have predicted.

"We want only those people who are really glad for us." Fiona's voice had been harsh. "I don't think that includes every little secretary and typist from your company, Grady."

"You don't understand, dear," he'd told her, half smiling at her wish to have everything just so. "A lot of these folks helped get the company where it is now. I *want* them to share in our happiness."

She had shaken her head with determination. Her hazel eyes had flashed daggers at him. "This event will be reported in the society columns," she hissed. "I will not be embarrassed by some snippy little underling trying to ingratiate herself into our lives."

There should have been misgivings then. Especially when his parents had shown up. His mother had never been one for society events and she'd stayed glued to her husband's side all night, afraid to say anything that might reflect badly on him. His father, Grady remembered, had been much the same. Only later had he found out Fiona's part in their discomfort.

The gloom of the thicket suddenly gave way and Grady realized that he was at the edge of the river. A small one, it was true. Still, it gurgled and ran along at a good speed. Crouching at the side, he stuck one hand in and smiled at the chilly temperature. Just what he needed to take his mind off the past.

A minute later he was fully immersed in the cool water. Its revitalizing freshness washed over every part of him better than the dinky shower in his camper ever could. He swam around for several minutes, letting the chilly temperature lower both his temper and his body heat. When at last he emerged, Grady grinned at the feel of the breeze caressing his skin.

"What can compare with Your creation, Lord?" he asked, staring at the huge moon overhead. He donned his clothes quickly and then found a huge warm stone to sit on as he stared out at the lush valley around him.

There was no doubt that Maggie's farm was demanding and she wore herself out trying to cover all the bases, but it was a lovely area and he couldn't imagine that she would ever really want to leave such peace.

"I don't know why I'm here, Lord," he mused, chewing

on a stem of wild oats. "I should be at home, trying to save what little there is left of my business." But the words rang hollow. Now wasn't the time. Hadn't Harvey told him that over and over again only this morning on the phone?

"You can't come back, Grady, old pal. We haven't got things in place yet. I'll let you know when. Just relax and get yourself healthy. There's always another empire to be built, you know." Grady remembered grumbling about the slow hand of justice and Harvey's laugh of derision. "For some people there is no justice," he said with a snort. "And I'm very much afraid that your ex-wife falls into that category, my man. The best we can do is salvage what we can and move on."

Grady had hung up, fury making it impossible to speak. But the words rang round and round his head like a bell that wouldn't stop bonging.

"Nothing can salvage my child. Nothing."

With a sigh of despair for a past that was too painful to dwell on, Grady clambered back up the hill, thankful for hard work and early mornings that made it nearly impossible not to sleep at night. He needed sleep. It was the only way he could forget.

Chapter Four

"Why, Margaret Mary McCarthy! My word, girl! I haven't seen such a handsome man in a month of Sundays! Wherever did you find him?" Minnie Hugenot flapped her two-inch, black, paste-on spider lashes provocatively at Grady, who was standing some distance away. "And such muscles, too. Oh, my!"

The obvious stare at Grady's biceps made Maggie blush. She'd never been so happy to have church over.

"Oh, for Pete's sake," Katy muttered, kicking her toe against the carpet of the church's foyer. "What a lot of fuss!"

Keeley elbowed her. "Hush up, Katy. Maybe Mom'll take the hint and see how cute Grady is."

"I thought you said she was going to marry Brian?" Katy glared at her sister in frustration. "Why does it matter what she thinks of Grady?"

"It just does, that's all. Anyway, Brian's away right now and Grady's here!" Keeley's voice dropped. "But we've got to get them together. I told you. That's how they do it in all the best love stories." Her smooth forehead wrinkled in thought. "I've got it! Let's ask Mom if we can go for a picnic when we get home. Then you can ask if Grady can come.

You and I'll go butterfly hunting and they'll be left alone. Grown-ups like that."

"I don't know," Katy began, and stopped when she had to move out of the way of Minnie's burgeoning hips. "I don't think Mom would like it much."

"Mom isn't supposed to know, silly." She tugged her twin over between the now-empty pews, and after casting a look to make sure no one could overhear, showed Katy the computer printout sheet she'd tucked into her white patent purse. "I got this off the Internet," she whispered, grinning. "I asked a question on this romance bulletin board and got a whole bunch of answers from a bunch of different people. I picked the ones I wanted."

"Keeley! If Mom knew, she'd…" Katy's voice died away from sheer shock.

"Well, she's not going to know unless you tell her." Keeley glared, advancing forward menacingly. "And you're not telling. Are you?"

"N-n-no. That is, not unless it doesn't work."

"If it doesn't work, we move on to step two." Keeley refolded the sheet and tucked it away again. "Let's face it. We have to do something. Otherwise our mother is going to make us move to Calgary!"

"Good! When are you leaving?" Johnny Applebaum's dirty face peered up at them from under the edge of the pew. "I can hardly wait!" He burst out laughing at their furious looks and dashed underneath the bench and out the other side. "I'm going to tell everybody you're going," he called.

"Come on, Keeley," Katy urged, ducking between Mrs. Simpson and Mrs. Anderson. "We've got to catch him before he squeals!"

"And then what?" Keeley gasped, lunging down the stairs. "You're not going to beat him up again, are you? Katy, you've got your best dress on!" In a desperate attempt to avert tragedy, Keeley followed her sister across the churchyard and into the Caragana hedge.

Maggie's anxious gaze followed her daughters out the door. She turned back to find Minnie watching her speculatively. "I expect Grady will be leaving before too much longer."

"You do rather seem to have a problem hanging on to the male of the species, don't you, dear? I hear Brian Dalgleish is away now, too." Minnie's voice was soft but the meaning was there, and Maggie felt herself flushing. "Now tell me, Maggie. Is my suit finished?"

"Yes, nearly," Maggie murmured, watching as the steady stream out the door lessened. "I wouldn't mind one more fitting before I do the finishing though. Just to make sure."

"I've never had a dressmaker who had to have so many fittings," Minnie said, looking down her long knobby nose at Maggie. "Perhaps when you get some more experience, you'll be a bit quicker at it."

Maggie stifled the words that rose in her throat, trying to remember that she was in the house of God and this was no place to make snappy replies. "It's only been two weeks, Minnie. And I did have some seeding to do."

"Yes, well—" Minnie searched through the crowd and began moving past Maggie "—just make sure I get *all* the remnants back. I don't want to find my suit as part of one of your little projects."

As her best paying customer sidled down the stairs, Maggie gritted her teeth. "One of my *little* projects indeed," she muttered angrily.

"Are you talking to yourself now, too?" Grady stood behind her, grinning like a Cheshire cat.

"No! I was just…" Maggie searched for the right words as she gathered up the girls' Sunday school papers and her Bible. "Never mind." She sighed and then peered around, remembering. "Minnie Hugenot went looking for you."

"Yeah, well fortunately for me, she's hard to miss and I avoided her." He looked very satisfied with himself. "Are you ready to go? I told the girls I was going to ask you if we could have a picnic. Since it's such a nice day and all."

Maggie searched his features, wondering what had prompted this sudden invitation.

"I could pick up a barrel of chicken. You wouldn't have to do anything. They come with plates, cutlery—everything."

He sounded almost desperate, Maggie thought. Maybe he was lonely. And the girls would love to have a picnic. Anything to get out of clearing the table and loading the dishwasher.

"All right," she agreed finally. "I was going to go to my parents', but I'll bet they'd enjoy the rest just as much, Mom's been out at my place so often lately, I'm sure she'd like to relax in her own garden." She felt his arm go under her elbow as they walked down the steep stairs. It had been a long time since she felt so protected. "I'll pay for half."

His hand fell away immediately once they reached the sidewalk and he whirled to face her.

"No, this is my treat." Maggie started to argue, but he stopped her with an upheld hand. "Please? Let me do this."

There was no time to say anything for Minnie bore down upon them like a two-ton truck, removing all obstacles in her way. Maggie nodded at Grady and turned her glance away as the other woman spoke.

"Mr. O'Toole," she cried in a loud, peremptory voice. "Welcome to our little church! As head deaconess, I would be delighted to welcome you to my home for lunch."

Maggie watched as Minnie waited breathlessly for Grady's answer.

"Thank you very much," he replied solemnly, although Maggie could see the glint of merriment dancing in his eyes. "But Mrs. McCarthy and her daughters have agreed to a picnic lunch with me."

"A picnic, eh?" Minnie's eyes were speculative. "It's too bad that I've already been asked to practice with the choir this afternoon," she murmured thoughtfully. "Otherwise I might have tagged along."

Maggie had to hide her grin at the obvious relief covering Grady's handsome face.

"Oh, that is too bad. Are you and the girls ready, Mrs. McCarthy? We should be on our way."

Maggie felt the warmth of his palm cup her elbow again and moved along at his bidding.

"I wish you'd stop Mrs. McCarthy-ing me," she grated when they reached his truck. "My name is Maggie to everyone around here. It has been since the day I was born, and I don't like to answer to anything else."

She stepped up awkwardly, hiking her slim straight skirt up in order to reach the high step of the truck. She'd had to beg a ride because the car had a flat this morning and she had no time to change it. Maggie just caught his assessing look at her bare brown legs and hastily smoothed the navy fabric over them.

"I know," she muttered defensively when he got into the cab of his truck. "I should have worn hose. But it's so hot! I don't think God cares about that stuff anyway. Especially not way out here in Willow Bunch!" She stopped the torrent of words just in time to notice the tic at the corner of Grady's mouth as he turned his dark head toward her and smiled politely.

"No," he agreed mildly. "I don't suppose it matters to God what's on your legs."

"Believe me," she mumbled, searching her purse for a tissue and mopping the moisture from her face, "if Nettie Fitzgibbons had noticed, I'd have had to listen to a decorum lecture. She used to measure my skirts when I was in fifth grade. I had to kneel on the floor, and if the fabric didn't graze the tiles, I was in big trouble."

"Such as?"

He actually sounded interested in her small-town history, Maggie noticed. She took another breath of the air-conditioned breeze shooting out the vents.

"Her favorite punishment was writing lines. I think she picked it because I had such terrible handwriting. Still do." She grinned, noticing the tiny flecks of silver that hid themselves in the rich chestnut darkness of Grady's hair.

He sat staring at her, his eyes full of something—longing? Maggie told herself not to be foolish. Nobody in their right mind would envy her dull, boring life!

"You must have had a wonderful childhood," he said, tilting his head to stare at the groups of people who still stood laughing and chatting on the lawn. "Everyone knows everyone else. There aren't any terrible secrets you have to hide." His voice dropped to a quiet hush. "I envy you your life, Mrs. McCarthy."

"Maggie," she corrected automatically, frowning up at him across the small space. "Why would you envy me?" She held up one hand and counted off each finger as she spoke. "I'm up to my ears in debt, doing something that is dirty and thankless and has a very poor return. My best horse has gone lame. It doesn't look like the wheat will be doing much unless we get some rain, and I can't sell what little I've got in the bins because I didn't get enough quotas last year."

"Still," he murmured, staring at the lush greenness around him with that starry-eyed gaze Maggie had seen before. "Just look around."

"I did," she told him succinctly. "Last night." She shook her head in disgust. "The pressure system is broken again, which means it's going to be another long, dry summer. The crops need to be sprayed within the week or there won't be any point and Buster McLean is all booked up. And the only thing that's doing really well in the garden is zucchini. Do you know how sick I am of eating zucchini?" Maggie lowered her brows and visually dared him to comment on how wonderfully versatile the vegetable was.

"Oh." He changed tactics. "Think of yourself then. Think of how…"

"What? Think of what? My fingernails, which are chipped and broken all the time, no matter what I do," she added in frustration. "That I haven't had a professional haircut in years? Or maybe I should remind myself of how wonderful it is to have clothes I've made myself. I mean, who wants to wear those designer silks and cashmeres anyway!" She felt the heat warming her cheeks but ignored it to focus on Grady and her pent-up wrath.

"As for a nice steady paying job in clean surroundings, doing something other than fighting the land or making pretty *useless* things for other people—well, how utterly boring!" The silence yawned between them as Maggie realized exactly how self-pitying she had sounded. "I'm sorry," she whispered, staring at her rough, reddened fingers. "I shouldn't have said all that."

"Why not, if it's the truth?"

Her head jerked up of its own volition and Maggie stared at him in surprise. "Of course it's true," she told him. "But it's not your problem."

"Is it that Brian fellow's?"

His question was impertinent and Maggie should have told him to mind his own business. Instead, she let him in on the truth.

"It could be. He's asked me to marry him. Brian even *wants* the girls. There are a lot of men who wouldn't be interested in a ready-made family."

"And there are a lot of men who would kill for one," she heard Grady mutter under his breath. But when he lifted his head, his face was free of any emotion.

"You must think I'm a terrible mother," she murmured, staring through the windshield at the children still racing around the lawns. "I love my daughters. But I want more for them than a meager, hand-to-mouth existence on that farm." She heard her own voice harden and felt the anger once more.

"I want Keeley to have the facilities available where she can learn all she wants about the latest in computers, not just play on a used one I bought from a friend. I want her to have a top-notch teacher who will help her with her piano. Mildred Springs does her best, but she hasn't had the training. Besides, Keeley's learned all she can from Mildred."

He listened, Maggie had to admit. Unlike her parents, Grady actually seemed to hear what she was saying.

"And Katy?" His voice was low and concerned. "What about Katy? Her whole world revolves around the farm and her animals. Would you ask her to give it all up?"

"No, of course not!" Maggie glared at him angrily as the prick of conscience nagged at her deep inside. "But Katy hasn't known anything else. Once she saw the sports that were available to her—the swimming and track and volley-ball that she could participate in, year-round—the farm would soon lose its attraction."

"Are you sure, Maggie?" He pointed to the little girl who sat sprawled on the church lawn, playing with five tiny kittens. "Are you sure that what Katy *really* needs is to move away from her friends and people she's known all her life into a nameless, faceless city?" He nodded toward Keeley, standing nearby, giggling with a group of girls.

The words cut at her, eating away the little bit of resolve that she'd gathered over months of soul searching.

"I don't know why I even told you," she told him. "You can't possibly understand what it's like. The eighteen-hour days, the unending bills, the tasks that really need doing but have to wait because you just don't have the energy or the strength or the resources to do it all alone." Tears welled in her eyes. "Alone—that's the worst part. Without anyone to talk it over with or discuss options, knowing the whole world rests on your shoulders."

"But you have your parents."

"Yes," she agreed tiredly, leaning her head back against the smooth leather rest. "They are wonderful. They help me out far more than I could have ever asked, and I love them dearly, but can't you see? They're getting older. They're tired. They need a break even more than I do, and I hate," she ground out viciously, "*hate* always dumping my problems on them when they've got their own lives to lead. They should be traveling south in the winter, like other retired couples." A tear dropped onto her open palm and she closed her fist around it in frustration.

When Grady finally spoke, his words were slow, as if he'd thought about them carefully first. "I know you don't think I understand. And I probably don't," he admitted quietly. "I cannot imagine how you've managed with small children and the farm and everything these past few years." He stopped and then went on more slowly. "But you have everything here. A family, a home, neighbors and friends you care about, a little bit of heaven carved out of this impersonal, industrialized, polluted earth." Grady's voice dropped to a whisper, as if he were speaking to himself. "I just don't understand how you can even think of giving it all up."

Maggie laughed mirthlessly, gathering her sweater around her. Suddenly the cab seemed cold. It mirrored her insides perfectly.

"I'd give it up in a minute," she whispered raggedly. "I'd gladly leave this place right now if I could be assured of a little peace and security in my future."

Grady shook his head. "There's no such guarantee in this

life," he told her harshly. "And I, of all people, know what I'm talking about."

Maggie stared at him, stunned by the anger and pain in his voice. But she was prevented from asking him about it by the simple reason that he opened his window and called to the girls.

"We want to get on the way for our picnic," he told them, smiling as if nothing mattered more than getting them a bucket of chicken and basking in the sun. "I think we should go down by your creek." He smiled as he helped each child into her seat. "That way we could swim if we get too hot."

Maggie took the high-pitched squeals of excitement in the back seat as agreement with this plan, but she couldn't forget the look of agony on Grady's face the moment before. Nor could she help noticing the way his features softened when he spoke to her daughters, or miss his tender touch on each blond head.

What is in Grady O'Toole's past that caused such terrible pain that only my life seems able to assuage?

It was a good question. Unfortunately, the answer eluded her.

Chapter Five

"Maggie McCarthy, I'm going to skin you alive!" Grady glared at the local crop duster as the words rolled through his brain. He was furious with her. "When did Mrs. McCarthy tell you not to do her fields?" he demanded with his lips pursed.

Buster McLean shifted from one filthy booted foot to the other, his gaze downcast. Not that it mattered, Grady decided grimly. The man wore a greasy cap pulled low on his forehead and it was difficult to even *find* his eyes, let alone read them.

"Well, like I said, it was right after I told her the cost. I do this to support my own farming operation, you see. I know Maggie needs the work done all right," he apologized, shoving his hands even deeper into jeans that seemed destined to pool around his size-sixteen feet. "But I gotta pay for the stuff out of my own pocket. That's why I need to be paid up front. If she can't pay, I can't spray." He grinned stupidly at the little rhyme and then shrugged as Grady lowered his eyebrows menacingly.

"How much?" Grady kept his tones low. When the answer came, he merely stared, eyes widening expectantly. "No," he said quietly, flicking the bug off his arm as if to emphasize his point. "I meant what is your best price on this particular job? And don't expect anyone to barter you down. Either you want the job or you don't."

Buster tugged off his hat and scratched his forehead with fingers that hadn't seen water in a while. He had beady little eyes, Grady noticed. They seemed to shift back and forth and around, everywhere but on him.

"You don't want terms?" he asked querulously.

"No terms," Grady agreed. "Mrs. McCarthy pays cash on the barrel head."

"Oh. Well, see, cash is a different matter altogether. Why didn't you say so in the first place?" And Buster named a figure that was considerably below his first one.

"Fine." Grady pulled out a check, filled it out and signed it with a flourish. "You'd better make sure it's a good job," he told the other man. "And she wants an early-morning spray, when it's calm and the kids are still inside."

"Doesn't everyone?" Buster slapped his filthy cap back on his balding head and stuffed the check into his pocket. "I suppose I could come over tomorrow about six," he offered, hitching up his pants.

"Make it five," Grady told him smoothly. "And I want a bill for that check. Marked 'Paid in full.'" He waited while Buster dug around in his truck for a pad and wrote out the receipt. "I'd appreciate it if you could go through me in any future dealings," he murmured, folding the paper and tucking it into his shirt pocket. "Mrs. McCarthy is pretty stressed-out these days."

"Ain't much of a wonder." Buster grunted, heaving his girth up into the seat. "Truth to tell, most of us figured she would have bailed out long ago."

"And as long as she was around and still kicking, I guess you just thought maybe you could keep skimming, is that it?"

Grady nailed the guy with his sternest look. "The way I figure it, you've been making things tougher for her instead of easier. So maybe, as a helpful *friendly* gesture, you can come by on Saturday. She could use your help at fixing up the barn."

Buster had the grace to turn red as a beet under such straight talk. "I never tried to take her," he blustered loudly. "It's just that with her having so many bills and all, I thought it would be best to add some interest and sorta make sure of things. It's just business." He blabbered on for several minutes before promising he'd be there.

"Well, thank you, Buster. That's right neighborly of you." Grady smiled in his best down-home fashion. "You might mention it to Burt Copperfield, too. I'm sure he'd want to help out. Say!" Grady opened his eyes up wide and innocent. "Isn't he the guy that did some plumbing work on the McCarthy house last fall?" He pretended to think for a minute and then shook his head ruefully.

"On second thought, don't ask him, Buster," he pleaded sadly. "The guy's useless. Why, I was down checking over the pressure system for Mrs. McCarthy late last night, and I have to say I never saw such a mess of a job in my life. And the price he charged!"

Grady suddenly slapped a hand over his mouth in embarrassment. "Oh, brother," he gasped in pretended chagrin, averting his eyes, "I hope I didn't say anything out of turn. You're not, er, friends, or anything, are you?"

"He's my brother-in-law," Buster told him, lifting his head a fraction to study Grady's face. "And he usually does very good work!"

"He is? He does?" Grady kept his face straight. "Oh. Maybe this was just a rare occurrence then." He tried to look apologetic. "Don't mention it, will you? I don't want to get anyone in trouble, although with that soldering, I don't know how he makes a living." He shrugged and let that sink in a little longer before turning away. "See you Saturday, Buster."

"Yeah." Buster's voice was thoughtful. "I'll be there." And he drove away at about half the speed he'd driven up.

"You do that," Grady muttered to himself as he watched the brand-new four-by-four pass through the gates. He pulled on the leather gloves Maggie had insisted he wear. He just bet Buster would be bringing along Burt, the plumber, as well. Grady grinned at the dog and tugged the roto tiller on once more.

Grady ploughed through the dark black topsoil around the spruce trees that framed the yard site. It would be interesting to see just what happened on Saturday, and he was looking forward to watching Maggie's face when it did.

That was, if he got back in time.

"I'm coming in on Friday, Harvey," he informed his lawyer minutes later on the cell phone he always carried. "I have to know how things stand, if I have a future."

"Don't be ridiculous, Grady." Harvey snorted. "Of course you have a future. Your trust is as secure as it ever was. She can't touch that at least."

"You hope! And my reputation? My business? My friends?" Grady said the words, knowing that it was fruitless to ask. Nothing could undo the damage Fiona had done.

"Your real friends are still here, waiting for you to call. Is it worth worrying about the others?"

"And Shaughnessy's? Is it going to fold?" Grady held his breath, his heart aching for the people who had worked so hard to help him build his company up from nothing.

"I closed it down, Grady. I handed out notices and laid everyone off so that they could at least collect employment insurance."

"You what?" Grady glanced toward the house to make sure no one noticed him.

"I had to, old son. They've tied us up for so long that business has really dropped, and no one was bringing in any new accounts. This way, your staff can at least try to get work somewhere else until you start up again. I sold all the equipment and furniture and used it to pay bonuses. Grady? Are you there?"

Grady sank down onto the ground, his heart racing a mile a minute. Gone. It was all gone. Without any pomp and circumstance. Without him even knowing it. Fiona had taken away his precious company without even really trying.

Harvey was shouting his name and Grady could hear the fear in his voice.

"I'm here," he whispered at last. "Just thinking."

"You scared me out of my tree," Harvey said. Grady could imagine his lawyer flopping into his black leather chair and grinned tiredly when a squeak of protest signaled just such an action over the phone line.

"Did Fiona say anything?" It galled him to ask it, but Grady swallowed his pride and waited for some indication that his ex-wife cared that his company was now defunct. Harvey's nasty little laugh made him suddenly feel better.

"Well, now there's the rub," Harvey muttered. "Her lawyers didn't even know till I'd cleaned the place out. Your staff was very good about keeping everything hush-hush. Everyone and everything was long gone by the time I got there to lock the door. Except for one thing."

Harvey paused expectantly and Grady knew he was supposed to ask the next question. Swallowing thickly, he held the receiver tightly and said it in a choked voice that gave away his inner agitation. "What was left?"

"The welcome mat!" Harvey chortled heartily at his own joke, making Grady's mouth tip in amusement. He could just imagine Fiona's lawyers in their three-piece pin-striped suits, outraged at letting the not-inconsiderable tangible assets of Shaughnessy's evade their greedy grasp.

"I told them they were welcome to it. With your compliments." Harvey's voice hardened. "I've filed petitions against your ex-wife and her legal eagles to hold them at bay while the board investigates your supposed crime. Just got the decision this morning. The judge agrees that they will have to wait a while until he can hear their case."

"And what do we do until then?" Grady noticed the school bus pulling up, and suddenly wondered to himself why this phone call had seemed so urgent as two excited little girls tumbled down the steps.

"Grady, my friend, we send dear Fiona her monthly installment on the settlement she was promised until such time as she marries again as per the agreement. And nothing else. Not a dime. You don't see her, you don't talk to her. You stay safely where you are until I get this straightened out."

Grady sighed, watching Katy throw herself into her mother's arms and the laughing embrace Maggie gave her that ended in both of them flopping on the lawn. Seconds later Keeley had joined in and they were madly tickling each other.

"I want it over, Harvey," he muttered, raking a hand through his hair. "I just want it finished. I want my life to begin again. If I have to pay her off to be free, then let's just do it."

"Not yet. First we'll see what they've got," Harvey suggested. "I have several investigators checking things out right now and I don't want you jeopardizing my work at this delicate stage. Just stay where you are and relax. I'll handle it for now."

There was a pause and Grady could hear the rustle of papers being shuffled. He was ready to sign off when Harvey's voice came back on the line. "By the way, where are you, anyway?"

Grady told him a little about the farm and Willow Bunch

but he didn't mention Maggie and her daughters He wasn't sure why, except that it was none of Harvey's business. Not yet anyway.

"It sounds wonderful," Harvey agreed. "Enjoy it while you can. And stay away from here."

Grady hung up after promising to do just that. He spent a long time watching the tall willowy woman chasing and tagging her giggling daughters.

Grimly he shook off the thought of the family he would never have, and yanked on the cord to start the tiller— Work, that was the only panacea. Work until he was too numb to feel the pain.

It might have been five minutes or an hour later that he became aware of the child on his right side, marching along as she kept step with him.

"Hi, Katy." He switched off the motor reluctantly. "How was school?"

"Boring. We had that stupid social test today." She kicked at a clump of dirt and then scrunched down to peer at the earthworm wiggling in the light. "Melinda Fairchild made fun of my braces again." Her voice was soft but full of defiance.

"And?" He frowned down at Katy's wide, easy smile. "What did you do?"

"Nothing!"

"Katy," he warned in a low menacing voice.

"I didn't!" Katy shrugged and stood, dusting her hands on her jeans. "Of course, she did get my gum stuck in her hair at recess, but that wasn't *my* fault. She shouldn't have leaned back when I was blowing bubbles. They had to cut it out and she has *very* long hair. Some of it's a little shorter now."

"Katy!" He tried to stifle the burst of laughter that rose in his throat at her innocent look and self-righteous tones. "That's terrible."

"So's she," Katy told him, snapping her gum with satisfaction. "She has more brand-name clothes than anyone and she still isn't happy."

"Things don't make people happy, Katy. You can have all the *things* in the world and still be sadder than a beggar." *If anybody knows that,* he thought, *I do.*

"I know," Katy mumbled, pushing her hair out of her eyes. "But sometimes it would be nice if stuff was spread around a little more, don't you think?" She pulled out a blade of grass and chewed on it thoughtfully. "Like if you took all the rich people and made them only half as rich, then there would be more for poor people like us."

"We are not poor, Katy McCarthy!"

Grady and Katy straightened guiltily, wheeling round to see Maggie standing behind them, hands on her hips as she surveyed her daughter with a frown.

"We have food and clothes. Warm beds to sleep in and Granny and Grandpa nearby. That's being pretty rich."

"I know, Mom." Katy hugged her mother's waist in apology. "And I'm not complaining. Honest. It's just that Melinda makes me so mad sometimes. She has so many toys and she won't ever share!"

"Yes, well, you remember that when Keeley wants to borrow something of yours," Maggie chided with a gentle smile, brushing the blond mess off her daughter's face. "Now go and do your chores and then you can play a bit before supper. *If* your homework is done."

"Okay." Katy went racing off toward the house, her voice carrying on the breeze back toward them. "See you later, Grady."

"I guess all my bellyaching has rubbed off on my girls," Maggie murmured, stubbing her toe in the ground. The action was identical to Katy's and Grady couldn't help but smile.

"It's not funny." She glared at him. "And just a few

minutes ago, when I asked Keeley how school was today she began weeping on my shoulder because Becky Snodgrass told her she knew her jeans were Elissa's old ones from last year and that they were supposed to go to the Goodwill pile at church." She glanced up at Grady, a tear poised on each long thick lash. "Why are kids so mean?"

The pain in her voice stung him and Grady could see that she barely had herself under control. He reached out and took her hand, patting it gently.

"Don't worry about it," he advised softly. "All kids go through this, but they survive. Yours will, too. Probably better than most because they already know what's really important in life."

"Is it so wrong to want them to have nice things?" Maggie's voice was ragged. "A few really nice clothes that they can take pleasure in, that would make their lives a little less dreary?"

"Maggie, Katy and Keeley take pleasure in every day. Look at them." He pointed at the pair gently petting the new foal. "What toy would you buy them that could ever replace that in their lives?"

"Yes, it's nice." She sniffed, leaving her hand wrapped in his. "But the other kids get to go to Calaway Park for their birthdays. Or they rent the laser tag place, or the water slides." Fresh tears rolled down her cheeks as she watched the girls carrying buckets of feed for the animals.

"All I can give them is a little party here on the farm with a cake and a dress I made myself. It's not fair," she railed in a tortured voice, her face an agony of pain. "I just want them to be happy."

Without a thought, Grady pulled her into his arms, pressing her head against his shoulder as her tears soaked his shirt.

"Of course it's not fair," he said gently, feeling her hands grasp at him. "Life never is. But we take what God gives us and we make the very best of it that we can. And hope that someday things will be better."

"I'm sick of waiting for someday," she mumbled against his neck. "I want them to remember their childhood as a happy time, blissfully carefree. Not an era when they had to watch and scrimp and save for every dime that came their way."

"Is that why Brian was out here again yesterday?" Grady had to ask the question. It had bothered him for hours. "Are you thinking of exchanging one set of problems for another?"

She pulled away at that, back as far as his arm let her, her blue eyes chilly in the extreme. "Brian's not a problem," she told him coldly. "He's a solution. He thinks he loves me. He and I and the girls could live quite happily together. We'd have everything we need. I could sell the farm and pay off the money I borrowed from Mom and Dad last year. Life would be so much easier."

"He only *thinks* he loves you?" Grady rolled his eyes. "But you don't love him. Do you?" For some reason he needed to hear her answer to that question. Badly.

"Brian is a wonderful man. So good and kind. He respects me and he wants to make a home for the girls. He has everything I could possibly want in a husband." She tilted her head back, defiance in her eyes.

"But do you love him?" Grady held her gaze, refusing to give up even when she pressed away from him and stood churning her fingers together. "Do you?"

"I can't let emotion sway me again, Grady." She shuffled her feet. "I did that when I was eighteen, and look what happened."

"So what happened? You were happily married and became a mother to two wonderful daughters, Maggie! Are you sorry?"

"No." She glared at him in frustration. "But now I'm alone

and I have to make some decisions about our future. I'm not sure I can last another year on this farm, living the way we have been." She met his gaze straight on. "I'm out of money, out of energy and out of patience. It's time for a change."

"And the biggest change would be for you, wouldn't it, Maggie?" he murmured, meeting her gaze. "You'd be free of this place and the memories it holds for you."

"Is that so wrong?" she demanded, head tilted back. "To start a new life for my family?"

"No, of course not. It's just that I think you're going to be disappointed. You can't run away from life, Maggie. You have to face it head-on."

"Is that what you're doing out on this farm looking like your world has fallen apart? Are you facing life head-on when you make those secretive calls on your telephone?" Her eyes slashed at him like cold hard steel and her words bit into him. "Practice what you preach, Grady."

He stared down into her beautiful face and wondered for the tenth time exactly why he was here. He was staying put as Harvey had demanded, but the longer he stayed, the more involved he became with this intriguing woman and her two delightful daughters.

"Well?" She was standing there, hands on her hips, demanding his response with that stubborn glint in her eye.

"You don't understand," he told her quietly, turning away to pull the tiller out of the soft loam. "And I can't explain. It's too personal."

"Too personal?" She laughed mockingly. "And you think delving into my life and telling me who not to marry and when and where I should live isn't? Oh, brother!"

Grady looked back at her, letting his eyes rove across her smooth clear forehead, the blond brows and glittering blue eyes. There was a smattering of very pale freckles on her nose just where that snobbish tilt began. Her wide laughing mouth was turned down in a frown and Grady could feel the sparks emanating from the silver glints in her hair. Maggie McCarthy was furious. And very lovely.

"I'm sorry," he said stiffly, turning away. "It's none of my business. Forgive me for interfering." With one motion he had pushed the tiller back and begun rolling it toward the shed.

"That's it? That's all you're going to say?" She stood in front of him now, anger bringing two pink spots to her cheeks.

Grady nodded. "Yes. That's it."

Her glistening hair spun round her shoulders in a cloud of gold as she whirled away. She'd gone only a short distance before she turned back. "I *am* going to have my life, you know. I *will not* grow old and withered and bitter, worn down by years of trying to make this place a go." She glared at him, hands clenched at her sides. "Maybe I was a fool to get married so young. And maybe I didn't know what I was getting into when I tried to keep this place going. But, believe me, I certainly know now and I no more want it for my daughters than I do for myself."

Grady forced his lips to remain shut, standing solemnly as she finished her tirade. He could see the tears trembling at the corners of her eyes and knew that at this particular moment she was at the end of her tether. She needed a break.

"I've tried," Maggie whispered brokenly. "I've tried so hard! But I just can't do it anymore. I'm worn-out trying to keep everything together. Is it so wrong to want a little space and time for me?"

The words were soft, not meant for his ears, Grady knew. And yet he couldn't let them go. Not without trying to make her see the whole picture.

"Maybe…" he murmured, keeping his eyes averted as she struggled to regain her composure, and then meeting those deep blue eyes with his own. "Just maybe this is your time. Maybe this is your shining moment."

Maggie laughed bitterly, glancing down at her torn shirt, faded dirty denims and ragged sneakers.

"There is nothing even remotely shining about me right now, Grady O'Toole." She exhaled in defeat. "And certainly nothing the least bit glamorous about farming. Don't make this into a Norman Rockwell painting, okay?" she warned sourly. "There is no intrinsic merit in driving yourself into the ground trying to make something out of nothing." She turned and began walking back to the house. He just caught her last words. "Believe me, I ought to know."

"Mom!" Keeley's voice carried across the yard and Grady watched as Maggie's proud head lifted. "It's Brian. He wants to know if we're free tonight. There's something he wants us to go to."

Maggie twisted her head around, her eyes meeting Grady's without flinching. There was something cold and hard in them that reminded him of Fiona, some determination that he knew he could not shake.

"Yes, I'm free," she called out. "We all are. It's time we had a little fun in our lives."

And as he stood watching, Maggie broke into a quick sprint that took her to the steps of her home. It was the first time, he reminded himself, that he'd seen her run for the sheer pleasure and abandonment of it.

"Help her, Lord," he murmured. "Keep her on your path. Whatever that is." Then he turned and headed back to the camper for a lonely supper on his own.

"What is going on?" Maggie stared at the crowd of men who were parking their trucks in her front yard. "What is everyone doing here?" she called loudly, drawing their attention to her. "Don't you know it's Saturday?"

"Of course we know. We thought we'd help out with that work on the barn," Chester Bird told her, buckling his tool belt around his skinny hips. "Been meaning to get here for a while. Today seems a good time."

"But…"

"And we thought we'd come along and help with any spring cleaning you want done," Minnie Hugenot added, wheezing out of her small car. "We've done everyone else's but we wanted to wait until you were finished seeding."

"But…"

"I reckon Grady could show us what needs doing on the barn," Slim Tattersall mumbled, his hat pulled low over his eyes. "The women brought lunch so we'll get to work right away. Gabby, you need anything for the house?" He watched impatiently, Maggie noted, not even offering to help as his tiny wife stumbled up to the step with several buckets and mops, a bag of cloths and several cleaners.

"No, thanks, Slim," she puffed, careening through the door with difficulty. Maggie moved to take the buckets and bags from her. "You fellows get to work. We'll call you when it's coffee time."

Maggie watched as Grady led the group of men toward the barn. Embarrassed, she noted the worn boards, rotting roof and wildly hanging doors. The barn was a wreck.

"Speaking of coffee," Nettie murmured, fanning herself, "why don't we start with a cup? That'll give Maggie and the girls time to get dressed. Had a late night, did you, dear?" Nettie winked in a totally unteacherlike fashion as her eyes roved over Maggie's tattered chenille housecoat.

"Can't really blame her, can you?" Minnie demanded, staring out across the yard. "Not with a hunk like that hanging around."

The rest of the group giggled and twittered, their glances openly curious as they went from Maggie to Grady and back again.

"Actually, the girls and I were out with Brian last night,"

she told them, trying to ignore the blush she could feel heating her cheeks at their knowing looks. "We went to the circus."

There was a long pause in the conversation then as the ladies digested this bit of information. Maggie waited for someone to ask when she was getting married, but to her surprise, no one did. Perhaps because of the warning glint in Henrietta Higglesby's dark brown glare. Of all the local ladies, Henny seemed to best understand how much Maggie needed to feel feminine and beautiful. It was Henny who gave Maggie the trial samples from her makeup selection at the drugstore.

"I think that's wonderful," Henny enthused, patting Maggie's shoulder gently. "You're just wearing yourself out on this farm. It's time you had a break. You take some time for yourself and the girls to enjoy."

"Thank you, Henrietta," Maggie said softly. "That's just what I plan to do more of this summer. We need a break."

"I don't know how on earth you do it all," Bonnie Copperfield muttered, urging everyone inside. "No wonder you're so thin. Come on, ladies, let's get to work."

In a daze Maggie got the girls up, had a shower, dressed and went down to her kitchen. Everything was out of the cupboards and Gloria Stampford was reaching from her perch atop the ladder to wipe out the highest shelf.

"I haven't done that in ages," Maggie warned. "It's probably filthy." It was embarrassing to have people see what a poor housekeeper she was, but there simply was no time to dust and clean with the animals and the children and homework and final exams.

"This is nothing," Gloria told her, grinning. "With my four, I barely have time to load the dishwasher. When Henny was cleaning out Jared's room, she found a frog under the bed! That was in March, so you know the thing had been there all winter."

"Yeow!" The screech came from downstairs and seconds later Bonnie Copperfield came racing up. "I've gotta get Burt," she called as she hurried out the door. "There's a leak down there!"

"It's been there for ages," Maggie tried to tell her, but Bonnie was halfway across the lawn.

"Let her go," Nettie advised, emptying her bucket of dirty brown water into the sink. "Bonnie will have Burt over here in a minute and he'll get it straightened out."

Maggie watched as they all went back to their jobs and decided it wasn't worth explaining that the leak had appeared *after* Burt's last visit. True to her word, Bonnie dispatched Burt and another man to the bowels of the basement and ten minutes later both men carried out several parts.

"These are defective," Burt told her, two red spots of color on his cheeks. "But don't worry. They're under warranty. The company will pay for the repairs. I think I've got some in my truck."

Relieved that for once there would be no extra expense, Maggie took her bucket outside to start on the windows and found two men on ladders painting the exterior of the house.

"No," she called out, hurriedly setting her pail on the railing. "I didn't order any paint."

"I did!" Elmer Palen peered down over the edge of the roof where he seemed to be replacing some shingles. "It's demo stuff that we're supposed to try out and report on. Grady thought this house might be a good test case since it's so old and weathered."

"Oh." Maggie frowned. *Grady thought that, did he,* she muttered to herself. "Thank you," she called a minute later, but Elmer just waved the hand holding his hammer.

"You can't get the woodwork wet if they're going to paint," Grady said from behind her. He was studying the workers around the barn with an absent air. "Maybe there's something inside that needs doing."

"You know very well that there's something *everywhere* on this farm that needs doing," she told him with a huff. "Did you call all these people? I will not be an object of charity with everyone feeling sorry for me!"

"I hardly think that's the case," he murmured mildly, his eyes meeting hers. "They're your friends and they want to help. Why don't you just relax and accept it?"

"Because it's denigrating!" She frowned fiercely. "Everything is run-down and shabby, as if I don't care how things look."

"Maggie?" Grady had his hand on her arm, warm and comforting. His eyes glowed with something that made her feel special and cared for. "Can't friends help friends without you taking it the wrong way?" His tone was softly chastising. "They've seen you slaving away here. They know how hard it's been, and they want to help. Try and graciously accept it in the same manner that it's given, will you?"

"Hey, Grady! Mac says the chicken coop needs some strengthening. Mind if I do that?" Buster McLean's voice broke into their conversation, his eyes watching as Grady's hand slowly fell away from Maggie's arm.

"That would be very nice of you, Buster," he agreed absently, but his dark caressing gaze stayed on Maggie.

"Okay, I'll do that, then." Buster hurried away as if he'd been bitten and Maggie could only stare.

"Buster? Donating labor? I don't believe it!"

"Well, believe it." Grady laughed. "And enjoy it. It may not happen again in this lifetime."

Maggie studied her new hired hand for several minutes, noting the way his hands were stuffed into his pockets, the way his shirt opened at the throat, showing the tanned skin there.

"Thank you," she murmured at last, leaning forward to press her lips against his cheek. "I don't know how you did this, but thanks." She turned away lest he see more of her tears.

"You're welcome." Grady sounded pleased and something else. It was that which made Maggie turn back and study his handsome face once more.

"Proud," she whispered to herself as she dusted the curio cabinet in the living room. "He looked as if he had some interest in this place and was proud it was getting fixed up."

And that was strange, wasn't it? Grady O'Toole had only shown up a few short weeks ago and she doubted he'd be staying on much longer.

"So why should he feel proud?" There wasn't any answer to the question that rolled round and round her head.

"Maggie? Can you come here a moment?" Henny called from Katy's room. "There's the strangest thing on this shelf."

Maggie climbed the stairs with a grimace on her face. She could only imagine what had made the woman's normally strong tones weak and breathless. Seconds later she understood completely. In fact, she felt a little weak herself!

"Back out and shut the door, Henny. Just go slowly. That's the way. There!" Maggie snapped Katy's door closed with a quick flip of her wrist and sagged against the wall. "No more pets, I told her. Not one more. And she promised she wouldn't bring anything else into the house. She promised!" Maggie let her weak-kneed body slide down the wall until she was sitting on the floor. Seconds later Henny was there, too, white-faced and shaking.

"I'm sorry, Maggie. I'm not usually so lily livered. But that…thing scared the wits out of me."

"Don't worry, Henny." Maggie patted the clenched hand. "I felt pretty scared myself." She stood up carefully. "I'll go get her," she murmured, praying her legs would carry her down the stairs. "Katy got it here. She can get rid of it."

"I'll go with you," Henny blurted, scurrying behind. "The girls probably need help downstairs anyway."

Maggie let her go, knowing the woman needed to calm down. She needed that herself, but first she needed to talk to Katy. She found her daughter behind the barn with Grady, cutting up some of the dead trees they had removed from around the garden.

"But why does the Bible say God is jealous?" the chirpy voice demanded. "God has everything, and if He hasn't got it, He can just make it, can't He? It doesn't make any sense."

"Neither does having a six-foot-long snake in your bedroom," Maggie murmured, her jaw tense. "But you've got one, Katy. *And* after I told you no more pets in the house."

"A snake?" Grady glanced from mother to child. "What kind of a snake?"

"A very long, fat, slithery one," Maggie informed him. "It nearly gave Henrietta Higglesby a heart attack, not to mention me."

"Oh, that's Bowie," Katy exclaimed, as if that told them everything they needed to know. She glanced at her mother and hastily added some more information. "You know, our classroom pet. It's a boa constrictor, Mom. I have to look after him this weekend. It's my turn."

"It was here last night? Uncaged?" Maggie sat down on the nearby bale before she fell down. "But I was walking around barefoot!"

"It's not poisonous, Mom!" Katy sounded aggrieved. "It gets things by squeezing them. Bowie caught a rabbit once and swallowed it whole."

Maggie shuddered, glancing up at Grady with her best pleading expression. "Please go with Katy and get that *thing* out of my house, Grady," she whispered. "Now!"

Maggie could see Grady's mouth twitch and guessed that he probably found the whole thing hilarious. But the thought of that slithering, slippery skin wiggling around through her home gave Maggie the creeps. She lowered her eyebrows and frowned. "Now, please!"

"But Mom!" Katy launched into her attack. "Bowie doesn't like it outside. He gets cold."

"Too bad. I want that reptile out of my home. Now."

They all turned as a series of shocked screams issued forth from the big old farmhouse. Seconds later a group of excited women poured out of the doors, pushing and shoving their way down the steps.

Grady and Katy headed toward the house at a fast clip, gathering male helpers as they went. Heaving a sigh of resignation, Maggie headed for the madly chattering ladies' group standing on her lawn.

"Slid right through the grate it did," Gloria Stampford gasped, her face white with fear. "I was just dusting Maggie's dresser when it slithered down in front of me."

"It's okay, Gloria. It's relatively harmless. Grady and Katy are going to get rid of it."

"Do you *like* snakes in the house?" Bonnie stared at her strangely, eyes wide and accusing. "I mean, how can you sleep, knowing that thing could slide up beside you and squeeze you to death?"

"Believe me," Maggie muttered, closing her eyes to relieve the throb at her temples, "if I'd known that snake was there, no one would have slept for a thirty-mile radius."

They all stood silent, watching as Katy emerged from the house with Bowie calmly curling over her shoulders and down her arms.

"We'll put Bowie in my truck until I can get a cage," Grady called. "Then I'll keep the snake in the trailer until Katy takes him back to school on Monday."

They watched as Grady tried to close the door of the truck. But the snake kept slithering out one crack or the other, obviously not thrilled with Grady's accommodations.

"If that isn't just like the tempter," Minnie declared, wiping her hands on her big checked apron. "Sneaking in when folks aren't looking. Just like a nasty thought or a hasty word." She beckoned to the others and stepped gingerly up the stairs. "I'm going to use that for my lesson on Sunday morning."

"See," Grady murmured in Maggie's ear as the rest of the ladies went slowly back to work. "There's some good to come out of even this."

"Yeah." Maggie rolled her eyes. "Now the entire congregation will be talking about the McCarthy snake house. Just what I need!" She stalked back up the stairs, conscious of the group of men who stood nearby, huge grins splitting their faces as they joked with Grady about women's squeamishness when it came to snakes.

"Why me, Lord?" she asked for the hundredth time.

"'This is the assurance we have in approaching God,'" she repeated to herself. "'That if we ask anything according to His will, He hears us.'

"Okay, Lord. I'm asking. Please don't let that snake escape," she begged, fervently scrubbing the bathroom floor. "You promised that if I'd ask, You'd hear me, and I'm really asking You now. I'm holding You to Your promise."

It wasn't that she didn't trust God, Maggie told herself later that afternoon as she peeked inside Grady's truck. It was just that she couldn't help checking to make sure that repulsive reptile hadn't somehow slid out. Satisfied that Bowie was still trapped inside the vehicle with the window open just a crack, she tried to slip away, only to find Grady planted in her path, grinning for all he was worth. She ignored his knowing grin and stepped around him.

"You have to have faith, Maggie," he chided quietly. "When you ask for something, you have to trust that it will be done."

Chastened, Maggie went back to work. "I know what faith is," she muttered to herself as she tugged clothes out of her closet and organized them into piles. "I do!"

"Who are you talking to?" Gloria asked from the doorway, wiping down the woodwork as she spoke.

"God, I guess," Maggie answered and then corrected herself. "Actually, I think I reminded myself of something." She glanced at Gloria and then smiled. "'Faith is the substance of things hoped for, the evidence of things not seen.' I think I'd forgotten how to believe. Thanks, friend."

Gloria grinned and waved her cloth. "You're welcome, friend. Now, you want to tell me about that tall, handsome guy in the cowboy boots?"

Chapter Six

"Mom? How many kids can we have to the party?" Katy peered up at her mother with a pleading expression she reserved for very special occasions. "It is our tenth birthday, you know, so how about ten each?"

"Twenty girls! Are you kidding? I'm not crazy yet!" Maggie poured herself and Grady another cup of coffee and stared at her daughters. "Although, if I fell for that line, I might just require the white-coated men." She noticed the glimmer of amusement in Grady's glowing eyes, and her guard immediately went up.

"Some people might even say this latest idea of yours qualifies you," he said meaningfully. "Taking on a whole pile of kids for two hours every evening? Nuts!"

"I happen to like kids," she told him sanctimoniously. "And they need to go to vacation Bible school. It's a rite of summer."

"Oh, I'm not debating that! But couldn't you have chosen a class to teach?" he asked with a twinkle in his eye. "Or taught a craft? Did you have to take on the directing of it?"

Maggie felt herself bristling and tried to control her temper. Over the past few weeks Grady had perfected the knack of getting her dander up, and lately he'd been doing it just for sport. Conscious of the girls, peering from one to the other, Maggie sipped her coffee slowly and counted to ten.

"I wasn't planning on directing the whole thing," she told him defensively. "Last winter, I told Nettie I'd help out. But with her in the hospital and Mrs. Enns getting that company from overseas, there doesn't seem to be anybody else to fill in. Besides—" she fixed him with a cooly sarcastic glance "—you should know how persuasive Minnie can be. She got you to take her to the Sunday school barbecue, didn't she?"

"Yeah, and she spilled ketchup all over his shirt!" Katy burst into a fit of the giggles as she remembered Grady's stunned face and pristine white shirt splattered with bloodred splotches. "It was so funny when she smacked that bottle and ketchup flew all over the place."

"Miss Hugenot did try to clean it up," Keeley reminded them, the beginnings of a grin tugging at her outer lips as she petted the kitten in her arms.

"Yes, I remember." Maggie blinked innocently up at Grady who had straightened from his lounging position at the far end of the table. "She almost had it off him and he was still wiping his face. That's when she knocked the bottle down and it dripped on his pants."

Katy and Keeley burst into peals of laughter at the look of disgust contorting Grady's handsome features.

"We were discussing vacation Bible school," he reminded them dourly. "And the fact that your mother doesn't have time to be running it. She's worn to a frazzle as it is."

"Well, thank you very much, Grady O'Toole!" Maggie stomped to the counter with her cup and plopped it into the dishwater, sending suds everywhere. "It's nice to know that I haven't lost that certain something every woman wants a man to notice—frazzle!" She stifled the ridiculous tears that begged release and scrubbed furiously at the cup.

Behind her there was the whisper of conspiratorial voices, but she resolutely ignored them, piling the lunch dishes in the sink with blatant disregard for their rims and edges.

"I'm sorry, Maggie," he murmured softly, his voice near the region of her left ear. "I didn't mean to upset you. Besides, you already know how lovely you are."

"I don't know anything of the kind," she replied, intent on keeping her face averted from him. "And I wasn't fishing for compliments. Weeding in the garden all morning is hardly the way to look alluring." She heard his quick indrawn breath and waited, but Grady merely picked up a tea towel and started drying.

"You don't need to try," he muttered after a few minutes. "You always look beautiful."

She twisted to stare at him and found his warm brown eyes fixed on her. There was a look on his face that told Maggie he wasn't lying and she held her breath as one tanned, work-roughened hand reached out to touch her cheek.

"You always look beautiful," he repeated softly. "It doesn't matter what you're doing. It's a beauty that shines through the field dust and the garden soil and the paint speckles."

He touched the tip of her nose where Maggie knew she had some remnants of the light blue wash she'd given her bedroom walls. And leaning down, he brushed his lips across hers.

Maggie was stunned at the reaction she felt from her toes upward. Her knees went weak and her hands moved of their own volition to tangle in the soft, worn denim of his shirt.

Grady pulled back a fraction to stare at her and then wrapped her in his big strong arms, his lips firmly on hers as he kissed her properly, his mouth warm and demanding.

Maggie kissed him back. There was something, some part of her that demanded she experience his kiss. It wasn't as though she hadn't wondered about him for weeks now, she told herself, as his arms pulled her even closer, his hands caressing her back in a soothing touch.

She had wondered exactly how it would feel to kiss him. And now she knew. It felt…wonderful!

"Mom, Mrs. Stone is here…" Katy's voice drained away as she took in the spectacle of her mother being kissed by Grady. "Uh, never mind. I'll keep her busy." Katy backed out the door and closed it carefully behind her.

"Well, that was embarrassing." Maggie laughed nervously as she pulled away from Grady and looked anywhere but at his eyes.

"I'm not sorry," he said gruffly. One finger tipped her chin up so his brown eyes looked directly into hers. "Although I probably should have waited until a more appropriate time. But Maggie, can't you see that you *are* a beautiful woman who deserves better than Brian Dalgleish?"

Maggie stared at the disgust on his face and in his tone, but not a word would come out of her mouth.

"You're not in love with him," Grady gritted through clenched teeth, swishing the towel over the rest of the dishes before he tossed it onto the counter and turned to face her. "I think you're blinded by the life you think he can give you."

"It's not such a bad life, Grady," she murmured, hanging the towel up and putting the dishes into their appropriate places. "It would mean opportunities for the girls."

"And you?"

"Of course me. I'd be able to work regular hours and be there when they needed me. We'd have a steady income, but most of all, Katy and Keeley would have some constancy in their lives." There was nothing more to do and she had to face him, but instead of finding his glance cool and condemning, his brown eyes were warm like liquid chocolate.

"Don't you have constancy here?" he asked quietly, his eyes penetrating the shell she tried to draw around herself.

"No! I have debts here. I have a lot of work. Sure, sometimes I even have some fun." She felt dread crawling up her spine again and finally, in a rush to have it out between them, spoke the word that haunted her. "But I have far too much fear to keep on living here."

"Fear?" His voice was shocked. "What in the world are you afraid of?"

"Margaret McCarthy, what is this strange child trying to do to me?" Emerald Stone burst through the door with Katy hanging on her arm and Keeley following behind. "I've been sitting on the veranda for almost ten minutes and the child just keeps babbling about you being busy. Now, are those dishes done, or not?"

Maggie nodded, knowing very well that it would do no good to argue with Mrs. Stone. Once she'd made up her mind, the matter was settled.

"Good. He," she nodded her head toward Grady, "has work to do, does he not?" Emerald stared at him balefully as if to say she knew very well that men had no place in the kitchen. "Then off you go! And take those two with you. Maggie and I have business to discuss and we don't need anyone around to bother us."

In five seconds flat, Emerald had shooed everyone but Maggie out of the house. She swiped her hands together in a dusting motion and breathed a hearty sigh before turning back toward Maggie.

"Now, Margaret, I would like to have a new outfit for my niece's wedding two weeks from next Saturday." And thus decreeing, Emerald pulled out ten meters of the boldest, ugliest fabric Maggie had ever seen. "If you could spare me a moment, I'd like to discuss cut and style with you."

"Of course, Emerald. It just so happens that I've got a few free minutes this week. I'd be happy to sew that up for you." Maggie tried to stifle the annoyance she desperately wanted to express. "Let's have a look, shall we?"

"She's a pain," Katy announced in a grim voice as the kitchen door closed behind them. "I tried to keep her away while you were kissing Mom, Grady, but she kept insisting. Keeley couldn't even hold her back."

"Nobody," Keeley said seriously, her face looking very adult, "and I mean *nobody,* can hold back Mrs. Stone when she wants something." Her big blue eyes were curious as they studied Grady. "Did you ever want something really badly, Grady? Something that you didn't get, even though you prayed and prayed for it?"

Grady thought of the tiny baby that had never had the chance to live. He thought of the years of dreaming of a family of his own. Dreams that had died in a miscarriage. "Yes," he murmured, folding her seeking hand in his own. "I have."

"You have? What did you wish for?" That was curious Katy, peering up at him in interest.

Grady couldn't help himself. He reached out and patted the little girl's bright curls, his work-roughened fingers catching on the delicate strands.

"A little girl," he whispered, his voice breaking despite his attempts otherwise. "A little girl just like you and your sister."

"Are you going to marry our mother?" Keeley stared at the two of them, her frown marring the pretty oval of her face. "She doesn't want to stay on the farm, you know. She wants to get away."

Grady saw her cast a look of longing around the familiar

landscape and wondered, for the first time, how Keeley would fare in the city. He searched for the right words.

"I think your mother has worked for a very long time to keep everything going," Grady said quietly. He sank down onto the lush green grass and waited for the girls to join him. "She's been trying to do everything."

"A farm does have a lot of work," Keeley told him seriously. "It's sort of like school. You can't always take a day or week off just because you want to."

"I know, sweetie." He smiled at her grown-up look. "And I suspect your mom hasn't had a day off in a very long time. She's always got another quilt to make, or books to work on." He cocked his head toward the house. "Or another dress to sew."

"She used to laugh a lot," Katy whispered, staring at her hands. "I can remember it. We'd make cookies at Christmas and Easter and stuff. I liked to put the decorations on." She scuffed her toe on the grass. "We never make cookies anymore."

"Katy McCarthy, that's a lie! Granny let us help her make cookies last week." Keeley's face was flushed and she glared at her sister. "That was the day Mrs. Bloomquist got the colors mixed up and Granny came out of the hair-dresser's with pink hair."

Grady swallowed the laughter that rose in his throat. *So that's what had happened.* He smiled, remembering that brilliant fuchsia hair that had covered Kayleen Davis's head for five days. It had been the talk of the town.

"It's not the same as having Mom though, Keeley. Mom never just cut the shapes out. She adds things and fixes them up so they're different than all the other kids' cookies. I took some to play school once."

"Things are different now, Katy. Dad's not here anymore and Mom has to run things by herself." Keeley's eyes narrowed, surveying the thick green crop across the road. "She's having enough trouble keeping things going. And if we could just get a really good harvest, maybe Mom wouldn't feel so bad all the time."

"She feels bad because she wants to give us things," Katy muttered astutely, glancing at them both as she snapped her gum once more. "But I don't care about fancy clothes and stuff. I wouldn't mind a four-wheeler, though."

Grady grinned at the obvious hint about an upcoming birthday. Katy took every possible opportunity to impress on him the importance of a girl's tenth birthday. Her veiled hints about appropriate presents had included an aquarium, an ant farm, new uniforms for the Little League team she belonged to and roller blades. A four-wheeler was her most ambitious hint yet.

"I don't think your mom would appreciate that, Katy." He mussed her curls with a grin. "Come on, girls. I need a little help with a project I'm working on. Only, you can't say a word to your mother. If she knew, I'd never live it down."

They danced around him like mosquitoes, trying to find out what he meant. But Grady just smiled and led them to a corner of the barn where he'd carefully hidden his latest labor.

"Uh…what is it?" Keeley peered at the plywood backdrop with its hinged sides. She struck her hands through the smoothly sanded holes and stared up at him, frowning. "You *deliberately* cut holes in this wood?" she asked in disbelief.

"Of course I did." He was strangely affronted that she didn't understand.

Katy glanced sideways at Keeley, who simply shrugged her shoulders and shook her head. Then they both sat down on a nearby bale of hay and waited for his explanation. Grady couldn't help feeling like a misunderstood schoolboy forced to stay late to explain his deeds.

"It's for vacation Bible school," he said at last, slightly exasperated.

"Oh, yes." Katy's big blue eyes were stretched wide open. "For Bible school," she said softly to Keeley, jabbing her sister in the side with an elbow.

"Uh-huh." They both stared at him in sympathy.

"Don't you get it? It's a backdrop for a puppet show!"

"Uh, Grady, our church hasn't got any puppets." Katy said the words slowly and carefully, her hand gentle on his arm. There was a soft sympathy shimmering in her gaze. "But it was very nice of you to think of it. Thank you."

"They'll have them by tomorrow," he told her smugly. "I ordered them from a place in Calgary."

"Wow!" Keeley, at least, appreciated his intentions. "So you can stand behind here and poke the puppets through and nobody will even know who's doing what." She beamed up at him. "It's great! What are you going to paint on here?"

"Well…" Grady scuffed his foot against the wooden floor in an imitation of Katy and drew in a deep breath of the fragrant hay smell. "That's a bit of a problem, you see. I can't draw a straight line."

"*Anybody* can draw a straight line," Keeley protested.

"Not me." Grady stared at his hands. "It's something to do with my eyes, they say. Even my glasses don't fix it completely. And I *was* hoping to have it ready as a surprise for your mom on Friday."

"What kind of puppets are they, Grady?" Keeley wanted to know, studying the smoothly sanded wood. "Animals or people or what?"

"The lady at the shop told me they're for a story about a missionary family living in the jungle of South America. There's a mother, a father, a boy and a girl and a dog named Luther." He watched her serious little face study the blank board before her.

"Luther's not a dog's name," Katy said disgustedly. "Where'd they get a dumb name like that?"

"It's not dumb," Grady murmured, hoping he wouldn't embarrass her. "Luther was the name of another sort of missionary a long, long time ago. Maybe that's why they called him that." He saw Keeley squinting at the board. "What do you think, sweetie?"

"I think we could do some trees and vines and stuff on here," she murmured. "But first it needs a white coat of paint to even things out. Can you do that?" She waited for him to nod and then continued. "I could draw some stuff on in pencil and then fill it in with paint later. Do you have paints?"

"No." He grimaced, stuffing his hands in his pockets. "I wasn't too sure what to get. Maybe we'd better take a trip into town to check things out. I'll just make sure that it's okay with your mom. You guys go and get into the truck."

"Can we stop for ice cream after?" Katy asked around the wad of gum that pouched out her cheek like a squirrel.

"Only if you get rid of that gum," Grady retorted, grinning. "I thought your mother asked you not to chew it anymore?"

"She says it's the kind that 'won't stick to braces,'" Keeley stated dourly. "It sure sticks to the desks at school."

"Katy!" Grady swung round to hide the grin that itched at his mouth when she hastily got rid of the ugly green glob. "You'd better not have any more when I get back," he ordered, striding off to the house before they saw him laughing.

Kids! Maggie sure had her hands full with this pair. And yet, she was so lucky.

Maggie snatched the sand pail full of water out of Greta Wilkinson's hand just before it was emptied on Grady's unsuspecting form and wondered why she'd ever consented to a beach party for the girls. This was more like a riot!

"Okay," Grady was saying. "Here's the raft." The words had barely left his lips when the raft lifted off the sandy beach and flopped down into the water. "Uh, you're welcome." He grinned, dusting his hands against his shorts. His brown eyes sparkled up at Maggie. "Just a little hyper, aren't they?"

"That's like being a little dead," Maggie informed him, sinking back down onto her beach chair. "Either you are or you aren't. There aren't any half measures. And I am," she added, closing her eyes and letting a sigh of tiredness escape. "Dead, I mean," she murmured, opening one bright eye to peer at him.

"Not quite yet." He laughed, catching the beach ball and tossing it back to the giggling girls in the water. "But relax for a while if you want. I'll watch them."

"All of them?" Maggie studied his face and privately wondered why Grady had hung around for so long. Sometimes, when his eyes got a misty, faraway kind of look, she was sure he wanted to be somewhere else.

"Okay, maybe not all of them. That Melinda kid asks too many questions. She's got more than Katy's even thought of."

Maggie groaned. "What did she ask now?"

"What does God do when he's on vacation?" Grady chuckled. "She didn't like my answer much."

"What did you tell her?" Maggie wondered out loud.

"That God doesn't take vacations. Even when we think He's busy somewhere else, God still hears His children and cares for them."

"Sure of that, are you?" she asked grouchily, thinking of the loan payment that would be due in September. It was a whopper.

"Absolutely positive," Grady said matter-of-factly. "But Melinda insisted that three weeks of vacation was the law and that God wouldn't be allowed to work it unless He got paid overtime." He shook his head at Maggie's wide-eyed look. "Then she wanted to know who paid God. Thankfully I didn't have to answer that."

"Why not?" She was almost afraid to hear this.

"Katy told her God got paid every Sunday when they took the offering!" He laughed heartily, his voice ringing out above the children's shrieks of joy, and Maggie caught her breath at the pure pleasure on his face. "Those kids are really something, Maggie."

"Yes," she murmured. "They are. It was really kind of you to give the girls those bikes. That's an expensive gift for one child, but two? You shouldn't have done it."

"Of course I should. How could I give one a bicycle and not the other? Honestly, for a mother, you're not well versed in fairness." He grinned knowingly when she sputtered angrily at the slur. "Anyway, it was either a bike or a four-wheeler, and I'm well aware of your feelings on that subject, Maggie McCarthy!"

"You wouldn't have! Would you?" Less certain now than she had been, Maggie frowned as she studied his face for an answer.

"I *was* considering it, but then I figured maybe you were right. They ought to be a little older before they go tearing around on one of those things. Next year, maybe."

Maggie couldn't contain her thrill of excitement at the thought that Grady would still be around next year. She and the girls had really come to rely on his presence.

"By the way," she murmured a few minutes later, "it's Friday today. How come you're not going in to Calgary for your weekly visit?"

He studied her for a few minutes as if he could see into her mind. Finally he spoke, but his words came out coolly, as if he didn't welcome her question. "Everything is at a standstill right now. There's no need. Besides I saw somebody locally."

She got lost in her thoughts of Grady and all the things they didn't know about him. Was he in love with someone in Calgary? Was that who he was making calls to? Or maybe he was really sick and had to go for treatment.

Maggie hated asking, but for the girls' sake she had to know. "Grady are you in some kind of trouble?"

"What?" He stared at her for one amazed moment and then burst out laughing. "You mean, am I visiting my parole officer every week?" He grinned. "Sorry to disappoint you, Maggie, but I haven't anything so exciting in my past." He took a deep breath and then lifted his head, his lustrous brown eyes meeting hers head-on.

"I had an investment company. Someone initiated a hostile takeover by spreading rumors that we were doing business illegally. I'm hoping to save what I can out of the whole mess. But I can't do that till my doctor gives me the all clear."

No wonder he had to work for someone else, Maggie thought to herself. *He must have lost everything but the truck and the camper.*

"I'm sorry," she apologized, her hand touching his gently. To her surprise he gathered it up and held it between his larger, work-roughened hands. "I had no right to pry. It's just that Emerald told me about Doctor Lee and I wondered if you were all right. Maybe you shouldn't be doing all that heavy work?"

"Good ol' Emerald." He didn't sound angry, and Maggie relaxed just a bit. "I suppose it's natural for people to speculate in a small community like this. That's something I'd forgotten about." He seemed lost in thought, unaware of her presence as he stared out at the glistening water rippling gently from a light westerly breeze.

"It's all right," she murmured finally. "You're entitled to your privacy as much as anyone else."

"You're a nice woman, Margaret Mary McCarthy. And trust me, in this day and age, that's a compliment!" He winked at her and let her hand go with a squeeze. "The truth is, I had a heart attack a while back. Stress induced, so they tell me. My doctor ordered me to rest and recuperate away from the city and my problems."

"A heart attack? So you decided to work on a farm?" Maggie shook her head. "That's really relaxing!"

"Actually it is," he muttered, staring at the calluses that covered his fingers and thumbs. "I do an honest job in the fresh air and the sun. A certain beautiful lady feeds me home-cooked meals and two little girls keep life from getting boring. I've never felt better. There's certainly no stress."

Maggie studied his tanned face, noting the healthy flush of color. "Grady, I don't think you should be—"

He cut her off. "I'm fine Maggie. Don't start fussing. And Doctor Lee checks on me. He says there's nothing on the farm that I shouldn't be doing. It's been really good for me." He lay back on the shore, his head cupped between his hands and stared at the sky. "What do you think that cloud looks like? I say it's a sailboat. One of the old-fashioned kind."

After a glance at the girls currently engaged in a sand-building contest, Maggie lay back on her towel and stared upward.

"No way," she disagreed after a moment. "See there." She pointed. "That's a puff of smoke from the dragon. There, underneath that ribbon. I can't believe you can't see it!"

"It's fairly obvious you don't know any science," Grady countered, shaking his head. "That's not a dragon. It's a dinosaur. Triceratops, I believe."

Maggie turned on her side to laugh down at him. "Triceratops, my foot! And I suppose you think the one beside it is a hippopotamus?"

He grinned, his breath near her ear. "Hey, maybe you're finally catching on."

She swatted his shoulder and found her fingers trapped in his. "I'll have you know I invented this game." Her voice died away at the look in his warm brown eyes, and she couldn't help leaning nearer when his mouth brushed across hers. It barely qualified as a kiss and yet Maggie hadn't felt this rush of stars to her head, or this giddy rush of feelings in a very long time. His mouth pulled away from hers but she couldn't break the intensity of his gaze.

"Are you married, Grady?" The soft words slipped out before she could stop them, and once said, Maggie sincerely hoped he'd answer her. The silence, however, was deafening.

"I was. Once." His voice was low and Maggie could hear the coolness. He was pulling away. Withdrawing. "We're divorced."

"I'm sorry. That must have been very painful." She wasn't sure just how to ask, but somehow she knew that it was important to know. "Do you have any children?"

His answer, when it came, shocked her to the depths of her being, and she felt as if the sun fell from the sky.

"Once I had everything. But now it's gone. Everything's gone." He got up then and strode down the beach, a lonely solitary figure, lost in the mists of pain she had glimpsed in his brown eyes.

"Oh, Lord," Maggie whispered fearfully. "Please be with him. Help him. I didn't mean to tear him up like that. I just didn't know."

Suddenly the pastor's words from last Sunday rolled through her brain. *I am, God said. I am in control. I am there when you think I'm not. I see. I hear. I know.*

It was a promise every bit as much as the rainbow that had covered the western sky had been a promise after the rain last evening. She just had to trust. Why was that so hard?

"Mom, we're starved. Can we have the wiener roast pretty soon?" Keeley stood staring down at her mother, her eyes swerving to where Grady walked far down the white sand. "Isn't Grady going to help?"

"Grady will come when he's ready, honey. But I think right now we should finish up here on the beach. You guys go gather some driftwood for the fire. Go down there." She pointed in the direction opposite of where Grady had walked. "I think there's a huge pile just over that rock. Okay?"

"Sure, Mom. Is everything all right?" Keeley's expression was worried and Maggie couldn't help the surge of love that she felt at the little girl's concern.

"Everything will be wonderful, sweetie. After all, God's looking out for us, isn't he?" She tried to sound sure of herself, but deep inside, everything was still a knot of questions.

"Yep! God, Granny and Gramps." Keeley grinned, pointing. "Here they come, Mom, and they've got presents." She swept up the beach and toward her grandparents with a whoop and a holler.

Maggie watched Katy follow and smiled at the looks on their faces as their grandparents wished them a happy birthday. But she couldn't help it when her eyes kept returning to the tall, lean, forlorn figure sitting hunkered down on a log, staring out over the water.

Chapter Seven

"Why? Just tell me why the woman ever volunteered for this," Grady demanded of no one in particular as he hauled in the tons of stuff Maggie had tossed into his truck bed that morning. "And how did she sweet-talk me into helping?"

"Grumbling and complaining are a sin." Pastor Jim grinned as he grabbed one of the largest boxes and lugged it inside. "But since you provided us with the puppets and backdrop, I expect the Lord will forgive you." He sidestepped Tommy Williams and set his box down in the foyer. "The kids are a little excited about vacation Bible school," he explained.

"A little?" Grady winced as a shrill voice bellowed out in the vicinity of his left eardrum. "What do you call 'a lot'?"

"Just wait until Maggie gets them involved in one of those stories of hers. They'll be as still as statues."

"This I've got to see," Grady muttered, carrying in another armload.

"You're not going to be able to see anything, Grady. You're going to be behind the backdrop. We're short a puppeteer," Maggie said as she walked over to the two men. Her bright eyes were studying him with a gleam that made his knees shake.

"Maggie, you promised!" he began. "You said that I wouldn't be needed in the school. You *said* that I could get started on that haying today for sure."

"But Grady," Maggie pleaded, her eyes imploring him with that wide-open appeal that Grady defied any man to resist. "You know I can't tell the story *and* manage a puppet. I'll help you with the haying this afternoon, I promise."

"You're not haying," Grady told her firmly. "It's far too hot, and besides, you've got that special quilt order to fill. I'll manage it myself. *If*," he hinted broadly, "I ever get out of here."

He tried to sidestep her but to no avail. Her fingers wrapped themselves around his arm and she hung on.

"Grady, I *need* you. Please?"

He tried his best to get out of it. "What about Emerald Stone? I thought she was going to help you?"

"Emerald fell and hurt her leg. Has to stay off it. Besides, she doesn't like kids. Please?"

Who, Grady asked himself as he let her lead him behind the curtains of the stage, *could resist the woman?* Not him, that was for sure.

He sat behind the curtain, waiting as he listened to Maggie try to bring order out of chaos. At last the group were singing merrily along to the chorus. Then Maggie began her segue into the puppet show. He'd heard her practicing it at home.

"Did you ever wonder about God?" There was a murmur of excitement throughout the room. "What kind of things do you wonder? Janice?"

"Is God really invisible, or is that just a trick?"

Maggie, no doubt through long years of practice with Katy, fielded that one easily. "Anyone else?"

"Instead of letting people die and making new ones, why doesn't God just keep the ones He has now?"

Since Grady had wondered that himself, he listened and

nodded at the pastor's answer. It *was* comforting to think that God had his child in heaven, watching over him.

"Okay guys, one more question. Tara?"

"I was just wondering how God could love everybody in the whole world. I only gots four people in my family and I have a hard time loving them all, 'specially at the same time."

"No, you can't." Maggie smiled. Grady could hear the mirth in her voice. "I have a hard time with that one myself, Tara. But that's because we aren't God. We're just humans. And today we're going to talk about God's love for a little boy who lives very far away in the jungle. His name is Tawi."

That was the signal for the puppets and Grady scrambled to get Tawi into place. Maggie—beautiful, *organized* Maggie—had taped the script into place above each hole and all he had to do was read his part at the appropriate place.

Ten minutes later he was drenched in sweat and profoundly glad he was finished.

"Now, that wasn't so bad, was it?" Maggie was smiling at him, and he couldn't help the charge of electricity he felt as he basked in that lovely smile.

"It was awful." He sighed, wiping his forehead. "I'll build the sets, I'll lug them here, I'll do all the grunt work. I'll weed the garden. I'll even paint something if I have to. But please, Maggie, please don't make me do that again." He folded his damp handkerchief carefully, stuffed it into his pants pocket and sank back on his heels, not caring a whit that he sounded like a whining six-year-old kid. If he remained standing, it would be a miracle.

"You did very well, Grady. Thank you for filling in." She wrapped her arms around his waist and hugged him. Grady, not caring who saw, hugged her back.

"You're welcome," he murmured when she finally pulled away. "I guess." The lemon scent of her hair clung to the air surrounding them. "Maybe it wasn't so bad. You need anything else?" *Like maybe another hug?*

"No, but thanks for asking. You go ahead and get started on the haying. "I'll see you at lunchtime."

Grady watched her walk away, his left hand slipping up to touch the spot on his cheek that she'd brushed with her fingertips.

"She's one rock-solid lady," Pastor Jim murmured, his eyes glinting as Grady's hand suddenly fell away. "Be an awful shame if she ever leaves."

"She wants to, though," Grady muttered, walking down the aisle with the minister. "She thinks she wants to live in the city and have a regular nine-to-five job."

"And I guess if things get much worse for her, she'll have to." Jim's voice was low and concerned. "I'd hate to see her leave the farm. She's carried a heavy load for so long, it'd be nice if she could get that crop of hers off and into the bin."

"It looks pretty good," Grady told him seriously. "Wheat's starting to form into good-size heads. Should be worth top dollar if we can get it off. I intend to ask some of the neighbors to help when the time comes." He glanced up at the blue sky. "I'd feel better if we could get that hay off, though. I don't think this weather is going to last."

"And Maggie's already obligated to vacation Bible school." Pastor Jim nodded. "Yes, I see your problem. But I might just have a solution." He studied Grady carefully for a long time and then nodded as if he was satisfied with what he saw. "You ever worked with kids who've been in trouble?"

"Yes. A little." Grady decided he'd have to give a bit of information. "My company used to take on some of the boys from the delinquent facility outside of Calgary. You've heard of it?" When Pastor Jim nodded, Grady relaxed a little and told him how many boys he'd trained and in what capacity. "Are these young offenders?"

"Well—" Jim scratched his head doubtfully "—they're young and they're certainly offenders. They spread graffiti all over the high-level bridge a few weeks ago, and even though they've cleaned it off, there's still the matter of stealing that car and spilling manure all over Highway 4."

"In other words, they've just started down the road to ruin," Grady muttered, thinking. "What have you got in mind?"

"Haying," said Pastor Jim triumphantly.

They spent the next few minutes deciding just how they'd handle the boys, and it wasn't long before Grady found himself agreeing to take on two extra boys. By one o'clock they were heading out to start the largest field. Maggie had frowned a little when the boys had shown up after lunch. But Grady had shaken his head and she seemed disposed to let it go. For now. He suspected the dearth of garden produce waiting on the vines behind the house had prompted her quick acquiescence.

"I want to go for as long as I can," he told her quietly. "If you could manage a meal in the field, we'd appreciate it. But if that's too much work, we'll catch something later."

She'd favored him with a dour look. "Six sharp," she told him firmly. "I'll bring it out. You'd better be hungry."

He'd saluted smartly and turned and marched across the yard to the twins' fit of giggles. Kent and Randy, the two troubled youths, followed quickly, their sour looks erased for now.

Maggie watched the three of them drive off, a light feeling in her heart. She hated haying with a passion. It was hot, dirty, dusty work. "Which, come to think of it, is what most of farming is about," she muttered to herself derisively.

Katy and Keeley stood staring at her curiously. "Are you okay, Mom?" Keeley asked at last.

"I'm wonderful! And so are you." She pressed a kiss

against their soft cheeks and replaced the hair clip hanging down Katy's back. "Now, here's the deal. If we can get those cucumbers and beans picked and put away this afternoon, we'll leave the peas till tomorrow."

"Gee, big deal," Katy muttered grumpily. "I thought maybe you had a surprise or something."

"Well, as it happens..." Maggie let the words hang, knowing her daughters wouldn't be able to resist her offer. "I thought maybe we could have a wiener roast by the creek tonight. You guys could toast marshmallows."

"Is Grady coming?" Keeley asked quietly amid her sister's loud jubilation. Maggie saw her tuck a piece of paper into her pocket.

"Maybe later. He wants to get the hay finished before it rains again. Why, honey? Don't you like it when it's just the three of us?"

"Yeah, I guess." Keeley's blue eyes were shaded by the sun hat she wore, and Maggie couldn't quite make out the strange look in them. "But it's more fun if he's there. Grady makes us feel like a family."

"And Mom's got somebody to talk to while we play," Katy reminded her. "The people said— Ow, Keeley, stop that!" She reached out and tugged her sister's neatly braided hair, sending Keeley off into a fit of anger.

"Girls!" Maggie raised her voice, her eyes open wide as she stared at them. "If this continues, we will not go to the creek or anywhere else. We'll finish hoeing the potatoes instead." Her daughters bent obediently and picked up their buckets, but not without angry glares tossed between them. Maggie walked behind them, her mind replaying their conversation.

"What did you mean, Katy? What people?" She saw Keeley's head give an almost imperceptible shake at Katy. "What did they say?" she asked more loudly.

"I can't tell you, Mom," Katy muttered, yanking the green beans off with a vicious twist that amazingly did little damage to the plant. "It's a secret. You know how you say we can have secrets if they're good. Well, this is a good one."

"Keeley?" Maggie fixed her daughter with a stern look but Keeley was busy hunting among the prickly vines for the pickling cucumbers she knew were used for dills.

"You said, Mom," was all Keeley would say.

Maggie sighed. Motherhood! It wasn't nearly as easy as it should be. But it was definitely worth it. "All right girls. But it had better be good." She watched them exchange a look that immediately set her motherly instincts on "red alert."

"Oh, it's good," they said. "Really good," Keeley added softly. "Some day you'll thank us."

"Oh, Lord," Maggie breathed silently as she picked heads of dill and shook off the insects that always hid among the seeds. "Please let it be a good surprise."

The creek had dwindled down from its raging waters of spring's runoff but there was still enough to let the girls paddle around and cool off from the hot afternoon. As they giggled and laughed and chased the dog through the shallows, Maggie wondered if moving them would be the right thing. They'd had such happy times here.

"Well, isn't this a pretty sight." Grady's voice was low and intimate as he folded himself down beside her in the gloom of the evening. "It's nice when summer evenings are so long that it's still daylight at ten, isn't it?" he murmured, dropping another log on the flickering bed of coals.

"The girls love it. I usually let them stay up fairly late. After all, they can sleep in." She studied his damp brown hair as it curled onto his forehead. "How did it go?"

"Actually pretty well. I was glad I took the time to sharpen those knives on that relic, though. They wouldn't have cut butter." He took the stick with the hot dog on it and began slowly turning it over and over, browning it evenly. "I don't really need this," he muttered, sinking his even white teeth into the bun he'd wrapped around it. "That supper was enough to feed an army. Those ribs were something else."

"I'm glad you liked them. It's the lemon that brings out the flavor. Were the boys a help or a hindrance?" Maggie glanced at the girls downstream where they'd built a dam. She knew the moment they spotted Grady they'd come racing back, chatting and teasing with him. It made these few times together oddly special.

"They're smart kids," he said, biting into his hot dog. "They just got onto the wrong track. We talked about that after supper. They're coming back again to help with the baling later this week. I said I'd help them with a computer project in the fall in return for their help during harvest. They figured it was a pretty good deal."

There it was again—that reference to a future here on the farm. Maggie hugged the knowledge to her and allowed herself to daydream as she stared into the flickering coals. It would be nice to have an evening now and then spent sharing the events of the day. Though the girls were still dependent on her, they were also more involved in their own lives. Particularly Keeley, who seemed to have developed more than her usual affinity with the computer lately.

"Maggie?" She turned at the light pressure on her arm and found Grady's face mere inches from hers.

"Yes?" She liked the way his grin tipped up the corners of his mouth lopsidedly when he smiled at her.

"You didn't hear anything I said, did you?" His eyes twinkled in the dusk of the sun setting over the riverbank. "You were lost in dreamland somewhere. Don't deny it."

"I wasn't going to." Maggie decided to just tell the truth.

"I was thinking how nice it was to talk to an adult again. Which reminds me... Where are the girls?" She turned to look around.

"Don't knock the solitude." Grady chuckled. "They're fine. They're catching worms. I told them I'd take them fishing tomorrow afternoon while I wait for the hay to dry out. With this heat it won't be long before we can start baling." His voice dropped to a whisper. "I like talking to you, too, Maggie. It's just one of the things I like about this place."

Maggie got lost staring into his deep brown eyes. There were secrets there, she knew. And hidden pain. But there was tenderness and joy, too. She could see it in the tiny crow's-feet at the corners of his eyes when they crinkled with pleasure. Suddenly his words sank in.

"Fishing?" she repeated dazedly. "You're going fishing and you didn't tell me?" A slow burn started deep inside her brain and spread to her heart. "You're leaving me out of it?" She tried to mask the hurt she felt.

"Of course not!" Grady stared at her. "I just didn't think... Do you want to come?" he asked curiously. "I've never met a woman who actually *liked* fishing. We're using live worms, you know," he told her seriously, his dark eyebrows raised in a question.

As if I was made of icing sugar, Maggie huffed mentally. The one pleasure she dearly loved and seldom afforded herself and he was going to leave her out?

"Is there any other way?" She shrugged away from the warm arm that had oh so carelessly draped itself around her shoulders sometime during the conversation and wiggled backward on the blanket. "I've been using live bait for years. My dad and I used to spend hours on the Little Bow when I was a kid. Those pickerel could hardly wait for us to toss in our lines."

"Pickerel?" Grady peered through the dusky gloom at her. "They're not usually found this far south, are they?"

Maggie tilted her chin in the air and tossed him a superior look. *A fat lot you know, Grady O'Toole,* she thought to herself. "Pickerel like cold, fresh water," she informed him. "And the Bow River is fed from mountain streams and glaciers. It's generally cold enough to support pickerel." She glanced up when he shifted on the blanket. "Of course, now I don't need live bait. I have a special lure that's never failed me yet."

"All right," he admitted with that warm laugh that skittered across her nerves and made her feel cared for. "I concede my ignorance. I'll even confess that I was crass and unfeeling not to invite you along. Am I forgiven?" He pulled her up, drawing her very close to his lean, muscular length. "Would you do us the honor of joining us for a fishing expedition on the Little Bow River tomorrow afternoon, Margaret Mary McCarthy?"

His voice swirled around her like a cool mist after a blistering hot day and Maggie felt her anger melt away as she stared into those warm eyes. He was so…what was the word? Comfortable? No, that made him sound like a pair of old shoes, and Grady O'Toole was not nearly so mundane!

"Yes, thank you," she murmured primly, to hide the thrill she felt when his hands squeezed hers like that. "I love fishing. It'll be nice to get my fishing rod in the water again." She watched as he kicked wet sand over the fire and made a trench so the few smoking coals couldn't spread. "I'd better get the girls home. Tomorrow's bound to bring a big crowd out for Bible school."

"Why?" Grady asked from his crouched position on the sand. "Wasn't most of the town already there?"

"Well, we had about three dozen kids today. By tomorrow, the word will have spread that we have puppets.

Besides, I promised a treat for anyone who brings along a guest." She laughed out loud at his shaking head. "It usually works fairly well."

"I can imagine." He dusted off his hands and plunged them into his pockets, studying her with an indulgent look that Maggie didn't quite understand. One hand came out to brush the blond fall of hair off her forehead. "Lady, you are a glutton for punishment."

"Aw, come on Grady," she teased, calling the girls once more. "The crop's growing like crazy, the weather's been wonderful. You've even got the hay off. Almost," she added at his frowning look. "Life is great. What could go wrong?"

"Don't even think about it," he muttered, shaking out the blanket and picking up the picnic basket. "By the way," he asked as the girls raced away in front of them, whooping through the thickly forested bush, "do you know what Keeley's been up to lately?"

There was something in his tone that had Maggie searching his eyes. "Keeley? No. Why?" Her heart thudded in her chest as she searched his face for some clue. "What's she done now?"

"Nothing that I know of. It's just that she spends so much time on that computer of hers. And then, when the mail comes, she's always there, waiting to sort it before Elmer even gets it in the box. She usually tries to hide it, but most days there's some envelope or letter packet for her."

"What do you suppose she's up to?" Maggie asked and watched the two blond heads tilt together as Keeley said something to her sister. "Maybe Katy knows."

"If she does, she isn't talking." Grady's face turned a deep red at Maggie's curious look. "I tried to pry it out of her days ago. No luck."

"Well, whatever it is, they'll spill it before long," Maggie muttered, grunting with exertion as she climbed the last steep hill. Grady's hand on her arm propelled her over the top. "They never could keep a secret for long," she panted, grinning at him happily.

They walked back to the house without another word, listening to the girls' excited jabber about tomorrow. When the twins had hugged Grady good-night and kissed Maggie, they climbed upstairs gladly, tired from their active day.

Maggie joined her hired hand on the front porch shortly after that and handed him a long, cool glass of ice tea. As she leaned back in the old willow chair, her eyes studied the star-studded beauty of the heavens.

"They're up to something," she confided, tilting her head toward the window that overlooked the front yard. "I can hear the whispers from here. I'll bet Katy lets the cat out of the bag tomorrow."

But Grady wasn't so certain. She could see it in the way he studied that window for a long time, sipping his tea absently. And he never even commented on the falling star Maggie pointed out to him just before the old mantel clock struck midnight.

But she knew exactly when his attention shifted from the room upstairs to her. She could feel the crackle of tension in the air as he watched her from under the brim of his cowboy hat. And when he stood up and slowly placed his glass on a nearby table, Maggie knew he was going to kiss her.

She stood and moved into his embrace easily, relaxing against him when his arms fitted themselves around her waist. She could smell the bracing scent of his cologne mingled with the blooming hollyhocks and taste the hint of lemon on his breath when his mouth closed over hers.

"You're a very beautiful woman, Maggie," he murmured as his fingers disentangled themselves from her hair a moment later. His smooth soft lips brushed her cheek in a gossamer caress that almost made her forget where she was.

Almost.

"You're lucky, too," he whispered, his arms looped gently around her. "You have what most people long for." The words were so quiet, she barely heard them. "Land, a family and a place to call home." For once she had no desire to contradict him.

They stood there, staring at the stars in each other's eyes for a long time before Grady set her away, his lips touching hers one final time.

"Good night, Margaret Mary."

As he walked across the yard to his camper and the lights went on inside, Maggie flopped back down in her chair. The old yearning for something more, something better, rose up inside, deeper and stronger than ever as she started out across the yard.

What she saw wasn't that great. A rickety old barn that had been patched and repatched. Rusty farm machinery that ran on a piece of gum and a prayer. A drafty old house that cost her a fortune to cool in the hot Canadian summer and even more to heat in the winter.

"It might be home for now, Grady," she murmured to herself as she slipped inside and tugged the warped door closed behind her. "But it's just a place to stay until I can find something better. Someplace where we can have everything the girls and I need. And I will find it," she added fiercely as she climbed the creaky staircase to her lonely room. "I will get a better life for my girls and myself. No matter what."

Chapter Eight

"Ah! This is the life." Maggie leaned back in her seat and jiggled her fishing pole slightly, waiting for the slight tug that would give her the next catch of the afternoon.

"Quit bragging," Grady muttered, casting out again. A disgusted look tipped his eyebrows down. "Two hours and not even a bite. What am I doing wrong, oh great fisherwoman?"

Maggie turned her face away, pretending to study her daughters as they searched the shallows near shore for minnows. The girls had long since tired of fishing with a pole and had opted for a swim, their minnow nets and the freedom to run and yell along the beach.

"I'm waiting," Grady muttered grumpily. "And if you even think about saying 'I told you so,'" he growled, motioning at the water, "I'll dump you overboard and return this monstrosity to your generous neighbor." His look grew even fiercer at the burst of giggles she couldn't contain.

"I'm sorry," Maggie said, laughing and lowering back into the chilly water of the lake the stringer holding the six lovely pickerel. "I told you, this is my lucky lure. It never fails to bring 'em in." She snapped it across the water with an expert flick of her wrist and glanced at him from the corner of her eye. "Would you like to borrow it?"

"No I would not." His voice was curt. "I'm using exactly the same lure. How many worms did you put on?"

"Didn't use 'em," Maggie asserted, jerking sharply on the line and winding it slowly in. "Don't need to," she said triumphantly as she lifted out another prime catch. She could feel his eyes studying her as she whipped the hook out of the fish's mouth and expertly strung it alongside the last. "It's all in the wrist action."

"How come it can't all be in the wrist when you change oil in your car, then?" he demanded, a trifle sulkily Maggie decided. "I've never seen anyone make that big a mess of an oil change."

"Changing oil is not my forte," she told him airily. It was hard to miss his "That's for sure!" seconds later. "You have some areas in which you don't exactly excel, either, you know," she reminded him primly.

"Oh, yeah! Name one."

"Well, for one thing, your color coordination is the worst I've ever seen." She nodded meaningfully at his faded pink shirt and bright red shorts. "The two of those do *not* belong on one body at the same time." She giggled at his offended look. "And especially not when the wearer is sporting such a sunburned nose."

"I got it this morning, teaching your children to water-ski," he reminded her sourly. "No, actually it was *trying* to teach you that took so long. I never had so much trouble with anyone else."

Privately, Maggie wondered if he spent as much time and attention on all his other students. Even now she remembered the touch of his hands on her waist as he'd carefully fastened the life jacket and lifted her onto the dock. She could feel the tingle of electricity between them and recalled the way he'd pushed her hair out of her eyes and hauled her aboard after she'd been swamped in the waves of another boat. She'd been freezing when she got out of the water. He'd rubbed the towel briskly over her back and shoulders, stopping only when his face had been inches from hers and the girls had started giggling.

"I knew you'd keep nattering about that," she complained now, flushing hotly at his raised eyebrow. "I don't think it's very polite."

"Neither is saying my clothes don't match," he retorted with a grin. "Especially when *you* spilled the bleach on my shirt!"

Maggie could feel the heat traveling up her neck to her cheeks. "You're the one who came rushing into the house and shoved a great huge slug under my nose. What did you think I'd do—eat it?" She eyed the chilly water of the lake for one mad minute, then tossed away the idea of splashing him. He'd only retaliate.

"How else was I going to get you to take them seriously? I told you weeks ago that they were into the tomatoes and the carrots. You just couldn't accept my superior knowledge."

"Superior knowledge!" Maggie could have laughed out loud. "What superior knowledge? You don't know any more about gardening than I do." With an agitated flick of her wrist, she jerked in the hook a little too firmly and then had the embarrassment of freeing it from her T-shirt.

"Actually, I do," he told her smugly. "My mother is the world's best gardener and she has passed on all her information to me. More than I ever wanted to know."

"Your mother gardens?" Maggie stared. "Why?" She couldn't imagine the parent of this tall, meticulous businessman pottering about getting her fingernails dirty. Once more she realized that Grady O'Toole was far more than just a farmhand.

"She loves it." He wound in his line and glared at the empty hook. "This is very, *very* frustrating," he grumbled.

"Here, use my rod and reel," she offered kindly, rising from her seat and moving to sit on the hull of the boat. "I've caught my limit anyway. I'll even leave the lure on." She grinned just to show there were no hard feelings.

"There's nothing wrong with this rod and reel or this lure," he contended angrily. "Your sister said they're almost new." He tossed it against the seat with frustration.

"Oh, well, you see, that's the problem. Fish know when you're a serious fisherman and when you're just playing at it." She grinned sweetly. "Borrowing a fishing rod? Well, that's pretty much playing around. Here, try mine. Please?" She watched as he cast the line one, twice, three times without a bite. Grady never said a word but she could feel the tension building at his lack of success.

"Well, there's one sure thing," Grady said, and Maggie turned to frown at him, sensing there was some important point he was trying to make. "There won't be any fishing like this if you move to the city. And I'll bet Brian doesn't find much joy in it, either."

It was like a challenge and Maggie flushed at the scorn in his voice. "Brian is a very nice man. He's been extremely considerate of us. And the girls like him well enough." She straightened her shoulders but kept her face averted from those knowing eyes.

"Is that enough for marriage? A father for your daughters whom they like *'well enough'*?"

"That isn't what I meant," she defended hotly. "Why can't you understand that I don't want to live and die without ever having done anything but slave away on this farm? I'm twenty-nine and I feel like I'm forty-five. The world is full of things that I've never seen or done. I'm dying here!"

"You're hardly dying!"

"I am dying inside," she muttered. "Do you realize that I'm almost thirty years old and I've never flown on a plane?" Maggie refused to look at him. "I've never been outside my own country, never been to a really formal occasion, never even eaten prawns!" She knuckled her fingers tightly, opening her eyes wide so the tears wouldn't fall.

"But you can plant a field of wheat straighter than an arrow, help a horse give birth, get a tractor running and with just a few kind words, can comfort any child that comes to you," he murmured softly from across the boat. "Isn't that worth something?"

"Don't you get it? When I finally die, I want to be somebody other than good old Maggie McCarthy from the farm. I want some exciting memories to take with me into old age. I want to experience life!"

He stopped winding for a minute. "Maggie, I didn't mean…"

"Yes, you did," she asserted, fixing him with a chilly look. "You seem to think that it's your right to comment on my wonderfully rustic life, my lack of choices. You have no idea what I need or want in my life."

"I know you think you're all alone in this. I know you think God has somehow abandoned you and left you to duke it out for yourself, but that's not true." His voice was solemn, softly chiding. "God never leaves us or forsakes us. He's always there. It's like that poem about the man who saw his life flashed in scenes and noticed that sometimes there was only one set of footprints in the sand of life. He thought he'd been abandoned. Instead, God had been carrying him through the rough parts." Grady lay her rod down on the seat and reached over, clasping her hands between his. "I'm here to help, Maggie. And you have lots of friends in town who would love to lend a hand. If you'd ask."

"I don't want to go begging my neighbors for help," she

informed him angrily. "I want to be independent and manage things competently on my own."

"Hmm." He frowned. "Nobody can do everything themselves, Maggie. And I can hardly imagine that Mrs. Potter thought of it as begging when she asked you to baby-sit her kids for a while last week."

"That's different!"

"No, honey, it isn't." He smiled sadly. "Everybody needs people in their lives. Otherwise they become self-centered and embittered. There's only one God, Maggie. The rest of us are mere humans. We need each other." He brushed one hand over the fall of hair that she could never keep clipped back and tipped her chin, meeting her gaze steadily.

"Can't you trust in God's promises, Maggie? Just a little longer?" he asked softly. His eyes were warm and she could have drowned in the peace she glimpsed there. "I care about you, Margaret Mary McCarthy. And the girls. I would never do anything to hurt you. Don't you know that?"

They were words that Maggie had longed to hear for so long. And she badly wanted to believe them, to relax into the kiss that teased her lips and made her crave more. But years of misplaced hope in a future that never arrived held her back.

"And what happens when you leave and go back to Calgary?" she whispered, drawing away from his touch. "What do we do then?"

She stared at him, remembering all the times he'd eased her load over the past weeks. Without even knowing how, Maggie realized Grady had assumed the hog's share of responsibility when it came to running the farm. She'd enjoyed this summer more than any other in a long time because of this man. But when he left, when he moved back to his company and his corporate business world, how could she go back to doing it all alone?

"You just keep trusting God to get you through this day

and then the next." He cupped her cheeks in his hands, his thumbs brushing over her sun-warmed skin. "But I've got to tell you, lady, I'm not going anywhere. I like being right where I am. As long as you want me around, I'll be here for you and the girls. You're going to have to tell me when to leave."

And then he leaned in and kissed her with a soft sweetness that brought tears to her eyes. She would have kissed him back, would have told him that she felt safe and comfortable with him. Except that there was a whirring sound behind him and Maggie knew only too well what that meant.

"A bite! You've got a bite! Grab the rod," she squealed in excitement as Grady turned around. "Quick! It's getting away!" She watched in dismay as he missed grabbing the pole and heard the scream of line spinning out over the water. "It's a big one," she half whispered. "Really big."

She made a lunge for the rod which was now wiggling across the seat. But her fingers missed it by inches as the nylon line suddenly jerked and the rod flipped over the side of the boat.

"My lucky lure." She groaned helplessly, watching it flash downward in the crystal-clear water as the partially hooked fish swept past the side of their boat in what she believed was gloating victory. "My rod and reel!"

There was a sudden splash, and out of the corner of her eye, Maggie caught sight of Grady, fully clothed, diving over the edge of the boat. She stared as he dove downward in the water, saw him grab at something and then surface, gasping for air.

"For goodness' sake, Grady, get out of the water! You'll freeze! It's gone," she hollered in helpless frustration, watching him glance down once more. "Forget it."

He muttered something and dove again, swimming so far below the surface, Maggie couldn't make out his figure in the water. She was almost ready to jump in after him when he came surging to the surface, gasping for air. She yanked and pulled, trying to help him into the ladderless boat.

"It's gone," he sputtered, blinking up at her sadly. "I searched as much as I could, but it's gone. I'm sorry, Maggie. I know it was special."

"Doesn't matter," she muttered, pulling up the anchor and starting the engine as he toweled off. "That's the way life is, right? Don't ever get too attached to something, because sure as guns, you'll lose it." She deliberately drowned his reply by revving the boat's engine and then headed straight for shore.

"I should have known better than to dream," she whispered to herself, pasting a smile on her lips as they neared shore and her twins who were waving madly. Somehow she couldn't bear to look at Grady's sad face.

Back in Calgary and for a few hours and Grady O'Toole was sick of its honking horns and rushing traffic. He was sick of meetings that never ended and this ridiculous mental boxing match that had been going on for two days now and showed no signs of a winner. If anyone could come out of this a winner!

"How much do you want, Fiona?" he demanded finally, cutting across her lawyer's oily tones. He met her green-brown gaze straight on and flinched at the avariciousness he saw there. "You've got your own money, you don't need mine. The company's folded. I'm being investigated for something you know never happened. My name and my reputation have been dragged through the mud."

A sudden picture of Maggie's clear blue eyes rolled through his brain and Grady straightened. It was almost harvest time, and even though he'd finished baling the hay, Maggie would need his help to get that bumper crop off and in the bins. It was time to buckle down to business.

"What is it that you want?"

"Grady, I warned you not to speak." Harvey's worried tones hissed in his ear, but Grady brushed him away, his eyes never leaving the beautiful red-headed woman across the room who was suddenly a stranger to him.

"You've taken everything that you could get away with," he said sadly. "What more do you want?"

Fiona made as if to speak, but her lawyer intervened and the woman whom he'd once thought he loved leaned back in her chair and smiled bitterly.

"Mrs. O'Toole has not come here to cause harm—" the lawyer began, but Grady cut him off.

"She's not Mrs. O'Toole," he said clearly. "She never was. Never wanted to be known by my name. Why start now? And quit making speeches. What do you want?" He silently prayed, adding to a long chain of prayers for wisdom and guidance, and then straightened his shoulders. "Let's get down to business, shall we?"

A tap on the solid oak door of Harvey's office stopped the other man in midsentence as his friend's secretary poked her head through the door. Harvey got up and left, returning moments later with his usual implacable smile. He sat down, tapped his file folder against the mahogany table and spoke.

"I'm afraid Mr. O'Toole is not prepared to offer your client anything further than the settlement previously agreed upon. We will be filing a petition in the morning to have him completely absolved of even that responsibility. We have nothing further to say on this matter now. Thank you for coming."

Grady stared at Harvey in amazement. He wanted this thing over and done with, regardless of what it cost. He wanted to be free of this place and its memories. He wanted, he realized in stunned surprise, to be back on the farm with Maggie and the girls and see the look in their eyes when they ate dinner together tonight.

He was in love with her.

The knowledge staggered him and he shook his head a bit to clear away the fog. He loved Maggie McCarthy. More than he'd ever dreamed. He wanted to be there for her, share the girls with her and make their own special memories on that farm.

"In that case, my client will be filing a new petition of suit in the morning against Mr. O'Toole and any assets he may have." Fiona's lawyer named an amount that staggered Grady and sent his gaze winging to Harvey. But that man was smiling slightly, his faded blue eyes glimmering with excitement.

"Will you now? I'm sorry, Mr. Faraday, but I think, under the circumstances, that it would be against your client's best interests to file anything at the moment. In fact, I have here a waiver against any such future spurious claims. If you'd care to sign."

"Don't be ridiculous! Of course she won't sign. What are you up to now?" Mr. Faraday's eyes shifted around the table. "What is going on here?"

"What has been going on is a little smear campaign by your client. I have just received word that Judge Ronaldson has dismissed all your actions against us and disallowed the restraints that were placed on Mr. O'Toole's company. Shaughnessy's is free to open up tomorrow morning and resume business as soon as possible. If you persist in further persecutions, we will be forced to take legal action against yourself and your client." Harvey twirled his pen pleasantly, but his eyes were cold and hard.

"This is preposterous! Why would the judge suddenly do this?" Faraday's face was a comic mask. "Are we now to add bribery to the list?"

Harvey's voice was very quiet but there was a shaft of steel through it. "Perhaps you might wish to ask your client that,

Mr. Faraday. It seems a witness has come forward. This witness swore to the judge that your client paid him sixty thousand dollars to falsify documents and spread heresay and rumor."

Harvey stood to his feet, gathered his papers and hooked his fingers under Grady's arm. "We'll leave you alone to discuss the matter," he said kindly. "I'm sure you have some questions that need answering."

As he stood staring at a woman he'd mistakenly thought he loved, Grady felt only pity for the angry, bitter woman who glared back at him.

"Why should you have all that money, Grady? You don't use it, you don't get any benefit from it. You just lock it away and pretend that it means nothing." Her face had drained of all color now and she rose slowly to her feet. "I could have used that money and doubled, no, tripled it. I could have made you the richest man in North America if you'd only taken my advice."

"You gained that advice in underhanded ways by manipulating people, Fiona," he told her quietly. "The money never meant that much to me. It's a legacy from a friend who wanted me to use it on something special. Once you could have asked and I would have given it to you."

She stared at him, hate broiling in her eyes. "For a child, Grady? Would you have given me your money if your child had lived?"

Pain came in waves then, rolling over him, almost knocking him down as he thought of the one thing he could never buy. Slowly he walked to the door, grateful for Harvey's support under his arm. He stopped there, and turning, let her see the agony and tears rolling down his cheeks as he thought of the child he would never know.

"Money is all you ever cared about, isn't it?" he said. "Being pregnant didn't stop you. You deliberately ignored all medical advice for the sake of a few more dollars. And it cost us our child, Fiona.

"I wanted that child, Fiona, more than you imagined. I dreamed of playing ball with him, of teaching him to swim, of handing over the company someday." The sheer pain of it made him stop and take a breath. He looked at her.

"Why didn't you stay in bed when you were supposed to? How much would it have cost you to leave the high-powered business deals behind? Why couldn't you forget about money for a few short months? Why couldn't you put the baby first?"

She shrugged. "I had a job to do." Her face held no remorse. "I never really wanted children anyway."

Grady winced. "I know that now. Too bad you didn't mention it before we were married."

"I didn't think it was important."

That one sentence said it all. There wasn't any point in going over it all again. Not now. It was too late, for all of them. Grady turned and left them all behind: Fiona, her lawyer and Harvey. He walked out of the office and into the street. With a rush of footsteps he was across the intersection and up the wide steep stairs of an old stone church that stood empty of afternoon visitors.

For a long time he sat, staring at the altar and the paintings of Jesus as a child, a young man and an adult. He knew he was crying, felt the tears dropping off his chin. But he didn't care. All that mattered now was the little body he'd never hold, the little fingers that would never wrap around his. The little voice that would never say "Daddy".

"Why?" he demanded at last, staring at the stained glass window so high in the ceiling. "Why?" The words echoed round and round the empty sanctuary until once more everything was silent.

Grady leaned back against the padded seat and breathed

in and out slowly, focusing on drawing fresh air into his tight lungs. As he did, his eyes fell on a picture of Jesus standing on a mountain, with crowds around. Underneath, words were printed, in a stylized hand, that he couldn't read from this far away. Slowly, unsteadily, Grady got up and walked over to the painting. Blinking to clear his vision, he focused on the script and then read it out loud in wonder.

"Who has known the mind of God? Or who has become His counselor? Oh, the depths of the riches both of the wisdom and knowledge of God! How unsearchable are His judgments and His ways past finding out."

"'His ways past finding out,'" Grady repeated to himself, thinking of all the things that had gone wrong without seeming reason. "You mean that I'm to trust that whatever happens, You're in charge?" he asked softly, staring straight ahead.

An image rolled through his mind, that of Maggie sitting in the boat listening to the smug, self-righteous words he'd offered, telling her that God was there, directing everything.

"Oh, I see." He sighed. "Practice what I preach, in other words." He gathered up his thoughts and once more focused on the beautiful picture hanging nearby. "'The depths of the riches of His wisdom and knowledge,'" Grady repeated, grinning now in spite of himself.

"I guess that means I can safely leave things up to You, right? Okay, God." He sighed again. "I'll try to let it go and focus on the future. I don't know what the plan is, but I trust You to handle it."

Satisfied, he walked to the door and stood staring at the city he'd lived in for so long. Suddenly he turned, walked back down the aisle and bowed in front of the cross.

"If it fits Your plans at all," he murmured softly, "could You somehow work things out for Maggie? I love her, God. And if this feeling is from You, You'll have to work through the situation for both of us. I'll trust You to do that. Amen."

And with a distinctly lighter heart, Grady walked out into the late-summer heat to head back to the one place where he still felt comfortable and at home. Maggie's farm.

But first he had a stop to make at a jewelry store. A very important stop. One that he fully intended would affect his future. If God willed.

Chapter Nine

"Anyone here?"

Grady could hardly believe it. There was no one home. He'd driven straight back to the farm, skipping supper in his urgency to return, and there wasn't a single soul waiting for him. Ironic, really.

"Trust," he repeated to himself as he changed out of the restrictive blue suit to his comfortable jeans and cotton shirt. "You've got to trust that all things work together for good for those who love God."

He grabbed three cucumbers from Maggie's garden and made himself a sandwich to accompany them inside the trailer while stifling down the worry that tugged on his brain. Where was she? It was getting dark and there was no sign of Maggie or the girls. That relic she relied on for transportation could have stopped anywhere between here and Timbuktu for all he knew. He decided to give her mother a call.

"Hi, Mrs. Davis? It's Grady. Have you talked to Maggie today?"

"Hello, Grady!" Kayleen's warm voice carried clearly across the line. "How are you, dear? It's lovely out tonight, isn't it? I was just telling Herman that it's the perfect night for a campfire. Perhaps you and Maggie could bring the girls for an hour or so?"

Grady swallowed, forcing himself to speak calmly. He didn't want to frighten Maggie's parents. Especially since he had nothing concrete to tell them. It was more a feeling, a nagging uncertainty.

"She's not here, Mrs. Davis. I was wondering if you had any idea when she might be back?"

"Grady O'Toole, I've told you more times than I can count to call me by my Christian name!" There was a short silence. "Not there? But I thought you had planned—no, wait a moment." There was some discussion that he couldn't quite hear and then Kayleen came back on the line. "Herman says she and the twins went to Calgary. To see Brian apparently. They're staying over."

The words were like a dagger through his heart. Grady thanked the woman and hung up, his mind unable to accept the reality of what this decision meant.

He had no future with Margaret McCarthy. She'd made her choice and it didn't include him. Well, then, he'd have to learn to accept that. But he couldn't help asking why. Why now, when he'd finally faced Fiona and all the pain of the past, and come out feeling almost whole?

He did the chores mechanically, barely noticing the soft nuzzles of the animals. All Grady could think about was the fact that Maggie was leaving the farm behind for the "good life" of the city. Keeley would get her piano and ballet lessons and Katy would rejoice in the variety of sports once she got over the initial shock.

And Maggie? Maggie would get a home with a man who could support her so that she wouldn't need to slave away thanklessly on this farm anymore. She would have the security she'd always craved.

"But she won't have love," he murmured, staring at the night sky in all its glory. But maybe he was wrong. Maybe she did love this Brian fellow and would be perfectly happy in her new life. Grady was surprised how much that thought hurt him.

When the chores were done, Grady finally sank into one of the big scooped-out patio chairs he'd purchased from a local welder. The wrought iron was hard and cold against his back but he welcomed that. There wasn't any point in fetching a cushion. No need to try and soften things. Reality was harsh and it was time he faced it.

"I'll buy the farm," he murmured to himself, staring round at the freshly painted house and neatly mowed lawn now visible in the yellowish glare of the yard light. "It's the perfect place to get back to what's really important in life."

There were two quarters of land adjoining Maggie's that Grady had noticed For Sale signs on last week. If he added those to what she already had, the property would be more viable as an independent operation. And they were already producing.

"Alfalfa would make a good cash crop," he considered, remembering the dehydration plant just a few miles away. The plans whirled through his mind with surprising rapidity, and he fell to daydreaming about this new turn in his life.

But the videotape of the future stopped cold when he remembered that Maggie wouldn't be there. No lilting laugh to welcome him back from the fields, no mocking grin when the twins covered him with straw, no flush of appreciation when he brought home a bouquet of wildflowers from the back forty.

"How can I do this, Lord?" he murmured as the air rustled through the trees. "How can I plan a future alone?"

Like a refreshing drink of water, the words memorized so long ago floated through his brain, full of calm and reassurance. "Trust in the Lord with all your heart. And lean not on your own understanding. In all your ways acknowledge Him and He shall direct your paths."

"It didn't take me long, did it?" he chastised himself. "This afternoon I was going to trust You and here I am tonight, doubting again." He got up and shuffled toward the camper door, knowing that Maggie wouldn't show up tonight.

"Well, then, Lord," he mumbled, getting ready for bed. "I'm leaving it in Your hands. You brought me here for a reason and I'm ready to be used however You desire." Grady shut off the lights and climbed into the small, hard bunk. He felt better after saying that, but sleep did not come easy.

Saturday turned out to be long and tiring. Slim Tattersall came out to help him work on the combine and Grady couldn't avoid the questions.

"Maggie away?" Slim's eyebrows curved upward comically. "S'pose she and them girls deserve a little holiday. They been stuck out here on their own for a long time. Do them good to get away."

"Yes," Grady agreed quietly. "It will. Do you think this thing is going to run without breaking down? I'd hate to be in the middle of swathing and have to stop because a belt breaks or something seizes up." The red herring seemed to work.

"Most everybody has a breakdown during harvest," Slim muttered, yanking on the tired old belt. "Best thing would be to replace what you can and have extra belts on hand. Be Prepared—that's my motto." He spared a glance for the farmyard. "Cleaned things up a fair bit around here, haven't you? Makes a change. Herman used to keep a nice yard when he was here, but when the younguns took over, things got pretty run-down." He fingered the rusty metal hood of the tractor and frowned.

"Don't know how Maggie kept it going. Roger was a nice enough fellow but pigheaded as the day is long. Wouldn't take my advice about buying that last quarter along the river. Said he had to expand. Then up and dying like that! Sure left his wife in a fix." He shook his head sadly.

Grady vaguely remembered Kayleen talking about how Maggie's husband had spent his insurance money on something nonreturnable. Was this what she'd meant?

"Surely she had some savings?" Grady suggested, slipping the oil cover back into place. "Everybody puts a little bit by, don't they?"

"I reckon so, if they can spare it." Slim scratched his almost bald head and then slapped his cap back on. "But those two took out a loan to buy out Kayleen and Herman. Said they wouldn't be beholden to them. Bank payments come due a lot sooner than you think." Slim's eyes were astutely studying the old farmhouse. "Then when you gotta pay a hired hand." He shrugged. "Maggie worked in town at the supermarket for a while but her help out here kept quittin'. Not much of a loss. Most of 'em weren't worth a plugged nickel, anyway."

"There now. I think that should do it. Want to try?" Grady slammed the cover down and watched his neighbor swing up into the old worn seat with an ease that amazed him. "Give it a bit of gas," he offered helpfully.

Slim fiddled with the choke and then pressed the starter but nothing happened. He clenched his jaw and tried again, finally eliciting a spark of interest on the fifth attempt. The motor spluttered indignantly for a few minutes, spewing out blue smoke in a huge cloud and then died.

"Thing's a pile of junk," Slim informed him curtly, climbing down. "Should have been retired ten years ago." He kicked one tire viciously. "Gonna take a pile of work to revive that hunk of scrap."

"I planned on that," Grady told him, grinning. "Want to help me out?" He waited for the older man's decision, ignoring the look of surprise.

"Didn't figure you'd be interested," Slim drawled, his eyes narrowed. "Big-city guys like you usually just buy what they need."

Grady stared. How did he know? "I, uh, that is, I'm not what you think."

"Sure y'are! I had some dealings with your company before it got shut down. Followed things real close." Slim chewed on the stem of wheat methodically before tipping his head back to grin at Grady. "Heard it's gonna be reinstated on Monday." When Grady didn't say anything, he continued. "S'pect you'll be moving on then." It wasn't a question but Grady answered anyway.

"No, I don't intend to go anywhere as long as Mag—Mrs. McCarthy needs help. I was raised on a farm and I've missed it." He opened the hood again and peered in at the rusted old motor. "I guess I'll have to lift this thing out, won't I?"

Slim shrugged. "Yep." His tone was quiet. "How come you don't just buy a new one? Seems to me you could afford it."

Grady stopped hooking the chain on the bumper, turned and met the older man's clear-eyed stare. Slim was concerned about Maggie, he could see that. And appreciate it.

"It's Mrs. McCarthy's farm, Slim. And she'd be offended if I bought something she couldn't afford. So I'm going to fix this machine if it kills me." He turned back to his work, hoping the man wouldn't threaten to expose him. He wanted to tell Maggie the truth himself. Sometime.

"Stubborn old thing probably will. Kill you I mean." Slim grinned from ear to ear, displaying a set of white, perfectly even teeth. Obviously there was more to the man than Grady had imagined. Slim's hand came out in a gesture of friendship. "If we're gonna tackle this brute, I'd better call Buster

McLean. He's the only one around here who's still got parts for these old clunkers." His hand was firm and reassuring as it gripped Grady's. "I don't aim to be telling anybody else's secrets," he added quietly. "I reckon you'll do the best you can for Mrs. McCarthy. Like you did with the spraying."

"Yes, I will." Grady met the older man's searching glance head-on. "The very best." After a long moment, Slim nodded. Then he was on the radio to his old chum, ordering him out to the farm.

"Now, Buster," Slim murmured half an hour later. "I don't want you taking any shortcuts. Me and Grady aim to fix this thing proper. And in time for harvest."

"By the look of that barley, that's gonna be pretty soon," Buster muttered, pulling on the chain that lifted the engine out of the combine. "Either pull or get out of the way, Slim. I got things to do."

"Like what?" Slim's disparaging look slid over the filthy overalls. "Change clothes, maybe?"

"Yeah! Give me that wrench, Slim." He smacked the tool against the metal several times, and when nothing happened, laid a solid blow against it. Something shattered and lay in rusty disarray at their feet.

"You broke it! We don't need a wrecking crew here, knothead!" Slim picked up the pieces and handed them to Grady. "Maybe you didn't get it. We're aiming to fix the thing, not bust it up."

"Sometimes you gotta break eggs to make an omelet," Buster announced, twisting his head this way and that. "Now this here's your problem. I might have one of these at the shop but I can't get it right now." He dusted his hands on his overalls and picked up his tool kit.

"Why not? You got a hot date or sumthin'?" Slim snickered. Grady saw the other man's barrel chest puff out and contented himself with watching this confrontation.

"You really are a silly old fool," Buster said, affectionately slapping Slim's thin shoulder. "The social's on tonight. Right after the chuck wagon races. I ain't aiming to miss that." He stomped out the door and lunged into his truck. "That guy with the real loud voice is singin' at the bandstand later, too. My wife's determined I gotta hear that." He shook his head mournfully. "I can't abide loud music."

Grady watched Slim's head snap back. The other man's face tightened, eyes wide as if lightning had struck. "Almost forgot." Slim handed Grady his wrench and stalked across the yard. "I'll have to do this later, son. I've never missed a chuck wagon race yet, and I ain't starting now."

They were both in their trucks, motors running, before Grady woke up. "Wait a minute," he called. "What races? Where?" He saw the pitiful looks they cast his way before Slim glanced across at Buster and shrugged.

"You better tell him, Buster. No sense in him missing all the fun." With a chuckle, Slim drove off down the driveway.

"It's the local fair," Buster said, wedging himself in behind the wheel of his truck. "Not the Calgary Stampede by any means, but our own little production. Since it's near the end of the season, we get a lot of the fellows from the chuck wagon and chariot circuits stopping off. Makes for some interesting races."

Grady was well acquainted with Calgary's annual event. Visitors from around the world had been coming for years to see professional riders rope calves and ride broncos. The prizes for most Stampede events were worth a lot. But he was interested in watching the way a small town like Willow Bunch handled such an event. Besides, it would get him away from the farm and his own morose thoughts.

"Where is it held?" He scribbled down Buster's directions and waved the big man down the driveway, wincing as Buster's souped-up engine roared away.

* * *

The fairgrounds were smack-dab in the middle of town, surrounded by tall, wavering spruce trees that were supposed to protect the residents from the noise of horns blowing and hooves digging into the watered-down dirt. If there were any residents at home, that was.

Grady could hardly imagine that any one of the five thousand residents of Willow Bunch had stayed away. They were jam-packed on the stands around him, avidly watching a tractor pull a huge load of cattle feed across a chalk line. The winner got to keep the feed.

"Come on, Travis! Put your foot down!" The tiny blonde behind him had a voice suitable for one of Maggie's opera singers, Grady decided, and then wished he hadn't thought of Maggie again.

"May I sit beside you, Mr. O'Toole?" Minnie Hugenot plopped down on the bench and offered him a French fry. "It's pretty warm, isn't it?" She glanced around him curiously. "Where's Maggie?"

It was the fifth time someone had asked him that in the last ten minutes, and Grady forcibly restrained himself from the curt reply that itched inside his brain.

"Uh, she's away, Miss Hugenot. I'm not sure when she'll be back." He tried to concentrate on the two massive tractors entering the track. "Sure good weather for a fair," he murmured, but Minnie ignored that.

"Don't you worry, honey," she consoled him, patting his arm. "Maggie will be here. She never misses the chuck wagons. Maggie and those girls of hers could outyell most of the folks here." As the woman behind him bellowed more orders to Travis, Grady rolled his eyes. "Yes, even louder than that." Minnie giggled.

"Hey, Grady! We're going to look at those newfangled foreign rigs Bob Reynolds just got in. Wanna come?" Slim stood at the bottom of the bleachers, clearly unembarrassed by the attention he was drawing.

But Grady barely noticed. His attention was centered on the slim, blond-haired woman carrying three cups. Two little blond heads followed closely behind.

"There she is now." Minnie beamed. "Maggie! Maggie McCarthy, you get up here and talk to this lonely man right now!"

And Grady was so glad to see her, he didn't care that half the heads in the crowd turned to stare at them. He tried to control the joy that sprung up inside by reminding himself that Maggie might well be tied to another man by now, but when his eyes caught a glimpse of her empty ring finger, he couldn't help the grin that spread across his face.

"Hi." Maggie leaned in front of Minnie to smile at him and Grady strove to remain calm.

"Hi, Grady," the girls chorused. Their faces were wreathed in smiles and Grady couldn't help wondering why they looked so happy.

"Hi, yourselves." He grinned back. And then stared at his hands, trying desperately to think of something to say other than, "Where have you been?"

"Hello, Miss Hugenot," Keeley murmured dutifully. She shuffled her feet for a moment and then grinned at Katy. "I think Mrs. Copperfield is looking for you to help her in the booth. They had a whole bunch of people lined up when we came past."

"Good gravy!" Minnie said explosively, hustling to her feet. "I just finished a shift! Folks seem to be mighty hungry today." She gathered up her huge handbag. "Still, it's for a good cause. Slide over here now, Maggie. That's right. Leave some room at the end so folks don't have to clamber over everyone. See you later."

As they wished Minnie goodbye, Grady couldn't help but

notice Katy's smug nod at Keeley. But there was no point in asking them what it was all about. He was pretty sure they wouldn't tell him anyway. He turned his attention where he'd wanted it in the first place. Back on Maggie.

"Did you have a good trip?" he asked softly. "Your mother told me you went to Calgary. Everything okay?"

Maggie's big blue eyes met his straight on as she nodded her head. "I think so," she murmured. Her voice dropped to a whisper. "I went to see Brian."

Grady forced his face to remain impassive and kept his rump planted right where it was even though he wanted to run howling into the hills. "Oh."

"I wanted to tell him that I couldn't marry him after all." She flushed under his intense scrutiny, but to Grady she was just more beautiful. "Then the girls and I had a little holiday at Calaway Park."

Grady listened as the twins burst into excited speech about their day at the amusement center. But while they talked about the rides they'd enjoyed, he concentrated on Maggie. And praised God that she hadn't been drawn in by the allure of Brian and all that he could offer her. Now, if he could just get a few minutes alone with her, maybe he could make her understand how much he'd missed her.

"Thanks for minding the farm for us," she whispered as the last tractor left the track. "I really needed a break and so did the girls. They haven't had a holiday in a long time." Her fingers squeezed his and Grady squeezed them back.

"You're welcome," he said softly. "You're very welcome." And when she would have pulled away, Grady hung on, enveloping her slender fingers in both his hands.

The chariot races took over then and Grady watched amused as Katy and Keeley alternately cheered and jeered the teams they picked to win.

"They have a small wager going," Maggie explained as

he watched Katy hand Keeley a pack of gun. "But they pretend they don't because they know I have a strict rule about gambling." She raised her voice on the last few words and was rewarded with two cheeky grins.

"Oh, Mom!" Katy rolled her eyes heavenward and snapped her gum at the same time. "It's just a game!"

But it was a good game, Grady agreed. "I'll take the red-and-white striped chariot, girls. I think those ponies are going to clean house."

The three females surrounding him looked at each other and burst out laughing.

"Oh, Grady,' Maggie said, wiping the tears of laughter from her eyes. "Thank goodness your expertise is farming and not horse racing." When she wouldn't explain further, Grady contented himself with watching the teams set up, mentally chiding the gorgeous brown geldings to prove her wrong.

"Can't beat that for a start," he informed them as the colorful rig rushed to the front. "Look how they're pulling away from the pack. I knew those horses could go."

And go they did. Across the infield, off the track, dodging chuck wagons that were just entering the ring. The driver seemed to be fighting with the horses as they pranced merrily past the stands. He finally lost his hold on the reins and fell out the back, losing his shoes and his baggy pants in the process. Underneath, he sported bright red boxers with a huge heart on the rear.

"He's a clown," Grady told them disgustedly. "A team like that and he's a clown!"

"A very good clown," Maggie corrected him. She was laughing openly at him now, her lips spread wide as her eyes glistened in the bright sunshine. Automatically Grady leaned forward and pressed his lips to hers, uncaring of the interested spectators surrounding them. The kiss lasted for only a second or two before Maggie pulled back, flushed with embarrassment. But for Grady, it was enough to start with.

"*Now* we're square," he murmured, for her ears only.

Maggie couldn't believe Grady O'Toole had kissed her in front of God and the entire population of Willow Bunch. Now everyone would be talking about them! Still, she couldn't help the hand that slipped up to touch her lips where his had rested.

"I, uh, I don't think this is a very good idea just now," she murmured, trying to control the heat in her face. "Everyone's watching."

Grady studied her serious face before turning back to the track. "Okay," he agreed softly. "But we need to talk. At least, I need to talk to you." She saw the uncertainty touch his face. "If you want to, I mean."

"Oh, yes, I want to," she agreed quietly, heart pounding as she considered all the things she wanted to tell him. "Later."

The chuck wagons ran faster that night than in previous years. Or it seemed that way to Maggie. And as she watched Katy's and Keeley's bright heads bent over in conversation with Grady, she whispered a prayer of thankfulness toward heaven.

This seems right, she thought, happily content to let the girls occupy his time. *He's kind and considerate. He knows by now that I haven't got a dime and yet he stays on. The girls like him.*

Those thoughts occupied her mind until it was time to leave the grandstand and move into the teeming crowd of people. At last they were on their way home with Grady's truck following close behind.

"Mom?" Keeley's voice was soft in the darkness. "Do you like Grady?"

"Of course I like him, sweetheart! He's been very good to us." Some motherly sense told Maggie what was coming.

"No, Mom! I mean do you like, love him? Like in the movies?" Keeley's serious face tilted upward, waiting. "'Cause if you do, well, Katy and I like him, too. We think he's great."

"I know you do, honey. And Grady is a really nice man. But I think it's too soon to be talking about love. We hardly know him."

"I know him really good," Katy piped up from the back seat. "He doesn't care if I ask questions all the time. Not like Brian."

Maggie frowned. "What questions did you ask Brian, Katy?"

"I asked him if he figured God meant for giraffes to look like that." Maggie could hear the snap of gum but ignored it. "Just seems kind of odd that He'd do it that way. You know?"

"What did Brian say?" Maggie could imagine that Brian had not understood the little girl's enquiring mind. It was one of Brian's shortcomings that she hadn't wanted to admit to herself.

"He said I was being sac...sac...something." She snapped her gum again. "But I wasn't, Mom. Honest. I wonder why, if God can create such a great invention as the photocopier, He would make giraffes look like they do?"

Maggie stifled her laughter and turned the car into her driveway. "Anything else?" she asked, tongue in cheek.

"Well, I said that if we came to live with him, Keeley and me would like our own bedrooms. I mean, you wouldn't want us to end up like Cain and Abel, would you? I bet if their mom had given them separate rooms, they wouldn't have killed each other." Katy stopped and Maggie could see her, in the rearview mirror, twisting her pigtail as she remembered that conversation. "He got kind of red-faced and told me not to be sac...that word."

"We're not going to live with Brian, Katy. I'm not going to

marry him, remember? So I don't think you have to worry about it anymore. You'll still have your own rooms here in our house."

"Yes!" Katy high-fived her sister in a jubilant cry of satisfaction, before yanking open the car door and racing over to Grady's truck. "We're not moving," she announced, hugging him tightly.

Grady's warm brown eyes met Maggie's, sending his own message, and she felt warmed by his gaze. "Yes, I know," he murmured, hugging Katy back. "And I'm glad. Very glad," he repeated as Katy raced around the yard, yelling at the top of her lungs.

The girls were overexcited, and it took an hour before they were finally settled in their beds. They insisted on Grady coming in to kiss them good-night, and Maggie noticed that he seemed thrilled with the idea. She stood outside Keeley's door, listening to their conversation.

"Are you going away, Grady? Or are you going to stay and help my mother with the harvest?" She sounded fearful, and Maggie wished she hadn't let the girls see how much the farm had taken out of her this year. At ten years of age, they shouldn't have to worry about her.

"I'm staying right here, Keeley. For as long as your mother needs me. You can count on that. And if you and Katy ever want my help, or just want to talk, I'll be here for you, too. No matter what happens. Okay?"

Maggie heard the heartfelt sigh clearly. "Thanks, Grady. It's just that I can't help wondering about things. You know?"

"I know exactly what you mean. And if there's anything else bothering you, you just ask me." There was a minute of silence and then Grady spoke again. "Keeley? Was there something else?"

"Well, I was just wondering." The little girl's voice dropped to a whisper and Maggie had to lean in to hear. "My dad died a while ago. And my mom's been alone ever since. She never complains or anything," Keeley rushed to explain. "But sometimes it would be nice if she had an adult to talk to, don't you think? Somebody who tells her she's beautiful and makes her laugh."

Maggie blushed. It was humiliating to have your daughter trying to match you up, and she was ready to go charging into the room when Grady spoke.

"I like your mom, Keeley. I like her very much. And you're right—she is very beautiful. But I think it would be best if I told her that myself, in my own way." Maggie heard the tender note in his voice. "Without the help of two little girls who are very tired and really need their sleep. Get my meaning?"

"Good night, Grady." Keeley giggled.

Maggie went downstairs to make tea, smiling as she filled the kettle. Her daughters might be meddling, but they weren't stupid. They knew when to back off.

"They're in bed and the lights are off," Grady said, walking into the kitchen. "But that's all I can guarantee."

"That's good enough for me." Maggie laughed. "Thanks. If you'll take the cups, I'll bring the teapot out in a minute." She deliberately kept her eyes focused on the counter in front of her, waiting as Grady stood watching her. Finally she heard him walk through the door and breathed a sigh of relief.

You can get through this, she told herself sternly. *Just pretend that you didn't hear a word.* But no matter how much she pretended, Maggie couldn't help remembering the look in his eyes earlier this evening when he'd kissed her.

"Oh, get on with it, woman," she muttered, grabbing the teapot and opening the door. "You're no schoolgirl!" She shivered as the warmth of the evening and the intimacy of being alone with him suddenly hit her.

"Whatever happens, Lord," she pleaded, "please help me say the right thing. Don't let me hurt him."

Chapter Ten

Grady wasn't on the screen porch. Instead he sat stretched out on a redwood lounger on the grass in front of the house. He'd pulled up a table and a chair for her, as well.

"It's hard to believe God made it all in six days, isn't it?" he murmured, staring at the star-studded, black velvet sky. "Perfection." He grinned at her, his teeth flashing. "And you look lovely, too."

"I always did think plain old denim and ordinary white cotton was my forte," Maggie scoffed, sipping her tea.

"It wasn't so much the color of the fabric I was referring to," Grady murmured, his eyes warm as they moved over her worn jeans and white cotton shirt. "You always look lovely. It's something that comes from inside, not from what you wear. You wouldn't be any more lovely if you were dressed in silk."

"Still," Maggie said with a laugh, "I wouldn't mind trying it out once." She stopped at the look on his face. "I'm sorry. That was rude." She inclined her head. "Thank you for the compliment."

"It wasn't really a compliment, Maggie. It was the truth. I've seen your real inner beauty every day that I've been here.

When you're talking with the girls, or leading Bible school or losing your fishing pole to a klutz. I think you're pretty special, Margaret Mary McCarthy."

"Oh. Well, thank you." Maggie placed her cup on the table and stood, trying to look nonchalant as she searched for another subject. Why was she so nervous?

"Maggie?" He was behind her, his hand on her arm. "I wanted to tell you something." She nodded her head and he continued. "I was in Calgary yesterday. The business with my company is all settled. Finally."

"So you can go back now?" It was hard, so hard to say those words. "Well, I wish you all the best, Grady. And I want to thank you for helping us out." She would have said more but for the lump in her throat. The silence yawned between them until she finally glanced up, surprised when his hands moved to her shoulders.

"I'm not leaving, Maggie. Not unless you want me to. I don't know what will happen about the company. I don't think I want to do that anymore."

"What *do* you want to do?" Maggie didn't know where the courage to say those words had come from, but she waited anxiously for his reply.

"I want to stay here, on the farm. I want to help you harvest this crop and watch the snow fly while we plan next year's. I want to watch the girls go off to school and be here when they get off the bus at night."

"Oh." She didn't know what to say to that.

"I love you, Maggie. I believe God sent me here, to meet you and the girls. I think He wants us to be a family and serve Him together. I think Katy has the right idea with her verse." His arms were completely around her now, holding her tenderly, his head just inches away from hers.

"Katy? What verse?" His eyes held hers, intent in their scrutiny. Maggie couldn't look away, even if she'd wanted to.

"'Two are better than one because they have a good return for their work. If one falls down, his friend can help him up. But pity the man who has no one to help him up…and how can one keep warm alone. Though one may be overpowered, two can defend themselves.'" He recited the words softly.

Maggie frowned slightly, trying to recall just where she'd last heard that.

"It's from Ecclesiastes," Grady murmured. "She painted it on a plaque at Bible school. I think we'd make a great team, Maggie." He kissed her tenderly, his lips asking a question Maggie knew she'd have to answer. "Maggie?"

Help me, she prayed fervently. *I can't make a mistake here.*

"I think I do love you, Grady," she murmured at last, watching the glow in his eyes dim just a little. "I like you very much. You're warm and kind and gentle and you've been here for me so many times." She eased away from him and took one step backward. "I think being married to you would be the most wonderful thing any woman could wish for, and I know I'd be happier than I've ever been."

"But?" He smiled at her grimly. "There is a but, isn't there?"

"But I don't want to stay on the farm, Grady. I want to be free of the never-ending debts and drudgery. I want to feel young and carefree, to go to a concert in the park, watch the girls enjoy life that isn't confined to good old Willow Bunch." She glanced up at him despairingly. "I've told you all this before."

"But we can do that, Maggie! We'll go for holidays and take the girls on weekend excursions. We can even go to Disneyland after Christmas, if you want."

"But I'll still be stuck on the farm." She felt terrible saying it, but she'd spent too many years denying reality. Now was not the time to start pretending life would be grand just because she married Grady.

Maggie watched the pain flood his eyes and knew she'd hurt him. "It's not you," she cried. "It's this place. I've slaved away here for years, trying to make a go of it, and it just isn't working."

"Maggie, the crops are going to be bumper this year! You'll be well on the way. And of course I expect to put some money into the farm, to share the load with you. We can have a wonderful life here, if you'll just give us a chance."

"You're not pouring more money into this place," Maggie informed him sternly. "Don't you see? That's been the problem all along." She shook her head firmly. "No, somehow we've got to become self-sufficient, and until I can contribute my share, I don't want to be dependent on anyone. It wouldn't be fair to dump all my debts on you."

"Maggie, I'm not trying to buy you!" His words were harsh. "I want to share the farm with you. I've got money, I can afford it. And we can make it into something to be proud of *together*. Don't you see?"

"No," she persisted stubbornly. "I don't. All I see is this huge millstone that will drag us both down, regardless of how wonderful things look now." Maggie felt her heart sink to her shoes as she said the words, but she refused to let that sway her. This wasn't God's will for her; it couldn't be. Not when everything that was in her cried out to get away from this place.

But what about Grady? a small inner voice chided. *Are you prepared to go through life without him?* A resounding no rose up in her throat and she struggled to understand the confusion in her mind.

"Please understand," she murmured finally, lifting her head to see the pain on his face. "I've worked so long to be independent. I need to know that I can take care of myself and my children no matter what happens." There was no point in prevaricating, she decided. He might as well know it all.

"I was devastated when Roger died. But it was worse when I found out how strapped we were financially. I felt abandoned and not very capable of standing on my own two feet." She sighed. "I know everyone means well. My friends have stuck by me when no one else believed I could put food on the table, and sometimes they've even put it there for me. But I'm tired of being the local charity case. I want to be able to hold my head up, knowing that my girls aren't being denied their chance."

She searched his face for some sign that he comprehended her feeling of failure. "Can you understand what I'm saying, Grady?"

"All I really want to know is whether or not you love me?" he reiterated firmly. "Everything beyond that we can work out."

"All right! Yes, I love you!" She glared at him in frustration. "But that's not the point."

"Yes, my darling Margaret Mary, that is exactly the point." She heard the relief in his voice and moved willingly into his arms as he tugged her close. His kiss was exultant. "If we start from the right place, God will lead us to the next step. You're not alone anymore, sweetheart. We're in this together."

As she returned his hug, Maggie considered his words. Maybe it was possible. Maybe love really could conquer all. Maybe this time, she didn't need to be afraid.

"Are you with me, Maggie, my love?" His voice was soft and cajoling and she couldn't deny him.

"Yes," she whispered at last. "I'm with you. But let's go slowly and figure out each step as we go along."

"All right!" He grinned at her, his eyes blazing with new light. "How about this?" Grady's hands enclosed hers, holding them tightly. "We'll be engaged. For as long as it takes you to see that this farm can be a wonderful home for us. Together we'll take that crop off, sell it, pay down your loans and then you're going to marry me. Deal?"

It sounded too good to be true. Grady, strong, reliable Grady would stay by her side. They would support each other. And, please God, if they got this crop off, they could start planning a future together.

"Deal," she murmured.

"See, I told you," Keeley whispered, poking her sister in the side. "The lady said *'get 'em together and keep 'em together'* when she sent that last E-mail. So far it looks pretty good."

Katy turned her eyes away from the window as her mother kissed Grady. "Yuck! I can't stand all that mushy stuff!"

"You don't have to," Keeley said reasonably. "They do." She leaned a little farther out the open window and smiled. She pulled her head back in at Katy's insistent tug. "What?"

"How do you suppose that woman knows all this stuff about making people fall in love?"

"She's a writer, isn't she?" Keeley reminded her sister. She pulled the curtain back into place and flopped onto her bed. "She writes about this stuff all the time."

"All the time?" Katy could hardly believe it. "Gee! How can she stand it?"

"Lots of people buy her books, dummy. She must know what she's talking about. I'm gonna ask her the next step." Keeley skipped over to her computer and flicked it on, waited a moment for it to boot up and then clicked on the E-mail icon. "It's a good thing I read that book she sent me. It had a lot of helpful hints in it."

"Yeah, but that was for *writing*," Katy reminded her. "This is real life. *And* it's our mother!"

"Still, everybody likes a happy ending," her sister muttered, typing out a few short sentences. "There, now she'll see where we are. I think we're past stage four, don't you?"

"Why don't you go in a chat room with her?" Katy demanded, popping another bubble. "Then you could ask all the questions you want."

"Because I don't want to! This is better." She frowned at the keyboard, erased a few lines and then continued tapping. "Anyway, I don't know how."

"Well, I wish you'd get it over with, that's all," Katy grumbled, tossing her ball in the air and catching it. "I wouldn't mind playing my computer games once in a while, you know. That *is* why I got them."

"This is more important," Keeley muttered. "Mom needs us now and we can't just desert her. Besides, *you're the one* who doesn't want to leave the farm. If Mom and Grady get married, we'll be able to stay here."

"Like you want to!" Katy sneered. "You know very well you've been begging for a new piano teacher for months. And there's no drawing teacher in Willow Bunch."

"No." Keeley flicked the computer off and swiveled around on her chair. "But I could go to the city once a week to take art lessons. Or piano. We wouldn't have to live there." She climbed into bed and made room for her sister to sit on the end. "The truth is, I don't really mind where we live. But I do want Mom to be happy and I think she would be with Grady."

"You like him a lot, don't you?"

"Don't you?" Keeley countered. "He's fun to be around, he knows about all sorts of things and he's not afraid to talk about God. I didn't like to ask Brian anything!" They looked at each other and grinned.

"At least he's out of the picture." Katy blew a huge bubble and let it snap all over her face. "That's what I think of Brian." She giggled, enjoying Keeley's look of disgust. "Why were you talking to Grady 'bout God?"

"Because I wanted to ask him something." She stopped abruptly but when Katy merely raised her eyebrows, Keeley continued softly, whispering so that they couldn't be heard. "You know how Mrs. Stone's been going over all those armies that God killed in the Old Testament?" Katy nodded. "That kinda bugged me. I mean, is that all God does—punish people? It goes on and on. 'He killed this bunch and smote that one.' It's scary!"

"Yeah, but they were fighting against God's people," Katy informed her. "God didn't like that. They deserved it."

"But that's just it. I do lots of bad things. I deserve to be punished, too." Keeley stared at her hands. "And I was scared."

"What did Grady say?" Katy was sitting up straight now, her gum forgotten as she studied her sister's face.

"He said that God is just like our father, only He's a heavenly father and that I should think of Him as my dad and not as a policeman."

"We don't have a dad." Katy's voice was flat.

"That's what I told him! So Grady explained some more." Keeley's forehead creased as she sought earnestly for the right words to tell her sister. "See, Katy, God doesn't like it when we do something wrong and He wants us to ask for forgiveness. But He doesn't hold it against us. He forgives us because He made us and loves us and knows that everybody makes mistakes. That's why He sent Jesus to die for us. Only you can't go making the same mistake over and over. You have to learn from it and not do it again."

Katy shuffled uncomfortably on the bed. "You mean like throwing spitballs in school?" she muttered at last.

"Yes, exactly like that." Keeley shook her head in disgust. "And come schooltime, you better not start doing that again," she reminded firmly. "You told the teacher you were sorry.

If you were really sorry, you'd stop. You can't be sorry if you keep right on doing it!"

Katy nodded. "Yeah, I get it," she muttered. "But sometimes I do things wrong even when I know better. Does that mean God won't forgive me?"

Keeley shook her head firmly. "Grady said that if we confess that we did wrong, God will forgive us and wipe our mistakes as far away as the east is from the west."

"I don't get it," Katy announced, her forehead wrinkled in puzzlement. "That's infinity. East doesn't ever meet west."

"I know. Isn't it great?"

They grinned at each other in sudden understanding and then guilt as they heard the front door open and shut. Katy wriggled off the bed and headed soundlessly for the door where she turned back to grin at her sister.

"I just hope Mom is as understanding when she finds out what we're up to," she whispered, grinning from ear to ear. "And if she's mad, I'm going to explain that it was all your idea." She scurried out the door and across the hall as the bottom step squeaked a warning.

"Mother! What's happened to your hair this time?" Maggie stared at the tiny woman coming through her kitchen door. "Ow!" She jerked her fingers back from the bubbling pot of raspberry jam and then resumed the steady stirring motion.

"Maggie, you've filled that kettle too full. I suppose you were trying to maximize the berries and minimize the sugar again?" Kayleen shook her head at the thick red mass and moved to pour boiling water over the jars in the sink. "I hope it gels," she muttered.

"If it doesn't, the girls can eat it on ice cream," Maggie told her, removing the pot from the element and then skimming the light pink foam off. "What happened?"

"Oh, I tried to get a perm. You know the Peters girl?" At

Maggie's distracted nod she continued. "Well, she's trying out for her licence this month and she wanted to practice one last time. I let her."

"And in the process you lost four inches of hair?" Maggie took the measuring cup from Kayleen's hand with a muttered thanks and began scooping the thick syrupy jam into jars, snapping on the lids as she went. "What really happened, Mother?"

"I just told you." Kayleen poured herself a cup of coffee and sank into the nearest chair, patting her shorn head. "She used too much solution and left it on too long. There wasn't any other option but to cut off the damaged parts."

Maggie poured the last of the jam into its container and slipped the lid on before inverting the jar on the counter and setting the Dutch oven in the sink. At last she turned and studied her mother thoroughly.

"I like it," she said finally. "It makes your eyes look huge." The soft feathery silver strands lay close against her mother's head, a curling tendril caressing her cheek here and there. "You look young and carefree."

"Your father will have a fit," Kayleen said calmly. "But he'll get over it. And he won't be able to gripe about how much time it takes me to get ready for church anymore." She smiled, patting the lavender sac at her feet. "He'll have even less to say when I show him my new nightie."

"Mother!" Maggie gasped, laughing appreciatively. "You are the most devious, conniving woman."

"It's not devious," Kayleen argued. "It's common sense. Herman likes me to look my best." She preened a bit. "And believe me, I do look good in that."

"Mother, have you lost weight?" Maggie studied the pronounced cheekbones and angular chin line. "Your face looks thinner."

"Why, thank you, dear!" Kayleen beamed. "I've lost

twelve pounds now. And I don't feel nearly so dumpy. I think feeling good about yourself makes such a difference to a woman's looks." Her eyes slid over her daughter. "You look pretty good yourself. Anything you want to tell me about?"

"No. Nothing." Maggie turned away to pour herself a cup of coffee and then sank down into a chair, ignoring her mother's knowing look.

"Margaret Mary McCarthy! You tell me right this minute what's put that sparkle in your eyes!"

"Or what?" Maggie giggled. "You'll put me over your knee?" She laughed out loud at Kayleen's glowering face.

"And don't think I can't," the tiny powerhouse threatened. "Now tell all."

"Grady has asked me to marry him." Maggie could hardly believe it herself. Was it any wonder she whispered?

"Excellent!" Kayleen rubbed her hands together. "When's the wedding?"

"Mother! We haven't decided on a wedding. I'm still thinking about things." The old yearning rose in her but she stifled it down.

"What's to think about? That man out there—" Kayleen jerked her thumb toward the barn "—wants to marry you. Presumably he loves you?"

"He says he does."

"Then what's the problem? Is something wrong, dear? Don't you love him?"

"Of course I love him. That's not it." Maggie flopped back in her chair and stared at the dingy old ceiling. "I'm just not sure. We're so different."

"Different? How?" Kayleen sat silent, waiting, Maggie knew, for her to open up.

"Grady wants us to stay on the farm. He wants to build it up. He thinks this place is better than sliced bread!" She glanced around the tired old kitchen dismissively.

"There was a time," Kayleen said quietly, "when you thought that way, too."

"Well, I've smartened up since I was eighteen. I feel like the farm is dragging the very life out of me," Maggie burst out. She grimaced as the pipes began a high-pitched whine. "Every single thing in this place needs fixing!"

"There's nothing that a new coat of paint wouldn't fix," her mother stated calmly, glancing around.

"Mother, get real! This ceiling's about to fall down from being waterlogged. And why? Because the toilet upstairs keeps plugging. There are trees growing into the sewer lines or something, and it'll cost hundreds to fix. The washer conked out again last night. It needs a new motor." She got up and walked to the living room.

"Why is it so dark in here?" Kayleen peered through the gloomy room and found the light switch. She clicked it several times. "The power's off."

"On purpose. Last night I woke up to the sound of voices. I thought it was a burglar but it turns out it was just the TV going on and off. Grady says there's some kind of short in the line and he turned off the breaker. Not before it burnt out the inside of the VCR though." She yanked the back off the black box and showed her mother the mass of melted wire inside. "I can't afford to get another one."

"Thank the Lord that it didn't start a fire before Grady found it, Maggie!" Her mother breathed a prayer of relief and tripped on the edge of protruding carpet. There was a tearing sound as Kayleen sought for a hold on something that might stop her fall. "Darling, I'm sorry. I didn't mean to tear it up but my heel caught." She would have said more but Maggie held up her hand.

"Forget it, Mom. It was old when we were kids. It should have been replaced long ago. I'll get Grady to cut it off and tack it back down." Maggie walked slowly back into the kitchen and sank into her chair. "Do you see what I mean? And that's only in the house."

"Perhaps your father and I could get you a new carpet. Something not too expensive but sturdy."

"No. Mom, you and Dad cannot keep spending your savings to get me out of a hole I dug myself into."

"If you can get the crops sold, you should be better off."

"If. If it weren't for bad luck, I wouldn't have any luck at all," Maggie scoffed bitterly.

"Why, Margaret McCarthy! We do not rely on *luck* to get us through this life. We rely on our heavenly Father." She patted Maggie's hand kindly. "Are you doubting Him?"

"I'm doubting everything," Maggie confessed. "I feel as if I'm dying here, Mom. Dying slowly, but surely."

"We're all dying, dear. From the day we were born."

"But don't you see?" Maggie explained tearfully. "I feel like I've never really lived." She swiped her hand across her cheeks. "I know you and Dad tried to tell me to get an education before I married Roger. You thought I should see something of the world before I decided on the rest of my life. You were right, Mom. You were right!"

"No, honey," her mother answered thoughtfully. "I don't think I was."

Maggie stopped midsob and stared. "What?"

"God has a plan, Maggie. We can't know it or understand it, but it's still there. I believe He wanted you to marry Roger and have those two darling girls. And hard as it may seem, I believe Roger's dying was part of His plan also. Now Grady's here. Is that coincidence? I don't think so. It's just another piece of the puzzle that He's so wonderfully fitting together."

"And what about me? What about this need I have to be free and young before I get much older?" Maggie made no attempt to hide her anger. "I want a place where I can be comfortable, not constantly looking ahead to the next chore."

"Well, darling, pardon me for saying so, but I think you're fighting against the plan. It reminds me a bit of Job."

"Job? You mean I've got boils and pestilence to look forward to?" Maggie rolled her eyes.

"Maybe." Kayleen smiled at the disgusted look on her daughter's face.

"Gee, thanks so much, Mother. Boils, huh? I feel much better now."

Kayleen continued, unperturbed. "Job had everything and he lost it. All of it. It wasn't because he was sinful or even that he did something wrong. He knew that. What he didn't know was 'why'?"

"Exactly. Why?" Maggie glared at her mother balefully. "Why me? Why now? Why here? Why?"

"Maggie, you cannot know the mind of God. You simply cannot because you are not God. The majesty and sovereignty of God isn't understandable to the human mind."

"In other words, there is no answer." Maggie frowned, trying to wrap her mind around the words.

"Yes, darling. There *is* an answer. But you may never know what it is. Then again, you may, some day, understand. But that doesn't matter."

"Well, then, what does?" Maggie looked at her mother.

"Handling each day that God gives you the best way you can. Problems will always come up, Maggie. You take them one at a time, do what you can and plan for the future to the best of your ability. There's only one sure thing in this life." She smiled. "The promise that whatever happens, God is still there, waiting and watching, ready to help us take the next step. He promised."

"You mean, why worry?" Maggie shrugged. "That's a pretty tall order."

"Yes, but you've got help." Kayleen thought for a moment. "Sweetie, if you spent your life worrying about

Mount Vesuvius, would that stop it from blowing up when the time came? Of course not. Worrying is only beneficial if it helps you change something. If you're worried that the electricity might cause a fire in your living room and burn you and the children, then, yes, you do something about it. But to fret and stew about things that may or may not happen is pointless."

Maggie felt her mother's hand on her head and leaned into that caress as if she were still a young girl, needing reassurance.

"Honey, God is all-powerful. Beside Him, we are nothing. But He promises that if we pray to Him, He will hear us. We can't even understand the miracles of nature and how He created them. But we do know that God is sovereign, in control and knows things we can only dream about. Our job is to follow where He leads us, one day at a time. Can you do that?"

"I'll try, Mom." She shuffled to her feet and moved toward the stack of pots in the sink. "I guess I've become a real whiner lately. It's a wonder anyone still speaks to me." She leaned backward into her mother's hug. "Thanks for reminding me."

"Don't give up, darling. 'Trust and see that the Lord is good.' I've proven it over and over in my own life." She picked up a tea towel and dried the pots one by one. "What's next on the agenda?"

"I've got to do something with that zucchini," Maggie muttered, staring out the window at the offending plants.

"I'll take some," Kayleen offered. "I thought it would be so wonderful to have only a flower garden after spending so many years planting that great huge plot out here. But you know, I really miss the first taste of those fresh vegetables. Next year I may plant some beets and potatoes in town. Just a few," she cautioned Maggie with a wink.

"Don't be silly! There's more than enough for you out here," Maggie chided. "Come on, let's go see what you'd like. We've been eating new potatoes for a while now."

"Your father loves those." Kayleen grinned as they walked along Maggie's garden. "I'll take a few. By the way, do you want to go blueberry picking tomorrow? I thought I'd get a few since Herman is champing at the bit to get out into the wilderness, as he calls it."

"Ha!" Maggie grinned, remembering this ploy from the past. "You just want someone to visit with while Dad disappears into the underbrush, searching for bigger and better berries." She watched her mother flush prettily.

"There are a lot of bears about, you know," Kayleen murmured. "It's dangerous to be alone in the woods."

"Oh, right!" Maggie giggled, digging another hill of potatoes. "If you take ten zucchini, I promise I'll come," she compromised and watched amazed as her mother picked out the largest specimens. "But not tomorrow. I promised I'd take the girls to get their school supplies. Can you believe school starts next week?"

"I can believe it," Kayleen said, nodding at the lush golden field across the road. "That wheat looks almost ready."

"It is. Grady says it could come off number one. Which would be wonderful since the price has jumped. Grady says it's gone up because a lot of people didn't plant wheat this year. I guess they remember last year's disaster."

"Does Grady know a lot about farming?" Kayleen studied her daughter curiously.

"Seems to. But he knows even more about the markets. He had a company in Calgary that did a lot of business in that area. He studies the papers for hours. He's even got next year's crops figured out."

"Had a company?" Kayleen repeated frowning. "What happened to it?"

"He sold it or something. It had to do with his ex-wife." Maggie set several beets into her pail and moved on to the carrots. "He hasn't said an awful lot about it."

"Does he have children from this marriage?" Kayleen's face was serious as she watched the object of their conversation emerge from the toolshed.

"No. I asked him that once and he got all cold and withdrawn as if he was hurting. I don't know what it's all about but I suppose he'll tell me when he's ready."

"Probably," Kayleen agreed. "The girls seem to adore him." They both watched as Grady hunched down to show Keeley something on her new bike. Katy moved to slide her arm around his shoulders and he drew her into his free arm.

"Yes, they do. And he really cares for them, Mom. I always wondered if Brian merely tolerated them for my sake."

"I never liked Brian," Kayleen said firmly. "He was too full of himself."

"Mother! You never said a word."

"Of course not." Kayleen carried her zucchini to the trunk of her car. "That was your decision, dear. I will always support you whatever you decide."

"Thanks, Mom. You've always been there for me." Maggie hugged the woman's narrow shoulders.

"That's what mothers do. You'll learn that sooner or later. By the way—" she helped Maggie store the other vegetables in a corner of the trunk "—your sisters are coming down for the long weekend. Beth can only come for Saturday, she's on duty after that."

"What about Cathryn and Dorothy?"

"The whole weekend. Kids and all."

"Put away your good china, then," Maggie ordered, her voice droll. "And make sure your insurance is up-to-date."

"Maggie, that isn't nice," Kayleen reprimanded, frowning.

"Nice, no. Truthful, yes." Maggie slammed the car door shut and watched as her mother put the car into gear. "Bye, Mom," she called. "And thanks. For everything."

"Patience," her mother reminded. "And trust in the promises."

"I'll try." She eyed the grain fields with a practiced look and reviewed this morning's grain quotes in her mind. "Although it would sure help my faith if we could get sixty bushels to the acre and haul it to the elevator without any problems."

Chapter Eleven

Grady winced at the noise emanating from the old farmhouse and grinned to himself. So this was what it was like to be part of a big family. The only child of only children, he'd never known the joy cousins found in each other's company.

"Bradley Richards, you are a bully! Leave that kitten alone." That was Katy, as vocal as ever when it came to her pets.

Here in the yard a group of children stood waiting their turn on the trampoline Maggie's sister had brought with her from Calgary.

"Until we get a fence up with strong sturdy locks, there's just no way I'm having that thing in my yard," she'd insisted. "The entire neighborhood comes over whenever they feel like it and we're liable if anyone gets hurt. Your girls might as well use it till then."

"If I had my way, I'd leave that thing here permanently," Dorothy's husband, Ron, muttered, grinning at Grady. "The thought of the lawsuits it could engender scares me to death."

"It's a crazy world when everybody starts suing everyone else," Matt agreed. He studied Grady. "Grady O'Toole. Aren't you the guy who owns Shaughnessy's?"

"I did," Grady told him. "Before it was closed down."

"We heard about that." Ron nodded. Both men were lawyers and Grady knew the news had probably spread through the legal community like wildfire. "Are you going to start it up again?"

"No," Grady murmured, searching but not finding anything but compassion in the men's faces. "The pleasure in Shaughnessy's has been lost for me. I'm thinking of staying on here."

"As what? Hired help?" Matt scoffed. "You're not a farmer."

"I could be. But I was thinking more in terms as a member of the family. Maggie's family." Grady watched as surprise lifted the men's eyebrows. "I'd like to take this place on and make a go of it."

"You do have a reputation of revitalizing broken-down companies," Steven Richards mused, glancing around the yard. "But farms?"

"He's going to need every bit of that reputation to revitalize this place." Matt frowned. "I thought Cathryn said Maggie wanted to move."

"That was the whole point of Brian, wasn't it?" Ron glanced from one to the other. "Can't say I miss him much. Grady's a much better asset."

"That depends." Matt grinned, rubbing his hands together. "Know any football?" he asked with a laugh.

"Used to play on the all-star team," Grady told him. "Why?"

"Because we haven't had a decent game of football in years, that's why," Ron said, tugging off his dress shirt so there was only a T-shirt covering his chest. "It's about time we brought back that tradition." The others agreed and within seconds they were searching for a ball.

He was in, Grady marveled. Just like that. No embarrassing questions. His connection with Maggie made him part of the family. It was a situation he wasn't about to question.

"You city guys think you can run in those fancy pants," he called out, noticing that they all stood waiting at the edge of the lawn. "Wanna borrow some jeans or something?"

"City guys? Buddy, all three of us were born and raised in the country. Cut our teeth on prime rib and T-bones. You'd better watch it." Steven was a different man without his horn-rimmed glasses, and Grady had to marvel at the speed with which he'd organized everyone into teams.

It was a hilarious afternoon. Grady caught as many passes as the next guy, but he wasn't used to running in his cowboy boots. After hitting the ground solidly for the sixth time, he sank to the grass and pulled them off, leaving his feet bare in the thick springy grass. It was a strategy that worked for he made two touchdowns in the next five minutes.

"Aha! The man's been holding back," Matt called, take a swig from his wife's full glass of lemonade. "You'd better give me a kiss for energy, darlin', or I'm liable to pass out here and now." Cathryn flushed a bit self-consciously and tried to turn away but he kissed her anyway, in full view of the crowd, and then went jogging back into the fray.

"Dad," Maggie's nephew, Bradley called. "You'd better get some energy from Mom, too."

Steven obediently walked over to his wife and took her in his arms, tipping her dramatically over one arm as he kissed her.

"Ooh!" the children cried from the sidelines.

"Hey, my dad's gonna make the next one. Aren't you, Dad?"

"Not unless your mother can outdo her sisters." Ron smirked, standing in front of his wife. "What say, Doc?" Beth never said a word, but Grady figured the kiss she planted on him should turn him into a Hercules.

That left him and there was no way Grady was kissing Maggie in front of this rowdy crowd. Unfortunately, the twins had other ideas.

"Come on, Mom! You gotta kiss Grady so he'll win!" Katy was hopping up and down in her excitement. "Come on."

"No, Katy. It's all right. I can beat these guys with my feet tied up." He didn't even glance at Maggie, but suddenly she was standing there in front of him, head tipped to one side with her ponytail dancing in the wind.

"What's the matter, Grady?" she demanded, hands on her hips. "You never minded kissing me before."

Everyone was staring at him and Grady had never felt more embarrassed in his life.

Grady kissed her the way he'd wanted to all day. He kissed her so completely, that it was some time before he heard the voices.

"So what is this?" Bradley the referee demanded. "Halftime?"

"I dunno. Maybe their lips are stuck together." Katy stood staring at her mother in Grady's arms. But she didn't appear to be the least bit worried.

Grady moved back slightly and stared into Maggie's wide blue eyes. She seemed as bemused as he as she pressed one hand against her mouth. The other hand lay against his chest, right over his thudding heart.

"I love you, Maggie McCarthy. And I don't care who knows it." But he said the words for her ears alone and was gratified to see the tiny flicker of a grin at the corners of her mouth.

"Nobody ever said I was shy, either," she whispered, and stood on tiptoe to reach his mouth. "I love you, Grady."

"We've got a game going here, folks. If you want to keep that up, I suggest you move off the field." Matt's tone was smug. "Maybe you should set a date."

"I, uh, think we should continue this later, Grady," Maggie mumbled, pressing away from him a second time.

"Yeah," he agreed. He let her go, but his eyes followed her figure and long legs to the edge of the grass.

"You okay?" Steven asked, clapping him on one shoulder. "I can get Beth's smelling salts if you want."

"Nah, leave him alone," Ron chided. "Maybe this'll slow him down a little and give us an edge. Us old married guys need an advantage."

"You should have slowed down a little," Maggie muttered as she stood many hours later dabbing liniment on his chest, reminding him of his childishness. She clicked her tongue at the bruise that stretched over one shoulder and down his torso. "Matt plays racquetball every day, you know. He's tougher than nails. And Ron lifts weights like a pro." She sniffed as he winced. "It's a ridiculous game anyway."

"It's a wonderful game," Grady contradicted, tugging her close. "I had a wonderful time with your family. But some moments were more memorable than others." He pulled her head down and kissed her softly. "Thank you."

"For what?" She stared at him curiously.

"For helping me feel like one of the family. I like your sisters and their husbands, Margaret Mary." His arms rested around her waist. "They're real people."

"That was evident by the amount of food they consumed. That huge bowl of potato salad Mom brought is completely gone. Ditto Matt's steaks and Ron's burgers."

"Did Steve really make that dessert?" Grady watched her nod. "It's hard to believe a man with that many degrees can do all that stuff. There's obviously more to a radiologist than meets the eye."

Maggie frowned severely. "That joke is growing very old," she warned him. "Find something new."

"This is new." He tugged her a little closer. "I can't remember the last time I had the pleasure of kissing you in private." He did it again just to make sure he hadn't lost the knack.

"And I guess that's going to have to last you for a while," she whispered, pulling away. "Here come the troops again."

Grady tugged on his shirt just as the door flew open and Katy popped her bright head in. "Aren't you and Grady ever coming out, Mom? The fire's just going good." She spied the bag of marshmallows on the table and snatched them up before racing away. "Hurry!"

"Maggie?" Grady watched as the woman he loved rinsed her hands. He dried them carefully and then slipped the ring he'd found days ago onto her finger. "Please marry me? Soon?"

She stared at the wide gold band with its brilliantly glittering sapphire and the ring of diamonds that surrounded it. As he watched, tears formed at the corners of her eyes.

"Oh, Grady," she whispered, throwing her arms around his neck. "Why did you have to pick today?"

"Because it's been such a wonderful day." He smiled, wiping away her tears. "And because I couldn't carry that around in my shirt pocket any more. I love you, beautiful Maggie. I want to marry you. I bought the ring because it reminds me of your eyes." He had a sudden thought. "If you want something else, we can always exchange it." She started crying harder and sudden doubt assailed him. "Maggie?"

"I will marry you, Grady. Soon," she blubbered. He handed her a tissue and waited till she'd mopped up her face. "I love you, too. But just for tonight, could this be our secret? Just between you and me?"

It wasn't what he wanted to hear, Grady admitted. He wanted her to be as pleased as he was. To shout it so the whole world could hear. But she hadn't said no. Maggie

McCarthy had said she wanted to marry him and that was what he wanted most of all, wasn't it?

"Sweetheart," he whispered, holding her tenderly. "We can do anything you want. I love you, and no matter what, I'll always be here. Count on that. Okay?" She nodded and he kissed her one last time before enfolding her left hand in his and walking back out to her family.

As they sat far into the night, singing old-fashioned songs around the campfire and toasting marshmallows golden brown, Grady held on to Maggie's hand and thought how lucky he was to be included in this big, boisterous family. The older kids tented in the front yard. The younger ones lay fast asleep in their parents' arms.

It was so exactly what he'd dreamed of for so long, he couldn't help but whisper a prayer of thanks. And when Matt led out in the doxology, Grady willingly sang along.

"God from whom all blessings flow," Herman repeated, snuggling up against his wife. "We have a caring God, don't we, my dear."

Kayleen pressed her head against her husband's shoulder and sighed. "Too big, too kind, too wonderful to understand," she agreed happily and then got to her feet as a baby cried out, shattering the solitude. "And I think it's time we went home." She pressed a kiss against Maggie's cheek and hugged Grady. "Thank you, my dears. We had a wonderful time."

Grady stood and watched everyone leave, holding Maggie protectively at his side. He waited while Katy and Keeley bid them good-night and went quietly up to bed. He even waited while Maggie fussed with the toys left lying around and dishes not yet put away. Grady stifled the small voice that asked why she hadn't told her parents or shown anyone the ring and concentrated on the here and now.

He waited as long as he could and then he grabbed her

hand and pulled her back to the fire pit, sinking down onto the blanket that still lay there. He leaned back against the chair and pulled Maggie into the circle of his arms, sighing deeply when she settled against him.

"What was that for?"

"That was a sigh of pure contentment," he told her seriously. "And when things get rough and you get mad at me and the girls won't listen, I'm going to remember this perfect evening when you and I got officially engaged. I'm going to think about how we all sat around the fire together and sang songs and I'm going to remember the way you kissed me good-night."

"I didn't kiss you good-night," she replied, frowning, tilting her head to one side to stare at him.

"I know." He winked at her, watching the glint of awareness light her beautiful eyes from inside. "But I have very high hopes that you will soon. Please?"

He would never tire of that lilting laugh, Grady told himself as she turned and wrapped her arms around him. Not ever.

Chapter Twelve

"Maggie, my love, that is the sweetest smell I've inhaled in years. Fresh apple pie!" Maggie watched as Grady closed his eyes and sniffed while curving one arm around her waist. "I can wait just long enough for you to kiss me."

Maggie complied and saw his eyes widen as he saw the ring he'd given her days ago, now strung on a chain around her neck. She tucked it back into the neckline of her blouse and flushed.

"I don't want to damage it by getting it full of flour and lard or ruin it when I do work outside," she told him, turning away to cut a piece of pie. When he didn't speak, she finally admitted the truth. "And I still don't want to tell anyone. Not yet."

"Waiting for a better offer?" he teased, but his laugh didn't ring quite true.

"No, that's not it," she told him seriously. She watched as he took the first bite and then poured two cups of coffee before sitting down in the chair across from him. She added two dollops of cream, which she knew he liked, and then pushed the mug across toward him. "I just want a little time to think everything through, Grady. Is that so wrong of me?"

"No, of course not," he mumbled. "It's good to be sure. I guess I just assumed that you *were* sure about us."

"I'm sure about loving you." She fiddled with her cup. "It's the rest of it that bothers me. I guess I just have to deal with this in my own way, Grady. Please don't be mad."

"I'm not mad." He grinned. "I'm the happiest man on this side of the planet. I've got what I always wanted."

"What's that?"

"Three gorgeous women. And a slice of the most delicious pie I've ever eaten. Life is good." He leaned back and patted his washboard-flat stomach.

"You're good for my ego." Maggie laughed. "But 'gorgeous'? I'm sure!" She touched the scarf that held her hair off her face and thrust out her stained fingers. "I've been fiddling with that auger all morning."

Grady winced and dropped his dark head into his hands in dismay. "Maggie, I asked you to please leave the machinery to me. I'll get to it."

"If we're going to start swathing this week, it needs to be done," she reminded him. "I want to at least start out with no breakdowns." He muttered something about her being the cause of the breakdowns, and Maggie glared at him. "I heard that."

"I'm sorry." Grady brushed a kiss across the top of her head in consolation as he took his dishes to the sink. "I'm going to do a round on that barley field now. I think it's about time."

"But what about the winter wheat in the south quarter? It should be ready, shouldn't it?"

"Not quite. Besides, I'd like to take it off straight if I can. This crazy weather we've been having isn't reliable enough to leave anything in the swath for very long." He walked to the door and stopped to look at the pail of crab apples on the counter. "What are you doing with those?"

"Oh, jelly, I suppose, though I don't know why. We'll never eat all the stuff I've canned and frozen this year. Just look at this." Maggie opened the pantry doors for him to see row upon row of preserves, jams, jellies and pickles lining the shelves. "That's a twenty-six-cubic-foot freezer over there and it's stuffed, too."

"I happen to love crab apple jelly, just about as much as I love you. Besides, now you'll be able to celebrate Thanksgiving with a full heart." He grinned, tugging his gloves out of his pocket.

"But I haven't even started on the pumpkins yet! What am I going to do with it all?" Maggie closed the pantry doors automatically as she glanced out at the yellowish-turning-orange vegetables that dotted the garden. "I could make a fortune at the farmer's market selling only pumpkins!"

"I don't think so. Everyone around here seems to have lots. I guess you'll just have to make a whole bunch of pumpkin pies," he teased, rolling his eyes. "What a hardship! But I'll face it like a man."

"Oh, get out of here!" She tossed an oven mitt at him, unable to stop the burst of laughter at his offended look. He advanced menacingly toward her and Maggie retreated. "No, don't you dare!"

But it seemed Grady O'Toole did dare and within minutes had her doubled over in laughter as his fingers tickled her mercilessly.

"Truce. Truce!" Slipping beyond his reach, Maggie wiped the tears off her cheeks and frowned. "How did you know about that particular weakness of mine, pray tell?"

"I have my sources," he whispered, advancing close enough to brush his lips against her ear. "Two short but very reliable and informative sources. No, don't put that…abomination over this gorgeous hair again. It should be illegal to cover such beauty."

Pleased that he found her attractive, Maggie tucked the scarf into her pocket. "Well, I have to do something with it," she muttered, blushing. "It's getting so shaggy."

"I like your hair long," Grady murmured, running his fingers through it. "It's beautiful. And so are you." He kissed her then. "Enough of this mushy stuff!" His eyes glittered as he set her gently away from him. "I've got to get to work. Are you going to be around?"

"Yes, I'm going to start on a new project. Why?" She hated to pull her hands away from his shoulders. She wanted to be held, safe and secure in that gentle embrace, just a little bit longer. Just long enough to shut out the worries that plagued her late at night when she was all alone and couldn't rush off to another job.

"Because I might need you to bring the truck over. If that barley's ready, I'll keep going." He waited till she nodded, then stepped back and picked up the gloves he'd dropped at her feet. "I love you, Maggie." With a peck on her nose, he was gone.

"I love you, too," she murmured. But Grady had left and the words hung in the silence of the kitchen. "There's no point in fussing about things," she reminded herself sternly. "The Father knows what you need before you ask Him. Now relax and do your part."

Maggie carried her coffee into her workroom and set about piecing together her Thanksgiving quilt. She made one every year and then gave it to the church ladies for the silent auction they held to raise Christmas funds for missionaries.

A pumpkin motif seemed appropriate and Maggie set to work planning the pattern, unaware of time until the door slammed open and Katy's voice echoed through the house. "I'm home."

"I can see that. How was school?" They talked for several

moments before Maggie realized that her older daughter had not come in. "Where's Keeley?"

"Um, well, you see, that is…" Katy stumbled over the words, her cheeks flushed, eyes downcast. "Keeley sort of had to stay after school."

"Keeley did?" Maggie stared. "Why?"

"I think she should tell you, Mom. I don't want to be a tattletale." Katy walked regally from the room, head held high.

"Since when?" Maggie called, but Katy ignored her, trudging up the stairs with solemn dignity. The telephone pealed out just then, preventing any further conversation.

"Mrs. McCarthy, this is Janice Fortescue. I thought I'd let you know that I'm keeping Keeley after school today." Maggie listened as the teacher spoke and felt the knot of tension in her shoulders wind ever tighter.

"No, Janice. That's perfectly fine. If you feel she deserves to then I support you wholeheartedly. I'll pick her up in half an hour? Thank you." Maggie hung up the phone automatically. "Katy McCarthy, you get down here right this minute!"

But Katy, it seemed, had snuck out the back door and was nowhere to be found. Maggie scrubbed her hands in the sink, soapy water flying everywhere as she mumbled dire predictions the entire time.

"Maggie?" The radio blared from the kitchen. "Are you there?"

"Yes, I'm here but not for long." Maggie forced herself to speak calmly and clearly. "I'm on my way into town to get Keeley. She had to stay after school."

"Keeley did? Why?" Grady's voice reflected her surprise.

"I don't know, Grady. But I intend to find out. By the way, if you see Katy around, grab her by the seat of her pants and hang on to her. I intend to have a heart-to-heart talk with both of them when I get back. Bye." She snapped the button down and then pressed it again, anxiety rising. "By the way, how is the barley?"

"Ready to go. That's why I was calling. But don't worry, Buster's here. I'll get him to drive over and bring the truck. I'm nearly full now. See you later."

"Yes, all right. I'll bring supper out at six. Bye."

"Maggie?"

"Yes?"

"I don't know how to say this other than to say, don't jump to conclusions, okay? Let her tell it in her own way."

"Grady, I'm the girls' mother! I've had ten years of practicing. I think I know how to deal with this." Upset that he would question her judgment put a harsh tone on her words.

"I know you can. Just calm down, okay? Nothing can be that terrible." When she didn't answer, he sighed heavily. "Bye, love."

"Goodbye." Maggie grabbed her purse and stormed out of the house. "As if I don't know how to handle my own children," she sputtered. "Who does he think he is?"

A tiny inner voice chided her for blaming Grady when all he was trying to do was help. He loved the girls and cared deeply for them. He loved her, too, the voice reminded Maggie.

Then he should trust me to do the right thing. The words rolled round and round inside her head, and suddenly Maggie realized that the same thing applied to her position with God. She was always telling Him what to do and how to do it, when she could and ought to be trusting Him to do the right thing.

"Sorry, Lord," she murmured, pulling into the school yard. "I've goofed again."

As she walked up the stairs and into the old, musty-smelling building, Maggie ordered herself to be calm and rational. The sight of her daughter, seated at the front of the room, head down as she read from a thick heavy book almost shook that determination, but Maggie held on. Barely.

"Miss Fortescue, Keeley." Maggie stood in the doorway. "What seems to be the problem?"

"I didn't mean to hurt her, Mom, really I didn't!" Keeley dashed into her mother's arms, sobbing as if her heart was broken.

"Hurt who? Keeley, what is the matter?" Maggie wrapped her arms around her daughter and held her tight, amazed to find the little body shaking.

"Keeley slapped Ginny Patterson. Ginny fell backward and hit her head on the cement curb surrounding the playground. I'm afraid she had to have some stitches."

"Keeley?" Maggie gaped at the daughter who had always been so quiet and restrained in her emotions. "Will you tell me what happened?"

"I—I s-s-slapped her." Keeley hiccuped and sniffled. "And I'm glad!"

"Maybe you are," Maggie muttered angrily. "But regardless of your feelings in the matter, we do not go around slapping people. What happened?" When Keeley didn't speak, Maggie glanced at the teacher.

"I'm sorry," Janice said, shrugging her shoulders. "You know as much as I do. Keeley won't say anymore."

"Yes, she will," Maggie muttered, pressing her daughter down in a nearby chair. "And right now, Keeley McCarthy. I want an answer."

"Ginny's mean and nasty," Keeley told them indignantly. "She steals and she lies!"

"That may well be," Maggie replied, and sat down. "But we're not going to go around decking every person we don't happen to personally like, are we?" She watched for the negative shake of Keeley's blond head. "Now what, exactly, did Ginny steal, and what lies did she tell?"

Maggie returned her daughter's stare with steely-eyed determination, holding her features in her best mother-the-discipliner look. "Well?"

"She said I was always gonna be an orphan, that nobody would ever want Katy and me for a part of their family." Keeley sniffed mournfully.

"But you know that isn't true. You and Katy and I are family. We have each other. You're not an orphan." Maggie watched the blond head bend. "What else?"

"Well…" Keeley stalled for time.

"Keeley, I was very busy when Miss Fortescue called. But I took the time to come here because I'm concerned with the way you've been acting. You know better than that. Now, what else?"

"She said nobody would ever marry you and be our dad 'cause they'd have to take on our ramshackle farm, and everybody knows we don't even have enough money to pay our bills, let alone buy anything new!" Keeley glared at her mother belligerently.

"I always pay my bills," Maggie murmured, softly enough that Keeley would hear, but fully aware of the teacher seated nearby, listening to this very personal discussion of her private affairs. She felt humiliated. "And nothing you've said so far explains why you slapped Ginny." Maggie thought over the conversation. "You said 'she steals.' What did she steal, honey?"

Keeley muttered something that Maggie didn't catch. "Pardon?"

"My papers. She stole my papers!" Keeley burst out angrily.

"What papers?"

"These papers," Janice Fortescue murmured, holding out a sheaf of white computer printed sheets. "I picked them up off the ground."

There was a look of shared commiseration on her face that

Maggie didn't understand. She accepted them and glanced down in perplexity. Her eyes popped open at the big bold title on the first page.

"How To Help Your Mother Snare That Man," she read out aloud. Her shocked eyes flew to Keeley's. "Where did this come from?" she demanded.

"I, um, that is, a lady I've been E-mailing sent it to me," Keeley mumbled, shame-faced. "She writes romances, Mom, and I figured she'd know a good way for you to meet someone. Then when Grady came along and you seemed to like him, I figured it would be nice to have him for our dad. You like him, Mom, I know you do." Keeley's belligerent voice was full of tears. "And Katy and I think he's the best almost-dad we've ever had. He really listens when we tell him stuff."

"But Keeley," Maggie gasped as she sorted through the documents that explained several ways couples could get to know each other better. "To talk to someone I don't even know, about my private affairs!" She stared at the pages with distaste. "I just can't believe you'd do this. Why, Keeley?"

"Because Katy and me want a dad, that's why. I'm tired of worrying about you and about what's going to happen when we leave here! I got sick of hearing you crying at night. You did, Mom," she accused when Maggie's head jerked upward. "Before Grady came, when you thought we were sleeping, you'd get up and go in the kitchen and make hot chocolate. I followed you once and you were crying." Keeley's eyes filled with fresh tears. "After Grady came, you weren't nearly as sad."

Maggie stared at the packet of advice for the lovelorn and tried to concentrate. "Ginny stole these?"

"Yes."

"Why?" Maggie stared at her daughter, hoping against all hope that Keeley wasn't going to say it.

"She was going to put them up on the bulletin board so everybody could see. She took them out of my backpack, Mom! That's stealing. And she read them without asking. Mom? Mom!" But Maggie didn't hear her. All she could see were the words dancing in front of her.

"Your mother has to decide for herself if she loves Grady enough to marry him. You and your sister can't help her with that, so don't add pressure to this important decision by bugging her. I know you love him a lot. You can tell him that, of course. But your mother has to think of the future and whether or not Grady would be a good husband and a good father to you two. Once she's married, it's too late to change her mind."

She had to get out of there, Maggie decided. Before she screamed or tore up the sheets or stomped her feet. "I'm sorry Keeley struck Ginny, Miss Fortescue. And I will make sure she apologizes. I believe you said you'd asked her to stay in every day at lunchtime?" Janice hadn't but that didn't matter. Maggie stood briskly as the other woman nodded her head in agreement with Maggie's form of reprimand.

"I'll take Keeley home with me now and together we'll work out an appropriate punishment. Thank you for calling me. Keeley?" She lowered her brows at her daughter's stubborn look.

"I'm sorry, Miss Fortescue."

"All right, Keeley. You go home with your mother now. I'll see you tomorrow."

They walked down the empty hallway littered with bits of paper and erasers that the caretaker was sweeping into a pile. The door clanged shut behind them and Keeley jumped at the loud noise.

"Mom? Are you mad?"

"Yes!" Maggie responded vehemently, slamming the car door shut behind her. "And I would appreciate it if you did not speak to me until I tell you to."

They drove home in grim silence with Keeley's whitened face peering steadfastly ahead. At home, she climbed out of the car and walked stiffly into the house and up the stairs, her chin held high. Maggie ignored the sniffles she heard and went through to the kitchen to spread the papers on the table.

It was awful, far worse than anything she had expected. There it was in plain black and white, for anyone to see. The story of their lives for the past three and a half months. Every time the girls had seen Grady kiss Maggie, or put his arm around her waist was recorded. The discussions Katy and Keeley had held to find out Grady's preference.

Here were questions about what the girls would call Grady if he married their mother, and on another page, questions about Katy baby-sitting any children she and Grady might have.

It saddened Maggie to see that her daughters had addressed this woman named Debbie about things they should have been asking her. Why had she thought to hide their engagement? The girls' lives were at stake here, too. She should have kept them informed about Grady's role in their lives.

But as the thoughts rolled around in her mind, Maggie knew the reason she hadn't discussed her engagement with her daughters. Or anyone else, for that matter. The truth was that she was scared stiff to think about a future on this farm.

"Grady is a good man," she told herself. "But he can't guarantee the future any more than Roger could. I might spend the next thirty years grubbing in this land. By then I'll be too old to do anything else. I want to live a little before I die!"

Maggie studied the words on the paper one last time. This Debbie person certainly knew her stuff.

"Your mother has to be absolutely certain that Grady is the man for her. And she has to decide it for herself. You and Keeley have to back her up in whatever she decides. But she gets to pick the man she's going to marry herself. Just as you two will pick your own husbands one day."

"Okay, Lord," Maggie murmured, gathering up the white sheets and stacking them into a little pile. "Here comes another test. Please help me get through it."

Maggie walked slowly to the bottom of the stairs. "Katy and Keeley, I'd like you both to come down here, please."

They came at once, Katy first, with Keeley slowly following behind. Both sets of eyes were huge with worry as they studied her face.

"We need to talk," Maggie began. "I have some things to say and I want you both to listen carefully. If you have questions, you can ask them when I'm finished. Understood?" The girls nodded.

"Good. First, I want to say that I am very hurt that you would speak to someone I don't even know about my private and personal life. I would never talk about Keeley's crush on Jeremy Benstat or about Katy getting her braces caught on the bedspread because those are things that should stay in a family." Both heads lowered.

"Secondly, I am very ashamed that my daughter would dare to slap another human being. That is not the way we solve arguments in this family and you know that. Don't you?"

They nodded slowly.

"Third, you've both done something very dangerous by putting our name and address on the Internet. You both know that there are strangers all over the world who grab on to something like that. For that reason alone, neither of you will be allowed to get E-mail or go on the Internet for the next two months." Not a protest issued from either mouth.

"Now, since you wanted to know about Grady and me, I will tell you on the condition that this news is between you and I. No one else is to know. And I mean no one." Maggie slipped the chain out from beneath the high-buttoned neckline of her blouse and held up her ring. "This is from Grady. He asked me to marry him. I haven't told him for sure when I would, because I wanted a little time to think about things."

"You and Grady are getting married?" Katy burst out. "That is so cool!"

"Katy! We're not going to get married right away." Maggie hated seeing the look of disappointment cross her daughters' faces, but she labored on. "There are some things I have to think about."

"Like what?" Keeley peered up from beneath her lashes. "You love him, don't you?"

"Yes, I do." At least she was sure of that much.

"Well, then?"

"Keeley, it's not that simple. I don't know that I want to spend my life on the farm. I'd like to live in the city, get a real job, maybe send you guys to ballet lessons, or basketball, or swimming and gymnastics. There are a lot of opportunities in Calgary that Willow Bunch doesn't have."

"Would Grady move?" Katy's normally boisterous voice was quiet.

"I don't know. I want the very best life for my children," she added. "I have to make sure that I'm doing the right thing."

"What about what God says?" Keeley demanded. "I know He would want us to stay here."

"But *I* don't know that, honey. I'm not sure God hasn't given me this desire to move because that's the best thing for us. Do you see what I mean?"

"Yeah, I guess so." Katy screwed up her face in concentration. "You mean you're not sure what to do."

"Exactly. So I've been praying that the Lord would lead me wherever He wants me to be. And now I need to listen for His answer."

"You mean we don't have any say about it?" Keeley frowned. "We have to go along with whatever you decide?"

"Of course you have a say. But ultimately the responsibility to raise you girls rests on me. I have to provide for you as best I can and I'm just not sure it's the best thing for either of you to stay cooped up on this farm. It's been very hard to keep things going these last few years. You know that."

"Boy, do we!" Katy rolled her eyes. "But Mom, Grady's got money. He could help us."

Maggie narrowed her eyes and frowned. "And you think that would be fair—to marry someone because he has money that we just happen to need?"

"No." Katy pouted for a minute before her eyes lit up. "But you said you loved Grady!" she crowed triumphantly.

"Yes, I do. And the money thing has nothing to do with that."

"I'm very glad to hear it," a low husky voice murmured from behind her. "It would be a terrible thing to be married for my money twice in one lifetime."

Maggie was startled by Grady's entrance, and his revelation.

"Is that what she did?" When he winked Maggie blushed.

"Are you rich, Grady?" Katy asked.

"Katy, me darlin'—" Grady laughed as he chucked the girl under the chin and sank into the nearest chair "—I'm as rich as a man can be. Your mother says she loves me." He winked at Maggie. "And I think you two beauties are the best thing since sliced bread. "I'm richer than Croesus."

"Who?" Katy was frowning.

"The guy who had all the gold," Keeley told her. "I read it to you last week, remember?"

"You mean you've got buildings full of gold?" Katy stared at him in disbelief. "And you're working as a farmhand?"

Grady stood and burst out laughing, the sound echoing around the room. "Katy, a man's wealth has very little to do with his bank balance. I have enough money to live on, but that's not important. Anybody can earn money." He hugged her close. "But not everybody," he whispered solemnly, "has the chance to have two lovely girls for his daughters."

"Is that what we'd be?" Keeley wanted to know. "Your daughters?"

"I'd like that very much," he murmured, glancing at Maggie. "But in here—" he tapped his chest "—you've been my daughters for a long time already."

"I love you, Grady," Katy burst out, hugging him tightly. He hugged her back, drawing Keeley into the embrace and then tugging Maggie nearer when she would have backed away.

"Group hug!" Katy called out.

Maggie good-naturedly let them maneuver her closer to Grady and returned the kiss he pressed against her lips, fully aware of two sets of very interested blue eyes.

"What are you doing here anyway?" Maggie demanded, pulling away. "I thought you were knee-deep in barley."

"Oh, I'd like to be! But that swather broke down. Again. Buster's gone to see if he can find a part." He tugged her close again, his eyes twinkling. "That leaves me with a little free time," he whispered loudly.

The girls cast each other knowing looks and moved toward the door. "We're going to do our chores," Keeley offered with a giggle. "So you guys can be alone for a while."

"Yeah, alone," Katy reiterated. They moved through the door jostling each other. A second later Katy's head poked back in. "Since you've got lots of money and we're going to be your daughters, do you think we could get a four-wheeler?" she asked in wide-eyed innocence.

"Katy McCarthy!" Maggie pursed her lips.

"Well, I was just wondering. I know money isn't everything, but it sure must be nicer to have too much than too little," she retorted before closing the door behind her.

"She's got you there," Grady said with a snicker, drawing Maggie into his arms. "That's one very astute lady. She'll make a wonderful businesswoman one day. You ought to be proud."

"Right now I'm embarrassed," she told him. "They're so mercenary."

"No, they're not. They're just sweet little girls who know a good thing when they see it. I must say, I have to agree. Don't you want to go along with their plans?"

"Ha! Plans? I'll show you plans!" Maggie lifted the stack of papers from the table and shoved them under his nose. "Sit down, Grady."

"Why?" He frowned, trying to read the top sheet.

"Because if you don't, you might fall down. It seems that you and I have been the subject of an Internet-generated romance plot. Women around the world have been advising Katy and Keeley on how to get us together."

He sank into the chair. "You're joking!"

"Not hardly. Those two 'sweet little girls', as you so sweetly called them, gave a romance writer our name. She passed on their questions. These are the replies." She dropped the sheaf on the table.

To Maggie's surprise he looked not the least bit angry. Instead, his mouth curved in what looked like a proud smile. "Grady, have you any idea of what you'd be taking on here?" she asked.

"No, actually I didn't," he murmured, studying the sheets more closely. "Not entirely. But you have to admit, at least it wouldn't be boring."

Maggie sagged back in her chair and closed her eyes.

Lord, she prayed silently. *What's the plan here? Please, please, tell me Your plan.*

The only response to her plea was Grady's muffled laughter as he read through the sheets of advice from the matchmakers.

Chapter Thirteen

Grady was worried. Katy and Keeley had hunted him down in Marty Shane's garage ten minutes ago. He could tell from their tone over the phone that something was wrong.

"Grady, do you know where Mom is?" That was Keeley, her voice betraying just a tiny wobble.

"She's swathing." A prickle of fear niggling up his spine made Grady's arm tense. "Did you try her on the radio?"

"For the past half hour. She isn't answering." Katy gave the information clearly. "Should I go and look for her?"

"No." Grady knew that was precisely what Maggie didn't want. "I'm leaving now. I'll be home in half an hour. Less, I hope." He shook his head at Marty's offer of a coffee. "You guys call over to the McLeans' and ask Buster to look in the west field that adjoins his. Okay?"

"Y-yes, all right," Keeley whispered. "Please hurry, Grady."

"I'm coming, sweetheart. You just remember that God is in control. Maybe you and Katy could say a few words while you're waiting. I'll be there soon."

He drove far faster than the speed limit, his powerful engine covering the miles easily. Precisely twenty-two minutes later he drove into the yard and squealed to a stop. Katy came racing out of the house, her little face white and pinched looking.

"Mr. McLean's away, Grady. Mrs. McLean said Timmy was sick so she couldn't help us. Keeley's trying some of the other neighbors." She threw her arms around him. "I wish she'd come home."

"So do I, honey," he murmured. "But right now I've got to go look for her. Run and tell Keeley we're going looking and ask her to stay by the phone."

Grady grabbed his tool kit from beside the combine and chucked it into the truck. Moments later Katy came racing back and they set off together.

"Do you think God wants my mom to go to heaven?" she asked in a hushed, frightened tone. "Maybe He needs her there."

"Nope. I think He knows that we need her here." Grady tightened his fingers around the steering wheel and drove faster than he'd ever done down the dusty rutted track. There in the distance he thought he could see the outline of the swather, but where was Maggie?

As they drew closer, Grady could see her bright red shirt on the ground. His heart sent up a quick prayer to heaven.

"She's on the ground, Grady. She's lying on the ground. What happened? Is she dead?" Katy rattled the questions off in a tense, tight voice.

"She's not dead." Grady surprised himself at his vehemence. "Stay here until I call you."

He raced across the furrows of perfectly cut barley, ignoring the chaff that flew up. As he went, he prayed.

"Please don't take her, Lord. We need her. The girls have already lost their father, God. They can't lose Maggie, too. I can't lose Maggie!"

As he got closer, Grady took note of her prone position.

No bones at odd angles, no blood on her face. No marks. He did a quick, thorough study and was just breathing a sigh of relief when his fingers encountered the blood on the back of her head.

"Oh, no," he breathed, feeling the sticky red stuff ooze through his fingers. He moved her slightly to one side and gaped at the pool of red soaking into her hair. "She's lost so much blood. Help her, God. Katy!" He yelled across the furrows and saw Katy's little body jerk. "Bring the first-aid box behind the seat," he called, more in control now. "Your mom has hurt herself."

Maggie's big blue eyes fluttered halfway open just then and she stared up at Grady groggily. "Oh," she murmured softly, "I prayed and God brought you." Her mouth curved in a smile. "I hurt my head."

"I know you did, sweetie. Just lie still and we'll get you all fixed up. Katy's here and she's going to help me."

"Katy came? Hi, Katy." The thick golden lashes flopped down once, twice, before Maggie refocused on them. "Is Keeley here, too?"

"No, Mom. She's at the house waiting, in case someone calls. Are you all right?"

"I'm fine. Just a little woozy. I'll sit up in a minute." Her eyelids dropped down once more. Grady was grateful they stayed closed while he pressed a gauze pad on the injury and wound a ring of gauze around her head to hold the pad in place.

"Bring the kit, Katy," he murmured softly. "I'm going to carry your mom to the truck. Then we'll put her in the back seat."

"What's wrong with her?" Katy frowned as she followed him over and held open the truck door.

"I'm pretty sure she's got a concussion. We'll take her to the hospital." He closed the door and climbed into the driver's seat. The ignition had barely turned over when the thready voice from the rear objected.

"I'm not going to the hospital. I just hit my head. It's nothing serious. I have to finish the field."

"Forget the field," Grady muttered brusquely. "It can wait. Your head can't. And yes, we are going to the hospital. Now be quiet!" He hadn't meant to say it so harshly, but he was angry. How could this happen to Maggie?

Grady contented himself with praying silently all the way back to the farm where they picked up Keeley and then headed to town. Katy quickly explained the situation and both girls sat silent, casting worried glances at their mother from time to time. Maggie said nothing and Grady wondered if she'd blacked out again.

At the hospital, doctors and nurses brushed him aside. "You'll have to wait with her daughters," the nurse told him. "I'm sure the doctor will explain once he's examined Mrs. McCarthy. Are you a friend?"

"I'm her fiancé," he burst out, pleased to be able to finally say the words. He didn't care if the whole world knew; he wanted some tie to bind him and Maggie together.

"Oh." The nurse studied him thoroughly. "Congratulations!"

"Thanks," he said, glancing down the hall at the flurry of activity around Maggie's room. "Will you let us know when we can see her?"

"Of course." She nodded. "But don't worry. Maggie will be fine. She's a very strong woman, you know."

Grady clenched his hands to keep from telling her that he didn't want Maggie to be strong. He wanted her to depend on him and let down that protective barrier she carried so well. Anyway, Grady half suspected that underneath all that bravado, Maggie's stamina was slowly crumbling. He'd seen evidence of it once or twice himself.

"Is Mom going to be all right, Grady?" Keeley's hand slipped into his. "She's not going to die, is she?"

"No, sweetie." Grady squeezed the tiny hand in his own and held on. He wrapped his other arm around Katy and held them both. "Your mom's going to be just fine. She hurt her head and it was a pretty deep cut, but the doctors will stitch it up. She'll probably have to rest for a few days."

"But what about harvest?" Keeley whispered, staring up at him with her huge blue eyes. "We've just got to get the crops off this year. It's our last chance."

"What do you mean, 'our last chance'? Has something happened, Keeley?" Grady peered down into the white and worried face.

"Go on, tell him, Keeley." When her sister didn't speak up, Katy grabbed Grady's hand and tugged him toward the chairs in the waiting room. "Sit down," she ordered in a tone he'd heard Maggie use before.

"I'm only telling you because I'm worried about my mom. Okay?" She waited for his nod of agreement and then continued. "Mom got a call from the bank yesterday. If we miss the next payment, we have to move off the farm."

"Are you sure?" He stared at the nodding heads.

"I picked up the phone and she was talking on it. I didn't mean to listen in, but she sounded so...mad," Keeley whispered. "I knew she was scared, though. Her voice was all shaky."

Grady thought back. So that explained the frenetic activity of the past twenty-four hours. "I'll worry about the harvest," he told them finally. "Don't bother your mother with any of this right now. She needs to rest."

"Here comes the doctor." Keeley sounded scared and Grady couldn't help but hug her close.

"Are you friends of Mrs. McCarthy's?" The doctor glanced from one to the other.

"You must be new here," Grady muttered, shaking hands with the young man who looked little older than a teenager. He introduced the girls and then looked the doctor square in the eye. "How is she?"

"She has a rather long cut on the back of her head which will need stitches. The scan seems to show no other injury, and since she is conscious and speaking clearly, we are hopeful that the cut is her only problem. I'm keeping her overnight just to make sure. Do you happen to know just how long she was unconscious?"

Grady shook his head. "No idea. I left her just after noon and the girls came home close to four."

"Well, her color is good and she's quite responsive, so we'll take that as a positive sign." He brushed a hand over the girls' hair and bent down to their level. "I have to put some stitches in your mom's head so that the cut she has will heal nice and neat."

"Then will she be okay?" Katy scuffed her toe on the floor.

"I think so, but I'm going to have her stay here tonight just to make sure." He studied them solemnly. "Do you think you can manage alone, just for tonight?"

"Of course." Keeley straightened her shoulders. "Grady will help us if we need it, and I can call Granny to come over. Just take care of our mother, Doctor."

"I'll do that." He stood and winked at them before drawing Grady aside. "Why don't you take them for some ice cream or something? It's going to be a while before they can see her."

So they did. Grady whipped the soiled seat cover off the back seat and stowed it carefully underneath so the girls wouldn't be reminded of their mother's injury. Then they ordered huge hot-fudge sundaes and took them to a nearby park to eat.

"Grady? Why does God let bad things happen to good

people?" Katy stared up at him with her guileless blue eyes. "Our Sunday school teacher said God is all powerful and that He can do anything. So why didn't He stop the accident from happening to my mom?"

Grady groaned mentally under the difficulty of answering such a challenging question.

"Sometimes things happen that we can't explain, honey. Things like that cut on your mom's head. Maybe she didn't take enough care putting the hood down or something, and that was the natural result. I don't know." He drew a deep breath and continued. "But the important thing is that God is still there and He can see us through all the bad times. He is in charge and if something happened, there must be a reason. We just don't know what it is."

"I think we should pray for my mom," Katy murmured. "And I don't want to pray out loud. I want to pray by myself."

"She says God can hear her thoughts," Keeley advised him.

"Of course He can. Why don't we all find our own little places here in the park and say a few words to God about your mother?" Grady watched as Keeley wandered away to find a tiny patch of sunlight hidden from the wind in the shelter of a big spruce tree. Katy found a crook in the arm of a huge maple and nestled herself against the rough bark before glancing toward heaven.

For himself, Grady preferred taking a slow stroll through the park. But he never let the girls out of his sight.

"I have to tell you, Lord," he began. "I don't get it, either. She's worked so hard. She's been true to you, raised her kids properly and kept their lives going even though it's been a rough, rocky road. Why is this happening?"

He sat on the park bench and waited, wondering how God would explain it all to him. Would he hear a still, small voice? Would there be a rustling of leaves and then some great enlightenment in his mind as he at last understood the mysteries of life? Grady grinned at his own silliness. And just like that the old memory verse rolled softly through his mind.

"Be still and know that I am God."

"I've got to hand it to You," he murmured. "No pomp, no circumstance. Just cold hard reality. I'm supposed to realize that 'all things work together', aren't I?" Grady grinned. "And if I admitted the truth, that's the way I like it." He got up and ambled down the leaf-strewn path for several more yards, absently studying the brilliant autumn foliage.

"Okay, God. You're the boss. You lead and I'll follow as best I can. Just keep showing me the next step to take, okay?" When a bird began singing from a perch high above his head, Grady took that as a sign of God's approval. "Keep on keeping on," he told himself and walked back to the girls.

Chapter Fourteen

"Ugh!" Maggie stared at the side of her head in the hallway mirror and shuddered. "Why did they have to shave it?" she asked miserably. "I look ridiculous."

"You look beautiful," Grady murmured from behind. "In fact you look fantastic. And did I mention alive?" His lips brushed her neck as he turned her in his arm. "Gloria Stampford's on her way out here. I met her at Riley's. She said not to fuss."

"I'm not an invalid, Grady," Maggie complained sourly. "I can make coffee."

"Yes, you can do that. And that's all," he warned. "I'm going to see Garret Fraser. We have to get that wheat off, and that relic in the yard isn't going to make it back to life for the occasion." He gulped down his coffee and headed for the door. "Rest," he ordered, grinning from ear to ear.

"Grady. How can I afford to pay a custom combining outfit?"

"How can you not?" he volleyed back. "We have to get the stuff into the bin somehow, darlin'. This will be the fastest. Bye."

Maggie went to her bedroom to change out of the clothes

she'd worn home from the hospital. When she came back into the main hallway, she found that Gloria had arrived.

"Maggie, honey, how are you?" Gloria stood in the doorway, a small black suitcase tucked under her arm and a grin spread across her face. She moved to examine the shaved area on Maggie's head and let out a whistle. "Those surgeons might stitch up a storm but they can't cut worth a whit." She giggled. "Sit down, girl. It's time for some professional help."

Giving Maggie no time to argue, Gloria took her hair scissors from her bag and began to cut away.

"Mom, you look beautiful!" Katy was the first one to comment on her new look half an hour later. "You can't even see where the stitches are."

"Thank you, sweetie!" Maggie hugged her daughter, her throat tight with emotion. "Mrs. Stampford came up with the idea of leaving the top part a little longer and cutting the back very short. The stitches are hidden underneath. It feels strange," she added, shaking her head carefully. "As though a weight's been lifted off my shoulders."

"You look younger," Keeley added, her head tilted to one side. "It makes your eyes look really big, too."

"I loved your hair long," Grady added from the doorway. "But you look beautiful this way, too. I must say, though, when you said you wanted a professional haircut, I didn't think you'd go to these extremes to get one."

Maggie rolled her eyes at his droll look as the girls giggled in the background. "Very funny," she muttered, marching over to turn off the oven and lift out a pan of rolls. "You should be in Hollywood!"

"Can't," he muttered, grabbing one of the still hot cinnamon rolls she'd put to cool on the counter. "More important stuff here. I thought I told you to relax." He glared at her but the effect was spoiled by the sticky sugar glaze that coated one cheek.

"Gloria mixed these up while I was resting," she told him cheekily. "She's gone home and they needed to come out."

He winked at the girls and lifted one hand to touch Maggie's forehead. "I don't think you're all well just yet." He grinned. "Who in their right mind would pick the hottest day of the year to bake?"

Maggie could feel the pink heat rising in her cheeks but she let his arm remain around her waist anyway. "It's going to cool off pretty soon," she murmured. "Fall evenings around here are always chilly. What about Fraser?"

"Starts in the morning," Grady told her, smiling at her sigh of relief.

"Wasn't he booked up?"

"Yeah, but the others agreed to wait until he was finished here. I think it's their way of helping out after the accident."

"I don't want charity," Maggie began, but Grady's fingers covered her mouth.

"It's not charity, Margaret Mary. It's an act of friendship by your neighbors. Treat it that way." His eyes were softly glinting in the warm kitchen and Maggie wondered if she would ever get used to having Grady there to lean on. "Why don't we have an early supper down by the creek, Maggie? The girls will help, won't you?" He tilted his head sideways as he glanced at the two.

Maggie saw wide grins split her daughters' mouths.

"With a fire and everything?" Katy asked. "All right!" She raced Keeley to the fridge and the two of them began pulling things out willy-nilly.

"We've got that jellied salad Mrs. Walton brought over. And Mrs. Enns-of-the—" She stopped upon seeing her mother's frown and reworded her sentence. "Mrs. Enns made these little sausage roll things. She said you just have to heat them in the oven."

"Gloria left some of her famous coleslaw," Maggie added,

trying to relax and enjoy the moment. "And Henrietta came by with a chocolate cake this morning." It would be nice not to have to cook a meal in this heat.

"I can make lemonade," Keeley offered, and began lifting the lemons onto the counter. "I'll put it in that big jug."

"And your mother will sit down here and rest while we get everything ready. Won't you, Maggie?" Grady chided, pressing her into the nearest chair. "Won't you?" he repeated more quietly.

"Yes, all right. But I really do feel fine. I'm just concerned about that barley." She clasped his arm. "Is the swather working again?"

"It's running, if that's what you mean," Grady mumbled, placing different items carefully into the big, old-fashioned picnic basket. "I think, under the circumstances, that's the best we can hope for. I'll start cutting again tomorrow while they're combining. We should be well ahead of the game."

But some niggling doubt, some bit of worry nagged at the back of Maggie's mind, preventing her from completely relaxing later, after the girls gobbled down their food and then raced with the dog through the now-shallow river.

"They sure love this place," Grady mused, watching Katy turn cartwheels on the sandy edge. He burst out laughing as Keeley tried and ended up toppling over onto her rump. His eyes moved and Maggie felt his intense scrutiny. "And regardless of what you say, I think you do, too."

"In the best of all possible worlds, I suppose I would like living here," Maggie murmured, fiddling with the hem of her shirt. "Given half a chance and a bit of modernizing, this farm could really be something."

"What was it like here when you were growing up?" Grady moved a little closer and slid his arm around her shoulders, hugging her against his solid warmth.

"I thought it was the best place in the world." Maggie let

her mind slide back to those halcyon days when life had been carefree. "I had tons of animals. We all did. My dad had more land than I have now and we had two hired men who helped him out. We were never rich but there was always enough for everyone. At least, I thought there was." She wondered suddenly, if her parents had struggled to pay the bills. Somehow she didn't think so.

"What do you remember most clearly?"

Maggie closed her eyes and let herself relax. "Thanksgiving," she murmured. "I always loved the fall, but Thanksgiving was my favorite."

"Why?"

"I don't know. The bounty, I suppose. There was always the excitement of getting the crop off and the feeling of satisfaction when it was all done. We all helped get the grain in the bins, and dug and bagged the vegetables. We had to drag them into the root cellar. My mother always had shelves of fruit and jellies and jams. Dill pickles were usually ready by Thanksgiving." She got lost in those memories of the past.

"What else?"

"Well, there were the decorations at church, of course. My dad would haul in a couple of bales as the background for our display. We'd get donated pumpkins and potatoes—all kinds of stuff that would go to the Bible school in the city after the service. Beth and I always dried and pressed a pile of leaves and we'd lay them around. My mom saved a pot of flowers for the center of the display and sometimes Dad would have a sheaf of wheat there, too."

"Was that when the Thanksgiving quilt tradition got started?"

Maggie started, staring at him in surprise. "You know about that?"

"Of course. Your mother." He waited for her to explain and so Maggie did.

"Actually, the quilt was my grandmother's idea. She always had her Christmas shopping done long before anyone else, and when the fall came along, she said she got itchy fingers and needed to give one more thing. So she began making a quilt that was sold to raise money for a gift for the missionaries." Maggie grinned. "I loved helping her with that quilt, although I'm sure it caused her a whole lot more work."

"Why?"

"My stitches weren't exactly even, Grady! I think she pulled them out every night after I left and redid them so I'd start the next day after school. We'd talk the whole time and she'd always have tea in real china cups and biscuits with crab apple jelly. Then on the Saturday before Thanksgiving, we'd spread the quilt out over the edge of the bales."

"You have wonderful memories, Maggie. Just as your daughters will have."

"If we stay." She murmured the words softly, but they came out stark and bare.

"What else do you remember?" he asked, ignoring her remark.

"The food, of course. After church we'd have a little snack and then we girls would help Mom for a while. Once things were ready in the kitchen, we could go outside and play until we heard the magic word."

"Which was?" he asked, following her prompt.

"Dinner. And what a dinner. We'd all hold hands and say what we were thankful for and then my dad would say grace. Then he'd carve the turkey that we raised on our very own land. There were potatoes and yams, carrots, corn, pickled beets, salad, sliced tomatoes, gravy, fresh rolls and pumpkin pie. All from our own farm."

"And pickles?" Grady teased.

"Lots of pickles," Maggie affirmed. "Mom and Dad and our grandparents would go sit in the living room and my

sisters and I would do the dishes. Then out came the croki-
nole board and we'd play Dad and the grandpas while the
ladies knitted or crocheted." Maggie patted her stomach.
"I'd usually sneak out to feed the horses a carrot treat and
work off some of the calories, but I remember lying in my
bed and listening to the house settling down, snug and warm
and safe."

"Is that why you married Roger? For the security?"

Maggie laughed derisively. "No! Who thinks about that
at eighteen? I married Roger because I was a starry-eyed
teenager who thought her life would be like a fairy tale." She
sat up, letting his arm fall behind her as she searched the
gloom for the girls. They were cuddled together with the dog
and Maggie had a hunch they were sleeping.

"Come on, Grady. We've been out here way too long." A
rumble of thunder sounded in the west and Maggie cast a
worried glance at the sky. To her amazement it was black,
the stars obliterated. The wind was rising, too.

"We'll have to run for it," Grady called as they each
grabbed a girl and helped her stand. "I think it's going to
pour."

"Come on, kids." Maggie urged them up the steep incline,
trying to ignore the dizziness that swam behind her eyes.
Lightning split the sky in a terrific crack, lighting up the yard
and the house. "Inside, quick." She hastened them through
the door and dropped the blanket on a nearby chair. "You
guys run up and get ready for bed. You should have been
there half an hour ago at least."

"Are we going to be okay?" Keeley startled as another
crack burst across the heavens. Her whitened face peered at
the door as Grady stomped in, setting down the basket before
shaking his wet head.

"We're going to be just fine, Keeley," he answered. "It's
just an electrical storm. Today was hot. The thunder and

lightning are because a cool air mass has moved in." Keeley glanced out the window at the sheets of rain pouring down. "Go ahead, honey," he urged. "I'll come up with your mother and tuck you in after a bit. Okay?"

"Yes, okay," she whispered, moving toward the stairs.

"Oh, and Keeley?"

"Yes?" She turned quickly, her eyes huge in her small pinched face.

"Unplug the computer, would you? Electrical outages are hard on them." Keeley nodded and continued up the stairs.

Maggie sank into a nearby chair with relief, closing her eyes to stop the room from whirling around her.

"Maggie?" She opened her eyes to find Grady's warm brown gaze fixed on her intently. "Are you okay?" His hand brushed gently over her head.

"I'm fine," she murmured. "Just a little tired. I should have slowed down a bit, I guess."

"No, I shouldn't have taken you down there. I knew you weren't feeling up to par." As the rain poured down, Grady moved over to partially close the living room windows. He stood there staring out at the darkened landscape for a few minutes and Maggie felt prickles of awareness creep up her spine.

"Grady? What's wrong?" She got up and walked over to see the yard for herself. The dusk-to-dawn yard light gave only a faint glow through the torrents of rain the wind was dashing into the ground. She knew exactly what he was thinking. "All that heat caused enough stress on the crop but this wind has to be murder." She moved toward the screen door and stood staring out. "I don't know how much of it will stay standing in this."

"It'll be fine once it dries out," Grady murmured, but Maggie could feel the tension in his fingers when they wrapped around her shoulders and drew her against him.

"We'll manage, Maggie. God's on our side." He hugged her. "Cooling off pretty fast, isn't it?"

They stood there, watching the rivulets form in the yard as the water took the path of least resistance to the ditches. Lightning crackled through the sky, momentarily illuminating the veranda and the rockers sitting there. Maggie would have liked to sit out in the air and watch, but now the girls had arrived and stood gaping at the sight, their mouths open in round O's of wonder. The rain slowed suddenly, rendering the night quiet.

"Is it over?" Katy asked, peering toward the barn. "Do you think my animals are all right?"

"They're fine, sweetie," Grady murmured, tucking her against his side. "It's just a little rain—" He stopped suddenly, and tipped his head to one side to listen.

And then it came, loud and almost deafening in its intensity as it hit the buildings with devastating accuracy.

Hail!

"No!" Maggie stared at the huge golf-ball-sized ice particles that drove themselves into the lawn. In a matter of moments the entire green expanse was covered in white balls. And it kept falling.

"It's like a snowstorm," Keeley breathed, staring at the whiteness that surrounded them. "You can't even see across the yard."

It was over in a matter of minutes. And before it had stopped completely, Maggie had tossed on her jacket and raced out the door. Her head ached with a viciousness that stung but she ignored it. The damage. She had to assess the damage.

She switched on all the outside lights she could find and then stood and stared at the mess. Her car was covered in pitted circles where the hail had dented the metal. The garden lay in ruins, sweet peas with flowers still clinging to their vines, now dashed into the black mud.

"Good thing I'd taken everything I wanted," she muttered, thinking of the pumpkins now hidden inside a corner of the barn. The barn! She hurried over, swinging open the door to study the damage.

"It's okay," Grady murmured from behind her. "That new roof can handle a little thing like a hailstorm. It's a good thing it's been replaced." And, in fact, the animals seemed perfectly comfortable nestled into the fragrant hay.

But now his words prodded her and all at once the full impact of a hailstorm penetrated Maggie's brain. "The crops," she gasped, staring at him. "What about the wheat?"

"Hail is usually localized to a specific area, Maggie. I don't think we've lost much." He grabbed her arm as a wave of dizzying relief washed over her. "Come on, you're going inside. We can't tell anything tonight anyway. Morning is soon enough."

Maggie let him lead her back to the house and drank the hot, sweet tea he brewed. She obediently swallowed two of the aspirin he handed her and kissed the girls good-night.

She was sitting in the living-room, when Grady came to speak with her. His eyes were shrewd and assessing.

"You overdid it, didn't you?" he muttered. "Maggie, you've got to slow down and start trusting God and His promises. You can't be everywhere and do everything. Whatever happens, we'll be fine. I have enough money for all of us to live on and I'm healthy enough. I can work."

"You're recuperating from a heart attack," she scoffed miserably.

"Which was caused by stress and tension, not hard work. You're going to be in the same boat if you don't let go and let God—" He brushed the strands out of her eyes.

"Let God what?" she queried grumpily, knowing he was right.

"Let God be God." Grady grinned. "Remember the verse

from last Sunday? 'The Lord is near to all who call on Him.'"
He winked. "That's what we should be doing instead of
worrying. Don't you think God knows how much you need
that crop?"

"Yes, I guess so." Maggie chewed on the tip of one fingernail. "But I guess I'm afraid He'll take away what I want
the most."

"Oh, Maggie!" Grady enfolded her in his arms. "You
break my heart. Don't you know that God never takes away
without giving something so much better than we can even
ask for."

"In my head I know," she whispered, holding him tightly.
"But in my heart, I'm so afraid!"

"Because you're tired and in pain and just plain worn-out.
Go up to bed, Margaret Mary." He kissed her softly and
walked to the door. "Everything will look so much brighter
in the morning. Good night, sweetheart."

"Good night." Maggie waited until he pulled the door
closed behind him, before she went to bed and let the doubts
and fears crawl through her mind once more. As she drifted
off, Maggie tried to pray. Strangely, nothing would come.

By the time Maggie awoke in the morning, the girls were
up, dressed and ready for the bus. Grady had fed them, they told
her.

After Maggie showered, carefully keeping her head free
of the water, she peeked out the window to see her yard in
ruins. Her gladiolus were no more. The huge castor beans
she'd planted were in tatters, bent over double. Tree branches
and twigs lay scattered across the yard and a window was
broken in the girls' playhouse.

She tied on her shoes and walked slowly downstairs,
holding her shoulders stiffly erect. "What's the damage?" she
asked once she'd reached the kitchen.

Grady's dark head jerked upward and he stared at her. She could tell from the drawn whiteness of his face that it was bad enough though his voice tried to deny it. "I'm not totally sure yet."

"It's pretty bad though, isn't it? I could tell from the size of those hailstones. I suppose Fraser can't start until tomorrow, when it's a bit drier." There was no response to this remark and from the corner of her eye, Maggie saw Grady's hand shake as he set down his coffee mug. "Grady? Tell me."

"Fraser's not coming."

"Not coming? Well, that's silly. You said he'd be over today. Surely he can wait one day. Can't he?" The last came out as a breathy whisper when she glimpsed the agony in Grady's eyes. "Can't he?" she repeated, begging for assurance.

Grady shook his head slowly. "It's gone, Maggie. It's all gone. The hail moved in a straight path across our land. It flattened everything. There's nothing to combine."

He didn't have to tell her. Maggie knew firsthand the damage hailstones of that size would cause. Still it didn't sink in. "But you said...you said we'd be okay. That it would be localized." She stared at him uncomprehendingly. "What about the Waltons? The Jeffers?"

"Waltons didn't get any hail," Grady murmured. "Jeffers lost part of a quarter of wheat that touched on to yours."

"So *I'm* the only one who got it all," Maggie demanded, fury strengthening her voice. "Good old Maggie takes the hit again! I have to see this for myself." She yanked on her jacket and stomped toward the door.

"Maggie, what's the point?" Grady's voice was full of tender concern and his hand brushed across her arm but she swiped it away.

"I want to see it," she grated, teeth clenched. "I want to

see for myself how badly *my* crops are damaged." She stomped down the steps and toward her old truck. Grady's fingers closed around her arm.

"Fine. But we'd better go in my truck. That road is awful."

Maggie climbed into his truck, ignoring Grady's helping hand. She sat straight and tall as he drove out, but her eyes were taking in every inch of the desolation.

"You were right," she whispered, shocked at the lush landscape now flattened. "I can't see a blade of anything still standing."

Grady said nothing. His lips were clenched tightly closed as he drove past acre after acre of ruined crop. He glanced at her once or twice to make sure she was okay, but not a word cut the silence in the cab. When he stopped at the last field, the prime wheat field that had been so thick and heavy, Maggie climbed out and walked over to the edge, tears streaming down her cheeks.

"I'm wiped out," she murmured, picking up a few broken golden heads and letting the big ripe kernels fall through her fingers. "There's nothing left."

His arms came around her then as he turned her and let her cry all over his shirt. "Don't cry, sweetheart. We can start again. You'll have the insurance money. That'll cover things for a while."

Maggie tore herself out of his embrace, white-hot anger rising up inside. "Don't you get it," she yelled. "There was no insurance. I couldn't afford it. I had to cut corners to make ends meet and that's one corner I decided was too expensive." She sniffed. "Just another in a long line of errors I've made."

"It doesn't matter," he murmured, trying to console her. "We'll make this place a partnership and I'll buy you out in a fifty-fifty split. We can plant again, Maggie. We're together in this."

"No, Grady." She said the words firmly, the decision already made. "I'm finished here. I've scraped and begged and borrowed for the last time. If you want to buy the place, fine. I'll sell it for whatever I can get. And then I'm leaving." She turned to stare at the mess that was her life.

"For where?" Grady was angry, too. She could hear it in the way he held his voice under control. "Are you going to run away when the going gets tough, Maggie? Refuse to find a solution to our problems? Are you going to dump me and ignore what you feel for me because it isn't convenient right now? Or were you lying when you said you loved me? Maybe you were just using me to help you out here?"

She swung around, furious that he would ask such a question. "I do love you," she said, her face heated with the emotions that whirled inside. "But I told you from the first that I had reservations about marrying you. I've tried, Grady. I've tried really hard. But God doesn't want me to be here. This is not where I belong."

"This is exactly where you and the girls belong. With me. Here, together, working side by side. So we don't have a crop this year. So what? We won't starve. I can give you designer clothes and a trip to Disneyland with the girls. We can redo the house and still have lots of money left over."

"It's not about the money."

"Sure it is. Poor little Maggie is destitute. She wants 'things' and can't get them. I've got money, Maggie. I can solve that problem without even feeling it. So why not marry me?"

"I don't want to marry someone for their money," she spat out, angry at his tone. "I've already had someone offer to *buy* me, and I turned him down! I want to go into a relationship knowing that I can hold my own. As an equal partner. Not like some kind of poor relation!" She stomped over to the truck and climbed in, slamming the door with a lot more force than necessary.

"But you would be my partner," Grady murmured placatingly as he got into the truck. "You own the farm. I would simply supply the capital to run it. When we earn some profits, we'd split them."

"I love that 'when' you threw in there," she scoffed. "Get this through your head, Grady. This place is a great big sinkhole when it comes to money. The more you put in, the more it demands. I just don't want to fight it anymore."

"But what about us?" The words were softly spoken as Grady shifted into gear and started across to the road. "What about me, Maggie?"

"I don't know." The tears started again and she let them fall. "I feel like I'm being torn apart, but in my heart I know that I have to leave here. This isn't where I should be anymore. Couldn't you come to Calgary, live there again?"

"And do what? I've sold everything, Maggie. I got out of my businesses because I wanted to farm. I feel like I've returned home when I come back here and look around. I don't want to run anymore."

"So I have to give up all my dreams because you've finally found this place? That doesn't seem fair," she complained.

"Maggie, I love you. If I really thought you would be happy living in Calgary or Timbuktu for that matter, I'd move there in a flash." He pulled into the yard and parked in front of the house. "But I think God brought us together here, for a reason. God promised to be with us all the time, not just during the good times. And I don't think He wants us to run away from our problems. He wants us to depend on Him."

"But that's just the problem!" Maggie stomped up the porch stairs and let the screen door slam behind her, knowing Grady was not far behind. "I've been depending so much, I haven't been facing the reality He's presented me with. Now it's time to deal with that reality, Grady. Head-on." She grabbed the telephone and dialed a number.

"Hi, this is Maggie McCarthy. I'd like an appraisal on my farm as soon as you can do it. No, just the land, buildings and machinery. There is no crop. Tomorrow would be fine. Thank you."

"Maggie, please don't rush into anything. Let's sit down and discuss this." He waited until she sank into a chair, his craggy face intent as he studied her. "I love you, Maggie. I love the girls. Please, let's make this our home and raise our family here."

"That was my dream once." She laughed harshly. "My children were going to have the same wonderful childhood that I once had. Well, you know what? It isn't wonderful. My kids aren't getting any great and noble life. They're getting a hand-to-mouth existence with a mother who can't even read the newspaper without bursting into tears." She saw the pain on his face and relented just a little, reaching out to touch his hand.

"I do love you, Grady. Very much, but I'm worn-out with trying to make a go of this place. I have to leave, to get a new perspective on things. I need a chance to prove to myself that I can be like other single mothers and support my family properly. I have to be worthy to myself before I can be worthy to you."

"And how long will that take? Six months, a year? What? I want to have a family, Maggie. And I want you there with me."

His disgruntled look made her smile. "Grady, I'm not going completely out of your life. Calgary isn't that far away. You can come and see us anytime. In fact, the girls would be upset if you didn't."

"They're going to be even more upset when they find out what you have planned."

Resolve straightened her backbone and Maggie got up from her chair. "I can't help that. I have to do what I think is best. For all of us. And with all that's happened, I think

God is directing me away from the farm. I don't know what's in store, but I'm willing to find out. No, please—" she held up one hand "—I don't want to argue anymore. This is something that has to happen. If we're meant to be together, God will lead us that way. You just have to have faith."

He snorted, slamming his hat on his head. "That's rich, coming from you. You don't have the courage of your convictions, my dearest Maggie. God brought us together. He put the love in my heart for you. And He did the same for you, only you're too chicken to hang around and find out what could grow out of that." He stomped across the floor and out the door, only to reappear seconds later.

"I'm buying this farm, Maggie McCarthy. I don't care what the price is, I'll pay whatever you want. And you can go searching for greener grass in the place you think is the answer to all your problems. But when the day comes that you realize that this is where you belong, I'll be sitting right here." He pulled her into his arms and kissed her thoroughly.

"I'm not giving up on you, Margaret Mary. So go, run to the city. Try and find your perfect life. And when it's all said and done, I'll still be here. Waiting. Because I love you too much to just let you go."

His dark brown eyes were liquid as they slid over her face, his fingers gentle as they brushed over her hair. Then, lips tightened, he was gone.

Chapter Fifteen

Maggie glared at the store clock, desperately willing it to move. When had time ever dragged like this? She flipped through the swatches of fabric she'd chosen for tomorrow's appointment and mentally chastised herself. At least she had a job. What did it matter if the customers chose the patterns and combinations and all she got to do was stitch them up? The money from this little quilting shop was hard to beat for someone with no previous job experience. The hours were certainly regular.

It's boring, a voice in the back of her head announced, laughing. *There's no creativity in this stifling little room. You can't even step outside and breathe in some fresh air.* The smell of diesel penetrated the air vents, testament to the bus stop outside the door. *And Grady's not here.* Maggie shoved the thought away and stitched a little longer on the gaudy pink-and-purple squares that her last client had selected for her daughter's wedding quilt.

Eventually the clock hands reached five o'clock and Maggie gathered her purse and coat and locked up. Her bus had just left, so she decided to walk a couple of blocks and catch the next one at the station down the road.

"I know I'm living in dreamland again," she told herself, peering into the big show windows with their displays of gorgeous silks in vibrant autumn hues. They were far beyond her price range, of course, and she couldn't afford the fabric, even if she sewed them herself. But it was fun to look, wasn't it?

"I'm doing all right," she'd said to Gloria Stampford last night on the phone. "The girls are fairly settled in their new schools and I've got a nine-to-five job." *Which isn't the least bit glamorous,* she wanted to add, but didn't.

The allure of the city had quickly lost its shine once Maggie realized how expensive everything was going to be. The rent on their tiny apartment took a huge bite out of her paycheck. The car wasn't working properly, which was probably good since parking near her work cost a fortune. Instead, she took the bus and got home two and a half hours after the girls. She had latchkey children, Maggie suddenly realized with a pang.

But all of that was bearable, or would have been. If only she didn't miss Grady so much. She wanted to talk to him about Keeley's rebellious streak and Katy's propensity to talk to anyone she met. She wished she could sit with him over a cup of coffee at the kitchen table, once the girls had gone to bed, and discuss her rather eccentric boss.

"You wanted to be independent," she muttered. "Don't go mooning over everything now." The truth was, she admitted privately, she missed his arm around her shoulder, his kisses, his laugh.

"Lady, are you gonna get on this thing, or study it for another half hour?"

Maggie came to and found the driver of the city bus glaring at her. "Sorry," she murmured, and climbed on, lugging up the steep stairs the few groceries she'd picked up at noon. She almost fell flat on her face when he jerked away from the curb and lurched into rush-hour traffic, but her fingers grasped the metal pole and she managed to stay upright The bus was full, of course, and there was no place to sit down. Weary beyond belief, arms aching from clinging to the strap, she climbed off at her stop aeons later and trudged up the street toward what was now home.

"Hi, Mom." Katy glanced up from the phone, greeting Maggie when she walked in. "I'm talking to Grady. Don't worry. He called me." Katy shook her head at her mother's warning look and turned back to the phone. "No, I can't go to the basketball practice when Mom's working and there's nobody to take me. I sure wish I could have my bike to ride around on, but there's no place to keep it at night, and people steal things. Mrs. Eversham in 108 got her lock picked."

Maggie stood upright in front of the fridge, tension racing through her. She hadn't heard of any break-in.

"Nah, they didn't even get it. Mrs. Eversham's got this really yappy dog, you see, and it set up a racket. She called the police." Katy stopped for a second, her forehead wrinkled. "Yeah, me and Keeley are real careful. Did you feed Laddie today? How is he?… Really?… You think they miss me?…I miss them, too."

A soft glow of happiness covered her daughter's generally sulky face and Maggie turned away as frustration overrode her. She wiped it away as Katy bellowed, "Mom! Grady wants to talk to you."

Maggie picked up the phone, every nerve in her body waiting to hear that familiar deep tone rumbling over the line.

"Maggie, are you all right? You're late tonight." He stopped when he realized what this implied. "I phone the girls quite often," he said at last. "I guess I've gotten to know your schedule."

"That's very kind of you, Grady," she muttered stiffly, furious yet relieved that he was keeping such close track of the girls. "How is everything?" She could hear hammering in the background and wondered who else was there.

"Everything here is fine," he said brusquely. "I'm having a few things done before the snow flies." There was a gap in the conversation then—a long, drawn-out silence that Maggie had no desire to break. Grady, it seemed was not so hesitant.

"When are you coming home, Maggie?" he asked quietly. "I miss you and the girls. The house is so quiet, I'm back in the camper just so I don't feel so lonely." He waited, and when she didn't say anything, continued on a harsher tone. "You've been there almost a month. Haven't you proven your independence yet?" There was a sting in his voice that touched a nerve.

"Grady, we've barely settled in. We're managing, but it's been a change for all of us."

"Yeah, I know," he grated. "Keeley's been in the principal's office three times, and now she's sneaking out at lunchtime to meet a boy from the high school."

"What?" Maggie stared at her daughter's back where it sat hunched over the computer. "I, I, uh, I'm dealing with it," she mumbled at last.

"Sure you are. Like you're dealing with Katy's F in math?" His voice was full of frustration. "Why won't you come home? I love you, Maggie! Why is that so bad?"

"It's not bad at all," she whispered, fingering the ring he'd insisted she keep on the chain around her neck. So she wouldn't forget him, he'd said. As if she could! "It's just that I have to do this, Grady. I have to stand on my own two feet here. I need to prove something to myself."

"Well, you're hurting all of us while you *prove* it," he ground out bitterly.

Maggie bit her lip to keep from crying out at the unfairness of it all. *Why, God,* she prayed silently. *Why is it always so hard for me?*

"You are at least coming home tomorrow for Thanksgiving, aren't you? After work? Your mother told me she'd asked you." His voice was calmer now, resigned almost.

"I—I'm not sure," she stammered, thinking of the strange noise the car had made last week on an outing to the zoo.

"Maggie, your parents are expecting you. They want to see you and the girls. They've missed you!"

"I've missed them, too," she murmured.

"If you don't come, I'll come and get you," he warned angrily. His voice dropped as he spoke again. "I'm sorry, honey. I didn't mean to yell. It's just that it's been so long and I miss you so much. And the girls. Please, say you'll come for Thanksgiving?"

"All right, if it means so much. But if you've missed us to that extent, why didn't you come for a visit? You know where we live, you moved our stuff here."

"There's nothing I'd like better than to drive in and see you all. We could go out for dinner. Maybe see a movie." His voice fell, the enthusiasm draining away. "But I can't get away. I've tried, believe me. But something always comes up."

Funny, Maggie frowned. He didn't sound very regretful.

"I know you'll think I'm nosey, but I'm still going to ask. Maggie, are you still standing on the promises of God?"

"I don't know what you mean," she lied, staring at her hands.

"I mean, are you certain that you're in the will of God? Have you really thought this out? Are you sure you're not making your own desires into your version of God's will?" His voice was soft, but the jab of guilt it dealt to her heart was not.

"What makes you qualified to judge me and my choices? Who are you to try and run my life, to make my decisions for me? Who are you to question me, Grady O'Toole?"

His voice was low and filled with sadness. "I'm the man who loves you, Maggie."

Tears formed in her eyes at the tenderness of those words, and she drew a shaky breath.

"I'm not trying to take over your life or tell you what to do. I'm not even asking you to come back—not if you don't want to."

Maggie pressed her fist into her mouth as if to staunch the pain. "Well, what are you trying to say then?"

"I'm just asking you to look into your heart and figure out if you really want to deny what God has given us—a second chance to love. I don't care about the past, Maggie. I don't care what could have or should have happened. I just want what's best for you and the girls. I want you to be happy. Are you happy, Maggie?"

On the other end of the line, Grady listened for an answer. When it didn't come, he quietly closed his cell phone. Behind him the hammers and saws resounded through the house as workmen tore out the old, water-ruined ceiling and installed a new dropped one. The aroma of freshly cut cedar permeated the house as the tongue-and-groove boards were fitted together in Maggie's studio. He'd had the skylights and east bank of windows specially installed so she could work in as much natural light as possible in her special room.

And it was Maggie's room. In fact, the whole house cried out for her presence. What did it matter that he changed the interior? She was still as much a part of this place as she'd always been. Would she ever come home?

"Lord, you know how much I miss her." Grady ambled down to the creek as he prayed, thrilled once more with the peace he'd found here. "And I do believe that it's Your plan for us to be together. So Lord, whatever it takes, that's what I'm prepared to do. If you want me to move to the city, I'll go." The word came out on a whoosh of desperation. "If you want me to go back to Shaughnessy's and restart the company, I'll do that. I've learned a lot here, Lord, and I could apply it to the markets."

He picked a cattail that had fallen over, its head top heavy and unwieldy, but his eyes were on the creek, remembering two small girls and their giggles of laughter.

"I don't understand Your ways, Lord." He stared at the serene sky and considered the vastness of it. "But you are God and it's not up to me to ask why. I'm nothing compared to Your majesty and power." Grady remembered the scripture he'd read that morning.

"Who gives intuition and instinct? Who is wise enough to number all the clouds? Who can tilt the water jars of heaven, when everything is dust and clouds?"

Another verse penetrated his brain. "God is not a man...nor a son of man, that He should change his mind."

"I'm like Job, God," Grady groaned, embarrassed at his lack of trust. "I have demanded answers too many times. You owe no one anything. Everything under heaven is Yours. This situation with Maggie is beyond my understanding and yet, You can use even this. Show me what to do and I'll do it."

The words came as if someone had spoken them in his ear. *Finish the work. What I have planned, that will I do.*

As Grady got up and strode back up the hill, he felt rejuvenated, renewed. Somehow God would handle this. And nothing any woman could do, even one as determined as Maggie, would stop God from completing His work.

Maggie shut off the alarm with a groan, reminding herself to speak to the super about the incessant parties next door. It had been well after three before she'd fallen asleep last night, and she had to get up before seven to get to work on time.

"Katy! Keeley!" She rumpled their sleepy heads and pressed a kiss to each cheek. "Time to get up and get ready for school." The girls groaned and rolled over, and Maggie took the opportunity to slip in and out of the shower. "Come on, girls. It's getting late."

Maggie sipped her coffee as she scanned the newspaper. The headlines didn't catch her eye, but the photo did. It was an old one of Grady. He looked younger in it, but not happier. Quickly she scanned the write-up and gasped.

Local entrepreneur Gradin O'Toole may lose everything in his bid to outfox his lovely ex-wife, Fiona Spenser, who has announced her intention to file another suit. This time the claim is against O'Toole's trust fund, gifted to him by the late oil tycoon, Harrison Fellows. Mr. Fellows claimed in his will that Grady O'Toole was the most honest broker he'd ever known and insisted on bequeathing his fortune to the Calgary businessman. The money has been tied up in litigation and now Ms. Spenser claims that the fund was improperly obtained when Mr. O'Toole prevailed upon the ailing magnate to adjust his will. Mr. O'Toole could not be reached for comment, but his legal counsel has issued a statement denying all claims.

Maggie couldn't believe her eyes. She'd let him buy the farm, glibly accepted that Grady was able to take over her mortgage and other debts! She'd let him blow his precious resources on that farm when she knew the place would only cost more money. And now he was going to lose whatever security he had—and all because of her and her determination to get away.

Why hadn't he told her about it?

The answer was clear. Grady's love was selfless. He wanted her to be happy. And was she?

Maggie glanced around the dinky apartment and grimaced. Yes she had a job that freed her at a set time each day, and they were near all the amenities. The little bit of money left after the farm debt was paid off she'd squirreled away for the girls' future educations. She was free of the farm.

And yet she had lost much more than she gained, Maggie realized. Gone was the relaxing cup of coffee in the sunshine whenever you needed a break. Fifteen-minute coffee breaks didn't allow for lazing in the sun and dreaming of the future. The people she'd met at the neighborhood church were friendly, but Maggie missed her lifelong chums and the knowledge that her friends would drop in whenever they got a free moment.

Her children came home to an empty apartment now and although she insisted they call her the minute they came in, there never seemed to be a second to lazily discuss their day while they played outside. The rules for surviving the massive city school terrified Maggie—knives, guns, drugs. It was all so much closer now.

But most of all, Maggie missed Grady. She missed knowing he was there to talk to, share her day with and discuss the girls. She missed his reassuring hugs and warm kisses. This terrible loneliness in a city full of people was the worst thing of all. Maggie picked up her Bible and let it fall open to Matthew, staring down at the words.

"If you, then, though you are evil, know how to give good gifts to your children, how much more will your Father in heaven give good gifts to those who ask him!"

"Mom? Aren't we having breakfast? And you're going to miss your bus if you don't hurry."

Maggie glanced up into Keeley's worried face, the words ringing through her head with bright clarity. This was her child and she wanted the very best for her. But what if she was wrong? What if moving the children away from Grady and the farm wasn't the best?

"Mom?"

"Yes, honey. Go ahead and eat. I'm leaving in a minute." She stared at Keeley's blond head for a long time, studying the gamine features closely. "Keeley?"

"What?" The sullen look was still on her daughter's face.

"Can I ask you something?" Keeley's eyes widened, but she slowly nodded. "Do you miss Grady?"

All at once the harshness fell away as tears rolled down the child's pale cheeks. Maggie gathered her up in her arms and rocked back and forth, holding the girl tightly against her. And she let her own tears fall.

"Oh, Mom," Keeley wailed. "I miss him so much. I wish I had him as my father."

"You do?" Maggie knew the girls adored Grady but apparently she hadn't realized how much they needed a father in their lives. "I didn't know you missed your dad so much, sweetie."

"It's not just that," Keeley mumbled, wiping her eyes. "It's because we were like a real family when Grady was there. Everything was fun and happy. You laughed a lot, Mom. And…" She stopped, glancing up through her lashes at her mother with a strange look on her face.

"Go on, sweetheart. Say the rest of it. You can tell me anything."

"Why won't you marry Grady? Is it because you really don't love him? Or is it because you're scared he'll go away like our father did?"

Maggie stared. "Why would you say that, Keeley?"

"Because that's how I feel. Sometimes it seems like everything is going really well and then all of a sudden, bang! Something goes wrong and you've got to start worrying all over again. And then I wonder if God even cares about what's happening."

"God always cares, sweetie. Of that I am very sure." Katy walked up slowly and Maggie held out her other arm. "I was just reading my Bible and I came across this verse." She read it to them. "Do you know what it means?"

"It means that if people can give good gifts, then God can give even more," Katy told them.

"That's right. And if He's in control, there's no need for us to worry about anything."

"You mean nothing bad will happen?" Keeley asked doubtfully.

"No, silly. She means that even *when* bad things happen, God is still there, watching out for us. And worrying about that guy downstairs doesn't make it any better or worse," Katy told her sister firmly. "Grady taught me that a long time ago."

"What guy downstairs?" Maggie studied her daughter anew. "What's bothering you, Keeley?" She watched the girl struggle to keep her face from showing her true emotions. "You have to tell me, honey. Otherwise I can't help you."

"I'm afraid, Mommy." Keeley buried her face in her mother's shoulder and sobbed her heart out. "I'm always afraid. At home there was Granny or Grady or even the Waltons to call if I got in trouble. But here there's nobody. At school the kids think I'm a geek because I get all A's. One of them stopped me in the bathroom and said if I answered the teacher's questions again and got them more homework, they were going to beat me up after school."

Help me, Lord, she prayed silently. *Give me the right answers.*

"Girls, God didn't give us a spirit of fear. It says in here—" she quickly turned the pages in her Bible to Second Timothy "—'God has given us a spirit of power and love and of a sound mind. We don't have to be afraid.'"

"But you are, Mom," Keeley protested softly. "You're

always afraid that we won't have enough money. And when we were on the farm, you worried that the crops wouldn't get off or that they wouldn't sell or that the rain wouldn't come or that the snow would come too early. Isn't worry like fear?"

From the top of her head to the soles of her feet, Maggie felt a deep profound sense of shame. Were these the values she had imparted to her children? Fear and worry?

"You're afraid to marry Grady, too," Katy accused "He told me that you didn't trust him enough."

It was true. It was all true. God help her, she'd been running because she was too afraid to stand still and let God handle it all. Grady was right. God had filled His side of the bargain. He'd sent Grady to help them through the tough times, to love her and the girls, to shore them up when they most needed it.

And because she wouldn't believe or trust in what was in her own heart, Maggie had thrown it all away for the foolish dream of security.

Well, she asked herself. *Are you secure now?*

"Mother, you've missed your bus!" Keeley was back to her usual responsible self and Maggie realized that it was something her child did to protect her, the mother.

"Don't you worry about me, sweetheart," Maggie murmured, hugging the little girl tightly. "I'm the mother here and I know when I've missed my bus. It so happens I don't care." She glanced from one surprised face to the other. "And you two aren't going anywhere, either."

"We aren't?" Katy frowned suspiciously. "Why? Did the teacher call you?"

"No, it's me," Keeley groaned. "I probably got suspended."

"Neither of the above." Maggie grinned. "Today this is one time you girls and I are going to have a day on the town.

We'll go to the Devonian Gardens this morning and drop out to Calaway Park this afternoon. And in between we're having lunch at McDonald's."

"We are?" The twins looked at each other and shrugged.

"Yes, we are. And then we're coming straight home to pack." Maggie watched the hope light up their eyes.

"You mean, we can go to Granny's for Thanksgiving?" Keeley's face shone one minute and then dimmed the next. "But what about the money?"

"For once, I think I'll depend on God to take care of things for me." Maggie grinned. "'…My Father will give you whatever you ask in my name. Until now you have not asked. Ask and you will receive, and your joy will be complete.'" She hugged each one. "Let's just spend a few minutes thanking our Father for the wonderful things He's given us."

She listened first to Katy's little prayer and then Keeley's, and then Maggie whispered her own. As the girls scurried out of the room to gather their jackets, Maggie closed her eyes.

"I believe You have a way planned for me," she said silently. "I don't know what it is and I don't know how I'll handle it, but I'm giving it all over to You. Forgive me for not believing when I should have and help me trust You more."

As they pulled out of the parking lot, Maggie found herself wondering how Grady would greet their homecoming. She could hardly imagine he would welcome them back now, with this new disaster looming on his own horizon.

Chapter Sixteen

"Sweetheart, your father and I would have come and picked you up. You didn't have to drive out here." Kayleen was frowning as she helped the sleepy girls out of the car.

"Believe me, if I'd known I'd have car trouble, I would have called you." Maggie stretched. "As it is, I'm dead beat. The traffic was awful. The girls conked out a while ago." She stared up at her parents' house and absorbed all the familiar details. It would be nice to sleep without the thudding of bass drums against her ear, Maggie decided.

Katy and Keeley were content to snuggle down in their grandfather's study, their eyes drooping closed almost immediately. Maggie smiled as she snapped off the light and gently closed the door.

"Now, dear, I've made a fresh pot of tea. Come and tell us all about Calgary."

Maggie fielded the questions as best she could, but just the same, Kayleen managed to acquire quite a bit of information. It was time to turn the tables.

"Mom, how's Grady?" Maggie tried to say it nonchalantly, keeping her eyes downcast.

"Why, he seems fine, dear." Her mother's bright eyes were

narrowed knowingly. "We've been out several times, your father and I, and the changes around the old place are amazing. Grady's been getting Elmer Hawkins to inquire into some different types of seed, and he's got next year's crops all planned out." Kayleen sipped her tea thoughtfully. "Did you know he has a degree in agriculture and another one in commerce?"

"No, I didn't," Maggie whispered, ashamed at the little she really knew about the man she'd fallen in love with.

"I can't imagine how a smart man like that got involved with a woman like her!" Kayleen flicked a finger at the open newspaper. "She's created such an awful ruckus around here that poor Grady's been afraid to leave the farm."

And it was all her fault! Maggie knew it as surely as if someone had screamed the words out. "I'm going for a walk, Mom. I'm just too wound-up to sleep right now. You and Dad go ahead if you want. I'll lock up when I come in." She slipped on her denim jacket and moved toward the door.

"Why don't you go through the park?" Kayleen murmured helpfully. "The leaves are a wonderful color right now, and this is perfect Thanksgiving weather."

Maggie walked out the door, barely catching her father's puzzled voice.

"There's not much to see in the park when it's this dark, Kayleen. And you sure can't tell the color of the leaves when it's almost midnight!"

Maggie smiled as she pulled the door closed and made her way to the street. Good old Willow Bunch, where you could still go for a walk in the park and no one would bother you.

"Maggie?" The voice was soft behind her left shoulder but she would have known it anywhere. Wheeling around, she came face-to-face with Grady's twinkling brown eyes. "Hi."

"Hi," she whispered, drinking in the sight of his wonderful craggy good looks and crooked smile. "How are you?"

"Lonely." His hands enfolded hers. "How are you?"

"Lonely," she murmured back, curling her fingers around his. Seconds later she was in his arms and his mouth crushed hers in a kiss that was long overdue.

"Maggie, I came as soon as your mother called. I couldn't stay away." They reached the park and found a bench by the playground. "When are you going to marry me? If Calgary's where you want to live, that's fine with me. I'll start a new company, find a new job. I don't care. As long as I'm with you."

"You're certainly not leaving the farm now?" Maggie gasped, turning to stare at him. She saw the love glowing in his eyes and almost forgot what she wanted to say. Almost. "I know how much you spent to buy the farm, Grady. You can't just dump that investment. Especially not now."

"Why not now?" he asked, puzzled. But Maggie was continuing.

"It's my fault you're in this mess in the first place," she stated firmly, although there was a little quaver in her voice. "I realize that now."

"Maggie, darling. What are you talking about?"

"I'm talking about me not seeing God's hand in things. About not trusting and believing that the God I serve is big enough to handle mortgage payments and broken machinery and hailstorms. Don't you get it?" Maggie frowned. When he shook his head from side to side she began again.

"I've been a fool," she stated baldly. "I got so caught up in my 'poor me' syndrome, that I couldn't see the bigger picture. You were right, Grady. I *was* running. As fast as I could. Nothing was going the way I planned and I lost my perspective on things. Somehow I figured if I could just get away from the farm, get that millstone off my neck, I'd find such greener pastures on the other side.

"So I refused to stick it out and discover what God had in

store for me. I figured if He wouldn't even save that wheat crop, I needed to take matters into my own hands. Maybe that would stop the fear."

"What are you afraid of, sweetheart?" His arm slid across her shoulders and Maggie snuggled into his warmth.

"The girls helped me see that I was afraid of everything," she told him. "Frantically worrying about the money and the bills and what was going to happen in the future made me crazy with fear." She glanced up at him. "I think I was afraid God would leave me to stand on my own two feet and face the mess I'd made of things. And now I've gotten you in trouble."

He frowned. "You have?"

"Of course, I know you'll deny it, but sinking all your money into the farm was the worst thing you could have done."

"It was?"

"Naturally! You're going to need that cash freed up to help settle the claim on your inheritance." She tugged a check out of her pocket. "I know it isn't much, but it's what was left from the farm." Maggie held it out toward him. "I'll pay you back as much as I possibly can each month, Grady."

"When are you going to get it into your head that I don't care about money?" His voice was harsh but a hint of pain shone from his brown eyes. "I didn't buy the farm so I'd have some hold on you. I bought it because I wanted us to live there and I thought once you had a chance to live out your dreams of fancy clothes and a nine-to-five job, you'd see that happiness—real happiness—doesn't have anything to do with money. It's a state of mind we choose when we depend on God.

"Don't you get it, Maggie? I love you. For richer or poorer. In sickness and in health. Until death do us part. And money or some silly legal case isn't going to change that. I love you. Period."

"I love you, too," she breathed, afraid to look away from those compelling eyes. "And it's not because of the money or anything else."

"Then why won't you marry me?" His voice was curt.

"I will." She grinned. "If you'll ask me. I don't care where we live, Grady. I finally realized that places and things don't matter a whit if you don't have someone to share them with. The girls taught me that. I think I was happier on that run-down, derelict old farm with you there, than I have been for a long, long time."

"Hey," he teased, pulling her close, "that's my home you're maligning." Slowly and carefully he lifted the shiny sapphire from the neck of her blouse and unfastening the chain, slid the ring free. "Maggie McCarthy, will you please, please marry me? Soon?"

"Yes," she cried, holding her hand out as he finally slid the ring into its rightful place. "As soon as you want."

"Tonight," he whispered before his mouth covered hers in a promise of a lifetime of love.

"Not tonight." She giggled. "I want to have my family around when I finally get to call you 'husband.' How about tomorrow?"

"Nope," he told her. "Tomorrow we're having a real Thanksgiving dinner. And it's going to be at my place. With my new family right beside me. Kayleen and I have it all planned. You and I are going to have Thanksgiving Monday all to ourselves."

Tears formed at the corners of her eyes. "You had that much faith in me?" She hugged him tightly.

"That and a whole lot more," he whispered. "'With God, all things are possible.' Didn't I tell you to stand on the promises? He will never let us down."

"Yes, you did," she murmured, tilting her head back for his kiss. "Thank you."

"You're very welcome. Now about a date for this wedding?"

It was a long time before Maggie heard the town clock chime one o'clock. Regretfully, she leaned back and closed her eyes.

"I've got to get going, handsome." She chuckled, when he tried to kiss her again. A new thought hit her. "Grady, what about Fiona and the money?"

"Nothing about Fiona and the money. She has no claim. I'm not destitute, if that's what you're worried about." His face mirrored his uneasiness at her grin. "Does it matter, Maggie?"

"Not to me. Not in the least! But maybe if you gave her some of it, she'd realize that true happiness doesn't come from money and things. We could do that, couldn't we, Grady? After all, we've got each other now and she hasn't got anyone."

Familiar and harsh, the bitterness rose in his face. "She lost my child, Maggie. She was pregnant and deliberately ignored the doctor's orders to take it easy. She wouldn't let me take care of her either. And she ended up losing the baby. My baby." His fingers clenched. "I don't owe her a thing."

"I'm sorry, Grady. So sorry." She slipped her hand in his, tears welling in her eyes as she felt the pain of it grab hold of him. She waited, long interminable minutes, for the grief to ebb. "I know how much you love children. It must have been terribly hard to lose that precious baby."

He nodded, mouth tight with emotion.

"But don't you see, darling? Giving away that money wouldn't be for her. Not really. It would be for you, to free you." She cupped his chin in her hand and forced his head up. "God can use even that sad thing to bring glory to His name. But to do it, you need to let go of the bitterness and hate. Let God worry about it."

She waited breathlessly as he sat there, staring at her, his body tense. Finally Grady closed his eyes and let out a whoosh of air, loosening his fingers as he did.

"When did you get so smart?"

"Just recently, as a matter of fact. I'm a quick study. I love you, Grady O'Toole."

"I love you, Maggie McCarthy."

Tomorrow came quickly and everyone rushed around the tiny bungalow to get ready for church. Grady showed up just as they were about to leave, and after thoroughly kissing her, to the delight of her family, helped Maggie transfer her Thanksgiving quilt to his truck. His fingers meshed with hers as they drove to the church.

"You finished it," he said as they spread it behind the jars of preserves and sacks of potatoes and carrots. "It's beautiful."

"Of course I finished it," she sputtered, half-indignantly. "It's a tradition around here."

"I love tradition," he whispered in her ear as the church began filling with old friends and neighbors eager to welcome her back. "Especially wedding traditions."

Maggie felt her heart fill as so many people greeted her. Then the service began and she couldn't help but pour her feelings of thanksgiving into the lovely old hymns and several new choruses. Pastor Jim gave each one something to think about as he spoke of God's faithfulness to His children, and Maggie dwelt on the verse he'd recited.

"'Though the mountains be shaken and the hills be removed, yet my unfailing love for you will not be shaken, nor my covenant of peace be removed,' says the Lord, who has compassion on you."

When they finally left the church with hearty congratulations ringing in their ears, Maggie's heart was full. She rode quietly down the old familiar road toward the farm, content with her life at last.

"Where are the girls?" she asked finally. "They love riding in this truck."

"They're coming with your parents in a while," he told her. "I wanted to have you to myself for a bit."

"That's nice." She snuggled against his shoulder with a sigh and then sat straight up. "Oh, my! This place looks wonderful."

The farm did look wonderful. The grass was lush and freshly cut, the fences were standing erect, the land was tilled as it waited for the spring. Her flowers still bloomed in the garden and a big pot now sat next to the front door. The screen porch had been repaired, with new corner posts, and everything bore a fresh coat of paint. Nothing had changed, and yet, Maggie realized, everything had changed. She was home.

"Oh, Grady," she whispered, stepping out of the truck into his arms. "You've done so much work. Everything looks cared for, loved."

"I do love it here," he murmured. "But I love you more." He kissed her quickly. "Come on, I've got to go check on the turkey."

Maggie would have liked to look around a little more, but he seemed impatient to go inside, so she went along. Nothing creaked or sagged when she stepped up and the brand-new door opened soundlessly.

"Welcome home, Maggie," Grady murmured, ushering her inside.

Maggie stared.

Everything gleamed and glistened, from the hardwood floors under her feet to the sparkling light overhead. It was the same and yet it was wonderfully different.

"Grady, what have you done?" she gasped, wandering

into the living room. Under her feet the plush beige carpet absorbed all sound. The room was an exact replica of a picture she'd once cut from a magazine, all neutral tones with an accent of plum and palest pink and touches of silky smooth oak here and there.

"I made a few changes," he murmured, stepping across to the gleaming fireplace. "The TV and VCR are in here." Panels slid open at the touch of his finger, revealing stereo equipment of every possible kind. Her plants still grew, lush and cared for, now along the window ledges.

"I have to check that turkey," he reminded her, crossing the hall toward the kitchen. "Come on."

Maggie did, staring at the burnished wood of the staircase as she passed. "It smells deli—" Her voice choked up. "Oh, Grady!"

"I wasn't sure about this room," he told her, his voice hesitant. "The others I took from pictures I found in your room, but you never had a kitchen picture. Is it okay?"

Maggie slid her fingertips along the smooth countertop and glossy oak cabinets. A wall oven was tucked into one corner and in another, a huge refrigerator. In the center of the kitchen was an island with a cooktop on one end and seating at the other. Six comfy chairs sat nestled there, waiting for occupants. Maggie could see beyond the kitchen to the dining room. A long, covered table sat glistening with linen, crystal, china and silver settings. In the middle lay a horn of plenty with fruits and vegetables pouring out.

"Maggie, you're crying! It wasn't supposed to make you cry." Grady wrapped his arms around her. "I thought you'd like it," he murmured, soothing her.

"I do like it," she said, hiccuping and sniffling inelegantly. "But you shouldn't have done it. It's too much. I don't need all this if I have you."

"Maybe you don't need it, but I wanted to give it to you. I just want you to be happy, sweetheart."

"I'm very happy," she whispered and burst out bawling when she sighted two clay figurines on the shelf above the sink. "Those are the girls'!"

"Yes, and they belong in our home, don't they?" He patted her back awkwardly when the words sent Maggie into fresh tears.

Grady didn't say anything but pulled Maggie into her workroom. Stopping just inside, she couldn't help but gasp. A huge ribbon was strung across the wall and the little gold letters on it spelled out Welcome Home Maggie.

Her fabrics lay on specially built shelves in a corner so that each color was displayed. The big tables had been refurbished so no fabric would snag or tear on that surface. There was a gigantic wall-to-wall mirror on one end of the room and a quilting frame that folded down from the wall. And everywhere there was that wonderful cedar smell. And there, propped against the wall stood a brand-new fishing rod and reel with a red-and-white striped lure attached. She picked up the tag and read "To my dearest love. Grady."

"Oh, Grady," she cried, "please say there isn't any more."

"Well, there's a Jacuzzi upstairs in the master bedroom," he told her, frowning when more tears formed. "And I put a—Maggie, will you please stop bawling!"

Maggie threw herself into his arms and clung for dear life. "I'm sorry," she murmured at last, swallowing the last sob. "I love it, really I do. It's wonderful. But it's far more than I ever needed or wanted, Grady. All I want is you."

"Well," he asserted, slightly disgruntled that his surprise had caused such a downpour, "you've got me. And this house. If you don't like it, we can change it."

Maggie burst out laughing and stood on tiptoe to kiss him. "We're not changing one thing, Grady O'Toole," she told him firmly. "Not one thing. I love it and you." She danced around the tables, laughing.

"God knew all this back when you first showed up in your snakeskin boots, looking for a place to crash for the night. He had it in mind all along. 'My unfailing love for you will not be shaken,'" she quoted. "Isn't God wonderful?"

"Awesome, as Katy says," he agreed, kissing her once more.

"They're kissing again." Katy giggled, entering her sister's bedroom. "I saw them in the kitchen."

Keeley switched off the computer and joined her sister, who'd stretched out on the brand-new blue carpet. "They'll probably do that lots now," she told her younger sister importantly. "Adults do that when they're in love."

"I guess that means we're moving back home," Katy whispered, rolling over to stare at the glossy white ceiling. "I'm glad."

"Me, too." They high-fived each other before Keeley poked her sister in the ribs. "After the wedding, it might be a good time to have another talk with Mom about babies. There's lots of room and I'd kind of like to have a baby brother."

"Yeah." Katy thought about that. "It's pretty cool how God worked all that out, isn't it?"

"It sure is." Keeley closed her eyes. "Thanks, God," she whispered. They lay for a few minutes, storing up memories.

"Do you think it's a sin to ask God for a four-wheeler?" Katy studied her sibling curiously.

"No, probably not a sin. But He's already given us all this." She waved a hand around. "Maybe you should wait a little bit. Like until after Thanksgiving anyway."

"Okay." Katy nodded. "But then you and I better get serious about it. Granny always says two heads are better than one." They grinned at each other, remembering how well it had worked in the past. "Besides, it's not that long till Christmas, you know!"

Epilogue

"Well, Mr. O'Toole, it looks like you've got yourself the son you wanted so badly." Maggie smiled, lifting their two-day-old baby up for Grady to lay in the nearby bassinet. "It's wonderful to be home again." She smiled at him. "I hope you're happy."

"I'm ecstatic," he told her, returning to press a kiss against her lips that only hinted at the fullness in his heart. "I have a gorgeous wife, two heartbreaker daughters and a new baby to make our joy complete. And I didn't care if he was a boy or a girl—you know that! God has given me everything I've ever dreamed of. What more could anyone want?" Grady sat down beside her on the sofa and pulled her against him, sighing with contentment.

"Mmm." Maggie relaxed against his shoulder, breathing in that strong, spicy scent that was pure Grady. "God *is* good," she agreed. "Although I think we might have some disagreement from Katy."

"Katy?" Grady sat up straight. "I thought she loved Jordan?"

"Oh, she does." Maggie smiled as she tugged him back to her. "I heard her thanking God for him tonight."

"But? There is a but, isn't there?" He looked worried, his forehead pleated in a frown. "What's wrong?"

"She really does love Jordan. They both do. But, actually, what Katy really hoped for was a four-wheeler."

Grady laughed appreciatively and then kissed his wife. "Our daughter has a lot to learn about the best things in life."

* * * * *

Dear Reader,

Okay, I admit it! I've often looked at someone else's life, home or job and wished I had it! Are we *ever* satisfied with our portion? Greener grass always beckons, and sometimes I have to remind myself to stop wasting time envying what I don't have and, truthfully, don't even need, and concentrate on the blessings I enjoy right now. When we do need something, isn't it so easy to complain and fuss instead of trusting God to supply all our needs?

There's a danger in worrying too much. We lose sight of the big picture and get bogged down in the little stuff. Stuff that we'll forget or maybe laugh over ten years down the road when our perspective has changed. Perspective means seeing the big picture, and the big picture is what most people remember after we've gone. So really, the only thing of significance is what we've done that lasts on in people's memories. When I was a child at Vacation Bible School, we carved out a verse on wood. It said "Only one life, 'twill soon be past. Only what's done for Christ will last." That's focusing on the present!

May we create memories of joy, love and gladness today in the lives of everyone we meet.

Blessings to you and yours.

In the exciting new FITZGERALD BAY *series
from Love Inspired Suspense, law enforcement siblings
fight for justice and family when one of their own
is accused of murder.*

Read on for a sneak preview of the first book,
THE LAWMAN'S LEGACY *by Shirlee McCoy.*

Police captain Douglas Fitzgerald stepped into his father's
house. The entire Fitzgerald clan had gathered, and he was
the last to arrive. Not a problem. He had a foolproof excuse.
Duty first. That's the way his father had raised him. It was
the only way he knew how to be.

Voices carried from the dining room. With his boisterous
family around, his life could never be empty.

But there *were* moments when he felt that something
was missing.

Some*one* was missing.

Before he could dwell on his thoughts, his radio crackled
and the dispatcher came on.

"Captain? We have a situation on our hands. A body has
been found near the lighthouse."

"Where?"

"At the base of the cliffs. The caller believes the deceased
may be Olivia Henry."

"It can't be Olivia." Douglas's brother Charles spoke.
The custodial parent to his twin toddlers, he employed
Olivia as their nanny.

"I'll be there in ten minutes." He jogged back outside
and jumped into his vehicle.

Douglas flew down Main Street and out onto the rural
road that led to the bluff. Two police cars followed. His
brothers and his father. Douglas was sure of it. Together,

they'd piece together what had happened.

The lighthouse loomed in the distance, growing closer with every passing mile. A beat-up station wagon sat in the driveway.

Douglas got out and made his way along the path to the cliff.

Up ahead, a woman stood near the edge.

Meredith O'Leary.

There was no mistaking her strawberry-blond hair, her feminine curves, or the way his stomach clenched, his senses springing to life when he saw her.

"Merry!"

"Captain Fitzgerald! Olivia is…"

"Stay here. I'll take a look."

He approached the cliff's edge. Even from a distance, Douglas recognized the small frame.

His father stepped up beside him. "It's her."

"I'm afraid so."

"We need to be the first to examine the body. If she fell, fine. If she didn't, we need to know what happened."

If she fell.

The words seemed to hang in the air, the other possibilities hovering with them.

Can Merry work together with Douglas to find justice for Olivia…without giving up her own deadly secrets?
To find out, pick up
THE LAWMAN'S LEGACY by Shirlee McCoy,
on sale January 10, 2012.

Love Inspired

After surviving a devastating tragedy, combat reporter Nate Garrison returns home to Starfish Bay. But his reunion with lovely Lindsey Collier is nothing like he's dreamed. Lindsey is now a sad-eyed widow who avoids loss and love. Knowing he's been given a second chance, Nate sets out to show her faith's true healing power.

Seaside Reunion
by Irene Hannon

Available January wherever books are sold.

www.LoveInspiredBooks.com

LI87715

Love Inspired
CLASSICS

#1 CBA Bestselling Author

DEE HENDERSON

brings you two heartwarming stories of love,
redemption and faith

The Marriage Wish
&
God's Gift

Available January 2012 wherever books are sold.

www.LoveInspiredBooks.com

LIC65151